CAT AND MOUSE

Also by Tim Vicary

The Blood upon the Rose

Cat and Mouse

Tim Vicary

SIMON & SCHUSTER

LONDON·SYDNEY·NEW YORK·TOKYO·SINGAPORE·TORONTO

First published in Great Britain by
Simon & Schuster Ltd in 1993
A Paramount Communications Company

Simon & Schuster Ltd
West Garden Place
Kendal Street
London W2 2AQ

Simon & Schuster of Australia Pty Ltd
Sydney

A CIP catalogue record for this book is
available from the British Library
ISBN 0–671–71816–9

Photoset in North Wales by
Derek Doyle & Associates, Mold, Clwyd
Printed and bound in Great Britain by
Butler & Tanner Ltd, Frome

Author's Note

Anyone well acquainted with the history of the suffragette movement will know that the action described in the first chapter of this novel was in reality performed by the suffragette Mary Richardson on 10 March 1914. It seems to me such an unusually striking and symbolic act that I have taken the liberty of borrowing it, and slightly changing the date, for the purpose of my story. My character Sarah Becket, however, is entirely fictional and intended to bear no other resemblance whatsoever to the real historical character Mary Richardson.

At exactly the same time as women were being imprisoned for demanding the vote, many influential men were strongly opposed to the government's policy of giving Ireland Home Rule. These men formed an army – the Ulster Volunteer Force – and threatened the United Kingdom with civil war if Ulster's status was changed. Unlike suffragettes, none of these men was ever arrested for this open defiance of Parliament, and their protest was largely successful.

Like the eternal war between women and men, the results of that protest remain with us today.

'The real cure of the great plague is a two-fold one – Votes for Women . . . and chastity for men.'

Christabel Pankhurst,
The Great Scourge and How to End It, 1913

'It is reasonable to assume that Germany had secret agents in Ulster in 1914.'

A.T.Q. Stewart,
The Ulster Crisis, 1967

PART ONE

Sarah

1

'Look out! Oh, sorry, ma'am, never saw yer.'

'What? Who are you – oh, I see. It doesn't matter.'

'Beg pardon, ma'am. I'm sure.' The two coster boys, grubby and boisterous in their flat caps and ragged, oversize jackets, scurried away across the square. As they went they winked and grinned at each other, knowing they had made a discovery. They were connoisseurs of street life and there was something about the woman that drew their attention. A few yards away they glanced back over their shoulders to make sure, and then, their suspicions confirmed, parked themselves calmly under one of the great lions of Trafalgar Square to watch. One of them shied a pebble at the pigeons as they waited.

There was nothing particularly strange about the appearance of the woman. She was fairly tall, about five foot eight perhaps, and quite slim. Between thirty and thirty-five years old. She wore a long grey ankle-length skirt belted at the waist, with a pleated jacket with puffed sleeves above, over a white blouse buttoned up to her chin. On her head was a hat with red and yellow feathers in it. Nothing unusual about that – they were the clothes of a respectable, well-dressed lady – perhaps even a rich one, for the fur of the muff she held in front of her to warm her hands in was expensive, thick and ostentatious. The muff was rather odd though, because it was a fresh, sunny day in April, and she had not chosen to wear a coat.

But it was the look on her face that had struck the boys.

When they had bumped into her she had at first stared right through them, then started away as though they were trying to attack her. The woman's face was pale, white as a cloud, the eyes in it burning like coals. An attractive face, perhaps, with smooth skin and soft curling brown hair, but that was not what interested the boys. It was the haunted look that riveted them, the idea that she might be a ghost, a woman who scarcely knew where she was.

'What d'yer reckon?' the elder boy asked, taking a bite from an apple which he had purloined from a grocery stall in Charing Cross. The odd behaviour of the woman was all part of the joy of observing the eccentricities of the rich. 'Going to kill herself, maybe?'

He glanced hopefully at the motor omnibus which was trundling towards them at nearly ten miles an hour, a few feet from the pavement where the woman stood.

'Dunno,' his mate said, judiciously. 'Be as good as that, anyhow. You wait and see.'

The other curious thing about the woman was that she stood absolutely still. All about her was movement. Nannies stood by their perambulators talking while their charges cooed at the sky or toddled across Trafalgar Square in pursuit of the pigeons. Amongst them passed office boys, servant girls, city gents in top hats and striped trousers hurrying to get somewhere. The street in front of her was thronged with motor omnibuses, hansom cabs, horsedrawn delivery wagons, and messenger boys on bicycles. All of them hooted, shouted, and jangled past each other. The woman seemed to stare right through them, intent on some vision only apparent to herself. In the whole square, she and the boys were the only living creatures that did not move.

As the seconds lengthened into minutes, the boys' attention deepened, hunters sure of their quarry. Once or twice she swayed, as though almost too weak to stand, then checked and held herself rigidly upright. But still she did not move.

When nearly three minutes had passed, the elder boy turned to his mate, a broad grin on his face.

'You wait, Jem,' he said. 'This one's going to be good.'

*

Sarah Becket did not know she was standing still. Her mind was too busy. It was focussed on one ridiculous, irrelevant thought that got in the way of everything she had planned.

She thought: the Gallery is too big.

She had seen the National Gallery many times before but never really looked at it. It was a place she had visited as a child in school parties to learn about art, and later, with Jonathan when they were courting, because it was a convenient, respectable place to meet unchaperoned.

She had never looked at the building itself before.

But today, with the meat knife scratching her wrist inside her muff, she saw it for the first time.

It had been built while Queen Victoria was still a child, three-quarters of a century ago – a huge, confident, proud building. There were two sets of stone steps leading up to the portico and the main entrance. The pillars supporting the entrance were as tall as forest trees. They were linked by a long balustrade to similar rows of columns away to the right and left. In the middle of the roof was a beautiful glass cupola. Everything about the building proclaimed the glory of culture and education. It looked as solid and immovable as the Establishment of the British Empire itself.

And she, Sarah Becket, a woman who had learnt all her life to obey and reverence everything this building stood for, was about to attack it . . .

I could always go home, she thought. No one need ever know, this is not planned or sanctioned by the movement as the other things were. I don't have to do this. I could go to meetings and large demonstrations where I would have the support of other women around me. That would be easier. I could do that as I have done before. Or I could just turn round now and go back to Jonathan and smile and keep my promise and stay out of prison and try to be a good wife and pretend I know nothing at all about where he goes when . . .

That's not the real reason. It's because I *can't* just do nothing, and leave Mrs Pankhurst to die.

She broke out of her trance and stepped off the pavement into the road. A bicycle bell rang furiously in her ear and a baker's delivery boy swerved round her, cursing and clutching at the loaves in the basket over his front wheel. Sarah stepped back, took a deep breath, looked around her.

If I cannot even cross the road I will never manage it.

She waited for a gap in the traffic, walked across, went up the left-hand set of stone steps to the main entrance. It was like walking through water . . . At each step the air resisted her, her muscles weakened, she wanted to turn and run or just fall down and weep.

Mrs Pankhurst was arrested again yesterday, she thought – the seventh time for the same offence. She could hardly *stand* last time I saw her. In prison she doesn't eat and walks up and down her cell for hours every night. She will be dead soon – she is giving her life for feeble creatures like me. I know what it's like in prison, I've been there. I must force them to let her out. I'm doing this for Mrs Pankhurst.

Not Jonathan. Forget *him*.

She walked through the great oaken doors. A uniformed commissionaire bowed stiffly to her. She found herself looking at his arms and face, thinking, he doesn't look an unusually strong man, or cruel. Will he hurt me very much, when I have done it?

Something not quite so polite, a little suspicious, came into the man's eyes. Women were suspected everywhere these days and Sarah realised she had stared at him a moment too long.

The shock gave her courage, made her begin to think clearly at last. It would be too, too stupid to come this far and *fail*, just because I acted feebly and looked like an idiot. After all, this man is just a servant, for heaven's sake.

She turned back and spoke to him. Her voice came out cool, distant, quite normal. A well-bred lady used to the deference of menials.

'Good morning. I've come to see the Spanish exhibition. It is here, isn't it?'

'That's right, ma'am. Upstairs, in room 17. Would you like a catalogue?'

'I would, thank you.' Then, as he turned to reach for one on the desk behind him, she realised the difficulty. How could she pay for and accept the catalogue while she was carrying the muff with the knife inside it? She had a small purse in there too, in a pocket in the lining, but the knife was two inches wide and over a foot long – far too big and heavy to fit into her purse. And if he saw it!

It was too late to back out now. Carefully, trying not to look as though she was fumbling, she withdrew the purse from the pocket inside the muff and held purse, muff and knife all in the left hand together, while she fished the money out with her right.

'Thank you,' she said. Even to herself her voice sounded small, nervous, flustered.

The commissionaire took her money and held out the catalogue.

It was a big catalogue, with expensive reproductions of the paintings. Oh God, she thought. I don't need this at all. But to go in without one would look abnormal, surely? And people everywhere are on the lookout for suffragettes. This is much harder than throwing stones or marching in a demonstration.

Clumsily, she stuffed the purse back inside the muff and took the wretched catalogue with her right hand. I should have planned this more carefully, she thought. In a minute I'm going to drop something or blush and then I shall have failed and look an utter, utter fool!

The commissionaire frowned, looked at the muff, and held out his hand.

'Let me take that for you, ma'am. I can keep it safe here while you're inside.'

'No! No – thank you very much, but I have – a disease of the hands. They get – unusually cold, even in this weather, and the doctor has ordered me to keep them warm at all times.'

Jonathan had once told her she had a devastating smile. She tried it out now, hoping that it would have the required effect and not display the sick, panicky desperation she felt inside. The point of good manners, her mother had always told her, was to shield the world from what you really felt.

'As you wish, Madam.'

The man bowed and turned away and Sarah walked swiftly into the gallery, up the stairs under the great glass cupola, and left and then right towards room 17. The incident had galvanized her. She felt rage begin to flow through her. Rage at herself for being so weak and foolish as to be nearly caught out at the entrance like a naughty schoolgirl, and rage, too, at the hundreds of thousands of ways in which women were put down, humiliated, treated like children every day until their only response was to fight back in some desperate way like the one she had planned. We are not trained for this, she thought, we have to learn it all from the beginning. It's mad, wicked, foolish even, but its only justification is that it must succeed! If I am going to do this thing I must do it well, carry it through to the end.

Room 17, to her dismay, was small and quite crowded. Ten or twelve people strolled about, consulting their catalogues, inspecting the pictures carefully. Nearly all of them were men – there were just two women. The women were listening attentively to a young man in frock coat and top hat, who was reading to them from his catalogue in a pompous, authoritative voice. What does *he* know? Sarah thought. Why should he have such a loud voice? If I spoke like that in here Jonathan would hush me – and yet those women are far older than that young man! And look at the pictures – nearly all of *them* are women! Women as nymphs and goddesses, half-clothed, looking seductive, tended by cherubs. They are pictures of naked women and this young man is explaining them to his lady friends!

And they are very, very beautiful . . .

Don't think of that now, Sarah told herself. It's not a matter to concern yourself with. Just find the one you came to see and do it.

But, just for a moment, she couldn't help it. She had not seen the exhibition before and the rich colours, the size of some of the canvases, overwhelmed her. Paintings that were hundreds of years old, and better, more self-assured than anything people did now. Their value was literally priceless – not only could no one reproduce one that was destroyed, no one today possessed the skill to produce anything remotely similar. At another time, Sarah would have walked slowly round the room, entranced.

But they are only canvas and oil paint, she told herself. People matter more. Real women who are denied things because of their sex, exploited because of their bodies. And especially

Mrs Pankhurst, who is a saint, and who is being tortured and killed by men like these.

There were three men in front of the picture Sarah had come to see. One of them was small and fat, with a huge round paunch and a large spade beard that spread halfway down his chest. He stood with his legs apart, contemplating the picture with his thumbs hooked into the pockets of his bright yellow waistcoat, and his top hat pushed to the back of his head. Beside him was a young man, thin and stooped, possibly his son. The boy kept glancing nervously from the picture to the catalogue and back again, as though to decipher something important he had not fully grasped.

The third man was tall, well-built, clearly affluent. His striped trousers and tailcoat sat on him comfortably, and he leant on a silver-topped cane with one foot crossed in front of the other, gazing at the picture with deep satisfaction.

Sarah hated him on sight, because he reminded her of her husband.

The picture itself, the *Rokeby Venus*, was of a naked woman. She lay on a couch with her back to the men in the room, gazing at herself in a small mirror held by a winged cupid. Her face could be seen in the mirror, calm, half-shadowed, relaxed. But the real beauty of the picture was the long, sensual, voluptuous portrayal of her back, which the artist had made so real that it seemed if one reached out and touched it, it would come alive.

A celebration of female beauty, Sarah thought.

She had read that phrase in *The Times*, and now that she saw the picture she understood what it meant. It was, undeniably, beautiful. It was also, because of its size, overwhelming. It frightened her.

It says, this is what women are, Sarah thought. I expect Jonathan would like *me* to be like that. I suppose I was for him, once . . .

The tall man sighed, turned from the painting, and glanced at the short fat man in the yellow waistcoat beside him. Their eyes met. The tall man nodded. 'Fine piece of work, old boy, wouldn't you say?'

Pleased to be noticed, the fat man grinned back jovially.

'Indeed! Most lifelike. Odd that the artist painted her with her back to the audience though, don't you think? I was just wondering to myself – if I tapped her on the shoulder, do you imagine she might oblige by turning this way for a second? The boy here is interested, you know, and would like to see more . . .'

Delighted by his own wit, the fat man began to wheeze and chuckle, his belly under the yellow waistcoat heaving and wobbling with amusement. At first the tall man seemed undecided how to respond to this unexpectedly indecent suggestion, but then he saw the joke and smiled conspiratorially.

'Anything to educate the young, eh?'

I expect that is the sort of thing Jonathan says when I'm not around, Sarah thought bitterly. And I'm sure father thought like that too. It was thoughts like that which destroyed mother's life, sent her scurrying to the doctor again and again. But I never thought Jonathan would go the same way. Until that letter. *Oh Jonathan! Jonathan! How could you?*

She glared at the tall man, thinking: I hope you die slowly like father did, mad, disgraced, covered with weeping sores! Christabel Pankhurst is right: the only way for women to get justice is to change the way men think. Make them chaste.

Her anger sent the blood flowing fiercely through her, but at the same time she felt quite calm. Time seemed to have slowed down. She dropped her catalogue on a seat and walked slowly forward towards the picture, both her hands inside her muff. The men glanced at her incuriously as she passed them, still absorbed in their joke. There was a uniformed attendant sitting on a chair near the door, ten, twelve yards away.

Everything was perfectly normal in the room. No one was taking any notice of her.

The picture was on an easel in the corner of the room. It was framed in glass. There was a red rope hung on short wooden poles a yard in front of it, to stop people getting too close.

Sarah stepped over the rope.

She thought: *Now*. Don't stop now.

She pulled the heavy knife out of her muff, lifted it, and swung it at the painting.

It was a heavy meat knife and it smashed clean through the

glass. Jagged splinters flew everywhere, bouncing off Sarah's skirt and jacket. She ignored them, dragging the knife down across the Venus's back. There was a small tearing sound.

'Hey! What the devil?'

She pulled the knife out and stabbed again. The canvas was surprisingly hard, but the knife was in and she began to pull, dragging it along the canvas to the right, forcing it in all the time so that it tore the canvas open. She was disappointed that she was now cutting the couch rather than the woman's body, so she took it out and jabbed again and again. Each time she tried to force the knife up higher, but it was heavy and her shoulder was aching with the strain. She was aware that people were moving, that she had no time left for another attempt. But that didn't matter – she had already cut it several times and this last slash was already a foot long . . . eighteen inches . . . two feet . . .

The seconds seemed to go so slowly. Sarah watched the knife blade ripping through the canvas and thought of nothing else, only that, I am doing it, it is cutting further . . .

Hands grabbed her shoulders roughly and snatched her away. The knife fell from her fingers. She spun round and saw it was the tall man like her husband, and then the short fat man had her arm too. They dragged her away from the painting and she tripped over the rope, stumbling against them.

'What the devil do you think you're doing, woman?'

Only then did she realise she must speak, explain the act as well as do it. With one arm twisted behind her and the rope tangled round her feet, she leant forward against the man and stared up into his face. Her eyes were near his chin, she could see a vicious, angry twist to his mouth. She took a deep breath and shouted as loud as she could.

'Free Mrs Pankhurst! Mrs Pankhurst is dying in prison. You must set her free!'

'She's a damned suffragette!'

'My God, look what she's done!'

'Get her over here!'

'Hold her arms!'

There were men all round her now, pulling, clutching, shoving, shouting angrily. The uniformed attendant had the fingers of one hand digging tightly into her arm and was blowing a whistle near her ear. Sarah continued to shout wildly, conscious that this was the last thing she had to do before they took her away.

'Votes for Women! Free Mrs Pankhurst! Votes for Women!'

Shouting was easy. Once she had started, her screams went on without conscious thought because they were only slogans. As she screamed she twisted her head to look back at the painting and exulted. There was a gash nearly two feet long right down the woman's back, with the ragged edges of torn canvas hanging down like flaps of skin from a wound. And half-a-dozen smaller slashes from neck to rump. Now they would see what real women were like – fighters, not their whorehouse picture!

'Free Mrs Pankhurst! Votes for Women!'

They manhandled her out of the room, through the other galleries, and down the stairs. Her clothes were ripped and stretched all ways across her body as it seemed every man in the place exerted himself to get a handhold. Halfway down the stairs they met the commissionaire who had sold her the catalogue. There were people everywhere, pointing and staring – even young coster boys from the street. Another attendant was blowing his whistle outside on the grand stone steps, waving to attract a policeman.

Then, mercifully, they marched her into a little office and shoved her roughly into a chair. A row of angry male faces glared at her. She gasped for breath, her face hot, her pulse racing angrily.

'What . . . what happens now?' she asked feebly.

'We're waiting for the constable, miss,' the commissionaire said firmly.

For a moment no one else spoke and Sarah thought: I've done it now – nothing matters any more. Then she saw the fury on the faces in front of her, and remembered Mrs Pankhurst walking endlessly, up and down her cold cell, all day and all night without food or friends or water. And the torture so many women had endured.

Her body shrank a little inside her clothes, and a shiver passed through her. Cold, like gooseflesh.

And she thought: this has only just begun . . .

2

The police cells were noisy, crowded, and squalid. But for Sarah they were the first refuge she had had all day.

She had probably waited for only a quarter of an hour in the room at the National Gallery, but it had been a frightening time. Every few minutes someone burst in from outside, to stare at her, shake a fist, or scream abuse. The manager, a small, dark, excitable man, had been near to tears. He had stood in front of her, shaking with rage, saying that the painting was a priceless, *priceless*, work of art, and that in his opinion she was a vandal and should be whipped – no, *hanged*, for such an act of desecration. The commissionaire had scowled also, and then there had been a stream of indignant men – and women too – some of whom had had to be restrained from spitting at her. And all the time the noise outside the door rose from a murmur to a menacing hubbub, and Sarah had begun to fear that she would be beaten or even lynched for what she had done.

Then the two policemen had come in.

They were big men, with impressive moustaches and shoulders that completely filled the doorway when they came through it. They exuded an air of calm and solidity. They were totally unexcited by what had happened. They contemplated Sarah with interest, and no anger whatsoever.

Her heartrate began to slow down.

She knew the drill, now. She had been through it several times before. There was nothing personal in it for the police. Many of them actually liked suffragettes. Within half an hour they had taken most of the preliminary details and were ready to take her away. One fastened the bracelet of a pair of handcuffs carefully round her right wrist. He attached the other bracelet to his own.

'You don't mind, I hope, ma'am? Just a formality really, but it's for your protection as much as ours. There's a biggish crowd out there.'

He was right about that. The entrance hall and the steps outside the Gallery were packed, and no one, so far as Sarah could tell, had a good word to say for her. People jeered, cat-called, spat – one or two pieces of fruit even came her way. She felt an intense gratitude for the calm solidity and bulk of the two constables beside her. Coster boys and street urchins followed them along the street, and women – *women!* – screamed abuse.

Surely someone will cheer, she thought. I did it for justice, for all womankind. There are so many of us – surely someone will understand?

Then she saw it. A green, white and purple banner waving above the crowd outside Bow Street Police Station, with a small, determined knot of suffragettes underneath it. As she was marched past they saw her, and a ragged cheer went up:

'Votes For Women!'

'Free Mrs Pankhurst!'

'Don't let them get you down, dear! We'll be out here, waiting!'

She didn't know them, but it didn't matter. Only a few seconds, but it was the most wonderful moment of the day. She was not alone, she was understood. And it was true, they would support her, just as she had slashed the painting to support Mrs Pankhurst. If they all hung together, and dared enough, they would win in the end – they had to! It was only justice.

Justice in Bow Street Police Station was bluff, calm, matter-of-fact. The sergeant at the desk raised an eyebrow briefly at her name and address, but no more. The details of the charge were taken and written down in a big ledger with a sigh. The constables were busy, they had seen it all before, they were ready for their tea. Sarah was taken down underneath the station to the cells.

She had seen cells before, too, many of them. This one was dark. There was a high window at the far end, but it was closed and black with grime. On the right was a wide, long plank raised from the floor, with a sort of wooden bolster for a pillow. Under the window, in the corner, a toilet. Nothing else. No light, no bedclothes.

It was cold, and there were shouts and banging from cells further down the corridor. It was what she had expected. Nothing would happen now for some time. Sarah felt suddenly overwhelmed by exhaustion. I haven't recovered from starving myself the last two times, she thought, and now it's all going to start again. Her legs trembled and would not hold her, and she had an irresistible urge to cry. But even that took too much energy – she could not sustain it long. When the weeping fit was over, she slumped down on the plank bed, put her hands over her ears, and tried to sleep.

Despite the noise, she must have slept for some time, for when she awoke she could see a light burning in the corridor through the little judas window in the door. And there was something else – a voice, a familiar sound – which had woken her.

Keys clanked in the lock, the door opened, light flooded in. And in the light, the silhouette of a man – tall, thin, bearded, in top hat and coat.

'Jonathan!' Of course, he would have to come. But she did not want to face this. Not now.

She had slashed the picture to avoid facing him.

'My God, it's dark enough in here! Can we have a light, man?'

'I'll fetch you a candle, sir.'

The door was left open behind him – clearly the constable did not fear she would run away. Sarah sat up, on the edge of the bed. She felt her face flushed, her hands trembling. Jonathan stood, the light behind him, as though waiting for her to get up and run towards him. As she had done when they were younger and still in love . . . If I run towards him now, she thought, I'll scratch his eyes out.

The constable returned with a candle.

'I'll have to lock you in, sir, I'm afraid. Regulations. But there'll be someone down at the end of the corridor. Just bang on the door when you want to come out.'

'I hope you can distinguish my bang from those of these other poor wretches, then.' But the urbane sarcasm was lost on the policeman. The heavy door closed behind him and they were alone.

They had been married eleven years and at first it had seemed a brilliant match. But they were both forceful people and over the past few years there had been increasing strain. Partly because they had no children. Sarah had had three miscarriages and she could not bear to try again. She knew how much he wanted children but she was afraid to let him near her, now. The love she had once felt for him had been tarnished by the pain.

She was glad of that now, after what she had discovered. He was no better than her father, after all. Perhaps no men could be trusted.

He said: 'Why did you do it? You broke your promise.'

'*I* broke *my* promise?'

'Yes. Sarah, you know you did. After the last time, you promised you wouldn't do anything like this again for three months. Damn it, you're not well, Sarah!'

'It's my body! *I* should be the judge of how well I am.'

Jonathan sat down on the hard bed – there was nowhere else – and put the candle between them. He was a slim, handsome man, still lithe even at the age of thirty-eight and he moved with the grace of an athlete. He had always defied convention by keeping a full beard, trimmed short like a radical. Lit from below by the candlelight, his face, usually kind, sensitive, curious, looked eerie and ghostlike. Like that of a stranger in the night.

He said: 'You destroyed one of the most beautiful paintings in the world.'

'Yes. You've seen it, then?'

'Seen it? I didn't have to. It's all over the evening papers. *Mad Suffragette slashes* Rokeby Venus. *Vandals strike again. MP's wife in scandal*. Here, look.'

She glanced briefly at the newspaper he gave her, then laid it aside. 'I gather you don't approve.'

'*Approve*? For God's sake, Sarah!' He stood up, took two fretful paces to the toilet under the window, then came and sat down again. Very carefully and pedantically, he asked: 'Do you really think that destroying a priceless work of art is going to make people respect the suffragettes, and regard women as responsible adult people who deserve the vote?'

It's the prison warders who are supposed to torture you, Sarah thought, not your own husband . . . She said: 'Yes, I do. Jonathan, you're a man. You probably don't see that picture in the same way as I do. I am sure it is a great work of art but it degrades women, too, because it invites men to see us as sex objects and nothing more. We want to be citizens, not odalisques!'

You didn't always want that, Jonathan thought. In the early days, when I used to come home late at night, and you would be waiting up for me, in that long silk gown . . . he sighed. This situation seemed to him to be a culmination of everything that had gone wrong in the eleven years of their marriage. It was not just the miscarriages, it was the way their minds no longer met. But it was not at all clear to him, even now, how they had got here. Still less about where it would lead.

'All right,' he said. 'You tell me, then. How am I to defend this in the House when the question comes up? My wife regards Velasquez as a pornographer, is that it?'

'No! Just say your wife regards paintings as less important than people. If they free Mrs Pankhurst and give us the vote, all these things will stop tomorrow. Jonathan, you know that! Until then, justice is more important than art.'

For a moment the coldness of her slogan hung in the air between them. Then the silence was shattered by a drunk battering his cell door with his boots further down the corridor.

Jonathan tried again. 'Of course I understand, you know that, but . . .'

'Do you? Do you really understand, Jonathan?'

'Look, you're my wife – I don't want you in a place like this! When they let you out under the Cat and Mouse Act last time I did my damndest to protect you – I even wrote to McKenna and told him you'd promised to stay out of trouble, in the hope they wouldn't arrest you. And now this!'

She hadn't known that but it made sense, like so many other things she was finding out about him. Jonathan was a Liberal MP, ambitious, eager for office; her suffragette activities were an embarrassment to him. He would do a deal behind her back if he could. Even with McKenna, the Home Secretary, who loathed all suffragettes.

She flicked her head back, to toss a loose curl away from her eye. 'A deal cooked up by men!'

His blue eyes widened, as they did on the edge of anger. 'For God's sake! It was a gentleman's agreement to protect you, Sarah! You're my wife. Am I not entitled to do that?' He reached out his hand, round the candle, and squeezed her shoulder. She flinched – it was the site of one of many bruises she had received that afternoon.

'Don't you dare touch me!' She jerked away from him, got up, and stood by the wall under the high barred window. The dim candlelight made it hard to see, but he thought she was trembling.

'Sarah? Why ever not?'

'Don't you *know*?'

He thought back over the past few years – the miscarriages, the frustrations, the way he had been banished from her bedroom. This was not the first such scene. Rage flared in him.

'No, I do not know. You are my wife and I have come here expressly to bring you comfort. If my offer is to be spurned then I –'

'You liar!'

She ran towards him suddenly and before he could get up from the bed she knocked the top hat from his head. He felt a hot, searing pain as she raked her nails down his cheek, near his eye. He lashed out to defend himself, pushing the palm of his hand against the first thing that he found, which was the soft flesh of her nose and mouth. She bit him, hard, near the base of his thumb. He yelled, lurched to his feet, and shoved her away. As he got up the candle fell over and went out. For a moment they both stood, blinded by the sudden pitch black. Each could only guess where the other was by the sound of laboured, frightened breathing.

He said: 'Sarah, please!'

'Leave me alone!'

A hand came suddenly out of the darkness and caught him a stinging crack across the cheek. He staggered and cried out: 'What the devil are you doing?'

A sound between a laugh and a sob came from somewhere just ahead of him, to his left. 'It serves you right! You *know* why!'

This time he had his own hands raised like a boxer, so when her hand came out of the darkness he managed to shield himself from the blow with his forearm and catch hold of her wrist before she could move away. He pulled her roughly forward and reached out with his other hand, trying to catch her other arm, but instead he found her hair. He wound his fingers in it and held on.

'Sarah, stop this. What are you doing?'

'Let go of me, you betrayer! *Guard! Help! Get this man out of my cell!*'

As she screamed he felt a sudden hard, agonising blow on his right shin, just below the knee. He let go of her hair and wrist and stumbled back, trying to get away from her. Then the door opened and a burly policeman stood framed in the yellow gaslight flooding in from the corridor. He coughed.

'Yes, sir? Madam? You called?'

Jonathan fumbled for a handkerchief and dabbed it across his cheek, to cover the blood. 'Yes, man. The candle –'

'Get this man out of here!'

'Beg pardon, madam?' It was not easy to see without a candle in the gloomy cell, but the policeman could make out the silhouette of the lady, shaking in the middle of the cell, and the gent, dabbing at his face with a handkerchief. She was a prisoner of course, but not the usual sort. 'But he's your husband, ain't he, ma'am?'

'He may be – but I don't want to see him! Get him out, can't you? I can't bear him near me!'

'Well, sir . . .' The constable hesitated. 'We usually only allow ten minutes as a rule . . .'

'Don't trouble yourself.' Jonathan fumbled for his hat on the floor, and dusted it off against his sleeve. 'It seems my wife is not well.' He stepped out, past the policeman into the corridor. Then, before the door was closed, he turned.

'I have no idea what is the matter with you, my dear, but I hope you recover. In the meantime, for God's sake be sensible in prison – and eat!'

Sarah's answer was not hysterical, as the constable had expected. Instead her words were very soft and determined, and they stayed in Jonathan's mind all night.

'Jonathan, go away, and let me face these horrors on my own. If I eat a single mouthful in here, you know I shall have betrayed the cause.'

3

When Jonathan had gone, Sarah paced the dark cell restlessly until the violence of her emotions began to subside. The drunk down the corridor sang in a loud, bleary monotone until a policeman hammered on his door to shut him up. In another cell a woman was cursing steadily, repetitively, with sudden loud bursts of fury when she shook the bars. In the occasional moments of silence Sarah could hear the hiss of the gas-lamp in the corridor outside, and somewhere, far away, another woman crying.

The top pane of her window was open and she guessed it must be just below the level of the pavement. Once, she heard the clatter and rattle of a tram approach, and the ding! of its bell as it stopped outside; at another time, the clop of a horse's hooves, and the shout of a man hailing a cab.

She thought of Jonathan, getting out of a similar cab a few miles away. In her mind she saw him drop coins into the hand of the driver. He would have to use his left hand, she thought. She had bitten his right! He would have a handkerchief round that and another to dab at his face. The cabman would notice but he would ignore it. He would raise his cap in gratitude for the tip, Jonathan would nod, the driver would shake his reins, and the cab would clop quietly away around Belgrave Square. Jonathan would sigh, and walk slowly up the steps to the front door. The door would open, and he would hand his top hat and gloves to Reeves, their butler, and go into his study, alone.

I wonder how he will explain those scratches to Reeves, she thought. Spot of bad luck, he might say, I picked up a cat and it scratched my face. Something like that . . .

And it's true, too, she thought grimly, except that this cat is his wife. The woman he promised to share his whole life with.

I don't feel like a cat, I feel like a coward, she thought. I should have told him what I know, why didn't I dare?

A little voice in her mind answered: *because you're not sure it's true.*

Of course it's true, it all makes sense, no one would send me a letter like that if it wasn't true. And it's not just the letter – I saw him with my own eyes. Anyway I don't want to think about it. I can't remember it all.

Remember it. You must. All of it.

She remembered what had happened two days ago. Two days! It seemed like a hundred years . . .

She remembered being in her own drawing room in the house in Belgrave Square. She could see the pale cream wallpaper studded with small, delicate patterns of roses and lilies; the long red curtains; the white sofa and armchairs scattered with red and yellow cushions. It was a cheerful room, flooded with sunlight in the late afternoon. A good place to convalesce.

She was sitting at a table near the window with Mrs Watson, her nurse. Mrs Watson was the main reason she had agreed to spend so much time at home, away from the WSPU offices. She was a friendly, businesslike woman, a qualified nurse devoted to the suffragette cause. She had first arrived when Sarah had been released, weak, delirious, exhausted, from her last stay in prison. The WSPU had wanted to take Sarah to a suffragette rest home in Sussex, quite away from her husband; Jonathan had wanted to keep her in his own house, quite away from all suffragettes. Mrs Watson had been the compromise.

At first she had seemed a triumph. Mrs Watson was undoubtedly a skilled nurse; under her care Sarah relaxed and grew better day by day. She was also a diplomat; after a few rather prickly exchanges, she had deliberately praised some of Jonathan's political work, and Jonathan had appeared to like and even respect her.

Sarah wondered now how much of that was a fraud.

The day Sarah remembered had been a Monday – two days ago. She and Mrs Watson had spent the afternoon going through a large amount of suffragette correspondence. It was useful work, but mundane – enquiries about membership, ladies wishing to subscribe to *The Suffragette*, queries about a forthcoming rally, and so on. It was, Sarah realised, part of Mrs Watson's therapy – work that made her feel part of the movement, without exposing her to any risk or undue physical activity.

It also kept her inside the house. Although she had seen no evidence of policemen outside, watching the house to see if she was well, it was quite possible that she would be re-arrested, under the Cat and Mouse Act, the first time she stepped out into the street. She was only out of prison because she had refused to eat while she was in there, not because she had completed her sentence. She had been released under McKenna's notorious *Prisoners (Temporary Discharge for Ill-Health) Act* – nick-named the Cat and Mouse Act. At any time the police could decide her health had recovered and re-arrest her to serve the remainder of her sentence. Then the whole dreadful business of the hunger strike would begin again. Mrs Pankhurst had been re-arrested six times like that, and she was so weak she could hardly stand.

About halfway through the morning, the second post arrived. Sarah began to open it. Among the standard letters to 'The Organiser, Women's Social and Political Union' and 'The Women's Suffrage Movement' was one addressed to her personally. The writing on the envelope was bold, black, confident: Mrs Sarah Becket, 30 Belgrave Square, London W2. It was a hand she did not know. She opened it curiously.

Inside was a single sheet of expensive, creamy paper, covered with the same bold black handwriting. Oddly, there was no address at the top. It began:

> *Dear Mrs Becket,*
>
> *I suppose you know that your friends in the WSPU have recently been poking their noses into things which concern them even less than the vote. They have been troubling several of us young ladies and asking*

for the names of our gentlemen friends, which is none of their business at all, especially when they stand outside the house where we live and work and try to put men off, so we have to move house. This does no one any good and makes us all poorer. In particular, they have been troubling Dr Armstrong too, who is a decent man and a good help to us.

Well, all this has got to stop. Tell your friends to stay away from our houses and Dr Armstrong or you will be sorry. Your husband gets the same treatment other men get, and whose fault is that? If you don't want to read about him in all the newspapers tell your friends to STAY AWAY. That's all.

There was no signature.

What did it mean? She read the letter a second time and this time a rushing noise roared in her ears as the meaning of the letter began to sink in. Young ladies with gentlemen friends . . . the house where we live and work . . . these could only be prostitutes, surely – but what had that to do with her or the WSPU or Jonathan? It was absurd to think that Jonathan had anything to do with women like that! But then, how did they know about Dr Armstrong? For there was a Dr Armstrong – Martin Armstrong. Jonathan had known Martin for years; he went to consult him sometimes for a stomach complaint he had. *What had treatment for a stomach complaint to do with prostitutes?*

Sarah's hand had begun to shake, and for a moment she had thought she was going to faint, but she recovered and held herself icy still. She looked across the table at Mrs Watson. Amazingly, despite the fanfare of shock and alarm in Sarah's head, Mrs Watson had noticed nothing. She was diligently writing, looking down, her head bent. For a moment Sarah had wanted to scream and thrust the letter under the woman's nose, but as Mrs Watson's pen scratched slowly across the paper, she changed her mind.

If what this letter said was true, no one must ever know.

Very quietly, she stood up, walked across the room, and stuffed it casually into the back of her writing desk.

Mrs Watson looked up. She was a good-looking woman of about fifty, with greying hair tied back severely into a bun, and round spectacles that made her look like a governess. Sarah was fond of her and they confided about most things, but this! What had the letter said? *Your husband gets the same treatment other men get and whose fault is that?* Her face flushed with anger at the thought of what it might mean and she felt a pain deep inside which almost deprived her of breath. But at the same time she felt an enormous sense of shame for Jonathan which said: no one shall ever know about this even if it is true. It is his shame and I shall never betray him.

It is my shame too . . .

It was an effort even to stand upright. Very carefully, keeping her poise one step at a time, she pulled the bellrope by the fire, and when her butler came, ordered tea. Then, as she and Mrs Watson sat drinking it, she forced herself to discuss the ordinary business of the day – subscriptions, replies to letters, arrangements for a demonstration next Thursday. The conversation seemed far away, trivial, a discussion between dolls in a children's puppet theatre.

All the time the words of the letter echoed in her mind. *I suppose you know that your friends in the WSPU have been poking their noses in . . .* But Sarah did not know. She knew that such work went on but she had deliberately not involved herself in it, because she thought it would be too upsetting, awake too many memories. Now she needed to find out, without letting Mrs Watson know why.

Casually, she said: 'I read the other day that some women are investigating prostitution in the East End. Do you know anything of that?'

Mrs Watson glanced at her in mild surprise, and Sarah thought: Am I so transparent? Did I shout? But it seemed Mrs Watson's surprise was only transient and she was quite willing to talk about it.

For some time, she said, ever since the Piccadilly Flat Case last year, the WSPU had been concerned at the outrageous double standards involved in high-class prostitution. In that case, a woman, Queenie Gerald, had pleaded guilty to keeping a disorderly house – a brothel – in a flat in Piccadilly. When the police had raided the place they had found three young girls there, aged 17, 18, and 19, and a detailed ledger explaining how they earned their money. There were also letters, many from a man who lived in the Ritz hotel, arranging appointments for his clients. As a result of the raid, Queenie Gerald pleaded guilty and was sentenced to three months imprisonment in the second division.

Several things outraged the suffragettes about this case. Firstly, the fact that it happened at all. Secondly, the fact that the madam of this brothel got off with three months, whereas Mrs Pankhurst, whose crime was to ask for political rights for women, had been sentenced to two and a half *years*. And thirdly, the fact that none of the girls' clients, believed to have been rich and famous men in the public eye, had been named at all.

'I remember it, yes,' Sarah said, 'Christabel Pankhurst has written a pamphlet about it, hasn't she? *The Great Scourge*. But what has that to do with us now?'

'Well, Mrs Becket, since then, several ladies in the Union – my cousin is one of them – have been watching houses which they believe to be bawdy houses. They want to find out how they are run and who uses them. Very unpleasant work – several times they've been approached by men themselves.'

'Yes,' Sarah shuddered. 'And?'

'Well, it's hard to find out much. Most of the girls are uncooperative, and when they think we're watching them they send their bully-boys out to harass our ladies and drive them away. But we're making progress slowly. One of the things we'd like to find out is who is making a profit and organising it. And another thing . . .' Alice Watson hesitated, peering at Sarah cautiously over her glasses.

'Yes, go on. What other thing?'

Mrs Watson sighed. 'There is a possibility that young children may be involved. Some ladies were watching a house in Hackney last week when they saw a middle-aged woman go in with two little girls, about thirteen or fourteen. She came out half an hour later with the same children dressed in gaudy clothes and feathered hats – not at all becoming. They got into a cab and our ladies tried to follow but they lost it in Kensington somewhere.'

'Children?' Sarah sat down weakly. 'You mean little girls are still involved in prostitution today?'

'So it seems. We can't tell for certain. The suffragettes went back to Hackney and knocked on the door and asked for the owner of the house. A man came out but he didn't help, far from it. He told them it was a respectable neighbourhood and called his manservant to throw them out.'

'How awful!' Sarah shuddered. 'But why didn't they call the police?'

She knew the answer even before Alice Watson confronted her with a resigned, reproving look. 'Call the police and expect them to take the word of two suffragettes against a male householder? Where would that lead? There was no proof that he had done anything wrong, and in fact very few men were seen going into that building, no more than any other house. So perhaps the girls worked elsewhere and were just brought to that place on the way. We need evidence before we can move, evidence that will stand up in a court of law.'

'Evidence of what, exactly? You say they saw these children come out.'

'Yes, but where did they go? There is no crime in dressing a child in gaudy clothes. We need evidence that the children are actually under age and being exploited; we need to know who is procuring them and how; and then, if we are lucky, we need the names of the men who go to these places, as well as evidence against the madams who run them. If we knew all that, we would have a scandal to shake the streets of London!'

'But what about the little girls? Surely they should be rescued, if possible. What about their parents?'

Mrs Watson shrugged. 'Probably most of them are orphans, or the children of criminals. Maybe some of the parents even profit by it. We think the little girls are taken from house to house, to meet the needs of men who are attracted to that sort of thing. I agree it is . . . not pleasant.'

Not pleasant. It most certainly was not, especially when you had just received an anonymous letter suggesting your own husband was connected with a scandal like this. And Mrs Watson's story seemed to parallel the letter so closely. But there was one vital detail missing from what Mrs Watson seemed to know. And that, Sarah thought grimly, is perhaps what I have received in a letter. Only it names my husband as an accessory to this crime.

She felt sick. Perhaps Christabel Pankhurst was right, all men are diseased in their minds. Could Jonathan really . . .?

'Are you all right, Mrs Beckett?'

'What?' She must have swayed, looked pale for a moment. If I go feeble now she'll start nursing me again and I don't want that. I'm tired of that, Sarah thought. She sat up straight on the sofa and smiled brightly. Whatever happens, whatever Jonathan has done, this woman must never know. No one must know, it is too foul, too shameful! Anyway, it may not be true. 'Yes, of course,' she said. 'I'm fine. But we've talked too much. Let us finish our correspondence, shall we?'

Now, alone in the police cell, her hand pressed against the cold grimy stone of the wall, she thought: that was the hardest moment of all, to get up and go back to ordinary letters and work through them as though nothing had happened, with the foul secret eating away inside me like a tapeworm all that time, and say nothing at all . . .

When Mrs Watson left, Sarah went into Jonathan's study and there they were, quite openly marked in his diary. Appointments with Dr Martin Armstrong. About once a week, regularly, sometimes more. For nearly a year now, usually on Tuesday or Saturday evenings. If it was for his stomach it clearly had not done much good – she had never thought of this before. She leafed her way back through the pages, appalled. Dr Armstrong's address was, 40, Roland Gardens, Kensington.

And Jonathan had an appointment for tomorrow afternoon . . .

As the night wore on, the drunk in the cell down the corridor stopped singing and only made the occasional loud, querulous complaint which ended with a kick against his door. More women had been brought in – prostitutes possibly, Sarah thought, for they cursed the constables with a cheerful, raucous obscenity, and mocked them noisily from within their cells. Sarah didn't know a lot about prostitutes and she didn't want to. No doubt they were exploited by men, but it was the class of women she found it hardest to feel sympathy for. Especially when they were assertive, and proud of what they were.

First her father, and now Jonathan . . . She didn't want to remember but now, in the lonely middle of the night, there was nothing else to think about. She had to. She thought back to the events of last night. After her conversation the day before with Mrs Watson . . .

She had only been out of the house a couple of times since her release from prison, and it had been difficult to arrange. She had had to face down Reeves, their butler, who was justifiably anxious for her health, and afraid that she might be re-arrested. She put on her oldest dark coat and a faded, flowery hat, took an old parasol, and slipped out of the side door where the deliveries were made. She had noticed no policemen in the Square, and when she had walked a couple of hundred yards she had hailed a motor taxi for Kensington.

She had found Roland Gardens without difficulty. It was an impressive street of tall, four-storey buildings, some still inhabited by wealthy families, others converted into expensive flats. Nannies pushed prams down it and ladies of Sarah's own class strolled on their way back from the park, talking idly. Nothing in the least unpleasant or disreputable or frightening anywhere.

Doctor Armstrong's brass plate was on a doorway about halfway down. When she had found it she walked quickly across the road, wondering where on earth she could position herself to watch the entrance. It was difficult, there were no restaurants or shops, nowhere obvious at all. Her only solution was to walk slowly to the end of the street and then, equally slowly, back up the other side. If I do this too often, she thought, people will start to ask questions.

The hansom cab arrived when she had just begun to turn to go back. A man got out, paid the cabbie, and walked briskly inside.

Jonathan!

She knew it was him even from a distance of a hundred yards. She would have known him anywhere – that brisk, lithe figure, the short beard, the casual tilt of the top hat. A gentleman calling for an appointment with his doctor. Nothing unusual about that, nothing suspicious. What could she do now?

Sarah walked slowly back down the street, thinking. She was not entirely clear why she had come. She had established that he did indeed come to see Martin Armstrong, but that was no secret – it was in his diary, openly admitted. What she really needed to know was what went on inside the house, and that she had no way of knowing. What had the letter said? *Treatment – he gets the same treatment as other men*? Something like that. But what did that mean? After all, one went to a doctor for treatment. Surely nothing indecent could happen in a proper consulting room, when Jonathan was there with Martin Armstrong?

What she needed to know was what was being said inside that house. What should she do? Walk up the steps and ring the bell?

And then go inside and say: 'Hello, Jonathan, I was just passing and I dropped in to see how your stomach is being treated.'

The idea was absurd. So was the setting. The street was far too quiet, too respectable, too prosperous. She walked up and down it again, flushed with embarrassment, keeping her parasol between her face and the windows of number 40. She began to think of going home.

Then, as she turned down the street for the fourth time, a man approached her.

He was a short, rather stout man, in a business suit and bowler hat. She had seen him leaning against a wall reading a newspaper last time she had come down the street. This time, as she walked past, he fell into step beside her.

'Nice evening for it,' he said.

'What?' She glanced at him, surprised, distracted. Just before he had spoken she had seen the door of number 40 begin to open. No one had come out yet but . . .

'I said it's a nice evening, dear,' the man said. She glanced at him and saw he was smiling in a way she didn't like. 'Got a place near here, have you?' He offered her his arm.

'What on earth did he mean? Despite herself, the polite gesture of a man offering a lady his arm was so compelling that she moved her own hand automatically towards his elbow, before she realised what she was doing and stepped hurriedly away.

'I think you're mistaken. I don't think we've met.'

The man stared at her, puzzled, his arm still raised and the unsettling smile still on his lips. They were rather thick lips, she noticed, and there was a boil on his neck.

'No, we haven't met yet, petal, but I want to know all about you. How much do you charge?'

Oh God. Understanding rose like bile in her throat. He thinks I'm walking up and down this street to solicit custom. She wondered whether to hit him with her parasol and then thought no, that will attract attention. And there is a man coming out of the doctor's surgery . . .

'Get away from me! You've made a mistake. I'm not one of those women. Leave me alone!'

The words sounded completely stupid, foolish, but what could one say? No one had ever approached her in that way before. She walked quickly away down the street and thank God, *thank God* the man did not follow. She could not walk very fast because she was still not fit, but no footsteps followed. As she went on down the street she came closer to number 40 and she saw the man who had come out cross the road in front of her. He reached the pavement on the other side and walked briskly back up the way she had come.

A well-dressed, burly man in morning coat and top hat, with thick eyebrows and moustache, heavy jowls, and a hearty confident stride. She had not seen him for nearly a year but she recognized him – it was Martin Armstrong . . .

She shielded herself from view with her parasol and walked to the end of the street. Her face was flushed and she was breathing deeply as though she had run a mile. As she stopped and looked back her legs trembled.

Now what? The man with the newspaper was still there. He stared back up the street at her, then snapped his paper shut and strode angrily away, out of sight round the corner. Dr Armstrong was getting into a cab.

I can't stay here, Sarah thought, I can't face that again. This is all a mistake, I'll just wait until Jonathan comes out and then I'll go home. I'll think about what to say to him later.

After all, what can I say? I received this letter and then I followed you to your doctor and saw you go in and then waited until you came out, and a man accosted me in the street. What sort of an accusation was that?

This is all nonsense. It's just a bad dream.

The flush faded from her face and her breathing returned to normal. Martin Armstrong's cab had long gone, and the street looked peaceful and empty. A nanny was pushing a pram down one side, and a little boy was riding a tricycle on the pavement in front of her. The gas lights were coming on in some of the windows.

Why hasn't Jonathan come out?

When you go to the doctor's it's never the doctor who leaves first, it's the patient. Martin Armstrong came out five minutes ago, and Jonathan's still in there.

Perhaps it's a partnership and he's seeing another doctor.

So why did it say *Armstrong* in his diary?

Grimly, she walked down the street for a fifth time, keeping her eyes open for the man with the newspaper. She had to see, she had to be sure. When she came to number 40, the brass plate was quite clear, as she had known it would be. *Dr Martin Armstrong, M.D. Private consultations.* No partner, no one else.

She stared at the front door, willing it to open, willing her husband to come down the steps towards her, to smile and put his arms round her and tell her it was all right. She thought if he did she might put her arms round him and kiss him on the lips. As she had not done for months.

Or slap his face right there in the street. She didn't know which.

Either way, she didn't have to choose. Nothing happened.

There was a light on in the hall but no lights on in the downstairs rooms, which were surely the consulting rooms. There were net curtains in the rooms up above, and window boxes and gaslight, but they were too high to see in. Most of the rooms had gaslight showing and, somewhere, she thought she could hear the sound of a piano.

She thought, this is a four-storey building, but there are no other names on the door, no other bells to ring. What does one doctor do with four floors?

She heard a car drawing up behind her and turned to see a black taxicab. She walked slowly away along the pavement and then stopped as though she were about to cross the road. The taxi drew up outside number 40 and a man got out. A well-dressed man with smart grey suit, top hat and a loud, cheerful voice. He paid the driver and then turned to hand out a young woman. As she stepped out he said something to her and she laughed.

There was something about the laugh that grated horribly on Sarah. It was high, falsetto, slightly tipsy. As though the girl was slightly drunk and determined to seem more so, to get the maximum amusement out of the man's joke and at the same time to seem silly, flighty, without a thought in her head but what he put there. As she came out of the cab she staggered and leant against him. He put his arm round her and led her up the steps.

The man did not need to ring the bell at Dr Armstrong's consulting rooms. The girl, tipsy as she was, produced a key.

When they had gone it began to get dark. Sarah crossed the road and looked back at the house. The curtains were drawn now but there were gas lights in every room except those on the ground floor. Although from this distance she could hear no sound, not even the piano, in the gathering dusk the house had an indefinable air of gaiety.

Sarah waited half an hour until the lamplighter came along the street with his long pole. By that time several men had passed, coming home to their respectable family houses and flats, and two had looked at her hesitantly, as though tempted to say something, before moving on. One other man, a distinguished man in top hat and grey overcoat, had run the doorbell of number 40 and been let in, but Jonathan had not come out.

Sarah walked home, feeling lonelier and angrier and more humiliated than she had ever felt since her father died . . .

She lay on her back on the hard wooden bed and stared up at the ceiling, where a glimmer of light from the street outside made shadows flicker in the gloom. The prostitutes and the drunk in the cells down the corridor were quiet now, and the shouts and laughter in the street outside were few and far between. Her body ached with the cold and she felt alone in all the world.

It's true then, she thought, the whole rotten system that men have set up oppresses women and destroys love. We *have* to get the vote, because that's the only way we shall ever change these horrors. Though just now she couldn't quite see how.

I slashed the picture, anyway, she told herself bleakly. That may do something for the movement but it won't help me. Because the woman in the picture wasn't just a whore as I said she was – she was me, myself, the woman Jonathan thought he had married. The woman I once thought I was. If I had stayed like that he would never have betrayed me.

She had not slept with Jonathan for over a year. It had been her own decision, part of her reaction to the trauma of her miscarriages, to her own political development. A grown man ought to be able to cope with that. If men behave like beasts they don't deserve our love.

The words rang hollow, even to herself. All that sleepless night she tried to warm herself with hatred of him but the flame refused to burn.

If he went to a whore she had only herself to blame . . .

4

The courtroom was crowded, but there were no women there at all. Sarah came into the dock up the stairs which led directly from the police cells, and she could hear the murmur of voices as she climbed the steps. The murmur changed to an indrawn hush, and then there she was. One moment in the cold, echoing, whitewashed underworld of the cells, the next in a warm, oak-panelled magistrates' court, warmed by the breath and bodies of fifty or sixty men crammed together around her on wooden benches.

She stood in the centre of it all, raised above them in the dock, with only the magistrates and their clerk at her own eye level.

Her hands shook as she grasped the metal rail on the front edge of the dock. She wondered what she looked like to all these men. A slim, tall woman with a pale face, dark, deep set eyes, and untidy brown curly hair, she supposed. Not very clean or attractive. She had washed and dressed as well as she could – one of the wardresses had given her a bowl of soap and water and a comb, and had helped her to straighten out her hat which had fallen off and been bent in the National Gallery. But the woman had not produced a needle and thread, and Sarah was conscious of several rips in her grey skirt and jacket. The men could not fail to see those.

Her hands shook, too, because she was already feeling weak after twenty-four hours without sleep or food.

They had brought her food last night, but she had sent it back untasted. She had resisted again today, though the smell of breakfast had been a much greater temptation than she had expected.

I am like an animal, here to be baited, she thought. I am their victim. They could tear me apart if it entertained them. But then, that is what all men are like, in the end.

She saw Jonathan, sitting down below on the benches to the left. Immaculate as ever in morning coat and top hat – tall, bearded, handsome. But the high wing collar only partially covered the medical dressing on one cheek, and the face which looked up at her was tired, drawn and pale like her own. She wondered if he had slept since he saw her, and if he was afraid of what she might say in court this morning.

They gazed at each other bleakly. When he tried to smile she frowned and he turned away, embarrassed, conscious of the long row of journalists eagerly watching from the side benches, ready to scribble in their notebooks.

She had prepared a speech, but everything seemed to go so smoothly she thought she would have no chance to give it. Jonathan had produced a lawyer for her earlier this morning, but she had sent the man away. He had suggested she plead *insanity*, for heaven's sake! Now, when they put the charge to her, she raised her head and proudly said: 'Guilty' in a clear voice which sent a buzz of comment through the court.

She had thought that would hurry things along, but it seemed that a great deal of time had to be given to the prosecution lawyer to ramble on stating perfectly obvious facts, such as the time of day she had entered the National Gallery and even the knife she had used – he held it up. When he called the manager of the Gallery into the witness box to explain the value of the painting, Sarah lost patience.

In a loud, clear voice, she said: 'I do not recognise the jurisdiction of this court.'

All the heads of the men, who had been concentrating on the oath the manager was about to take, turned her way. the manager's mouth was actually open in surprise. The clerk of the court scowled.

'Please be quiet, madam. You will be given your chance to speak in due course.'

'But I don't want to be given a chance to speak, I want to speak *now*! I have been here many times before and listened to *you* – now it is *my* turn. Freedom of speech is not a thing for men to grant to women – we have it of right. And I say here and now that I do not recognise this court, because it is a court composed only of men, granted its powers by a parliament composed only of men, which in its turn was elected by male voters only. Whereas half of the citizens of this country are women . . .'

'Madam! You will be silent!' The clerk banged furiously with his wooden gavel, and the policeman in the dock moved to Sarah's side and held her by the arm. But he hasn't got my mouth, Sarah thought, that still works.

She raised her voice and spoke louder into the uproar.

'That man there is only going to testify that the painting I slashed was priceless, which we all know anyway. What he won't tell you, because no one will ask, is that it was a painting of a naked woman lying voluptuously across a bed, which was painted with the clear intention of giving lascivious pleasure to men – the same men who not only deny the vote to women, but refuse to pay them equal wages, live off their sweated labour in laundries and brush factories, and seduce the daughters of the poor into prostitution. I know that happens, and I am quite sure that many men here know that it happens, too. Even my husband knows it is true. He is as bad as the rest . . .'

Heads turned, swung towards Jonathan. The reporters scribbled frantically. *Oh Jonathan, Jonathan!*

'And the painting which was exhibited by that man there . . .'

The noise was so great now that she wondered if anyone could hear. The policeman, embarrassed, began to drag her by the arm sideways out of the dock. But she caught hold of the brass rail and clung on. Perhaps no one would hear her but it was *her* trial, she would speak when *she* wanted to! She saw the reporters scribbling away in shorthand below her to the right, and a great feeling of joy and defiance bubbled up inside her. This was what she had come here for! Whatever they did to her later, tomorrow people would read her words in the papers and understand what she had done, and why!

'You men care so much about that painting which is just a

matter of canvas and paint, and nothing at all about the real living women that are all around you! What do you have to say about Mrs Pankhurst and all my sister suffragettes, who are locked up in prison and tortured as I suppose I shall be, tortured until they can scarcely walk? Do you care about the damage you do to their bodies? Bodies of real living women, not paintings! We are your mothers, your sisters, your wives – don't you think we deserve the same right that you have – the right to vote for the government whose laws we live under?'

The policeman had been joined by a colleague, who managed to prise her hands free from the rail, finger by finger, bending them back until they almost broke. The first policeman wrapped his arms round her waist and lifted her bodily backwards out of the dock. For a moment she struggled, kicking the shins behind her, but it was futile. The bearhug drove the breath from her body, and the second policeman held her wrists to prevent her fighting back with them.

The last thing she saw as she was carried backwards like a naughty child out of the dock was Jonathan. He was on his feet, angrily shouting from the far side of the court. She wondered if he had understood that she knew his secret. She had shouted it out clearly enough. But even if he had, there was nothing he could say to her now.

The policeman lugged her down into the bare whitewashed staircase leading to the cells. The walls echoed with laughter from the courtroom above. That hurt her more than anything else had so far. It's all for nothing, she thought. I'm just a freak, a monster to these men.

A child who got married and thought she was loved. A doll that thought it was human . . .

The collecting cell below the court was a long narrow room with wooden benches down either side and a toilet at one end. There were several women there when Sarah arrived, and more appeared throughout the afternoon. Most had been convicted of various petty crimes, and some were merely being remanded in custody until a later trial. There were pickpockets, prostitutes, thieves – several only fifteen or sixteen years old. Some were in despair, others proud and defiant. All, at one time or another, felt the need to use the toilet at the end of the room, in full view of the rest.

Shortly after Sarah had been brought down, a policeman had come in to tell her her sentence. 'For cutting the picture – five months. And for contempt of His Majesty's Court of Justice – one month. All in the third division. *Consecutive*!'

He said the last word with malicious relish and emphasis and one of the other women grinned as he went out.

'Must have hurt his pride, dearie, when he had to carry you down. Or did you catch him a good one in the cockles?'

'What? No – no, I don't think so,' said Sarah dazedly. Six months! She could never survive that long! But then she wasn't going to have to. They would let her out because she wouldn't eat.

She gazed at the woman vaguely, wondering what such a large, blowsy, motherly-looking woman could be doing here. 'What are you charged with?'

The woman laughed, her double chin wobbling up and down. 'Solicitin',' she said, shortly. 'Picked me up in Piccadilly Circus.'

'Oh, I see,' Sarah said bitterly. What man could possibly pay to make love to a woman like that? She must be at least forty, and plump in all the wrong sorts of places. Did Jonathan betray me with a woman like that? she wondered. Or with a child? Both ideas were equally grotesque.

Something in her expression seemed to offend the woman. 'There's no need to turn up yer nose, milady. Suffragette, are yer?'

'That's right.'

'Going to starve yourself to get out?' The rest of the women in the cell were watching with interest now. Previously, when Sarah had been arrested, she had had other suffragettes around her. She had never been quite alone like this before.

'Yes, I am. I shan't be in here for six months, whatever they say. I'm not going to do anything they tell me.'

The woman raised her eyebrows. The others in the cell contemplated her with a flat, incurious stare. Not exactly hostile, but there was no sympathy there, either. No sense of sisterly solidarity.

'I wouldn't like to do that,' the woman said. 'Hunger strikin', an' all that. They're pretty bitter about that in Holloway now, you know. Some of the doctors used to be sorry for the suffragettes once, but they left. Governor slung 'em out.'

Sarah had no response to this, and for a while the conversation lagged. More women came in as the court continued its process up above, and by midday the cell was quite full. There were women of all ages – a grandmother of sixty with wrinkled face and black teeth, convicted of stealing fruit; a young servant girl with wide, scared eyes and a pinafore over her drab grey dress, who had taken the spoons and a silver teapot from her employer's house; shop-girls who had stolen from the till or walked out with clothes stuffed under their skirts; a middle-aged woman with a swollen lip and black eye who sat in a corner and glared at a girl with a scratched cheek on the far side of the room, ostentatiously ignoring her.

And then there were the prostitutes. As well as the fat blowsy woman who had spoken to Sarah earlier there were half a dozen girls aged between about sixteen and twenty-five who had been picked up for soliciting in the streets. Most still wore their finery, splashed round the hems with the mud of the gutters and crumpled after a night in the cells. Most had hard, strained faces, some garishly covered with too much make-up, smeared from the night before. None of them were in the least bit beautiful. The make-up made it worse.

Two of the older ones were crushed up against Sarah as the cell filled. They glanced at her curiously, taking in her fine, good quality clothes, the plain gold ring on her finger.

'Lady, are yer?'

'Yes. I'm a suffragette.'

The fat woman on the other side of the cell laughed, a deep, throaty, suggestive chuckle. 'Not just any suffragette, neither! She slashed the picture in the National Gallery, she did! You mind your manners, Sal – we got a top-notch dafty 'ere!'

'You may think it's crazy, but I did it out of principle. You ought to understand.'

'Oh yeah? Go on, tell us, then.'

For a while Sarah tried to explain. The oppression of women, the low wages, the exploitation, the futility of their lives, the way the whole of society worked to the advantage of men. She was not a great orator, and had only spoken in public once or twice before, but here in the crowded airless cell she provided a welcome distraction. Her audience was captive, but sullen, frightened and cynical too.

'Look at us all here now! How many of you would be in prison at all if you were paid a decent wage by men instead of half what they get? If you had a proper education, if there were women lawyers as well as men – if the laws were made by women? If women had the v –'

'Sal would!'

'What?' Sarah shook her head, confused, as the fat woman's laughter interrupted her. She was pointing at one of the two women sitting beside Sarah – a slim woman in a blue print dress, handsomer than most of the others, who might have been pretty if it were not for a certain hard strength to her chin, and the plucked eyebrows which Sarah loathed.

'Sal likes doing it, lady! Can't get enough! She'd be 'ere whoever made the laws – wouldn't yer, Sal?'

'You shut your mouth, you old pissbag! If I had a decent flat of me own I wouldn't need to be 'ere at all, 'course I wouldn't! Just because no one but a blind drunk beggar's been near you in the last . . .'

The two women got up, facing each other, and in a moment the cell erupted into conflict, which lasted until two large policemen waded in to restore order. Quite how serious the turmoil had been Sarah was not sure, but it was obvious no one was prepared to listen to her arguments any more. She relapsed into silence, and desultory conversation resumed all around her. After a while she became aware that the two women beside her were discussing children. Sal, the woman next to her, was advising her friend about her daughter.

'I told you, didn't I? They'll look after her. She's a looker, isn't she?'

'I know that, but not yet. She can show it off if she wants to, but she's just a kid. Thirteen next July. I wanted something better . . .'

'Like what? Look, face it. She's got six months now to fend for herself without you – what's the choice? She could go into service and get up at five every morning shovellin' ash out of grates, and then scrubbing floors and polishing silver all day till eight or nine at night – would that make her happy? Or she could get a job wearing the skin off her fingers stuffin' bristles into brushes ten hours a day for one and six a week – is that what you want?'

'It's straight, in' it?'

'Yeah, it's straight. Straight way to death by exhaustion, I say. I know, I done it, dearie. Look, if Mavis has come and asked you already, your kid must be a looker, mustn't she? It's her chance, ain't it – are you going to stand in her way? That Mavis, she may look like a pig but she gets some of the best clients in the business, she does. Listen, there's a kid I know, Rachel Hargreaves. Mavis took her on a couple of years ago. Found her in that charity hostel when her ma was in Holloway – Lord knows what Mavis was doing there. Anyhow, she started her out at that place in Hackney, Red Lion Street, the one that doctor owns, Armstrong. Just like your little one she was, couldn't have been more'n thirteen then, and now I swear she earns more'n I do. In demand all over the place, top hotels, Kensington, the lot – sends her old ma four or five quid a week, never mind the rest.'

The other woman wavered. 'I could do with that, God's truth I could. And my Linda would send it to me, she's a good girl, she is.'

'Well, there you are then. Play your cards right and you never need work again. *And* you'll get a good bonus for her being pure.'

The other woman sighed. 'I know, I know. I just wish it could wait a year or so, that's all.'

'Well, it would have waited, if you hadn't quarrelled with your Dan and got forced out on the street again. But you're getting on, dearie, we all are, you got to look out for number one. At least this way your kid has a good lie in, keeps her looks, and has a *chance* of going somewhere . . .'

The cell door opened, three more women came in, and Sarah lost the rest of the conversation as she had to move up along the bench. But she had heard enough. There could be no misunderstanding what the two women had been talking about. They were talking about selling a young girl into prostitution through the services of some woman called Mavis. And they had even mentioned a doctor called Armstrong – where was the place he owned? Red Lion Street, Hackney. Could there be two doctors involved in this with the same name? Surely not! It was too much of a coincidence to be a mistake.

I suppose this is the evidence Alice Watson wanted, Sarah thought. If we could just produce those two women in court, get them to swear on oath what I have just heard them saying, then the scandal would be proven. Or even just tell Alice the name of the street in Hackney and the fact that Martin Armstrong owns a – a brothel there. If it is him . . . All we would need then would be the names of the men who are actually paying to seduce – is that the word?

Paying to deflower – to destroy – to ruin *thirteen year old girls!*

Oh Jonathan, Jonathan! In the overcrowded cell Sarah felt herself trembling, sweating, scarcely able to breathe. She tried to imagine what would happen in a bedroom in that house in Kensington when a man – a mature man, bearded perhaps, distinguished, socially secure, thirty-eight years of age perhaps, *my husband!* – came into a bedroom with a thirteen-year-old girl. A child who might be his daughter . . .

It can't happen.

It does. Those women were talking about it, just now. Men pay extra because the girl is pure, a child, a virgin. Some of these men must be fathers, with daughters of their own. As that woman is a mother, who is selling her girl.

Not my Jonathan. Please God, let it not be him.

Let there be some mistake. Oh dear Father in heaven – *why is God a father, would He have done this too?*

My father did . . .

Sarah sat very still, trembling, her hands clasped so tightly in her lap that her fingers were white and bloodless. She closed her eyes and tried to pray, not knowing what she believed in any more.

Certain only that hell was all around her . . .

At four o'clock they were marched out, thirty women together, to the Black Maria. Sarah had been arrested twice before, but for some reason she had always been taken to prison in a cab, never one of these until now. The Black Maria was a motor coach, a little longer than an omnibus, but with a single deck and no windows. One by one, two policemen ushered the women in through the doors at the back.

When it came to Sarah's turn, panic seized her. There was no room inside! The door at the back opened into a long narrow corridor, almost entirely filled by the bulk of the policeman crouching in it. His head was bent because of the low roof, and he was holding open the door to a small cubicle, a cupboard, on the right.

'Here you are, Ma'am. First class passengers step this way!'

'But – I can't!' She began to back out. It was too small, too cramped!

'Here, George, catch her back! This one's leery!'

The policeman behind caught her waist, and between the two of them they manhandled her through the little door into the cupboard, like grooms dealing with a skittish horse. 'It's all right, dear, you'll get used to it!'

'But I can't! I can't breathe! I –'

The door closed in front of her. They had sat her on a small plank, facing the closed door and the corridor she could no longer see. She had to sit, there was no choice. The cubicle was not high enough for her to stand up, or wide enough for her to turn round in. Her knees touched the door in front of her. And it was quite dark. She heard the door at the back of the vehicle slam shut, and total darkness enveloped her.

There were women all around her, in other cubicles, but she could not see them. One or two were cursing and crying, but several called out mockingly to each other. They have been here before, they are not afraid, Sarah thought. If they can bear it I can – I must. I can't set out to battle for women's rights and then not be able to bear what a common streetwalker can.

It was the darkness that saved her. After a moment's panic she found it relaxing, comforting even. Do nothing, she thought. Feel nothing, don't move. And then, as her eyes grew accustomed to it, she saw a marvellous thing.

On the back of the door in front of her, an image appeared. Very faint at first, a blur of light where there had been utter blackness before, but then it grew clearer. It was round, about the size of her hand, and there were shapes moving in it. As she felt the Black Maria lurch out of the gates of the police station into the street, the shapes of the images in front of her changed, growing one minute dark, then lighter again, and with little blurs of different colours moving this way and that.

It fascinated her, and she forgot to be afraid. What could it be? The images seemed to be moving along the top of the picture, while the lower part was brown or red, like the upper stories of buildings. Very like . . . In fact – they even had square shapes like windows which moved across them. And below, something blue, like a streak of sky – except that it was right at the bottom of the picture instead of at the top!

Then something clicked in her memory and she realised what she was looking at. She had seen something like this before, as a child. Her father had taken her and her little sister Deborah to an exhibition of photography, and there had been something – what was it called? A camera obscura – that was it! She had sat inside one with Deborah, he had drawn the curtain, and when their eyes had become accustomed to the darkness the same thing had grown on the wall in front of them – a picture of the world outside, but upside down, because the light came in through a pinhole in the wall behind them and changed places somehow.

Sarah laughed, and the panic drained out of her like bathwater. She felt clear, clean, relaxed. That was it – the little figures moving busily across the top of the picture were people on the pavement, and there were vehicles bustling past them, upside down! For a while she watched them, entranced, smiling to herself in relief. The discovery had released her from fear, like a children's story at the edge of night.

But it was like childhood in another way too. It came back to her now, with the pain of a memory that had not been released for over twenty years, what it had been like in that camera obscura. At first she and Deborah had been fascinated by the tiny figures; but just as now, they had been blurred, difficult to make out clearly. And when you did make them out, they were only ordinary people in the street, after all. So she and Deborah had started to talk, in hushed whispers, about a secret they had learnt about their father.

What was it, that secret? The memory came back to her with such painful clarity – she could even feel the print dress with ruffled sleeves she had worn, feel the way her feet only just touched the floor from the high seat. How old had she been? Eleven? Yes, she had had her birthday a few days before and Deborah had given her the butterfly brooch she was wearing. She could see it now, so painfully clear! And outside the booth, her father, in tweed coat and flannels, for it was a holiday, and he was trying to be jolly. She could even smell his cigar.

But what was the secret they had talked of?

The Black Maria lurched over a bump in the road, and the picture on the back of the door in front of her changed. They were going over the river, Sarah realised. She could see ships. But for the moment it didn't matter. Her mind made this memory seem immensely important.

Deborah had – met someone, that was it! A woman – the two girls had been watching a woman in the pinhole picture inside the camera obscura, going along upside down in front of them, and she had been wearing a purple coat – that was what had reminded Deborah of it. Deborah had seen this woman a week or so before, and she had been totally mad. Deborah hadn't actually spoken to the woman – she had been playing with a hoop in the park at the time – but she had seen the woman come up to their father and speak to him. She was rather a poor woman, Deborah could see that, but she had been wearing this gaudy purple coat which made her stand out. And she had called her father by his Christian name – *George* – just like that, as though she knew him! She had even put her arm through his, tried to walk down the path with him – it was terribly funny!

And all the time Deborah had been bowling her hoop along between the trees, watching, and seen their father go awfully red, because of course it made him look ever so silly. Then he had given the woman some money and spoken sharply to her, to make her go away. When Deborah had asked him about it he had said she was a poor madwoman, who didn't know who she was, and ought to be in hospital.

Yes, that was it! It came back to Sarah now, all in a rush. She remembered Deborah telling her about it in the camera obscura, and the two of them had started giggling. Their father had pulled back the curtain to ask what was so funny and they had danced out, still giggling, linked his arms, one on each side, and dragged him away to the ice-cream stall. They were both pretending to be that silly woman, without letting their father know. What a strange daddy he was! All you had to do was come up to him, link his arm, call him George, and he would give you money. Or ice-cream.

It was an exquisitely painful memory. Sarah could even see her father – young, as he had been then, with brown hair and slim waist instead of the paunch and bald head he developed later. No sign of that embarrassing rash on his neck which he had covered up with a scarf as he grew older.

The rash that was the first visible symptom of the syphilis that killed him when she was nineteen . . . The shock had turned her mother into a permanent hypochondriac who always wore black and hardly ever left the house until she died too, nine years later. It had made Sarah fear and distrust all men, until she had met Jonathan.

The most painful thing of all, was how she had once loved her father. So long ago – she had been so innocent. He had been a jolly man who bought them ice-creams and swung them up on his shoulders and made them laugh, and never looked worried or tired or ill as their mother often did. That was before she had learned what men were really like. Before she had learned what he had done to her mother . . .

Because he did what Jonathan was doing now.

The Black Maria stopped in a traffic jam under a railway bridge, and the tiny pinhole of light failed utterly. Sarah Becket sat hunched on the wooden seat in her cubicle, rocking from side to side to calm herself. A thin shabby woman crushed into a box in a coach full of boxes. Some small boys, passing outside, casually threw handfuls of gravel onto the vehicle, and it thundered on the roof like hail . . .

5

Holloway. Sarah knew they had arrived even before the door at the back of the Black Maria was opened and light began to seep in. This time, when the vehicle stopped, the engine was switched off, and in the sudden quiet she heard the distant thud of a heavy gate shutting outside.

The first of many, she thought with a grim shudder. She pictured the massive, metal-studded gates she had seen when she had been imprisoned here before, and remembered how she had felt then. Hopeless, forgotten, alone. But she had starved her way out and she would do it again. She took deep, steady breaths, to calm herself for the struggle ahead.

Her compartment door was thrown back with a crash and she was hustled out with the others into the dazzling grey daylight of the prison yard. She stumbled, hands in front of her eyes, blinking, and before she could fully recover she was led through a prison door, down a noisy echoing corridor, to a room where her name was entered in a ledger.

Here the policemen delivered her, like a parcel, and the prison wardresses took over. She looked at these women curiously, searching for the least trace of sympathy. On her last two visits there had been none. And yet, she thought, wardresses need the vote too. We are all women here, it is the men who are the enemy. But these wardresses did not even look at Sarah or the other prisoners. They stared somewhere above her head, or to the side, and spoke in loud harsh voices as though addressing someone who was deaf, or stupid, and far away.

'Out of the door, turn right, down the stairs to the washroom!'

'Will I be allowed to –'

'Button that lip! No one to speak unless spoken to!'

All this in that rude, harsh, impersonal voice, with no eye contact at all. A shove on the shoulder – from a *woman!* – and Sarah was out in the corridor. The wardresses seemed worse than she had remembered, harsher, as though those with any hint of sympathy for the suffragettes had been weeded out. There has been a change here, she thought, this place is worse than it was . . .

In the washroom the wardress took her into a cubicle with a large enamel bath. She turned the taps on with a quick, assertive flick of her wrist and then stood facing Sarah with her hands on her hips. She was a young woman, Sarah noted, not more than twenty-five, well-built, with strong arms and a rather wide, plain face. She was staring at a point slightly to the right of and above Sarah's head.

'Right then, you. Strip!'

Sarah considered. She had submitted to this last time but it had left her feeling foul, humiliated. The bath had evidently not been cleaned for some time. There was a grimy ring around the sides and a broad streak of rust leading to the plughole. The water coming out of the taps had a yellowish tinge, and a froth of grey bubbles was forming on its surface.

If I am going to resist at all this time, this is where I start, Sarah thought. If my maid had run me a bath like this she would have been sacked on the spot. And this surly girl is no more than a jumped-up maid, even if she has power over me. I must win her over. After all, my protest is for women like this, too. She decided to try humour.

'Is this really necessary? It doesn't look as though I shall derive much benefit from it.'

The young woman's eyes flickered for an instant in her direction, then resumed their stony stare at the wall.

'All prisoners wash on arrival. Regulations.' The wardress stepped slightly to one side and Sarah saw the usual torn, greyish towel on a chair behind her, next to a green chemical-looking bottle. 'Make sure you wash your hair, too. Nit shampoo.'

'There is absolutely no need for that, young woman! The idea is absurd!'

The grey bubbles on the surface of the water were now halfway up the side of the bath. Splashes and groans came from some of the neighbouring cubicles, but no words. Sarah did not move. Surely this young woman realised that she was talking to a lady – a Member of Parliament's wife, no less! Perhaps that was why she was rude and abrupt; it was a sign of nervousness. She looked as though she might have a pleasant face, if she did not scowl.

Sarah smiled and said: 'You know I am a suffragette, don't you? I am only here because of a protest to get votes for all women. You should support me in that, you know. If you oppress me, you only oppress yourself.'

The wardress glanced at her, briefly, and something like fear or fury flickered behind her eyes. Then she reached down to her belt, raised a whistle to her lips, and blew it.

The sound in the small echoing room was piercing, an assault on the ears. Before it was over the door was flung open and a second wardress appeared. She was slightly older and shorter than the first, with iron-grey hair and the forearms of a washerwoman.

'Yes?' She glanced at the younger wardress.

'Suffragette. Won't bath.'

Without another word, or looking her in the eyes, the second woman strode straight up to Sarah and began to undo the buttons of her blouse. Sarah was appalled. It was like the behaviour of her maid but utterly, horribly different. Did this monstrous woman think she was a doll, perhaps, or a baby? Feebly, Sarah stepped back and raised her arms to push the woman away, but there was a wall behind her and the women were used to this, knew what to do.

Each of them gripped one of her arms with one hand, and continued unbuttoning with the other. Then the blouse was pulled down, off, thrown on the floor.

'Skirt next.'

One woman pinioned her arms, the other unfastened her

skirt, flung it down. And so on with her petticoat, camisole, corset, undervest, stockings, drawers. The two women were grimly efficient, relentless, swift. They undressed her with hardly a word between the two of them, and never a glance in her face. Just a slight grunt of effort as they pulled and tugged at the fastenings. As though she was just a huge doll being undressed in nursery by – what? Monster children, without words or souls?

As the clothes came off Sarah felt a sudden enormous urge to laugh. It was so ridiculous – it was not even humiliating, it was absurd! Here she was now, a grown woman of thirty-three, the wife of a Member of Parliament, being stripped quite naked in this grubby little cubicle by two – underservants, they might be, if they did not work here. Factory girls, coalheavers! Women whose husbands Jonathan was elected to help. Women she wanted to get the vote. It had the unreality of a dream.

Her body was limp in their hands, without will, stunned. She lifted her foot like an obedient mare as they nudged her leg and pulled off her shoes, stockings, drawers. It dazed her. Nothing in her social training had taught her how to deal with this.

The laughter which welled up inside her came out more like a sob. The older woman slapped her smartly across the face, as one might treat a hysteric. Then they both dragged her by the wrists to the edge of the bath.

'You do what you're told here, first time. Get used to it.'

Sarah lifted a foot and stepped into the grey, tepid water. They let her go then and she sat down. The grime spread up over her waist to her breasts and she felt grit scratch her bottom and thighs.

'Every time I've bathed here I've come out more filthy than when I went in . . .' The mocking, superior tone returned to her voice, despite herself. It was the only way she knew to deal with such a situation. But even to herself it sounded feeble, false.

'Head up!' The younger woman lifted a large white enamel jug from the floor, filled it with bath water, and raised it above Sarah's head.

'Oh no!'

Fingernails dug into her shoulders as she tried to get up. The water did not fall and Sarah stopped struggling. She spoke in the words of a child.

'Please! I don't –'

'Regulations.'

As the fingers let go the water sluiced down, drenching her hair, getting into her eyes. Then, while she sat shuddering, something cold on her scalp.

'The nit shampoo. Rub it in well. Then rinse your own head in the bath water.'

Miserably, she did as they said. She understood now. She was quite naked, dripping, a baby in front of them. Covered with shampoo and dirty water in a mockery of cleanliness. And she had to co-operate with the process, wash her own hair. Each movement that she made to wash herself in this grime humiliated her more than when they had pushed and shoved and undressed her.

After the first grimy rinse, a thin smirk of satisfaction flickered across the face of the older woman, who was still staring away from her at the wall over the taps.

'All for your own good. A clean prison is Holloway. No germs, no diseases. They all learn, in time. I don't think you'll have any more trouble now, Miss Harkness.'

It was always the same, on the first days. They brought you the best food, carefully cooked, to tempt you to break your fast. The porridge was in a clean china bowl on a tray, with a little jug of cream beside it, and a bowl of sugar.

Sarah had never imagined that porridge could smell so good. Before her first prison sentence, she had scarcely thought of it, except as a solid, reliable food which she had for breakfast on cold mornings. Now, after two full days in prison without food, the steaming bowl of hot porridge filled her cell with a scent like that of the food of the ancient gods.

She crouched at the end of her wooden bed, her knees clasped to her chin, savouring the memories the smell brought with it. It reminded her of the cold, early spring mornings on holiday in Ulster. Days when she and her sister Deborah would get up at first light to go across the fields to see their ponies. Their breath would steam in the crisp morning air, and frosty grass would crackle underfoot as they ran.

We were such friends then, Sarah thought. And Deborah is probably walking across her own fields now, at Glenfee, while my bones ache from the cold of this wretched cell. She remembered the little girl who had run beside her, all those years ago. Deborah had always been such a cheerful, obedient child; it had been a pleasure to play with her. She had worshipped that pony, Blaze, which she had had to ride in the holidays. Probably it was then, when she was twelve and Sarah was sixteen, that Deborah had first met Charles.

Strange, Sarah thought. For a moment a tall, handsome young man rode into her memory – a young soldier with a lopsided smile and a proud new moustache, riding a bay hunter towards them across the fields. If anyone had seen us then, they would have expected Charles to marry me, not Deborah. I was sixteen, but she was only a child – even on her pony her head only came up to Charles' waist.

Oh, I wish I could go there again . . .

The cell door crashed open. A wardress came in and scowled at the uneaten porridge.

'Not eating your breakfast again, I see?'

'No. I told you, I shan't eat anything until I'm free.'

'We'll see about that.' The wardress picked up the porridge bowl and carried it out. 'It's a long time, six months, you know.'

But I shan't be in here that long, Sarah thought. Three days already. They daren't let anyone starve to death in prison. They let me out after a week last time. I can last that long.

If only it wasn't so infernally cold . . .

Resolutely, she swung her feet over the side of the bed and began her daily walk. Four paces from the window to the door, four paces back again. Already she had worn holes in the lumpy stockings, but the prison shoes were impossible to walk in – two sizes too small, and stiff as iron. The clothes were little better: a rough serge dress with arrows stamped all over it, and a ragged, yellow-stained apron and cap. Already she felt so grimy she would have welcomed a bath even as filthy as the one she had had that first day. And always she was cold. On the first day she had huddled on her bed with her blanket round her, but the wardress had taken that away during the day because she refused the 'hard labour' of sewing.

She paced up and down. She had not properly recovered from her previous fast, and her body felt curiously light and weak. But the walking made a little warmth flow through her. By counting the paces she could work out how far she had gone. Three miles this morning, she decided, then she would rest and write another text on the wall. Already there were two. She scratched them on with a slate pencil she had found, and then made them stand out with an ink she made from soap and the grime of the cell floor. On the first day she had written 'Votes for Women' and yesterday a text from Joshua, 'Only be thou strong, and very courageous.' Today she thought she might quote the Irishman, Wilde: 'Stone walls do not a prison make, nor iron bars a cage.'

That's right, she told herself. This is my morning walk and I have to make myself see the grass, hear the birdsong, feel the sunlight. Perhaps, when I am out again, I will confront Jonathan more calmly with what he has done, make him understand and stop it.

Make a new start . . .

There was a clatter in the corridor outside, and the cell door opened again. Two wardresses came in – one of them the big young slab-faced girl like a coalheaver who had forced her into the bath. This girl, Miss Harkness, took Sarah by the arms, pushing her back towards the window so that a man could come in behind them. A third wardress came in behind him, pushing a trolley.

'What do you want now?'

The wardresses ignored her. The doctor said: 'You haven't been eating, Mrs Becket.'

'I refuse to eat anything while I'm unjustly imprisoned.' The words came pat, she did not think about them. But she had seen the trolley and, despite herself, her thin body began to tremble uncontrollably. *This is not supposed to happen. They don't do this any more. The whole point of the Cat and Mouse Act is to get away from the horror of . . .*

'Then we must feed you.'

She did not look at the man at first; all her attention was

focused on the trolley. There was a white enamel jug on it, a bucket, two large mechanical devices rather like clothespegs, one wooden and one metal, a funnel, a jar of what looked like glycerine, and a rubber tube. The tube was about half the width of a garden hose and very long. It lay there, curled round and round and round on itself, like a sleeping cobra.

If I have to face this, she thought, I will. Maybe it's only a bluff anyway and when I refuse they will go away.

'I don't want to be fed, thank you.'

'Then will you eat your breakfast?'

'No.'

She dragged her eyes away from the trolley and looked at the doctor. He was a well-built young man, not much taller or older than she was herself. He had a solid, square, dependable face, with a luxuriant brown moustache. Sarah could imagine him preening it in the mornings and dabbing at it genteely as he sipped his soup. It was a pleasant, presentable face, like that of thousands of other normal young men.

The face said: 'Lay her down on the bed.'

'No!' Sarah struggled, but the wardresses were ready for her. They each held an arm and backed her towards the wooden bed until it touched the back of her knees, and she sat down. A moment later she was lying on her back. Each wardress held one of her arms immobile with a hand and a knee. She stared up at the young man, who had one of the mechanical clothespeg things in each hand.

'I shall have to use one of these, Mrs Becket. They are gags, to hold your mouth open. The steel one is more effective, but it will hurt, so I would prefer to use the wooden one if you will co-operate.'

Sarah said nothing. She began to writhe and kick but it did her little good. Miss Harkness, the heavy slab-faced girl, sat on her legs, while still keeping a grip on her arm.

The young doctor sighed. 'I'll try the wooden one first, anyway.'

The third wardress held Sarah's head, and the doctor began to try to force the wooden thing into her mouth. Sarah pressed her lips together as hard as she could. Even as she did it, she could feel the lines of tension spreading out from her mouth, all over her face, and the thought flashed through her panic-stricken mind that she must look like a grim, disapproving old spinster. But the young man peeled her lips back with his fingers, and thrust the wooden gag between them. It banged against her teeth. He changed his grip, and with the wardress's help, used his strong fingers and thumbs to try to lever her lower jaw down. Slowly, horribly, she felt a gap opening between her teeth.

He thrust part of the wooden gag into the gap, and reached behind him for the tube. But as he did so his grip loosened slightly. Sarah bit the edge of the gag with her teeth, twisted her head violently, and spat it out with her tongue.

The sudden twist had wrenched her neck. But there was no time to think of that. The wardress gripped her head firmly by the hair and ears. Sarah stared up, helpless, at the young man's reddening face.

'All right, it'll have to be the steel one, then, if that's the way you want it. I warn you, Mrs Becket, the more you resist, the more this is likely to hurt. This thing is just a device to hold your mouth open while I feed you, nothing more. But whatever you do, keep your tongue down when I put it in, or it'll get trapped. If you behave sensibly, no one will hurt you.'

'You're already hurting aaaaaauuugghch!'

It was a mistake to open her mouth. He must have been watching for that, and he was quick – much quicker than she had imagined. The steel gag was in her mouth, filling all of it, hard cold sharp metal forcing her tongue down and her jaws apart, banging against her teeth. She tried to turn her head but the big young wardress held her firmly, immobile. The young man was bending over her, intent like a dentist, twiddling with some knobs or levers that set the thing more firmly in place, stretching her jaws apart to the maximum extent. She tried to spit it out but there was no way. Her tongue was flattened, trapped.

Satisfied, the young man turned away, back to the trolley. There was nothing Sarah could do – arms, legs, head, all were gripped tightly by the wardresses. She tried to scream, but a high, thin, gurgling sound came out, terrifying her. Even her voice was imprisoned by this gag, and the scream brought saliva into the back of her throat, so that she thought she would choke, drown in her own spit.

The young man turned back, the tube in his hand. He was rubbing glycerine from the jar around the end of it.

'I'm going to pass this tube down into your stomach, Mrs Becket, and then feed you through it. It isn't dangerous, but I advise you to lie still and co-operate if you don't want it to hurt.'

The tube came towards her, like a black snake in his hand. Sarah's eyes were wide open, and she screamed again – she couldn't help it. And then it was in – going in, down into her throat. Despite the glycerine, the end of it scratched, but it went past her throat and on down, more and more and more of it. The tube filled her throat so that she could make no noise, only suffer. She felt herself begin to vomit, but the muscles contracting around the tube had no effect on it so that nothing came up. More and more tube went in. Her wide lidless eyes stared at him as he methodically fed it in and in and in and she thought, that must be two feet, maybe three, nearly a yard of tube inside me, surely he can't possibly need so much, when will he ever stop?

Her body tried to vomit it out again and her throat gurgled and she nearly choked. She thought, what if I can't breathe? They'll suffocate me and there's nothing at all I can do. She took great desperate snorts of air through her nose and thought: how thin my nostrils are, how easily they could get blocked. I had a cold last week – please God don't let me cry because my nose often gets blocked then and I'll die!

The young doctor stopped feeding the tube into her. He picked up the funnel and jammed it into the other end. Then he held the funnel and the other end of the tube with his left hand, directly above Sarah's face. With his right hand he picked up the white enamel jug.

He looked down at her and smiled!

'Here you are, Mrs Becket. Your breakfast. Best beef broth with egg whipped into it. Just the thing to put strength back into you and bring you to your senses. I'm going to pour it slowly into your stomach through this tube. All right? You'll feel better afterwards.'

He began to pour. She didn't, in fact, feel anything at first. Just a slight warmth and swelling inside the tube as the soup went down inside her throat. Then, as he went on, there was an ache and a bloating feeling inside her stomach. She tried to shift her legs to ease the discomfort, and became horribly conscious of the heavy wardress sitting on them. Please God don't let that woman move, she thought – if she puts any weight on my stomach, I'll drown in all this, something will burst and I'll die . . .

There was a gurgling sound from the funnel at the top of the tube, and the young man put the enamel jug down with a clang.

'That's it, then, Mrs Becket. Now, I'll just take this tube and gag out, and leave you in peace to digest your meal.'

He began to haul the tube up, hand over hand like a sailor hauling an anchor out of the sea. Sarah became aware that she had a headache, and a rising tide of nausea was flooding through her. Her face, her neck were sweating. Still she could not move. The doctor bent over her and began to fiddle with the knobs of the steel gag, to loosen it from her mouth. As he pulled it out, the nausea became unbearable. She retched, and a stream of brown vomit shot out all over him.

The wardress let go of her head, and the doctor started back. Sarah was aware of the foul stuff all over her face and hair, and she struggled onto her side, her hands free for the first time. Feebly, she tried to brush the vomit away. It was on her face, her dress, the bed, the floor – everywhere. She saw it was on the doctor's coat and hands too – he was cursing and mopping them with a handkerchief.

Sarah sat with her head in her hands on the edge of the bed, wondering if more would come. She wanted to do something about it, clean it up, but for the moment she was too weak to move.

One of the wardresses took the bucket from the trolley and placed it in front of her. Then she opened the door, went out into the corridor, and came back with another prisoner, a sad, grey-haired woman in a serge dress covered with arrows, who had a mop and bucket of water in her hand.

'There! This prisoner's been sick. Clean it up, will you, quick as you can!'

The doctor stood by the trolley, mopping his coat. He glared at Sarah in disgust. 'Look at what you've done now, you stupid woman! Mess everywhere! If you can't take the punishment, you shouldn't commit the crime. Learn to eat, or we shall be back again tomorrow, and every day from now on!'

He marched out. The three wardresses stayed, watching the elderly prisoner slowly, methodically mopping the floor. She did it without comment, never raising her head to look at anyone. Sarah felt immensely sorry for her.

'I'll clean it up myself next time,' she whispered. Her voice was so faint that she wondered if anyone could hear it. She looked up at the wardress who had held her head. 'Do you think . . . I could have a bath, or a wash at least? This stuff is in my hair and on my dress.'

'Bathtime's six o'clock. You'll have to wait till then.' The young slab-faced wardress glared at her, then relented slightly. 'But I'll see you get a bucket of water and a towel. Whatever 'appens, 'olloway's a clean prison, we can't change that.'

'Thank you.' Sarah gazed down at the woman scrubbing the slimy floor, and shivered. She felt so cold, feebler than she had ever been in her life. It has happened now, she thought slowly. I have suffered, as other suffragettes have done. And I am still alive.

This is what men do to women. When we protest and stand up for our rights they don't understand or respect us at all. This is the only way they can fight back.

Does Jonathan know they are doing this to me?

When the floor was clean the young wardress sent the elderly prisoner to fetch a bucket of water and a towel. Then they all went out and left her alone.

For a long time she sat without moving on the edge of her bed. Even to move a finger was an enormous effort. But then the smell and the stickiness of her hair became too much to bear, and slowly, very carefully, she knelt down on the grimy floor in front of the bucket, picked up the cake of grey, gritty soap, and started to wash her hair.

Much later, she dragged herself to her feet, and, with the towel wrapped like a turban round her head, began to totter the four steps from window to door, and back again.

Again. And again. And again.

Three miles a day. Making herself see the grass. Hear the birdsong. Feel the warm sunlight on her back.

Remembering Glenfee . . .

PART TWO

Deborah

6

Deborah Cavendish stood on the verandah at Glenfee, waiting.

Her home, Glenfee Lodge, was a three storey red-brick building of some fifteen or twenty bedrooms, standing in ten acres of parkland on the edge of Strangford Lough. In front of her the lawns sloped down towards the lough, and in the orchard the apple trees were resplendent with blossom. Away to her right, gardeners were raking out nursery beds in the walled vegetable garden and planting out seedlings from the cold frames; and all around them, birds flitted to and fro, seeking bits of straw and twigs for the nests they were building in the luxuriant creepers that festooned the south wall of the Lodge.

She was a fair-skinned woman, tall and slim like her sister but with full breasts and a delicate, motherly face that tended to freckles if she was out too much in the sun. Unlike Sarah she had long fair hair which was wound into an elegant coiffure parted in the middle and swept back round the top of her head, like a turban. It was a style that was supposed to be fashionable, but Deborah was not quite sure if it suited her or not. She was never sure of things like that. She only knew that it took her maid half an hour's careful work each morning to pin it into place, that it made her look very similar to the fashionable ladies in *The Times*, and that it was very easy to pin a hat on to. She would have preferred to wear her hair long and loose over her shoulders as she had as a girl, but of course no married woman of twenty-eight could do that, it would cause a scandal.

So Deborah wore her hair up and the hairstyle made her hold her head up too, making her delicate face look rather proud, anxious, on edge. She had a straw hat on and a full-length white dress with a high collar. There were white gardening gloves on her hands, and she was carrying a basket of tulips and late daffodils which she had just picked and was intending to arrange in the house. She had caught sight of herself in a mirror before she went outdoors and thought: I am dressed like a bride today.

Not that Charles will notice . . .

But he *has* to notice me sometime. Sometime *soon*. If he doesn't, it will be too late.

I may look like a bride but I feel like a whore . . .

Deborah had seen the first swallows earlier in the week, and as she watched, one swooped in under the eaves of the stables to where they had built a nest of mud every year since Deborah's marriage.

Nine years, Deborah thought. Which means those swallows must have hatched how many chicks under our roofs: twenty, thirty? But they can't be the same birds – how long does a swallow live? We have reared generations of swallows while I just have the one son . . .

But an afternoon like this was made for hope. She looked beyond the lawns to the sparkling blue waters of the lough, where the brown and white sails of fishing boats bobbed up and down; and then glanced left, along the dusty white coast road to Killyleagh, where two horsemen were riding towards the house.

She watched as they passed through the gates and rode up the drive. They were a handsome pair – the tall man on the bay hunter and the boy on the dapple grey Connemara pony. As they came nearer the man saw her and waved, and her heart leapt. Perhaps it would really work this time, she thought. It had been a difficult few weeks, these Easter holidays, but now that Charles was back from Egypt at least he had made a real effort to spend time with their son, Tom. And through spending time with Tom he had spent a little more time with her, too – more time than she could remember for many years. She waved back, enthusiastically. Perhaps this time . . .?

As they came closer her son nudged his pony into a trot. He

halted on the drive just below the verandah and looked up, beaming. She smiled down at him.

'Did you have a good ride?'

'I'll say! Mother, I jumped the three hedges down by the copse, *and* the ditch! He never stopped once – ask Father if you don't believe me!'

She glanced at Charles as he drew up, grinning, beside Tom. Charles Cavendish was a tall, lean man, ten years older than his wife. He had a thin brown face with a hooked, aquiline nose, high cheekbones, and a short dark moustache. Over the years the face had become thinner, more leathery with exposure to wind and sun. When he smiled, as he was doing now, the smile always rose more to the left of his face than the right, giving an engaging, boyish look. But I see it so seldom, Deborah thought.

'Quite true, m'dear, every word! And you needn't be frightened, either – the boy's got a seat like a trooper and the pony's a genuine smasher! We'll have him out with the hunt this autumn!'

'Well done,' she said, gamely. The thought of her little boy flying through the woods with the hunt appalled her, but only briefly; she had far too many other worries now. And besides, if Tom was happy – that was the whole point of this holiday. To bring them together as a family again. Before it was too late.

A stable lad ran up to take the horses, and Charles dismounted. But Tom stayed on his pony.

'It's all right, Harry,' he said. 'I'll ride him down to the stables and untack him. I can, can't I, Father? I like doing it, and you always say a good soldier has to be able to do everything for his horse.'

'Yes, of course. Be sure to walk him round until he's cool, then rub him down. Harry'll show you.'

Charles smiled, watched them go, and came up the steps to his wife.

'It seems that the present was a success, then,' she said.

'Certainly. He's a grand little pony.'

'I'm glad. Tom will have something to boast of, at least, when he goes back to school.'

'Yes.' He paused just below the top step, and looked at her, still smiling. I remember he smiled at me like that on our wedding day, Deborah thought. Nine years ago this May, in the church in Downpatrick. Sarah said I was a fool to marry so young but I defied her. We came back here afterwards in a black shining landau and stood on the steps of this house to welcome our guests to the reception. The photographer from the *Belfast Times* took a picture and printed it next day, saying we were the handsomest couple in Ulster.

Now the smile looks more like that of a general, a commander. Weighing you up even as he looks at you. Yet there is that haunting loneliness somewhere deep behind the eyes, too. It's been worse these past two months than ever before. I wish he would let me in to touch that. Ease the pain of whatever it is that gnaws him . . .

'Well . . .' As she spoke she thought she sounded almost flustered, not quite knowing how to deal with the unexpected intimacy of such a short, friendly moment. He had been away so often in their married life, they had spent so little time together. If I'm not careful I'll blush, she thought, and that would be really foolish. It's so important. 'I've spent all the afternoon getting Tom's clothes packed. I think he'll find they're in apple-pie order.'

It was Tom's third term at boarding school, and tomorrow she was to take him back for the start of the summer term. It seemed that an eight year old boy needed a quite extraordinary collection of clothes and kit to last him through the next twelve weeks – cricket flannels, house blazer, rowing strip, straw boater, black gown, house tie, house cap, and a complete selection of new shirts, knickerbockers, socks, boots, stiff collars, and suits, to replace those that his wrists and ankles were suddenly poking out of. Deborah had spent most of the last week buying and labelling these things, and was heartily sick of them all.

'Good. Let's hope he keeps them like that. He can be a scruffy little beggar if he wants to. Not with the pony's tack so far, but with his own things. Would never do in the army.' Charles stepped up onto the verandah and strolled beside her into the house. They went up the main staircase together, to the first floor where their two suites of rooms opened one off the other. He said: 'The fields are looking good, too. If this weather holds we should have a good year.'

'I hope so. We've had a good crop of daffodils anyway. And a few early tulips – look.'

He glanced at the basket she was carrying over her arm. 'So I see.' They reached his bedroom door and he turned to go in. 'You'll want to be arranging them, I suppose. I'd better get out of these clothes and change for dinner.'

'Of course.' He was wearing his riding boots and jodhpurs, and she could smell the scent of leather and horse-sweat on him. As he opened the door she said: 'Charles.'

'Yes?'

'Do you – mind if I come and talk to you while you change?'

As soon as she had said it she felt her hand shaking; it was not the sort of thing that happened between them once in a year, even. But then, it was the sort of thing that other married women must say, all the time; and she had a feeling, growing in her, that today was going to be different, lucky. It had to be, if their marriage was not going to fall apart for ever.

Charles hesitated, then shrugged. 'Why not? I have a screen, though I don't use it very often.'

As she came into her husband's bedroom she noticed, as she always did, how bare it was, devoid of almost all the things that give a room comfort. There was a faded Persian rug on the floor, but it only covered a quarter, perhaps, of the floor space. There was a desk and a chair by the window, with a selection of framed photographs of his army career on the wall around it, and one or two of him with elephants and a tiger he had shot; but none of her, or his parents, or even of Tom. There were no other pictures at all; just a couple of crossed African assegais over the mantelpiece. Other than that, there was a bookcase, a wash-stand with a jug and ewer, two leather armchairs, and a bed.

A small dressing room opened off the main bedroom. Charles went in there, hunted around a moment, and then brought out a faded screen, painted with incongruous Chinese scenes, which he erected in front of the ewer and washstand. Deborah put the flower basket down on one of the chairs and sat on its arm.

'Yes, my dear, what is it you want to talk about?'

Again the smile, briefly, but now from a disembodied head that glanced politely at her from over the top of the screen.

Deborah heard the sound of a belt and buttons being undone, and the head moved out of sight for a moment into the dressing room.

'Oh, I don't know. Nothing in particular. Just to talk, that's all.'

She felt foolish saying it, but there was no rebuff. He grunted, in a way that might have meant amusement, and then there was the sound of water being poured from the ewer into the basin, and splashing.

'Talk away then.'

Deborah felt nervous, but also determined. There was nothing unusual about such a scene really, she told herself; in some marriages husband and wife must often be together like this. He has been back in Ireland for two months now, training his wretched Ulster Volunteer Force; he *must* take notice of me sometimes. He *has* to, if our marriage is to be saved. It's almost too late already . . .

She stood up and walked towards the window, suddenly conscious of how her clothes restricted her. She was still wearing hat and gloves, and was encased from neck to toe in a dress with a corset beneath it, whereas Charles, splashing in a basin a few feet away behind the screen, must be stripped – to the waist at least. She wondered what his body looked like. She had not seen it for – so long . . .

She peeled off the gloves and flung them on the bed.

'It's a beautiful day, isn't it? I was watching the swallows – do you know they're back, building a nest in the stables again.'

'Are they?' Charles grunted, and there was more splashing. 'I didn't look.'

'Well, they are.' Charles's windows looked out of the back of the house, across the park to the south-west. Here, too, all the oaks, elms, and horse chestnuts were bright with new leaf, and the crisp spring sunlight sent a gleam of hope over all the world. There were fallow deer in the park, and away in the distance, towards the hills, what must be new lambs dancing madly around their mothers.

She turned back to the bare room, unpinned her hat. A tress of hair fell loosely down the side of her neck. 'I was thinking of the day we were married.'

There was no response. The splashing had stopped and there was the sound of brisk towelling. A tousled head glanced over the screen at her briefly. 'Oh, were you? Why, for God's sake?'

'Because – it's a happy memory, or should be. I always think of it at this time of year. And especially with Tom being here. Here am I sorting out cricket flannels half as big as yours, and it seems only yesterday he was in nappies and little dresses. I've still got all those baby clothes, you know.'

The towelling had stopped. Charles turned round and leaned over the top of the screen, looking at her. He must still be naked, at least above the waist – she could see his arm and shoulder. Muscles flexing under the pale smooth skin.

He frowned and shook his head. His mouth twisted, as though he might smile again. 'You're in a funny mood today, Mrs Cavendish.'

She met his eyes, and hope fluttered inside her. 'Oh yes, I suppose I am, Charles,' she said. She took two steps towards him, and put up her own hand, timidly, to touch the hard smooth muscle of his upper arm. For a moment they stood there, either side of the faded Chinese screen. She looked into his eyes and they did not turn away. Something dark fluttered behind them.

The screen was still between them. With her left hand, she tried to push it aside.

'Charles,' she said. 'Let me come in.'

It was difficult to move the screen. There was a hinge in front of her, and as she tried to drag the screen aside it bent between them, pushing them apart. Then, as she stepped behind it, it tottered and collapsed on the floor.

She put her arms on his shoulders. He had not begun to dress, he was quite naked. His shoulders felt hard and smooth beneath her hands. She wanted to look at his body but she was too embarrassed, nervous. She was shaking all over with excitement and fear and she did not know what to do next, not at all. They had not made love for over a year and never in his room, certainly never like this in the afternoon. But you *must*, a voice inside her cried. We have been married for nine years and I need him. If I have another child it has to be his! I want us to stay a family.

She slid her arms around his neck and put her mouth up to be kissed, and when his lips did not move towards hers she found them with her own and then – thank God! – his arms went around her waist and pulled her hesitantly towards him. The kiss was clumsy, hesitant too, but it was a kiss for all that, and the shaking in her faded and was replaced by a soft, melting sensation throughout all her body and in her loins especially. She pressed her loins against his and there was a slight answering pressure but nothing hard there, not yet, oh but there will be Charles, there must be soon my lover, my husband. She slid one of her hands down his spine, over the firm, smooth muscles of his lower back, down to the rise of his buttocks, and then . . .

There was a knock at the door.

Charles jerked away from her as though her dress were full of needles. She stared at him, her face flushing. Don't answer it, Charles, she thought, please! Just this once, tell whoever it is to go away. Her eyes met his. She saw the doubt in them, and shook her head, ever so slightly. *Please.*

The knock came again, discreet, insistent, intrusive.

Charles hesitated for another long moment, watching her. She saw something fade in his eyes. He picked up a towel, wrapped it round himself, and turned away.

'Yes,' he called. 'What is it?'

A man's voice answered from outside the door; Charles' ADC, Simon Fletcher. 'Telegram for you, sir. It looks as though it's from UVF HQ. I thought I'd bring it up straight away, in case it's urgent.'

'Bring it in for me, Simon, would you? I'm just getting dressed.'

'As you like, sir.' The door opened and a tall, fair-haired young man came in. He wore well-tailored khaki battledress and had a cap under his arm. He came into the room without hesitation, as though he knew it well, and walked straight towards the screen in the corner. Then he saw it lying on the floor, and at the same moment realised Deborah was there. He stopped, and blushed.

'Oh, excuse me, Mrs Cavendish. I didn't know . . .'

'Never mind her, Simon,' Charles said irritably. 'Give me the telegram now.'

Simon Fletcher held the envelope out and Charles ripped it open. While he was reading, Deborah stood quite still, shattered, staring at Simon. For the moment she could not bear to look at Charles. Simon Fletcher was an unusually fair-skinned young man, whom she had first met two months ago when Charles had returned to Ireland and taken command of the local UVF unit. Simon was unfailingly polite to her, and seemed devoted to her husband. But somehow she had never liked him. He always seemed cold to her, self-centred, like a walking statue conscious of his own beauty. But it was gracious of him to blush, at least, when he walked in on the scene of her humiliation.

Charles held out the telegram. 'You were right, Simon, it *is* urgent. Here, read it yourself.'

Simon Fletcher took the telegram and pursed his lips in a slow, elegant whistle. It seemed to Deborah an odd, strangely familiar thing for a young man to do in front of his commanding officer. Especially when the commanding officer was dressed only in a towel.

'Yes, sir, I see. Will it be a big operation, do you think?'

'We'll soon find out. Go down and order the motor, will you. Then come back up – I may need to send a reply.'

Even when Simon Fletcher was gone Charles did not look at his wife. Instead, he picked up the screen and began to get dressed behind it.

She heard the hurried movement of trousers being pulled on, and asked: 'Why did you let him come in?'

'What?' Charles glanced at her over the top of the screen, as though he had only just remembered she was there. 'What the devil do you mean?'

'Charles, when a man and his wife are together in his bedroom . . . you could have told him to leave the telegram outside.'

His voice was cold, distant, as though the matter was already past consideration. 'It was important, Deborah. A top priority message from UVF High Command. He was right to bring it to me immediately.'

'It could have waited ten minutes!'

Charles was nearly dressed now; he had a shirt on and his tie was slung loosely round his collar. He came out from behind the screen and stood very straight in front of her, quite hard and stern, like a commanding officer cashiering a subaltern for theft.

It was a manner he had which she had never been able to cope with. His eyes did not meet hers; they glanced at her briefly then gazed away over her head, troubled, clouded. He spoke to her like an adult rebuking a child.

'Deborah, whatever came over you just now, it must never happen again. Quite apart from Simon Fletcher, this house is full of servants. If any one of them was to find out how you'd behaved we'd have to replace the lot of them at once! You'd never live it down – never!'

He was right, she supposed; according to his code of conduct it probably was unseemly for a married woman to behave as she had done. But in comparison to other things – to the way she had behaved at other times, in other places . . . *Oh God no don't think about that not now!* She felt at once the cruel, inhuman injustice of it, and a terrible mocking hysteria that would turn the world upside down if she let it. If she once began to laugh it would turn into a scream and she had no idea where that would end . . .

She dug her fingernails into the palms of her hands and said: 'But *why*, Charles? You're my husband, aren't you? And I *need* you!'

'Not in the afternoon, woman, damn it! If I, as a man, can control my baser feelings, surely you can do the same! When I married you I thought you were at least guaranteed to act like a lady, but it seems I was mistaken. Or is this another of your advanced ideas about how the modern female should behave?'

For a moment she felt a wild urge to spring forward and sink her nails into his neck, but she never did things like that. Anyway, he was far too strong; it would only lead to further humiliation. Deborah burst into tears instead. He was her husband, so of course he was right, but if only he *knew*! She was trying to *save* their marriage, not destroy it.

But if what she feared was true then perhaps she had done that already.

If she had it was his fault too. It would never have happened if he had been a real husband to her, the one she had wanted and thought she had married, nine long years ago. Or had she expected too much – things that no respectable woman should ever want? Tears of humiliation filled her eyes.

'But if not in the afternoon then when, Charles? *When?* You haven't been a husband to me once since you came home, have you? Why is that? Perhaps you don't like me but I need you, Charles, sometimes I do! If only to have another child – I can't do that on my own, can I?'

She hadn't meant to say that. But then she hadn't meant to do any of it. She turned and walked out of the room. He was right – she had lost control and now the results would lie like a sword between them for months, perhaps years.

When her child was born he would know it could not possibly be his . . .

When she had gone, Charles Cavendish stood for a moment, rigid, unmoving. He was not a man who liked emotion. He tried to damp it down, and, when he could, ignore it. It had got him into too much trouble in his life already. He walked slowly over to the window, and leant his head on the cool glass, staring out across the park at the trees of his estate.

She is my wife for all that, he thought, the mother of my son. I should respect her, love her if I can. When we were first married . . .

It seemed unimaginably long ago. He remembered how he had walked down the gloomy reverberating aisle of the church in Downpatrick with Deborah on his arm, out into the sudden glare of the sunlight where the honour guard of his regiment waited, with an arch of gleaming sabres raised. He had shivered then, and hesitated, struck by the irrational fear that one of those blades held by his brother officers would fall and strike him dead. But of course it had not. His friends knew nothing, they had only grinned and wished him luck. And as he had stood with that young, slender, happy fair-haired girl on his arm waiting to be photographed and the proud tearful smiles of their families around him, he had thought, with a sense of wonder and guilt and hope: I have done it now, and *no one knows!*

I can start a new life. Have a wife and family like other men. No one raised any objection at the wedding. No one knows what I was.

For a few months it had seemed like that. He was not given to dancing but when he had first courted Deborah it was that which had first attracted him. He had asked her to waltz and foxtrot with him and as they proceeded round the floor he had had the impression of a young woman who was lithe, agile, almost *boyish* in the way she moved. Quite different from the usual soft, scented, simpering girls he so loathed and avoided. With a girl like that he had thought it might almost be possible. And when they were married and he came to her bed he had found it as he hoped; her body next to his was slim, long-limbed, hard, with little fat anywhere and small breasts which she was shy and ashamed of and which he ignored altogether. And so he was able to do as she expected and give her a son.

But with the baby, her body changed. Her skin bloomed and her breasts swelled and although he understood it was a natural form of female beauty he did not want or dare to touch her any more; and after the baby was born she remained the same. His child-wife had blossomed into a mother, an adult woman with more generous hips, fuller breasts, a softer, looser stomach – and, in the early years, an embarrassing love and admiration for her husband. Despite a most earnest struggle with himself, none of those things, in the end, were what Charles Cavendish wanted.

And so over the years he had taken every opportunity to be away from home, with his soldiering and his polo and his secret. A secret that, until two months ago, he had guarded more carefully than anything else in his life. Even now, he was sure, Deborah had not the slightest suspicion. Despite my neglect, he thought, the poor woman still appears to be attracted to me. And, Lord knows, she's right in what she said about another child. Of course it's my duty. It's not completely impossible, even now. If Simon hadn't knocked on the door just at that moment, I might well have . . .

As though to mock him, the knock came again. Charles jumped, turned abruptly. 'Yes? What the hell now?'

Simon Fletcher came in. 'I'm sorry, sir. The motor's ready. I thought you said . . .'

'Oh, yes, of course I did.' Charles waved his hand dismissively in front of his face, as though to brush his emotions away. 'You saw the signal – meeting in Craigavon by six o'clock. You were right to bring it straight up.'

'Yes, sir. I thought it looked urgent. It'll be about the gun-ship, I suppose – the *Clydevalley*, won't it?'

Charles paused, his tie half-tied, and raised an eyebrow. 'Now, you're not supposed to talk about that, Simon, you know.' So far as Charles knew, only twelve men in the whole of the UVF High Command knew that the *Fanny*, the ship that was bringing in 20,000 new Mauser and Mannlicher rifles from Germany, had evaded the British Navy and was preparing to transfer her cargo into the coaster *Clydevalley*, which was due to bring them into Larne tomorrow – the 24th of April. The men on the ship knew, of course, but apart from them only the most senior UVF leaders: Sir Edward Carson, Sir James Craig, and a very small, select committee of officers.

Charles was on that committee. Simon Fletcher was most certainly not.

Simon smiled – a peculiarly beautiful, winning smile, which he knew Charles could seldom resist. 'Yes, sir, I know, of course. Mum's the word.' Then, seeing Charles still lost in thought, fumbling with his tie, the young man walked over, took the tie out of Charles's hands, and fastened the knot for him. 'There.'

He stepped back, still smiling conspiratorially. 'I thought you needed rescuing, anyway.'

'I . . . what the devil do you mean by that?'

Charles's voice was friendly, like an uncle addressing an indulged nephew, but there was an edge to it, too, which Simon had not expected. The smile stayed on Simon's face, and he lifted his chin very slightly, in a way that displayed the smooth line of his jaw to better effect.

'I thought you were being – bothered – that's all. By your lady wife. I know how you say she fusses.'

Very suddenly, something snapped inside Charles. There was something about the insouciance of the tone, the self-consciousness of the pose, that hurt him deeply even as it appealed to him. *Because* it appealed to him, and Simon knew that and was using it.

He turned away, strode to a chair, picked up his jacket. 'She is my *wife*, Simon. Don't speak of her in that way!'

'But why ever not? I thought you liked me too! Isn't that why you told her women shouldn't behave like that, wantonly, in the afternoon? After all, men do, don't we, sometimes?'

'You . . .' There had never been, until now, a moment when Charles had hated Simon Fletcher. He had met Simon on the ship returning from Egypt and it was only the third time in his entire adult life that he had succumbed to his attraction for young men. He had been virtually celibate for so long; he was still uncertain how he had fallen for this boy. At times he was appalled by the shocking risks they ran, at others enormously grateful. He had felt emotions he had forgotten he had ever known – tenderness, fascination, lust, extreme love. Exasperation, sometimes, even jealousy. But never, until now, anger. It hurt him more than he had thought possible. '*You were listening*, outside the door?'

Simon saw it had been a mistake. He had only meant to tease, to flirt a little with his power over this man. The smile faded. He tried to look contrite, succeeded only in looking devious and unrepentant.

'Only for a moment. You were shouting so loud I could hardly avoid it.'

'I don't believe that.'

The two confronted each other, very still, silent. Charles had never said anything like that to Simon before. He felt the house echo round him with the importance of it.

'You're shouting now.' Simon's voice was sibilant, a whisper. 'If you're not careful the servants will hear.'

And that would be the end of everything, Charles knew. Sodomy was not just a social disgrace, but a crime for which they could both be imprisoned. He would be cashiered from the UVF, unable to take up public employment or appear in society again. At school, his son Tom would be mocked, bullied, scorned. His wife could even divorce him.

An affair like theirs was only worth the enormous risk if there was love, complete trust, mutual respect. If that was gone . . .

From somewhere outside himself, Charles heard his own voice speaking again. It sounded like an echo from inside a bell; he had no idea whether it was really a shout or a whisper.

'Simon, I think if this is the way you behave, it is time for us to end – what we have had. It has been a beautiful, a very good relationship but we always knew it could not last and this is the time to end it. I will give you good references, you will find a good post . . .'

'No!'

'What do you mean, no?' As an army colonel, Charles was not used to having his orders questioned by anyone, certainly not by a young man scarcely half his age. But then, no one else had ever had such power over him. 'If I say it will end, young man, that's what will . . .'

'I am not just a toy, you know, to be picked up and thrown down at your whim! What the hell do you think you're talking about, Charles? I . . .'

'I've told you never to call me that here! If anyone heard . . .'

'I don't care if anyone hears!' The whisper was low, but the words were lethal. 'You think that just because one day you grow tired of me, because that woman flaunts herself at you, you can throw me out in the street? Do you know what would happen if you did that?'

'You would find another job, as I said. A good one, Simon, I promise. And I suppose, in time . . .'

He paused. The vision was too painful. He didn't even want to think it. Simon was less squeamish.

'Oh yes, in time, another lover, you suppose.'

Again the silence fell between them, long, terrifying. Had anyone heard them? Charles wondered desperately where Deborah would be at this moment – to say nothing of the butler, the housemaids, his son Tom. *Oh no, please not Tom!*

Simon said: 'It wouldn't be such a long time as you think, either.'

The smile had quite gone from the young face now. Simon looked as beautiful as ever, but cold, clean, deadly. He was not blushing. Nothing of what he said embarrassed him.

'There *are* plenty of other men, you're right. I met one in Bangor the other night. A journalist, foreign correspondent, can you believe that? Just over from Europe, special assignment, lonely. I could have him any time I wanted. Is that what you want – *Charles*?'

Charles flushed. Despite his sense of danger his voice was

enormous. 'You mean you have . . .?'

'No, no.' Simon had his finger on his lips, shushing Charles, almost smiling at the outrage he had provoked. 'Of course not. I'm not a tart, not unfaithful, don't think that, old boy. I'm just telling you. I can spot them, where ever I go. It's not hard. And I need it, you know that. I *like* what we do together.'

Charles's anger was beginning to cool into a terrible sadness. Of course he had suspected that Simon might think and behave like this, but he had never seen it before. He never wanted to again. And yet, at least Simon had been faithful. And even now, he was so beautiful. I will never find anyone like this again, Charles thought, so how has it come to this?

He said, huskily: 'We don't talk of it.'

The sardonic smile had returned to Simon's face. Tinged, too, Charles thought, with a hint of sadness.

'No, not until now. But if you do send me away, you must know what you're losing.' He paused; an idea came into his mind. 'I can't help being what I am – I thought you loved me for it. But if it *were* a journalist, Charles, a foreign correspondent eager for things to tell his readers . . .' The young man bent his beautiful, Grecian head to one side and tapped it gently with his finger. 'There are a lot of things in here that I know now, because of you. I wouldn't want to let them out, by mistake. It could have serious results, not just for you, but the UVF.'

Another silence.

Far away, Charles could hear the sound of the car, its engine throbbing outside the front door as the chauffeur brought it round. And the shouts of young Tom on the stairs – he had probably seen it.

He said, very softly: 'Are you threatening me now, Simon?'

Simon stepped towards him. Suddenly, amazingly, the young man's eyes were shining. Could that be tears in them, after such a statement? If they were he ignored them, met Charles's gaze without blinking.

'What I am saying, sir, is that I don't want to go. I don't want to end what we've had, I don't want to be sent away. If I am sent away I don't know what I'll do. It could be anything. But there's no need for it, no need to think of that. Is there?'

'Yes, Simon.'

'No, Charles! There is not! Please sir, think of *me* for a moment! I'm not just some guttersnipe you picked up in a bar – I need you, I like you, I admire you! I help you in your work, don't I? I like being in the UVF, I feel proud! If I . . . if I said something wrong about your wife, I'm sorry, I apologise. I'll never do it again. I was jealous, that's all, I didn't mean it!'

For the third time that day, someone knocked on Charles's door. 'Car's ready, sir!' It was the butler, Smythe. Charles heard his own voice saying: 'All right, Smythe. Thank you. Be down in a jiffy!'

And then felt his own arms go out, to hold the young man by the shoulders. It was strange: when they were dressed, either in civilian or army clothes, they never touched. Perhaps because of fear of discovery, perhaps because there was no social convention for it. They didn't know what to do.

But, as he felt Charles's hands on his shoulders, Simon stepped forward, and for a moment the two embraced.

And Charles thought, he didn't know why, of Christ and his apostles in the garden of Gethsemane. Simon Peter. Andrew.

And Judas . . .

7

On the morning her son was to go back to school, Deborah Cavendish got up early. Young Tom was in the breakfast room before her, hurriedly bolting a slice of toast and gulping a glass of milk at the same time, under the indulgent eye of a housemaid. He had already been down to the stables to see his new pony fed. His fair hair stuck out sideways and there were several wisps of straw on the stained baggy trousers and riding jacket he was wearing. That high, narrow forehead, the hooked nose, the intense proud face: all those things are like Charles, she thought. But not the grey-green eyes, the unruly fair hair, the freckles – that's me, my side of the family.

He looked at her apprehensively.

'Please, Mother, don't make a fuss. Father promised I could have one last ride on Bramble before we go – and there's acres of time, really there is! I'll just ride up through the woods past the ice house and then down to the three oaks. I promise!'

Deborah looked at her only son and sighed. It was a wonder to her how quickly the little baby who had smiled at her from his cot had grown into this gawky, tousle-headed ragamuffin. The older he got the more mess he made, the more energy he had. Only the smile was the same.

I wonder what the next one's smile will look like?

Not today. Forget that now.

Above all, this morning, Deborah wanted to see her son smile and be happy. Even if that meant she had to deliver him to his school appallingly late, covered in dust and straw. So she sighed, touched his cheek with her fingers, and said: 'All right. Just an hour now. Mind you keep your word, young soldier!'

'Yes, Mother.' The light of relief came into his eyes. He dodged away from her caress, embarrassed, and turned swiftly towards the door. But when he got there he glanced back, and she was rewarded with the smile she craved. 'It might even be less than an hour, you know. Father says he's the fastest pony he's seen in the County Down.'

'You just mind you stay on his back, now.'

'Like a leech!' He gave her a mock salute, and was gone. As he went out of the door she thought: If I lose him, I'll lose part of myself.

She poured herself a cup of coffee and sat with it cupped between her hands, her elbows on the table, staring moodily into space. Thinking back over the past few months. About the man, James Rankin, who had made her pregnant . . .

Deborah first met James Rankin on the back of a cart in Dublin.

She was there to be thanked in Rankin's speech. She had been asked to make a speech herself but she had declined because she was too shy. When she saw how many people had come to listen, she was glad she had refused.

The cart was parked in the middle of Sackville Street. It was surrounded by a sea of people, completely blocking the road. Faces and hats everywhere – workers in flat caps, young men in straw boaters, office clerks in bowlers, a line of officious policemen in the high pointed helmets of the Dublin Metropolitan Police. And women – mostly poor women in shawls with babies on their hips, but others in small round hats, wide straw hats with flowers on, some large ones with ribbons tied under the chin. And under the hats, faces, silent, hopeful, angry, desperate, puzzled, ecstatic, disapproving – listening intently to Rankin.

Beside him on the cart, Deborah listened too, rapt. She thought he was the most magnetic speaker she had ever heard.

He was a big man, young, with a huge powerful chest and a strand of long dark hair that fell forward over his forehead and which he flicked back constantly as he spoke. He had thick eyebrows and an unusually swarthy, lean, gypsy-like face. He wore a workman's flannel shirt, hobnail boots, and trousers tied round his waist with a piece of rope. As he spoke, he radiated an electric animal energy. When she had been introduced to him a few minutes before he had smiled cheerfully at her, and she had realised that his dark face had the most startlingly pale green eyes she had ever seen. A peculiar shudder had gone through her, and later, when he glanced her way once or twice during his speech, she had the odd feeling that the whole performance was for her and no one else.

It was in the early months of the Great Lockout in Dublin in autumn 1913. The Irish Transport and General Workers' Union encouraged their members to call for decent wages, and the bosses locked them out. Rankin was speaking of the injustice of it, the low wages the workers had always been paid, the threat of starvation stalking the streets of Ireland's capital city.

Deborah knew it was true. She had come to Dublin earlier that summer, as a delegate from South Down branch of the Irish Women's Guild, to see what could be done for children in this dreadful situation. In Dublin she saw people crammed into the most appalling tenements – one, sometimes two families to a room, with no sanitation or running water. Barefoot children played in the streets, sometimes paddling in sewage. And yet often both parents were out at work, for ten, twelve hours a day. The father earned perhaps one or two pounds a week, a lot of which he spent on drink, to escape the awfulness of his condition. The mother earned a quarter of that.

With her son away at boarding school and Charles abroad in Egypt, there was little to keep Deborah at home. So she offered her help to the women who were working in the Dublin slums. At first they were suspicious of her, because of her wealthy unionist background, but she rolled up her sleeves and overcame that. She helped to run soup kitchens and cheap medical dispensaries for the poor. She visited evening schools which tried to teach illiterate women and girls to read.

As the dispute went on, thousands of starving men, women and children began to roam the streets of Dublin. Boatloads of food came from trade unions in England, and Deborah herself spent large sums having food brought in from Glenfee. She helped cook it in the strike committee's kitchens. But the bosses were adamant, and as the starvation worsened she conceived the idea of taking thirty poor children back to Glenfee for a fortnight's holiday, where they could be fed and well treated and taken off their desperate parents' hands. She imagined her great house filled with noise, laughter, children.

She brought her friend Annie Haines and three other members of the Women's Guild down to Dublin with her. It was then that she met Rankin. The day before they were to collect the children, the union had asked her to share a platform with him, to explain what she was doing and where the children would go.

But before she was able to speak, the crowd was attacked by mounted police.

She had seen them gathering at one end of the street during Rankin's speech. Suddenly, a trumpet blew, and people started to scream. The horsemen began to trot forwards determinedly into the crowd, and a second detachment appeared, too, at the opposite end of the street. Two, perhaps three thousand people were trapped between them. As Deborah stood up someone pushed her and she fell off the cart onto the road. A man trod on her – a heavy hob-nailed boot stamped on the side of her knee. She tried to get up but tripped on her long skirt and fell. Boots kicked and stumbled over her. Her elbow and neck were bruised, her right knee wouldn't work. Then, as the hooves and batons were all around her, a man bent, put an arm round her shoulders, heaved her to her feet.

'Are you hurt? Can you stand now?'

The pale green eyes, the dark floppy hair. Rankin. She shook her head. 'I'm sorry, no, I don't think I can.'

He pulled her wrist forward, bent, swung an arm behind her knees, lifted her onto his shoulder. Then he pushed and shoved his way with the rest. They were in a maelstrom of hurrying feet and legs and hooves and screams and sticks. Deborah was terrified. Once a policeman grabbed her hair so that Rankin staggered backwards; but he swung round, punched the policeman in the mouth and kicked his shins until he let go. The crowd swirled them apart, and Rankin saw an alleyway and carried her down it, through a maze of sidestreets to a small square. There was a church in the square, and a couple of shops and a pub and a boarding house – and a blessed absence of noise. He lifted her down. She stumbled, and leaned against a wall.

'Are you all right now?'

'Yes, I think . . . thank you.' She put her hand gently to her head and tottered sideways.

'You're not, though. You're white as a sheet. Look, I'm staying in that boarding house over there. Come inside and have a sit down. Will I carry you across?'

'No, it's all right, I can . . .'

But he picked her up all the same. More gracefully this time, with one arm behind her back and the other behind her knees, so that she had no choice but to put her arm behind his back and look up into the dark face that was so close to hers. He looked tired, strained, with beads of sweat on his forehead and down his cheeks; but although he had already carried her half a mile he was not breathing heavily. His arms and chest were so strong, she felt like a child again. He smiled at her briefly as he pushed open the door with his foot.

'Not how you go home usually, is it?'

'No.' Charles had never picked her up once, in all their married life. Only her father, long, long ago, before he died. But she was not a little girl with a hoop now.

Rankin took her into a living room, set her down carefully on a sofa. 'Now let me look at you. Where is it you hurt?'

'It's my knee, I think. I can't let you see that.'

'What? Modesty is it now? Stuff and nonsense! A knee is only bones and skin, we all have them, don't we? Where do you keep yours now, let me take a look.'

Abashed, she lifted her skirt for him, and there was the bruise, red already and turning purple on the side of her right knee. She felt embarrassed and ashamed of it, but his fingers were surprisingly gentle for such a big man. He flexed it carefully to see if it would move.

'You can bend it, that's something, so I doubt it's a break. But you'll not be walking on that for a few days. Where are you staying?'

She told him. Annie and the other women were in a church

hall away on the other side of town, past the streets they had just escaped from. They were due to collect the children there tomorrow morning and take them north by train later that day.

'You'll never get to them now, with the peelers all over the town and your knee wrenched like that,' Rankin said. 'You'd best stay the night here. Mrs McCafferty'll find you a bed.'

'Oh, but I can't . . .'

'You can't do much else, as I see it. Or is this place too poor for a fine English lady like you? Is that it, now?' He looked at her more carefully than before, and she felt he was seeing her for the first time. Hearing the upper-class twang of her accent, seeing that even the drab, everyday clothes she wore had been sewn by a skilled seamstress. Deborah blushed. It was the sort of implication she came up against often in her work with the poor; it was important to knock it on the head at once.

'No – of course I'd be honoured to stay if Mrs McCafferty can have me. It's just that I must get a message to my friends, and – I don't want to cause any trouble.'

He laughed, his teeth gleaming unexpectedly bright against the dark skin of his face. 'You have already. It's not every day I pick up a pretty English lady in the street and carry her home. You'll be breaking my heart next, Lord save me!'

And that, of course, was the moment when she should have crushed him. Turned a cold shoulder, shown that any kind of innuendo from a working man to a fine married lady like her could not possibly be tolerated. Only – she did not want to. His smile was so open, friendly; those pale green eyes twinkled in such a cheerful, mischievous way that she wanted to laugh instead. For a moment the laughter bubbled up inside her and she struggled to hold it down. But she was so unused to men flirting with her – or even paying her any attention at all of that sort since she had been married to Charles – that she did not know what to do. It seemed wonderful, a blessing.

'That's what I like to see.' The smile on Rankin's face widened as he saw her lips twitch. She allowed herself to laugh with him, and felt enriched.

'Well, I'm afraid I'm not much of a fine princess for you,' she said. 'With a torn skirt, grimy hands and a sprained knee. But I can offer you my thanks, if nothing else.'

'Sure and that's all I want, for now. In a way I saw you more as a sort of female pied piper, come to take ragged children to your country home. Is that the great plan?'

'Yes. Why not?'

He frowned and said: 'I don't know. Sounds a bit like the bountiful lady of the manor, to me. I hope the little chiselurs are properly grateful to you. Will you be teaching them to doff their caps and drop a curtsey before they come home?'

'Of course not!' She glared at him, offended. 'What do you think I am? I want to help these children, make them happy. Put a little good food in their bellies for a week or two. Is that something to sneer at?'

'Perhaps not,' he said slowly. 'Though they may not be as grateful as you'd think, that's all I'm saying. And you'd best watch out for the Catholic priests. Splitting up families, they'll call it. Taking the little beggars away from their loving homes to a world of sin.'

'The more fool them. My house, a world of sin?'

He smiled at that, and sent a boy across the city on a bicycle with a message for Annie Haines. But by the time Annie arrived the knee was so stiff that Deborah could not bend it at all. They called a doctor who advised bed rest with no movement. So the two women decided it was best if Annie and the others went on north with the children, and Deborah followed when her knee was strong enough for her to be of some use.

Mrs McCafferty gave her a comfortable bedroom with a sitting room overlooking the square, and ministered kindly to her needs, so in the end she stayed for a week, that first time. Rankin was frenetically busy, out early doing what he could for the strikers and their families, and meeting committees late into the night downstairs, but nonetheless he contrived to spend an hour or two with her every day. In that time she told him, gradually, the story of her life.

For that was what it became. She did not stop when she had explained her presence in Dublin. She went on, to talk about her childhood in London, her holidays as a young girl in Ulster, her sister Sarah and the terrible year they had had when their father died, her time in India when Tom was born, her dislike of living as a soldier's wife, her loneliness in her marriage, her desire to fill her big, empty house with noise and laughter and children. He seemed genuinely to want to learn about her.

He sat on a chair beside her bed, sometimes flexing her knee with his big gentle hands to see how far it would bend, or letting her lean on his arm as she learned to hobble across the room. She was flattered. She was unused to talking about herself to anyone, and certainly not to a handsome, vibrant, powerful young man. All the time he watched her with his lean dark face and pale green twinkling eyes. Even when she was serious they seemed to sparkle with some inner amusement.

'Are you laughing at me, James Rankin?' she asked him once.

'Me?' He feigned surprise. 'Not a thought of it, woman. There was never a more serious moment in all my life.'

She didn't know how to take that either, but she was aware that she was playing with fire. It was a most improper situation, especially for a married lady like herself, to have a young man, a working class trade union leader, sitting alone with her for hours on end.

As he listened to her story, a tremor of excitement and fear went through her. I am in this man's power, she thought. I do not have to tell him any of this but I want to. I have never had any man ever listen to me like this before – and I like him!

Rankin laughed easily, an infectious chuckle resonating deep in his chest, and she liked to hear it so much that she was always searching through her childhood for amusing stories to tell him. When he laughed, she laughed too, and it was an enormous release to her, something she had not done so freely and openly for years. She longed for it like a medicine.

She had forgotten life could be funny. She had not known a man could be a friend.

When she could walk a few yards with a stick she said she ought to be going home to see how much of Glenfee the children had wrecked, and whether the week had given her butler grey hairs. That night Rankin asked if she would mind if Mrs McCafferty served them supper together, at the table in Deborah's sitting room. It was to be a celebration, he said, to mark the end of a notable week in both of their lives.

When Deborah agreed, she knew it was wrong. It was a quite improper, daring suggestion. But she knew that if she refused, she would regret it for the rest of her life.

Whereas if she agreed . . .

They went out for a walk together while Mrs McCafferty set the table. James had put on his best clothes – tweed jacket and waistcoat, flat cap, leather belt round his trousers, polished boots, a bright green silk scarf round his throat in place of a tie. He had three scarves like that. They were his one luxury – something that set him apart from the other trade union leaders. They made him instantly recognisable when he stood up to speak.

Deborah limped beside him, leaning on his arm for support. Her knee was still stiff, so they moved slowly, to avoid further slips or damage. The square was not far from the Liffey, and they made their way carefully down to the quays. The sun was setting behind the tenements to the south of the river, and some seagulls were squabbling over some rubbish a boat had thrown in the water. There were barefoot children in flat caps and ragged oversize clothes trying to beg from passers-by, and on the far bank a boy of about twelve was scavenging in the mud by the river, looking for money or cans of food or scrap iron to sell.

They sat on a bench and watched him. 'He was here yesterday and the day before that,' Rankin said. 'He works hard at it. He must find something, sometimes.'

'It's admirable,' Deborah said. 'But it's a disgrace as well, that a child should have to do that to live.'

'One day he won't,' said Rankin thoughtfully. 'If we win this strike then we'll have forced the transport owners to give us a decent wage, and that'll make all the other bosses afraid as well.'

'Do you think that'll happen, really, James?' They had had many discussions like this. She thought of the industrialists she had met at dinner parties in Belfast. Some of them determined, thick-necked, stubborn men with big bellies and loud voices. Others better bred, casual, lean, arrogant, intimidating as Charles was. But both groups equally certain that the world belonged to them. Not to ignorant, uneducated workers.

James turned to look at her. They were sitting very close, and he had his arm casually along the back of the old wooden bench behind her. The setting sun tinged the dark skin of his face a rich rose colour. The pale green of his eyes reflected the darker green of his neck scarf, and as always, a lock of his dark hair flopped forward over his forehead. It's the passion in him, his naive enthusiasm that makes him different, she thought. This is a man who wants to set people free, not control them. If he chose to write instead of speak he would be a poet.

'Men may be born in the gutter but they needn't die there,' he said, passionately. 'I *have* to believe that. Even if we don't win this strike, we'll win the next one. It's going to happen, it's *got* to. One day there'll be justice and wealth for all. In our lifetimes. You wait and see.'

'You speak as though it were a religion.'

'It's better than a religion for me. I'm talking about heaven on earth now, for all men – and women too. So we can have what we want and truly deserve.'

He smiled at her and she felt, as so often before, the magnetism that flowed from him like an electric current. Her lips went dry with sudden terror, and she thought, with awful clarity: It does not matter really what he says or thinks. It is the man himself I want. And even to think that is a terrible, dreadful sin.

Please God let him dare to ask me.

Later, as they ate and drank in her room at Mrs McCafferty's, the conversation drifted between them more quietly than before, as though they were both waiting for something which it was not time to mention yet. Mrs McCafferty came to clear away and bring them coffee, and they sat in the old armchairs on either side of a small crackling fire. They talked about the strike, the prayers suffragettes were offering in church for Sylvia Pankhurst in Holloway prison, the war in China, the parade of the Kaiser's troops and the flight of a huge new Zeppelin airship in Germany. As they talked, the light gradually faded and the room grew dark, shadowy, mysterious. The lamplighter went past outside, rattling his pole. Rankin bent forward to light a spill from the fire and carried the flame to a small cigar. As he flicked away the spill and exhaled they looked at each other, silent for once, like two old friends sharing a secret joke.

She said, only a little nervously: 'I am glad we thought to celebrate our time together like this. You may not believe it, but I have never had a man as a friend before.'

He smiled, his teeth flashing white in the semi-darkness. 'Sure and isn't a good man the best sort of friend to have, for an independent lady like yourself?'

'Perhaps. But there are certain rules of propriety, you know, even in these modern days.' It was after eleven o'clock. There was another long silence. Slowly, she stood up, listening to the sound of her dress rustle as she moved. It was her last attempt to resist what she knew was going to happen – and wanted. It was the sign that the evening was over and that he, as a gentleman, should leave.

But he was not a gentleman. She had known that from the very beginning. He put down his cigar, stood up, and faced her. *Please*, she thought.

He did not touch her. Instead, very quietly, he said: 'I will go if you want me to, now.'

So the choice was to be hers, after all. She knew very well what she ought to do; but she did not do it. It is my life, she thought. And for once, I do not care.

'No,' she whispered, very softly, like a sigh. 'Don't go.'

She lifted her hand to his cheek, and she remembered, long after, how surprised she was at the roughness of it, where the bristles were. Then, only then, he kissed her. And although he was not rough he was so big, his chest and arms so strong from the years he had spent as a boy heaving bricks, that when they were naked in bed together she felt smothered and crushed by a giant. Without his clothes he was a bear of a man, with broad, powerful shoulders and a deep barrel chest covered with a cross of dark soft curly hair which went down in a thin pointed line across his hard flat stomach to where she was too shy at first to look. There was fine downy hair on the back of his neck too, and on his buttocks and thighs. His skin was much darker than hers. He was like a great woolly bear with soft dark hair, pale green eyes and bristly scratchy cheeks which he rubbed against her face and between her breasts – and he sucked her breasts too! No one had ever done that except her baby, Tom, for the first few desperate, disappointing days before she gave him to a wet nurse in India. Now, she gasped and then cried out because of the force with which Rankin did it and the pleasure it gave her. Charles had scarcely looked at her body and had ignored her breasts – this young giant wanted to kiss and rub her and stroke her all over, as though each and every part of her were soft and beautiful to him. At first she was shocked, then overwhelmed. His delight in her body made her feel beautiful. Waves of pleasure flowed through her, and as she looked down at his dark arms and legs entwined with hers, she thought: he is beautiful for me and I am soft and smooth and pale and beautiful for him too, and I have dared to do it and we are both here, *alive*, now.

And then, as he moved gently inside her, something began to happen which had never happened with Charles and which she did not know *could* happen to a woman except secretly, alone, by herself. She wanted to resist but he was kissing her and inside her at the same time and it was so *good* – and then she gasped and cried out aloud and it was too late, far far too late to be ashamed now.

Then to her dismay and amazement he rolled off her and lay beside her stroking her gently with his hand, there between the legs where she was still so damp and tender – something which she had thought no man could possibly know about, ever, but before she could push his hand away she came again, better than before. He laughed, lying next to her, kissing her breasts, and, after a while, he began again but this time she pushed his hand away and said: 'No, please, I can't!' and snuggled up to him, amazed and exhausted and utterly, totally relaxed.

It was cold in the bedroom. He rolled on to his back and she wrapped herself round him. She was overwhelmed with terror and joy and gratitude. All week she had secretly wanted him, but she had had no idea it would be like this. In bed with Charles she had always felt ashamed, confused, embarrassed. Sex was an animal function he wanted to get over quickly and have done. She had always known, secretly, that there was more pleasure to be got from her own hand, but had felt intensely guilty about it. Now – now she was in bed with a man who not only knew her secret, but laughed and loved her for it.

She had her head on his shoulder, her leg with the stiff,

bruised knee laid carefully over his, her breasts nudging softly against the smooth skin under his arms. Her fingers played with the curling hairs of his chest and she said, timidly: 'I used to dream of men like you when my father read me fairy-tales, you know. The prince who would kiss me awake.'

She felt the laughter resonating in his chest beneath her arm.

'What's so funny?'

'Well, now. I've been called many things in my life but never a prince before. I'm a barrel-lifter, that's all, a worker with a big mouth who joined a union.'

'What does that matter?' She raised herself up on her elbow and looked down at him, smiling, her hair loose, drifting in his face. 'I'm a lady. I know about these things. If I say you're a prince you are a prince to me!'

His smile flashed up at her. 'Sure it's nice of you to say so then, ma'am. But a great ignorant lump like me mostly feels like one of them goat fellows in the classy pictures, a satyr, when he thinks about it. Though you ladies seem to like it.'

You ladies.

A thin cold needle of jealousy pierced her. She had come so far, risked so much. Don't betray me now, please!

'What ladies?'

'Oh.' He frowned, and put on a deliberately broad accent to make a joke of it. 'Sure I thought there was six of ye in here at least, with all the gasping and moaning you're after doing.'

It was meant as a joke, she saw that; but it was clumsy, it hurt. Not a prince after all but a peasant. *Oh God, what have I done?*

'Don't!' she said. 'James, please, don't laugh at me.'

'I'm sorry.' He saw his mistake at last. As she tried to turn her head away, he held it between his hands, forced her to look at him. 'There's only one woman in this room and she's the most beautiful I've seen in years. Deborah, believe me.'

I want to believe you. I have to now, she thought. It's too late for anything else.

'But have there been other ladies?'

Of course there have, she told herself. How could he possibly have known how to make love like that if I was the first? And didn't I like it?

His fingers stroked her face. 'I never said there hadn't, now did I? Though they weren't all what you'd call ladies, exactly. But why talk of them? They're all past and gone, over, finished with, done. We're here, you and me, now. That's all that matters, today.'

'Yes.' She smiled and kissed him, and the film of tears cleared from her eyes. She saw him clearly now. Not a prince after all. Just a big, beautiful man, who had charmed his way to her bed and blessed her, more than she had thought it was possible to be blessed. But a man who would leave her, one day, as he had left all the others.

Over, finished with, done.

After all, who was she to be jealous, a married woman who had invited him to her bed of her own free will? Whether she had been right or wrong it had been a blessed gift, this night. She would not wish it undone if she could. Whatever the future might bring, it had changed her, changed her utterly. She would never be the same woman again . . .

Deborah returned to Glenfee and saw the slum children in her husband's house. Her servants looked scandalised and exhausted, Annie and her other women friends triumphant but harrassed. Six windows had been broken, five chickens and two ducks killed, and there were muddy paths all over Charles's carefully planted lawns and through the vegetable gardens. But the children themselves had filled out. Their faces were flushed, excited – and some, at least, had made valiant efforts to mend the things they had broken.

The next few days were filled with large, disorganised games of cricket, drives to the beach in the dogcart, huge noisy meals on trestle tables in the main dining room, and stories in the evening in the library, when thirty children sat round her on the floor, their eyes glittering in the candlelight, while nightjars shrieked in the dusk outside and bats flittered across the lawns. And then the last, exhausting struggle to pack them all off to bed and plan more activities for tomorrow.

At the end of that fortnight she returned with the children to Dublin. Annie and her helpers had decided they could not keep the holidays going non-stop, it was too exhausting. They would allow themselves a week's grace in between each group, to tidy up and prepare for the next.

And so Deborah was able to see Rankin again. For three blessed days of that week she returned to Mrs McCafferty's. Days full of guilt, passion, and laughter.

Passion made her bloom. As the weeks went by she returned a third time, and a fourth. Their bodies became accustomed to each other, the pleasure greater, more protracted. Afterwards she lay in his arms, relaxed, purring like a cat. She walked along the streets singing to herself, she looked in the mirror and saw her skin smoother, softer than before. Almost as soon as she left him she began to ache, and when she had been home in Glenfee for a few days her skin became tender all over and she longed for his touch. And that was part of the pleasure, too.

Best of all was the laughter. From the first day she had seen him, James had laced the passion of his political speeches with wicked mockery of his opponents. It was one of the things that made audiences love him. Now she found herself saving up little anecdotes about the children to tell him, so that he would reward her with that deep-chested laugh she so loved. He was not embarrassed by anything they did, not the sex or the secrecy. He was liable to find any of it amusing at the most inappropriate time, so that more than once she found herself naked in bed and laughing helplessly on top of him.

And then the laughter would fade and they would come together seriously, the more relaxed because of the previous release of tension.

She had not thought she could ever be so happy.

In November the Catholic priests brought an end to the children's holidays at Glenfee. As Rankin had predicted, they saw such things as sinful, dangerous, a threat to the family. Poor families were afraid of the Church and refused to send their children any more. Deborah was furious.

If there is one part of society more than another dominated by men,' she said, 'it is the Roman Catholic Church. The priests pray to the Virgin Mary and have no idea, none, what it means to be a poor young mother with a starving family.'

'No more have you,' said Rankin quizzically, watching her through his cigar smoke as she paced up and down her sitting room in Mrs McCafferty's boarding house. 'Not really now, have you? With your big house and fine clothes and rich husband.'

She stopped pacing, turned, glared at him, her head slightly on one side like a sparrow. She had been unpinning her hair and was brushing it as they talked. It hung in a shining rope over her left shoulder, lovely in the lamplight. She wore a pale pink ruffled blouse and light blue ankle-length skirt. Her face was flushed, her eyes alight with anger.

'Of course I understand! I'm a woman, aren't I?'

'Sure you are that. It was the first thing I noticed about you, so it was, now you come to remind me of it.'

She giggled, and stepped out of his reach. 'And that means, James Rankin, that I understand more about bringing up children than any priest in black skirts ever will. Or you, come to that. Don't you laugh at me, now.'

'Never in life would I dream of it, ma'am. Surely not.'

At Christmas her son Tom came home. For three weeks she devoted herself entirely to him. Because of the love James had given her, she felt better able to be a mother to Tom than she had for years. She took him to the theatre and the pantomime, rode in the woods with him and cooked sausages on fires of driftwood on the cold winter beach. She invited his friends round for the day to play rugby in the grounds, hide and seek in the dozens of rooms of the house, and cricket with a soft ball in the library when it rained. She listened to his stories of school and marvelled at the lanky, freckled, confident youth he had become at eight years old.

Charles sent presents from Egypt for Christmas – a jewelled necklace and bracelet for her, a complete boxed set of lead soldiers in the livery of the Egyptian army for Tom. She watched him play with them on the carpet by the fire in the library, with shoeboxes and logs under the rug for hills, and thought: will Tom grow up cold and distant to me too, like Charles? Or if I give him love and attention now, will that change things?

Deborah tried, sometimes, to explain to Tom what she had been doing for the strikers' children. He listened and nodded but showed little real interest, and she wondered: does he think his mother is mad? Or is he just polite and bored because it is too far outside his own range of experience and interest? I wonder what he'll think when he's older.

What would he think if he really knew . . . Stop it! Don't even think that, ever.

If you make a mistake he'll have to know.

I'm discreet, I won't make a mistake. Ever.

Perhaps you already have.

Of course not. I'm careful. I do what the book says, don't I?

Since that first time, when she had taken herself by surprise and been lucky, Deborah had been most careful to avoid the chance of becoming pregnant. In her work for the Women's Guild she had realised the crucial importance of the forbidden idea of birth control, and had bought and read Knowlton's book on the subject. At the time it had seemed to her ironic that she should spread this knowledge, discreetly, among poor girls who seemed to have no trouble having babies, while she herself, after nine years of marriage, had only one. But since that first night in September she had obtained a sponge and used it carefully, every time, without a word to Rankin.

Who had not asked.

So I *am* careful. We've been making love for three months and I'm still not pregnant, she told herself that December. And if I've fallen in love that's not a mistake – it's a blessing. I know it won't last but I'm in control, no one is going to get hurt. It's my life and I know what I'm doing.

Don't I?

Towards the end of the Christmas holiday there were moments when her body began to ache for him unbearably. Her breasts became hard and tender when she thought of him and when she was alone in her bedroom she ran her hands down her stomach and remembered what Rankin's hands looked like, felt like . . .

When Tom had been back at school for some weeks she had a letter from Charles.

It was dated 28 January 1914. From Cairo, where he had been for the past year and a half.

> *My dear Deborah,*
> *You will no doubt be surprised to hear that I am resigning my commission in the Army forthwith. This is*

not through any disgrace or conflict with senior officers here, but simply out of a fundamental disagreement with Liberal government policy. A number of the Irish officers here have been following the Home Rule affair with considerable concern, and we have come to the conclusion that we can no longer stand aside when the government itself is intent on destroying the Union which is at the heart of our Empire. General Richardson has been kind enough to offer me a commission as colonel in the Ulster Volunteer Force, and I shall be returning to Glenfee on the next available boat.

I shall, of course, expect to find you by my side, doing such female work as will best help to assist the Union.

Your loving husband
Charles.

When she got off the train in Dublin, she was shaking with nerves, and guilt, and desire for comfort. She met Rankin outside the station and shook hands with him, smiling, as they always did, so as to give nothing away to anyone who saw them. But the touch of his hand made her tremble, and their fingers caressed each other as they parted.

She took Charles's letter from her bag and showed it to him as they walked west along Eden Quay. He laughed.

'Well, what are you going to do then? Go home, like a good little woman, and iron his army shirts?'

'Don't be silly, I can't do that! Anyway, I don't care one way or the other about the Union.'

'Well, you could always defy him. Forbid him entry to the house unless he changes his politics.'

'He is my *husband*, James. It's his house, not mine.'

'Your husband . . . Yes. So he is.'

He sighed and put his arm round her, and for a moment, indiscreet though it was, she leant against him. Perhaps it was her own tension, but she felt that his flippancy disguised some change within him too, something not quite as she had expected. After twenty yards she broke away and said: 'James, is there anything wrong?'

'No.' The sparkling green eyes met hers briefly, then looked away, into the distance. 'Why should there be? Other than the fact that this strike is ending, and we have been beaten.'

'I know.' She saw the lines of strain around his eyes, and thought of the hundreds of speeches he must have made, the weeks and months of committee meetings, marches, pickets, food collections. All for nothing, in the end. He looked thinner than before and there were streaks of grey in his hair. She wanted to take him home to Glenfee, give him a week of decent food, hot baths, warm bed . . .

Not now. Not with Charles coming home. She could never have done it anyway because of the servants.

'I'm so sorry, James. But you did your best – no one can do more than that. There'll be another chance, another time.'

For the transport workers' union, at least. Not for us.

'Oh yes.' That wonderful, magnetic smile came again, almost as she had remembered it. But a little fainter, more weary than before. 'Always another chance. And there were good things that came out of this time too. Like meeting a fine English lady with a generous heart . . .'

He took her hand and they walked through the quiet streets to Mrs McCafferty's boarding house. On the way it began to rain, and by the time they got there her hat and coat were dripping, and they were splashing through puddles on the cobblestones. Inside, a fire was already burning. She took off her hat and coat and hung them behind the door, then stood facing the fire, spreading out her skirt and watching the steam rise from its hem. She thought: I have a week here at least. A week until Charles's boat arrives.

He slipped his arms round her, kissed her under the ear.

'Come to bed, my lovely.'

She laughed, turned, looked up at him. 'What, so early, James? We've only just arrived!'

'Yes, I know. I need you.'

And looking into his face she could see it was true – and it was the same for her, more urgent even than it had been the first time. So they kissed, and he unfastened her damp skirt and blouse and laid her back on the bed straight away, with no precautions, like two strangers meeting in the night. And that is what he is going to become, she thought, starkly. Now Charles is coming home I will have to bring this to an end. This is one of the last times. Soon the smell of his skin, the rasp of bristles on his cheeks, the taste of his lips, his hands on my breasts, his penis swelling there inside me will be all gone, memories, dreams in the night.

Over, finished with, done.

Afterwards, they took off their clothes and got into bed and he lay with his head on her breast, asleep, while she listened to the rain rattling the windows outside and the crackle of flames from the coal fire. It was late afternoon; somewhere downstairs Mrs McCafferty was preparing the evening meal, and there was the murmur of talk from men in the bar.

When he awoke, they made love again, slowly, leisurely, unspeaking. Then he got up and began to wash in the basin in front of the fire. She lay back on the pillows, watching him. Sad, motherly, content. A lake of grief filled slowly inside her, with the thought of what she had to say.

She thought: I can't do it. I've changed my mind, I won't tell him. I'll run away from home and stay with him for ever.

The idea flooded through her like a revelation. It would be simple, terrible, permanent. It was a huge relief to her. The problem of how she would deal with Charles receded, became tiny, insignificant. A ship hull down on the horizon. This is where I belong, she told herself. Here, now, in this room with the only man who has ever loved me. How could I ever have thought of leaving him?

As he pulled his trousers on he stood quite still and looked at her. The skin of his deep, hairy chest glowed rosy in the firelight. His face was dark, lean, his jaw shadowed with the afternoon's growth of stubble. His hair was still tousled by their lovemaking and the firelight flickered softly in his eyes. She thought: he is like a beautiful savage. A Celtic chief from long ago.

He said: 'I shall always remember you like that.'

'Me?' She had not considered her own appearance. 'Why?'

'Warm and happy like that in bed.'

She smiled sadly. 'And I you. Why do you talk of remembering, James?'

'Ah well, you see. That's because . . .' He came and sat on the side of the bed, took her hand. For a moment he stroked it, thoughtfully.

Then he said: 'I have to go away.'

Five words. Once when she was a little girl she had been bitten by a snake. It was a very small snake, an adder only eighteen inches long with fangs like tiny needles in a jaw no wider than a man's thumb. Her arm had swollen like a balloon, her heart had thumped like a trip-hammer and she had been unable to move for hours. She had nearly died. Afterwards, her father had shown her the dead snake and she had thought: all that pain and paralysis came from a drip of venom half the size of a raindrop. She thought now: he means for ever.

'Away? Where?'

'To England. London, at first.'

'Oh!' Relief flooded through her. 'Then I can come with you.'

'No, Deborah.'

'What do you mean, no? Why not?'

He bowed his head, stroked her hand in his. 'It wouldn't look right. There's a big dispute blowing up in the docks there and I'm to help, if I can. Some of the boys in the union, they see affairs like ours as a – well, a diversion – but there are others with strict moral standards. The two of us coming would just create scandal – they would hold it against me and I'd never get started.'

She understood that. 'I didn't mean I'd get off the train on your arm, of course not. But soon, when you've found somewhere to stay.'

'Maybe. I don't know.' He paused and looked up. She felt her heart beat fast, as it had when the snake had bitten her. 'Listen to me, Deborah. The dear knows we've had a fine time together and I wouldn't have missed it for the world. But I hope you've not imagined . . . it can't last for ever, you know.'

'No,' she said. 'Of course you're right.' Her mouth was quite dry, the words did not come out as they should. She slipped her hand out of his and sat up straight in the bed. 'James, I came here tonight to tell you the same thing.'

He stood quite still. 'The same thing? What do you mean, woman?'

'That we can't go on. My husband is coming back and – it is foolishness what we're doing, as you say. Only . . . I wasn't going to say it, because . . .' Tears overcame her. She shook her head for a moment to be rid of them. Then looked up and said: 'Like you, I wouldn't have missed it for the world, my lover.'

There was a silence. Some workmen's boots clattered on the cobbles outside and there was a laugh from downstairs in the bar. Deborah waited, her eyes blurred, smiling nonetheless.

He said: 'You were going to leave me? To go back to your husband?'

She nodded. 'Please don't be angry, James. *But I can't.*'

He picked up his vest and pulled it on, over his head. It was nothing, but the action seemed callous, unconcerned, as though she did not matter to him any more.

'You have to accept it, Deborah. I know it's hard at first but it's for the best in the end, believe me. You must have known. You're a fine lady with a house to keep up and a husband coming home, and me – what have I got to offer? A series of rented, secret rooms, the chance of prison or being beaten up in a strike, a scandal in the end. It's foolishness, Deborah! Plain foolishness, what we're doing!'

'And you have other women?'

'No!' His back was to the window so she couldn't see his face clearly, and she was glad of that. She didn't want to know what he looked like when he lied.

There was a silence. Deborah waited, her eyes quite dry, unweeping. She felt like a woman turned to stone.

'Well, yes, of course there are one or two.' He shuffled, turned his back on her, to stare out of the window. Then whirled round again, defiant. 'We're adult people, Deborah. I never made any promises, did I? We both knew what we were doing.'

'Did we?' Deborah spoke with an immense weariness, like one already dead. And I would have given up everything for you, she thought. Pointlessly, she asked: 'What did you think you were doing, then, James?'

For answer, he came and sat down again on the bed. A faint trace of a smile crossed his face. Magnetic, gleaming, as before. Its insincerity terrified her. Under the covers, she moved her legs aside, to avoid any possible contact with him.

'I thought I was making love to one of the most beautiful, generous women I had ever met.'

'Oh, for God's sake!' She flung the covers aside and got out of bed, naked. Took her coat off the hook behind the door and wrapped it around her.

Rankin continued, stubbornly. 'A beautiful, generous, rich woman who needed an affair because her husband was away and unkind, but who knew what the rules were and would not make a fuss when it ended.'

'Rules, James?' She whirled round and glared at him. 'You, a man who wants to turn society upside down, talk to me of rules? I thought you believed in the freedom of people to make their own choices in life, to become what they really want to be! Haven't I heard you say that, ten or twelve times a day?'

'Of course. But . . .'

'But what? But you've changed your mind, you don't like me any more, is that it?' Even as she said it she thought: I sound hysterical. But it doesn't matter, I don't care, if he leaves me now there's nothing left at all . . .

'But I want to be free to go away to London, that's what I'm saying. I want the freedom to go there without feeling obliged to you or any other woman. That's the freedom I need in order to lead the workers properly, don't you understand? Deborah, I'm not a husband, I could never be that sort of man. For me the sort of freedom I was talking about means just that. Freedom from any permanent ties.'

Silence. A coal fell in the fire and Deborah noticed it was mostly smoke now, rather than flame. She shivered inside her coat.

'And what about *my* freedom?'

He sighed. 'That's a matter for you. But the world's not perfect, we both know that. Think what you have to lose – a husband, a son, money, a place in society. One day you may be grateful for what I'm saying now.'

It was true, she thought. The cruel truth she had come to tell him. But even more true if he didn't want her. Numbly, she asked: 'When do you go to London, James?'

'Tomorrow. There's a ferry to Holyhead at seven.'

She could still be hurt. 'So you knew that all along and you still brought me here to bed before you told me. Is that it?'

'So we had something good to remember from today. Yes. Why not?'

'I see.' There was a dressing table in the corner of the room, where she kept a hairbrush and a few items of makeup. She sat down on the stool in front of it and began to brush her hair, mechanically, like an automaton. As though her own face in the mirror was of paramount interest to her suddenly, and he was of no concern at all. If I concentrate on small things, now, I will not break down, I will get away with some surface pride, at least.

'Look, James, I want to get dressed now. On my own. So if you don't mind, I'd like you to put your clothes on, go downstairs and tell Mrs McCafferty I won't be staying to dinner. Then send her boy out to call me a cab. I'll be going straight back to the station tonight.'

Like a whore, she thought. That's what they do, isn't it? Go to an hotel with a man for an hour or two in the afternoon, then take a cab on to their next appointment. Only I have nowhere to go.

Nowhere in the world that matters, any more.

When he had gone she stared into the mirror hard. Defying her eyes to mist over, refusing to let the tears come.

Not in front of him, she thought.

Not in the cab, or on the train.

Not until I get home, to Glenfee . . .

8

On the night she had left Rankin and come home to Glenfee Deborah had shut herself in her bedroom and cried herself to sleep. For the next few days she lay in bed until noon, staring at the ceiling, numb, unweeping. Then she got up and wandered through the grounds, or rode out on lonely bridleways by the lough.

It had been a wet spring, that year of 1914, and she had stayed out longest on those days when a cold east wind howled in across the sea from Scotland, chilling her to the bone and making the great elm trees roar above her head in the storm. When at last she came home, shivering and drenched to the skin, she sat up alone in her bedroom and drank, for the first time in her life, a whole small bottle of gin each night until the room swam around her and she could scarcely stagger to bed.

Perhaps her body had known why she was doing this, but her mind had not. Not then, not yet. She had just wanted to dull her mind of all thought, so that she would remember nothing, grieve for nothing. The third time she did it, she caught pneumonia, so that when Charles came home, brisk and bronzed and full of energy for his new post, he was confronted with a wife who shivered in an overheated room and stared at him like a stranger. Mercifully, he paid no attention to her feverish mutterings; once the doctor assured him she would live he ignored her, and got on with his work.

Not until Charles had been home for three weeks did

Deborah first suspect she might be pregnant.

Even then, she could not be sure. She had been delirious for too long to be certain if she had had her last period or not, and she dared not ask her nursemaid. Only, she felt different: her breasts heavier, her skin, despite the fever, richer, smoother.

It must be an illusion, she thought. No foetus could survive an illness like that. I'll find out in a few days, a week at most.

Then the morning sickness began.

If Charles had been the least bit interested in her he could not have failed to notice, and for two weeks she was convinced that he knew and was avoiding her for that reason. Then one evening he said: 'You look blooming, my dear. It is good to see you fully recovered,' and she realised he had noticed nothing, nothing at all. After all, they slept in separate rooms, and he was usually up before her in the mornings, off to his soldiering.

It was then she realised she had to seduce him.

At first the idea disgusted her. This is what it means to be an adulteress, she thought; to behave like a common whore, slinking from one man's bed to another. From the man you love to – but she clenched her mind tight, shut Rankin out. After all, he had not loved her either, that was just a delusion. He had used her for a while and left her with this child – and it was the child, now, who had to be protected. It was her duty to find it a father.

But the only possible father, Charles, refused to be seduced.

She ordered tempting meals for him, and dressed attractively: he returned late, tired and dusty from soldiering, ate quickly and went straight to his bedroom. She tried talking to him about their early years, about his campaigns – he answered briefly, with impatience, as though forced to explain difficult things to a child. She walked into his room late one night in a silken nightdress and he asked her, irritably, to leave. She did not know what to do. They were out of the habit of making love – they had not done so more than a dozen times in the last six years. She had thought this was because he was abroad so much, but the truth was, he intimidated her. He was ten years older than her and had always been cold, distant, superior. Now, when she needed him most and loved him least, he terrified her. Even to touch him set off an earthquake of fear.

Yesterday afternoon she had tried again, one last time. And failed, because Simon had interrupted them. That was my last chance, she thought bitterly. I don't think I could bear him to touch me now even if he wanted to, which he doesn't. If it wasn't for Tom I wouldn't care.

Now it's only a matter of time. The very fact that I can face breakfast today means that the morning sickness is passing. In a month or two my belly will start to show and then even Charles will realise. Almost certainly he will divorce me.

When he does it will be in all the papers. *Unionist Officer's Wife Gives Birth to Trade Union Leader's Bastard.* What will Tom think of that? How will *he* feel? Probably I won't be allowed to see him again, anyway, to find out.

It's Rankin's baby but he won't want it either. He almost told me so. *'I want freedom from all permanent ties,'* he said. It's so easy for men. Just make love and walk away. Or in Charles's case, just walk away.

None of her thoughts were new or helpful. They just went round and round in her mind endlessly, like flies trapped in a jar. She sipped her second cup of coffee and stared gloomily at the wall.

Tom clattered by outside the window on the grey Connemara pony, waving happily. Deborah lifted a hand to wave back, tried to smile, and Charles came in.

He was wearing his UVF uniform. He had just shaved and his hair was neatly brushed and slicked back with oil. He glanced at her briefly, as though surprised to find her there. Then he took a plate from the sideboard and helped himself to kedgeree from a silver bowl that was kept warm over a spirit lamp. He sat down opposite her and poured himself some coffee.

'Tom gone riding, has he?' he asked.

She sipped the dregs of her coffee before answering. I suppose I should be grateful he speaks to me at all, she thought.

'Yes. If we're to reach the school by two we don't have to leave before eleven, at the earliest.'

Charles frowned. 'You'd better not start too late. Something's come up – I shall need Simon and the motor early this evening. Top priority.'

'Oh yes?' Deborah did not feel particularly sympathetic.

'More important than taking our son to school?'

'Different.' He frowned again. 'You know military priorities have to come first.'

'Oh yes. Always,' she said.

If there was irony in her tone he did not seem to notice. As usual, his manner was calm, brisk, energetic. As he forked the kedgeree into his mouth she watched the way his lips moved, clean, quick, precise, never spilling a grain of rice or fish. She tried to remember when those lips had last kissed her, before yesterday, and failed. I wonder if he has a mistress somewhere. Is that it? If so, the woman must be made of stone.

As Charles ate he scanned the newspaper swiftly, turning to the centre pages of *The Times* for the main news. Deborah got up and strolled to the window. The ash tree at the end of the drive was just coming into leaf. She could see the tiny figures of Tom and Bramble three fields away, trotting towards the lough. I'm going to lose all this, she thought . . .

Behind her, Charles said, 'My God!'

'Sorry?' She turned slowly, mildly surprised. He sat with his fork suspended in the air, halfway to his mouth, while he pored intently over an item in the paper in front of him.

'This,' he said. 'I don't believe it. She must be a madwoman!'

'What on earth are you talking about, Charles?' She walked to his side, looked over his shoulder. Usually he would have resented such intimacy as an intrusion, but this time he pointed, jabbing the page with his forefinger. 'Look there! It's your wretched sister, damn it!'

As she read, Deborah's mouth went dry. She bent closer, holding on to the table for support.

SUFFRAGETTE OUTRAGE IN NATIONAL GALLERY
ROKEBY VENUS SLASHED
MP'S WIFE ARRESTED AGAIN

She read the rest of the article, transfixed. It was Sarah all right – her sister. How could she do such a thing – take a knife in her hand, a great meat cleaver from the kitchen, and walk into the National Gallery and slash . . .

She sat down weakly on a chair. 'But why?' she said. 'What a dreadful thing to do. Sarah . . .'

Charles gave a short, contemptuous laugh. 'I always said the woman was deranged but look at this! It's the act of a savage, a hottentot!'

Deborah tried to collect her thoughts. 'It's not savagery, Charles. I don't agree with it but there's reason behind it. It says in the article, it's a protest against the imprisonment of Mrs Pankhurst.'

'And that's what you call reason? It just goes to show what lunacy this suffrage business is. Give us votes or we'll tear the place to pieces. Even *you* show more sense than that.'

Anger flooded through her. She thought: Sarah wasn't really free even before she did this. She could have been rearrested at any time under the Cat and Mouse Act, to complete a three month sentence for breaking a window in Regent Street. And now this! The poor brave fool. What have I been doing all this time, while she has been risking her life for her beliefs? Getting myself pregnant like any stupid servant girl. While my husband, this man, dares to mock . . .

She glared at him. 'It's no different to what you do, is it?'

'Me? What are you talking about, woman?'

'Marching up and down in your UVF uniforms defying the government. Saying that if a law is passed through Parliament you won't accept it, you'll fight instead. Where is the difference between that and what Sarah does?'

'All the difference in the world.' He shook his head in wonder. 'Deborah, you don't know what you're talking about.'

'Of course I do. Listen, Charles, I'm not saying I approve of what Sarah did, I don't. Picking up a knife and slashing a painting like that – of course it's wrong. I agree women should have the vote but we should convince people by speeches and demonstrations. But I understand why she did it. When we put our arguments forward reasonably no one listens to us. Whereas you men, you say if Parliament passes a law you don't like you won't accept it. You get guns and march up and down like soldiers, and because you're men everyone listens to you. We can't do that.'

He was actually smiling, as though what she said was

patently absurd. 'The UVF is a disciplined military force, Deborah. We don't go round slashing pictures or setting fire to pillar boxes, for heaven's sake!'

'But still . . .'

'Nonsense! It all goes to show how absurd all this suffrage talk is. You don't understand politics and no one expects you to, Deborah, because it's not your business. Neither does Sarah, it seems.'

There was a silence. I suppose the man of the house has spoken and that is the end of the matter, Deborah thought. But she was not prepared to go on with it. This is the first real conversation I've had with him since he came back. And all it's going to do is drive us further apart . . .

He pushed the newspaper away. 'Anyway, I can't stop here talking about this. I have to be at local HQ by nine. Sir Edward Carson is coming here tomorrow and I have to plan all the troop dispositions for his escort, for one thing.'

'Tom will miss you if you go now.'

'I've got to ride the way he's gone. I'll meet him on the way to the three oaks and say goodbye to him there.'

'Good,' she said softly. 'He'll like that. The boy worships you, you know, Charles.'

A strange expression crossed his face. A mixture of emotions, it seemed to her – part anger, part pride, part guilt. He said, irritably: 'So he should, damn it! Boy's got a soldier for a father, he ought to be proud. I hope one day he'll join a good regiment, as I did. He's got the makings in him.'

That's why we send him to a boarding school at the age of eight, she thought. To knock all the female nonsense out of him. It's as though men and women are brought up as different tribes!

Her mind still full of the appalling daring of Sarah's action, she said: 'I just wonder if you're setting him the right example, that's all.'

She hadn't planned to say that. But, now that it was said, she did not regret it. It was too late for regret and tactfulness now. She had tried all that.

He put down his cup of coffee softly, and glared at her. 'Just what the devil do you mean by that, woman?'

The look frightened her, as his anger always had. But she was too tired, too weary of trying to please and entice him over the past two weeks, to care any more whether he was upset. The way he had spurned her yesterday had hurt and humiliated her more than anything he could say now.

She said. 'I'm not your woman, I'm your *wife*. Remember? We're supposed to love, honour and respect each other. And what I meant was, that I don't see how you can be a proper father to the boy, because you're never here.'

'Never here? I've been here almost every day of his school holidays, haven't I!'

She nodded. 'Yes, you have. And that's the first time for the past four years, isn't it? For most of that time you were in Egypt. So it may be that he sees you as a hero but he hardly knows what you're like. Neither do I, if it comes to that.'

For once, she thought, I have astonished him. The dark eyes in Charles's lean, aristocratic face stared at her. For a moment the mouth under the carefully trimmed military moustache was open in shock. Then he said, sharply: 'I don't know what you mean. As a soldier of course I am away a lot. It's part of the conditions of the service. The boy understands that and respects it, as I respected my father. As for you . . .'

He hesitated, perhaps unwilling to hurt her. But contempt, it seemed to Deborah, was the only response she could get out of him these days. At least it was a sort of recognition, better than being ignored. So she said: 'Yes, Charles? As for me?'

He got up from the table, clasped his hands behind his back and strolled to the window before answering. Like a man searching for the right words to lecture a platoon of soldiers, Deborah thought, almost amused. Perhaps I should stand to attention.

At the window, Charles swung round abruptly to face her.

'As for you, Deborah, from what I hear you have hardly been at Glenfee yourself, for most of the past year. Instead of attending to your duties as Tom's mother and mistress of this house, you have been running away to Dublin, involving yourself with this ridiculous notion of feeding the children of illiterate strikers and filling the house with street urchins who smash the windows and uproot the trees. That is scarcely better than your sister! Certainly not the sort of conduct that qualifies you to criticise me, I would have thought. When we married I had hoped for better from you.'

When we married. The cruel arrogance of the man. As though I am a child, a servant in this house. Deborah was sure her face had gone white. She said: 'You had hoped for what, exactly?'

'A mother who would not embarrass my son, at least. How do you think the boy feels, when he hears of these foolish antics? A mother who spends her time in the slums of Dublin and fills the house with paupers. Whose sister slashes pictures in London. What do you imagine Tom thinks of that?'

'Nothing very much, I suppose. I have tried to explain it to him, and he seems to understand.'

'Oh, does he indeed?' Charles shook his head. 'Well, let me tell you, madam, the boy is deeply embarrassed. He tells me so on our rides. What do you think his schoolfriends would say, if they found out the way you behave?'

Very coldly, Deborah said: 'I am sorry if he feels like that. But if he does it is a failure in his friends, not in me. I only do what I think right and just.'

And look where that lands me, she thought. Making a gift of myself to a beautiful handsome devil like James Rankin, who cares for the future of all mankind but doesn't care to commit himself to any one woman in particular. Men always win.

Charles said: 'Well, if you think such foolish behaviour is just, that only goes to show how far women are from understanding the world of politics. I suppose we should be grateful you don't actually perform these unwomanly acts of vandalism yourself.'

Deborah's hand shook on the table in front of her. She felt a surge of anger welling up inside her, changing as anger so often did with her, to tears. To prevent herself from crying she stood up and gripped the back of a chair.

'So what exactly *would* be womanly behaviour as far as you are concerned, Charles? You seem to know so much about it and yet take so very little interest. What would make me a proper wife again, for you?'

For a second he flinched, as though something had struck

home. Perhaps because of the desperate appeal underneath her shaky façade of anger. But he recovered quickly. He looked away from her with a mocking, dismissive laugh.

'I should have thought that was obvious. Take care of this house – it is large and complex enough to absorb your energies, surely? Be a mother to Tom, without embarrassing the boy. And, if you really need any other interest, support the Union. That is the really important question in politics these days. If you knew anything at all you should know that.'

He glanced at his watch, as though the conversation was over.

Suddenly it came to Deborah what she had to do. There was no point staying here, having fruitless arguments like this. Brooding, waiting for her stomach to swell and her life to disintegrate around her. Sarah is in prison – she needs my help.

And Rankin is in London, too.

She said: 'I shall have to go to London, Charles.'

'London? What the devil for?'

'To see my sister, of course. Give her what support I can. And Jonathan. He'll be dreadfully upset about this.'

He considered her without answering at first. As though weighing up, quite coldly, the advantages and disadvantages of what she had said. Perhaps he wants me to go, she thought. He can't *like* having me here.

'You feel it is more important to help them, then, than to stay here and give your support to me?'

Those cold blue eyes, watching hers. Bitter, clouded, distant.

'Do you really want my support, Charles?'

'It would be the proper, decent thing. What a wife is expected to do. Support the Union.'

He didn't say it with anger. She thought, for a fanciful moment, that it sounded a little like an appeal from somewhere far away. So she waited, to see if he would say any more. Even now, if he would come to her, their marriage might be saved.

Nothing.

'Charles, I don't give a fig for your Union.'

She hadn't meant to say that, either, or known it was coming. But as the words came out they sent a strange thrill through her. As though they were not about the Union of England and

Ireland at all, but about her own union with Charles.

As though she had slashed a picture herself.

'I see.' Charles stood quite still in the doorway. Like a man who knows he is wounded, but is not quite sure yet where he has been hit. Her odd, defiant words echoed in their ears.

Will he forbid me to go? she thought. At least that will show that he cares.

'Then you will not be here when I get back?'

'No, probably not. I shall catch the first ferry tonight after I've taken Tom to school. If there's time, I'll ask Simon to drive me to the harbour.'

'Very well. I wish you a good journey, though I fear you will find it a wasted one. If Sarah's sent to prison you probably won't even be allowed to see her.'

'I shall see Jonathan, anyway. And he may find a way. He is an MP, after all.'

'Much good may it do him!'

Charles turned on his heel and walked away without saying goodbye. As the heels of his riding boots clicked away down the corridor, Deborah thought, is this how it all ends, then?

I may never meet him again.

She walked upstairs to the tall window on the landing to watch her husband ride away down the drive. As he had promised, he met Tom in the five acre field and the horses stood together for some minutes while their riders talked. She wondered if they were talking about her.

As she watched, she repeated the words softly to herself. They had, she found, an almost sensual taste on her lips, like sharp, bitter chocolate.

It's true what I said.

I don't care a fig for his Union.

Tom's school, St Andrew's Preparatory, was on the banks of a small river flowing down to Lough Neagh. It was in a rambling, shabby Stuart manor house, with a number of stables and cottages round it, and a sixteenth century Protestant chapel. Simon Fletcher drove Deborah and Tom towards it down a long twisty rutted drive, full of potholes which threatened to destroy the Lancia's suspension at any minute. As the chimneys of the old house came in sight beyond the cricket fields, Tom pointed eagerly ahead.

'Look, Mother! There are some boys already practising in the nets! I think that's Randall – yes, it is! Randall and Carter. They're in my house team. We're going to win the cup this year, I bet you anything!'

Deborah looked – not at the nets, where several youths in white flannels were queueing up to bowl or bat, but at her son, whose face shone with excitement. She felt at once glad and empty. Glad that Tom was so excited, that he liked the place and seemed so eager to return here; but empty, sad and lonely for herself.

All the way, on the two-hour car journey, she had tried to talk to him. He had shown great excitement when talking about the school, or his friends, or his pony, or his father. But when she had tried to sound him out about what he really felt about the things Charles had mentioned – her activities in Dublin, the holidays she had arranged at Glenfee for poor children – the curtains had come down behind his eyes. He said little, he lost interest. It was obvious he did not want to talk to her about these things. This had happened before, and she had always assumed that it was just because he was too young to understand. But perhaps Charles was right, perhaps he was embarrassed or ashamed. Once she asked him.

'Tom, when you're at school, do the boys ever talk about the sort of things I'm involved in? Working for poor children, things like that?' She had not dared mention Sarah.

He looked at his hands, then glanced away over the fields, where a herd of cows was making its way slowly down to a ford by a stream.

'Sometimes,' he said. 'Not much, though.'

'What do they say?'

'I don't remember. Silly things, really. Oh, look, there's a heron!'

She looked, saw the big grey bird flying laboriously up, away from the cows, along the line of the stream. She said, softly: 'Am I an embarrassment to you?'

For a moment she thought he was not going to answer. He followed the bird with his eyes, ignoring her. It was a silly question, she thought, unfair to him. Then he said: 'Carter said something once, but I punched his head. He won't do it again. Look, there! It's going down, into that pond!'

And with that she had to be content. So he had stood up for her, after all! She felt a sudden urge to hug him, thank him for his loyalty, but she resisted. That would have embarrassed him surely. Instead, she talked about the heron, and cricket, and the difficulties of Latin prep, and the mice they fed with breadcrumbs in the dormitory, and secret midnight fishing trips down to the river, until the school came in sight along the dusty track and they were there.

They met the headmaster, Dr Duncan, on the front doorsteps where he stood with the matron to welcome returning boys. He was a beefy man with a round, genial face and imposing mutton-chop whiskers. He bowed to Deborah, ruffled Tom's hair, and shook Simon Fletcher by the hand. He seemed impressed by Simon's UVF uniform, which, as always, was immaculately pressed, despite the long journey.

'You gentlemen are well organised then, from what I understand?' Dr Duncan said.

'Oh yes, sir,' Simon answered. 'We do our duty and the UVF are well prepared. At least in County Down.'

'Glad to hear it. Though perhaps I shouldn't say so.' Dr Duncan met Simon's eyes for a moment, then winked at Tom. 'Ticklish business, this politics. But if men don't stand up for law and order and the United Kingdom when it's threatened, then we don't deserve to live here. That's what I expect your father says, eh, young Cavendish?'

Tom smiled proudly. 'Yes, sir, of course. Father's a colonel in the UVF now, you know, sir.'

'Jolly good show! Excellent.' Dr Duncan beamed at Deborah. 'Which probably means that Mrs Cavendish is kept busy as well, if I know anything. Eh, what? But I expect you'll want to be away up to your dorm.' He turned to Simon. 'Can you manage that trunk, young man?'

'Just about, I think so, sir,' Simon said, unstrapping it from the back of the car. Deborah marvelled at him. He had been silent for most of the journey, but now he seemed so suave, polite, more at home here than she felt herself. But then it is a male institution, she told herself. Mothers are an embarrassment. Even those without advanced views.

'Splendid! House assembly at four o'clock then, young Cavendish, with high tea immediately afterwards. Till then you're free to meet your friends and swap stories of the hols, eh, what!' Dr Duncan beamed again, then turned to watch a pony and trap which was approaching with another pupil up the drive behind them.

On the return journey Deborah sat beside Simon in the front of the car. At first neither spoke much. Deborah was thinking of Tom's face when she had left him. He had been standing in the middle of a group of his friends, his grey-green eyes alight, cheerful, not apparently concerned at all that she was leaving. Anxious for her to be gone, in fact, so that he could immerse himself into a world of boys. And so she had kissed him, very lightly, on the forehead, knowing that even so small a display of affection was an embarrassment in his boys' world. And now she would not see him for at least a month.

Perhaps longer, Deborah thought. Perhaps much longer. If I stay long in London the baby will start to show and there will still be no agreed story with Charles. When he finds out poor Tom's world will absolutely fall apart and it will be entirely my fault.

'He seems happy there.' Simon's words broke in upon her thoughts. She glanced at him. He sat quietly beside her, his eyes on the road, his handsome, classical profile smooth in the afternoon sun. She wondered that he had spoken at all; he was normally so quiet, reserved with her.

'Yes. Yes, I think it's a good school.'

'He'll be better off there, with all the trouble at home.'

Simon's tone was quite neutral, but Deborah felt a blush spread across her face. Did he know, then, about the argument she and Charles had had this morning? About the other disagreements between them, and her reasons for going to London? And if he did know, was he actually going to have the insolence to discuss these things?

As coldly as she could, she said: 'I beg your pardon? What trouble do you mean?'

He took his time answering. They left the rutted track and

came on to a metalled road. 'The UVF, of course. What else? The conflict with the Liberal government and the British army.'

'Oh, that.' Her blush faded. 'Why, do you think there'll really be fighting?'

'It's possible, yes, of course. Why else would we be doing all this training?' Simon glanced at her, a faint smile on his thin lips. A rather mocking, patronising smile, she thought. As though to imply, this is something you don't know anything about, because you're only a woman. And then – was there something else, behind that?

'Let's hope both sides come to their senses first,' she said. 'It won't do anyone any good, to have loyal Irishmen and Englishmen fighting each other.'

'No, of course not,' Simon agreed.

It seemed a banal enough conversation. Deborah thought: I was a fool to blush, I've misjudged this young man again. He's a decent enough young boy, polite, helpful, well behaved. I'm just jealous of him because he broke in when I was trying to seduce Charles, and because he always has Charles's attention when Charles is playing soldiers and I'm shut out.

Then Simon said: 'It's rather like a marriage, isn't it?'

'I beg your pardon?'

'A marriage. The Union between England and Ireland is like that, don't you think? Two unequal partners linked together by law. So long as both sides want the same things, everything's fine. But when they don't want the same things they quarrel and things fall apart. Sometimes, one partner even goes off with someone else. Then there's dreadful trouble.'

She stared at him, her heart beating quickly. There was a superior, knowing smile on Simon's face. Surely he was not just making conversation now – he *was* dangerous, after all! But what did he mean? He couldn't know about her and James Rankin , that was impossible. So . . .

The answer ran through her like lightning. *Charles must have a mistress – and this young devil knows about it!* He's gloating – trying to tell me without saying so in so many words. The smooth little swine!

The car rattled on past fields of cows and sheep, through a village. Neither of them spoke, but twice Simon glanced at her, smiling coolly. At last she said: 'You're not talking about politics at all, Simon, are you?'

'I beg your pardon, Madam?' This time it was his turn to try to look confused. But it was definitely there, Deborah thought. Behind the smooth face and raised eyebrows, a smile of deep inner amusement. Mocking. It's true, he's patronising me, she thought.

'You're trying to tell me something about my husband, aren't you?'

Simon's frown was almost a parody of concern. 'No, Mrs Cavendish, of course not. I was only trying to discuss the politics of the Union. No more.'

It was an utterly miserable situation to be in. Deborah could not prove the young man was lying, laughing at her. If she went on and challenged him he would only act as though she were deranged, and yet she could not retract what she had already said. Nor could she order him out of the car or drive it herself; she did not know how to. She had to sit beside him for the next two hours.

'All right,' she said. 'Have it your own way. I don't believe you, but in any case it's none of your business. I'd appreciate it if you would keep your thoughts to yourself for the rest of the journey.'

And that, at least, he did. But nothing she could say or do could keep the cool, knowing smile off the young man's lips, or the look of mocking contempt out of his eyes . . .

9

It was half an hour before the speech, and the streets of Newtownards were already so crowded that it was almost impossible to move.

Werner von Weichsaker sheltered in a bank doorway and watched the hordes of people flowing past. He was a tall, angular, bony man, wearing a long belted raincoat and a flat tweed cap. The face under the cap was lean, hungry, alert – like a wolf sniffing the air for prey. He had a prominent nose, strong clean-shaven jaw, thin lips, slightly sunken cheeks, and eyes of a pale, unnatural shade of blue. Many people were fascinated by those eyes, but few could meet their gaze for long. The blue was so pale, and there was a strange white ring within it, around the iris; when he became angry this widened, like the sun burning through mist on a midsummer's day, and people tended to look away, lest they were burnt also.

Now he was not angry, merely amused and observant. He surveyed the crowds of Ulstermen and women in front of him, and thought, this must be the strangest form of loyalty the world has ever seen.

The street was like a river, with waves of cloth caps and bowler hats streaming up and down in swirls and eddies between banks of low, grey, slate-roofed houses. The faces of the men were solid, heavy, rural, reddened by the endless wind they met every day in the fields. Dour, heavy-featured farmers for the most part, with big noses and solid jaws. They wore thick, serviceable suits, broad leather belts, and strong hobnailed boots. Grey clouds blew briskly over the smoky rooftops, but no one seemed downcast by the weather. Everywhere there was laughter, shouting, the hum of anticipation.

Werner heard the sound of music further up the street, and immediately the current of people began to flow towards it. He stepped from his haven in the doorway and went with the stream, letting it carry him where he wanted to go, into the main square.

Here he saw the band. It was composed entirely of men and boys in the soberest and most respectable of clothes imaginable – black suits, bowler hats, shining polished shoes. Their faces, too, were straight, solemn, unmoving. Yet beneath this sobriety was something fervent, powerful, messianic. Over his dark suit each man wore an embroidered sash of brilliant red, white, or orange; gleaming silver fifes made piercing, defiant music; and the shattering *boom*! of the great Lambeg drum throbbed through the crowd with enough force to make the bricks dance in the walls.

Every building in the square was bright with Union Jack bunting, and the platform behind the band seemed composed of nothing else. Werner smiled ironically to himself. These men are rebels, he thought. Every one of them. Rebels whose first thought is to pledge loyalty to their King!

'Come along now, move back there, sir, will you?' There were very few police in the square, but Werner was shoved firmly backwards by a line of men who were clearly soldiers. Few of them wore uniform and most held wooden staves rather than rifles, but their military bearing was unmistakable. Their sergeant was a short, solid, bullet-headed type recognisable anywhere, and behind him and his corporals, the whole operation was directed by a mounted officer.

But it was not the sergeant Werner had come to see. It was the officer. Werner saw him, and knew him instantly. As he stared, the pale, hot ring widened in his eyes.

A lean, athletic individual, the officer sat with one hand on his hip, coolly surveying the scene. He had that air of unconscious arrogance so natural to the British army, and clearly assumed that all matters in the square were completely under his control. From time to time a runner pushed his way up to him, saluted, and ran off again with fresh orders; and once the officer urged his horse forward into the crowd, pointing at something casually with his swagger stick. Immediately a file of soldiers rushed past him and made a space for two elderly ladies who were in danger of being crushed.

That's the man, Werner thought. That's why I'm here. Charles Cavendish, colonel in the Ulster Volunteer Force. Once soldier of the British Empire, an officer trained at Sandhurst. And before that again, head of house at Eton, captain of cricket, senior prefect, the prototype of the English public schoolboy.

The sort of man Werner hated now, but had once longed to become.

Even now, as a grown man, the memories made him blush and shake with rage.

Long ago, Werner's father, a German diplomat, had convinced himself that the English public schools were the finest educational institutions in the world. It followed, therefore, that his son should have the benefit of going to one. So, when he was thirteen, young Werner, wearing the high top hat and stiff collar of a freshman, had walked proudly with his father through the medieval gates of Eton College, the finest public school in the world.

And there, Werner's hell had begun.

In the first place, his English, although carefully nurtured by six months of private lessons from his English governess, Miss Brinton, proved woefully inadequate. His accent was ludicrous and he didn't know the right name for anything – words like 'tuck', 'fag', 'skive', 'creep', and 'Pop' meant nothing to him. He had not been to a prep school, so he knew nothing of their traditions, either. He couldn't play cricket or rugby, he had hardly even been away from home before. And, worst of all, he had an innate conviction of his own superiority.

That conviction was both the one thing that kept him going, and also, if only he'd realised it, the main cause for all the cruelty he received. The English boys might, perhaps, have tolerated a foreigner with all Werner's manifest shortcomings, if only that foreigner had had a sense of humour and a willingness to laugh at himself and try to learn; but Werner had none of these virtues. When the others mocked him he stiffened; when they ragged him and tried to teach him to hold a cricket bat he lashed out and hit them with it. One boy was quite badly injured and had to spend a week in the infirmary, but Werner, even when ordered to by the housemaster, failed to apologise. From that moment, his fate was sealed. He had rejected the boys' crude attempts to teach him, insulted the English national game, and spurned the advice of authority. He was on his own, an unrepentant hyena in the lions' den.

It did not take him long to realise how lonely his fate was to be. It is not pleasant to get into bed at night and find that your pillow crackles and is full of snails, to feel woodlice creeping out of your nightshirt pocket as you sleep, or to get up in the morning and step in a dog turd inside your own shoe. There were other games too, such as being tossed in a blanket, roasted in front of a dormitory fire, trussed with your elbows to your knees and made to cockfight, which had a long history in the British public school. Werner suffered every one.

There was a day when the senior prefects found young Werner, with his hands tied behind him, his head jammed in the bottom of a sash window, and his trousers around his ankles. The boy's face was weeping bitter tears into the quadrangle, but the prefects didn't see that, because his head was outside the room; what they saw, as they came into the room, was the boy's smooth, wriggling buttocks. On each buttock an eye was painted – an eye with fetching long lashes. The eyes were painted so cunningly that they appeared to wink at the prefects as the owner of the buttocks struggled and strained to get free.

And so the prefects' first response was to laugh. That laugh mortified Werner to his core, for these were the very type of young men, only a year or so away from a commission in the army, whom Werner had so far worshipped. One day, he hoped, he would become one of those godlike figures himself. But after this . . .

Of course, the prefects had released him, and officially disapproved, but not before one – the head of house, Cavendish – had placed his large hand on the wriggling buttocks in a casual, intimate, patronising gesture that was somehow worse than anything that had gone before. And when Werner was free, and they saw who he was, they showed scant sympathy.

Especially when he spat at them.

For although Werner could not prevent these things happening, his spirit was never quite broken. That was the one thing he had to hang on to, and the thing that ensured that the torments continued. He even struck back once, arranging for a dead snake to rot slowly in his principal tormentor's mattress. But that only made things worse.

It led to the incident, finally, when they broke his hand. The day when they pegged him out on the grass, below the bank at the far end of the cricket pitch where no one would find them, and put ants in his hair and slugs up his nose in an attempt to make him say foul things about his mother. When he would not, and insulted their own mothers instead, they brought the big cricket roller, the one that weighed half a ton, to the top of the bank and held it there, poised above him, insisting that if he defied them it would be the last thing he would ever do.

The boys holding the roller had all been tense, sweating; it was a threat bigger than they had ever made before. Werner, pegged out on the ground below them, had realised suddenly that it was a moment of crisis. If he defied them this time they would never be able to threaten him with anything so awful again; he would have won.

So he had looked up at them, shadowy figures blocking out the sun at the top of the bank, and sneered; and the sneer had driven them wild. They realised what it meant, just as he did.

Now, or never again.

Their leader, Rickman, had screamed: 'I warned you, Kraut!' and told the others to let go. Perhaps he meant, as he afterwards said, that only those at his end should let go, so that the roller should go near Werner's head and give him a fright; or perhaps he thought he could let it roll a few yards and then stop it.

Whatever Rickman thought, he was wrong. Once released, the roller was unstoppable. Standing in the doorway of the small Ulster town of Newtownards, Werner saw it again now as he did in nightmares; the sheer vast metal bulk of it trundling slowly but with inexorably increasing speed down the bank towards his head . . .

He always woke up then, in dreams. At the time he had shut his eyes. So he was never quite sure how Rickman and the others had managed to lug the lumbering monster to the side, so that the ton of smooth iron missed the thin bones of his skull, and only crushed the bones of his right arm instead, pegged out as it was above his head.

His right hand had never worked properly again. He flexed it now in front of him. Shrivelled, weakened fingers that could never fully bend or straighten, a thumb that could not be persuaded to touch his palm. The legacy of an English public school.

But at least his broken hand had been the last of the torments. There had, of course, been a scandal. Rickman and two other boys had been expelled. When Werner had returned from hospital, he had found himself treated with a wary caution. Most of the boys had heard the story of how Werner had defied his tormentors, and that gained him some respect, even among those who disliked him. And the whole school had had some very strong warnings from the headmaster. Werner was placed under the specific protection of the head of his house, Charles Cavendish.

That, for a while, had been Werner's dream. Cavendish then seemed just the type of English gentleman he himself longed to become. Tall, slim, good-looking, with a casual grace that made him naturally good at all sports. The school had an army cadet corps, and Cavendish was a leading light in that – marksman in the shooting team, a skilled horseman, clearly officer material. Werner became his personal fag, shining his shoes, cooking his toast, lighting his fire, cleaning his study – duties he would have resented doing for anyone he had not so admired.

At first Cavendish was kind to him. He took an interest in the boy's welfare, made sure he was bullied no more. He helped him with his Latin, watched him encouragingly as he painstakingly practised the skill of writing with his undamaged left hand. Werner glowed as the tall young man leant over him, his hand on the back of his chair, passing friendly comments as the clumsy letters formed. Sometimes Cavendish would put his hand on Werner's shoulder. Once he held his hand to help him shape the letters.

One evening, when he had locked and bolted the study door, Cavendish ran his hands through Werner's hair, and kissed him . . .

It became a nightmare for Werner, worse even than what had gone before. Because he liked and admired Cavendish, he did, at first, the things that the elder boy wanted. They were not painful, they were done and asked for in a friendly way, they seemed to give pleasure. But the more Werner agreed the more Cavendish demanded, and so the study came to seem to him like a trap, in which his former hero lurked with soft, insistent lips and hands that stripped off his clothes and touched him everywhere, in places that no one should ever want to go, and . . .

Werner had been terrified. He had felt dirty and powerless and utterly invaded, and still he smiled at Cavendish and consented because the elder boy to him represented power and protection. He knew what they were doing was wrong, but he thought that if he complained to the Headmaster he would be disbelieved and sent back to Cavendish to be caned. Either that, or the Head would believe him. And then they would both be expelled, and Werner would be sent home to his father with a letter that said . . . Great God, he would endure anything in the world other than that! So he went every night smiling to the Spartan study of his casual English sporting hero, and shut his mind and allowed his body to do things and have things done to it that he never, ever, wanted to remember again.

Until the summer came and he returned to Germany. There, for the first time, the father saw the full extent of what had happened to his son's hand and was stricken with guilt. If he had not sent the boy to such a school, he thought, it would never have happened. He praised his son for his courage in the face of adversity and tried to make it up to him in any way he could. He bought the boy a pony – which Werner's hand made it hard for him to ride – took him everywhere with him to military revues, let him fly in one of Zeppelin's new balloons. But all the time he saw the grief in the boy's eyes. So when he asked Werner what he really wanted and the boy said simply 'to leave that school', the old man was uncharacteristically sympathetic. Werner was enrolled in a Prussian military academy near his home, and for the next five years, forgot all about England.

Until, at the age of eighteen, he tried and failed to achieve his lifelong ambition – a commission in the Imperial German Army. Predictably, he was turned down because of his hand. But then, a wise general had offered him a chance to put his education to some use, in gaining revenge on the society which had maimed him.

Officially, he had been appointed a foreign correspondent for a Swiss newspaper, the *Neue Zuricher Zeitung*. Secretly, he had also been awarded a commission as a lieutenant in the Army Intelligence Service. It was not what he had hoped for, but at least it was in the service of the Kaiser, with military status of a sort. And it was something at which, to his surprise, he had proved unusually good.

So good, in fact, that a couple of weeks ago he had been invited to meet two of the most powerful men in Germany.

General Eric von Falkenhayn was Minister of War to His Imperial Majesty Kaiser Wilhelm II of Germany. General Helmuth von Moltke was Chief of the Imperial General Staff. Werner had been summoned to see them to discuss a report he had written about the possibility of civil war in Ireland.

Werner's report explained the British government's intention to end the Union of Great Britain and Ireland, and establish a Home Rule Parliament in Dublin. This parliament would take over responsibility for most Irish affairs and would, inevitably, be dominated by Roman Catholics. The majority of Irishmen supported this idea but a vociferous minority, particularly concentrated among the Protestants of Ulster, vehemently opposed it. Home Rule, they said, would mean Rome Rule. No Protestant could be expected to accept that.

So their leader, Sir Edward Carson, had stated publicly that if the Home Rule Bill were passed, the Unionists of Ulster would not accept it. They would form their own Provisional Government of Ulster, loyal to the King, but not to his Liberal government. They would defend themselves with their own army, the Ulster Volunteer Force. 100,000 of them had signed a Covenant to this effect. Andrew Bonar Law, the leader of the Conservative Party, had spoken in support of this Covenant, and General Wilson, the Chief of Military Operations at the War Office, had signed it – as had many other prominent members of the British Establishment, including Lord Milner, Rudyard Kipling, and Edward Elgar. The commander-in-chief of the Ulster Volunteer Force had been recommended to Sir Edward Carson by one of Britain's greatest military heroes, Field-Marshal Lord Roberts of Kandahar.

'So when the Home Rule Bill is passed through Parliament later this year,' Werner had told the two generals, 'it is quite likely that there will be civil war.'

'So I understand,' von Falkenhayn had answered smoothly, staring thoughtfully at the pale blue eyes of his intelligence officer. 'But, Major von Weichsaker, I am less clear about the timing of this civil war, and its likely outcome. You state in your report that it will come soon, I believe?'

Werner nodded. 'Within the next few months, Herr General. The Home Rule Bill has been through the Commons and rejected by the Lords twice; it is due to be introduced in the Commons for the third time in the next few weeks. The Government of the Realm Act states that the Lords can only reject a Bill twice. So unless the government loses its nerve, the Bill will become law before the summer.'

'And the government shows no sign of losing its nerve?'

'Not at present, Herr General. On the contrary, they are becoming more aggressive. The day before I left, the First Lord of the Admiralty, Winston Churchill, spoke in Bradford. He called the Unionists "sinister revolutionaries", and "anarchists", as I recall. He is believed to speak on behalf of the Prime Minister.'

Falkenhayn smiled. 'I read that speech. It seems Mr Churchill has a longing for war, and if he cannot fight Admiral Tirpitz, he will fight the Ulstermen instead. But . . . do you really believe this Ulster Volunteer Force can offer serious resistance?'

'I believe so, Herr General, because of the moral force on their side. They are, so far as I have seen, very well disciplined, but lacking in military equipment. Many of them drill with sporting rifles and shotguns, even wooden guns. I saw one machine-gun only. So in any full-scale conflict they would undoubtedly be defeated. But equally, there is great reluctance among the British Army to fight them, and they have enormous support among the Protestant population in their province. So I believe that the regular army will fight half-heartedly and the Ulstermen will resist with passion, making the struggle a more equal one.'

'And how long will it last?'

'That is much harder to say. It depends on moral as well as military force, as I said. If the Ulstermen were better armed, it would last several weeks. A month even.'

Von Moltke had spoken for the first time. Ten years older than von Falkenhayn, he was a blunt, crusty soldier of the old school. Werner had the impression that he regarded undercover intelligence work as an unnecessary evil, and wondered if he had even bothered to read the entire report.

Moltke scowled. 'Surely we can arm the rebels, Major? Isn't that what one normally does in situations of this kind? Ask Tirpitz to organise a shipload of machine guns? A few free gifts to friendly natives – why don't you go ahead and organise it, man?'

Werner smiled. 'I have indeed thought of that, Herr General. It is mentioned in my report. A consignment of 25,000 rifles and two and a half million rounds of ammunition to leave Hamburg within the next week. The Ulstermen believe, of course, that they have organised this all on their own, but with General von Falkenhayn's consent, my colleagues and I have, er, taken a few steps to clear the way.'

Moltke beamed; he was genuinely delighted. 'Excellent! Excellent! And are there more on the way?'

'Not so far, Herr General. This is the maximum the Ulstermen believe they can handle at present. And it remains to be seen how they can land them. After all, we cannot be seen to help them openly. They may behave like rebels, but they regard themselves as loyalists; they distrust Germany as much as the Liberal government does. As I say in my report, any suggestion that we were openly involved would be likely to unite both sides against us.'

Moltke nodded, convinced but disappointed. Falkenhayn picked up Werner's report from the table, and leafed through it thoughtfully.

'It seems to me, Major von Weichsaker, that what we are discussing is a situation of enormous potential for the Empire of His Majesty Kaiser Wilhelm. I fully appreciate the detailed study you have given to it, and I think that both General Moltke and I accept the point you raise that it is politically impossible for us to be seen to interfere openly in this conflict. But . . . I think perhaps General von Moltke would like to explain to you why this civil war is so crucial to the fortunes of Germany.'

Moltke had lumbered importantly to his feet. It was not the first time in the interview he had done this; it was as though the constriction of a chair and a desk were too much for him, and he yearned to be back in the saddle at the head of his troops. He strode to the large map of Europe on the opposite wall, and slapped it emphatically with his riding crop. The end of the crop landed on the Belgian border.

'You see this, von Weichsaker, don't you? The weak point in the French defences. All along the French border with Germany the French Army are prepared – perhaps to attack us. It would take millions of men to overcome them. But if we sweep around the outside, through Belgium, there will be no resistance, none. The French have no fortifications at all on their Belgian border. We shall be in Paris within a month, and the French will be annihilated. Then we can regroup and concentrate our forces on our destiny, which is in Poland and Russia, to the east.'

Werner had smiled, perhaps a trifle too complacently. 'Yes, Herr General, I realise that.' It was not only he who knew about the Schlieffen plan; knowledge of it was so widespread amongst senior army officers that Werner would be surprised if the French did not know of it also. Even if they hadn't found out, they ought to have been able to work it out for themselves. They had maps in France, after all, didn't they? That was why the French had been so keen to get the British to sign a guarantee of Belgian neutrality. And to get the Germans to sign it, too.

Moltke waved his hand again, imperiously. 'You realise it, Major, yes. But you do not think about it enough. You do not realise its importance. Whereas I, who will have to implement this plan, think about it day and night.'

Werner had sat back in his chair. It was the first indication he had had that he had been summoned to discuss matters far wider than Ulster. What has this got to do with my report, he had wondered.

'Over a year ago, in December 1912, I wanted to implement this plan.' Moltke continued. 'The army was ready, we could have crossed the Belgian border and smashed the French in a few weeks. I recommended action, but the Kaiser overruled me because of the navy – Tirpitz told him they would not be ready for another eighteen months, when the Kiel Canal would be opened. That will be in June of this year – 1914. That gives us just two months from now – do you understand me? Then, if there is the slightest pretext, I shall recommend that we move – through Belgium, into France. You follow me so far, Major?'

'Perfectly, Herr General.'

'Good! And as an astute intelligence officer you will know that the neutrality of Belgium is guaranteed not only by the French, but the British.'

And ourselves, Werner thought. Poor Belgians . . .

'So, when we invade Belgium, we shall find ourselves fighting not only the French, but the British Empire too, unless . . . ' Moltke scowled ferociously at Werner, as though to ensure his full attention. Werner watched him with his pale blue eyes and thought, this is it. This is why they are so interested. A pulse of fear and excitement began to throb urgently in his throat.

Moltke thwacked his riding crop across another part of the map – the British Isles, where the coast of Scotland reached out towards Northern Ireland. 'Unless this civil war that you talk about has begun before we move. Preferably by the middle of May. In which case the British will be too preoccupied with killing each other to be able to send any effective help to Belgium at all.'

Werner nodded, and stretched his aching right hand carefully across his thigh. 'I see, Herr General. But . . . '

'But nothing!' A grim smile crossed von Moltke's face, a smile of almost boyish enthusiasm like that of a hunter who has seen his quarry. He returned to the desk, and thumped his open palm down hard on it, flat on the top of Werner's report. 'The answer

General von Falkenhayn and I want begins with "so", not "but"! That is why we have summoned you here. It is obvious to us that we should do everything in our power to foment this civil war, in the interests of the German Empire! It is less obvious to us that the man Carson will be foolish enough to begin such a war on his own. So what I want from you, Major von Weichsaker, are constructive suggestions as to the best ways in which we can act! What plans do you have for this?'

Werner had paled. His right hand had been aching badly by then, and a pulse was beating irritatingly under his arm. He felt like a young recruit being bawled out on the parade ground by the sergeant-major. Only these were the two most important sergeant-majors in Germany.

Feebly, he said: 'None at the moment, Herr General. As I said, we have helped them with the purchase of arms, and beyond that there are many difficulties . . . '

Von Falkenhayn frowned and tapped a pencil irritably on his desk. 'There are always difficulties, Major. But the world does not belong to men who can point them out. It belongs to men who can overcome them.'

'Yes, Herr General.' Werner remembered admiring his father when he had said something like that, years ago. But to start a civil war, all on my own . . .

'I am glad to hear you agree,' von Falkenhayn continued. 'You can have all the resources you want, but I want a coherent plan worked out, and the details back here on my desk a week from today, do you understand? The civil war in Ulster must begin in the summer of 1914, so that the German Army is free to march through Belgium without interference from the British. From now on, as far as you are concerned, this has priority over everything else. That will be all, Major. Dismiss!'

Werner got to his feet, saluted, pushed his chair carefully to one side, and turned to the door. His hand was hurting him abominably, and he was sure his face was pale.

As he reached the door, Falkenhayn spoke again. 'And, Major?'

Werner turned. 'Yes, Herr General?'

To his surprise, Falkenhayn had been smiling; a bleak, ironic smile. 'If you do provoke this war, Major, then you may consider it the crowning success of your career.'

And if I don't?

Hemmed in by a crowd of loyal Ulstermen, Werner remembered the approval his slim plan had met with when he had presented it to von Falkenhayn a week later. Now he wondered if it could possibly succeed. Can one man, all on his own, push these people over the brink into open armed rebellion?

Perhaps I won't be needed. The guns are on their way, the soldiers are well-drilled. They might do it all on their own.

A clergyman had mounted the platform behind Cavendish and begun speaking. Werner let the familiar phrases about religion and loyalty roll over his head, and concentrated instead on the faces of the people in the crowd. Dour, heavy-featured farmers for the most part, with big noses and solid jaws. Most of them wore flat caps or bowler hats, they had heavy, serviceable suits, broad leather belts, strong hobnailed boots. They listened to the preacher earnestly, in silence, taking in every word.

Hardly the sort of people one would want to take to a concert of chamber music, Werner thought irreverently. But in truth he liked the Ulstermen. They took life and religion seriously, they meant what they said. Not the sort of people you would want to get into an argument with, if you could avoid it. As soldiers, fighting for what they believed in, they would be unbeatable. What was it the leader of the Conservative party, Bonar Law, had said? 'Ulster will fight, and Ulster will be right.'

The UVF soldiers, in particular, impressed him. Cavendish had deployed them well, in positions where they could guard the platform and the entrances to the square. They were relaxed, proud, and well-drilled. It was clear that no one in the crowd resented being controlled by them. They obeyed orders quietly, quickly, without fuss. Cavendish has them eating out of his hand, Werner thought. Just as he organised the prefects and monitors at school.

If these people knew what he was really like they would tear him to pieces in seconds.

Werner heard cheering approaching from a distance. Hooves

rattled in South Street; the UVF soldiers sprang smartly to attention; and Sir Edward Carson himself came into the square.

Sir Edward Carson, the MP for Dublin University who wanted to save Ulster from an Irish Parliament. The brilliant lawyer who had been offered the job of Home Secretary, and turned it down. The puritan advocate who had demolished the Irish wit Oscar Wilde in court, and put him in an English gaol for homosexuality. The leader of the Ulster Unionist Council, who proclaimed that Ulstermen were so intensely loyal that they would set up a Provisional Government of their own, rather than accept the decision of Westminster.

The man who could, if he wanted, plunge the United Kingdom into civil war.

He was sitting in an open coach, waving and doffing his top hat to either side. The coach stopped, the soldiers presented arms, and Carson got out and returned their salute. Werner noticed the cool pride on Charles Cavendish's face as he nudged his horse through the crowd to clear a way for the great man to the platform, and he nearly laughed aloud at the irony of it.

Carson, the scourge of Oscar Wilde, with a guard of honour commanded by Charles Cavendish!

What would he say, if I told him?

In the centre of the platform, Carson turned to face the crowd. The noise was deafening. Werner watched, open-mouthed, pretending to cheer with the rest. What was it about this man, he wondered, that appealed to these people so much? Clearly it was not physical beauty. Despite his expensive, well-tailored clothes, Carson was a big, burly, truculent bull of a man with a huge, heavy, pugnacious jaw and a solid, square, lowering face. Like a bare-knuckle prize-fighter in top-hat and mohair suit.

It was the conviction in him that set the man alight. Carson believed in himself utterly. He had accepted his role as these people's Messiah. He held up his hands and bade them be silent, and the cheering stopped. The huge Union flag behind him rippled in the wind as they waited, attentive. It was so silent that Werner could hear the sound of a rooster crowing half a mile away in a farmyard. An inner light of belief and happiness burned under Carson's heavy features. The man is a prophet, Werner thought – a prophet at home amongst his own people.

The voice was as big as the man. It filled the square and echoed down the side streets. He reminded his listeners, first, of their history. 'We are the people who made this land,' he said. 'It is ours, and we will hold it. Our ancestors came here three hundred years ago, from Scotland and England, to keep this country loyal to the crown. They were threatened; sometimes they were attacked and murdered and massacred; but they survived. They survived because of the strong Protestant character that was in them – a character of godliness and thrift and self-reliance and courage and the knowledge of right and wrong – those were our ancestors' virtues! And when they were betrayed by an unjust Catholic King, it was not the Protestant people who were cast out, but that bad king. James II. You know the story well. At the siege of Derry and the Boyne and Aughrim – did our forefathers surrender then? Did they listen tamely to a discredited ruler from Whitehall, who planned to hand over our land to Rome? Or did they gird up their loins and march with King Billy to smite the unbeliever hip and thigh, banish him to the wilderness? Answer me that!'

A wild burst of cheering filled the square. Werner glanced around him curiously. He had been here often enough to know how those words – 'Derry', 'Boyne', 'King Billy' – could excite the Protestant people of Ulster, but he still found it curious. So long ago, and yet for Carson and his audience, it seemed, so closely remembered . . .

As close to their hearts as the Bible. Part of it, almost.

Carson surveyed his audience, smiling grimly. When the applause had died down he continued, his voice strong, steady, hypnotic, telling them that they faced the same choice today, of an unprincipled government which schemed to deprive them of their rights without even daring to put the issue before the people in a general election or a referendum. He told them of the great rallies there had been in support of the Union, in Hyde Park, and at Blenheim Palace.

'I tell you this, my friends. We will maintain our fundamental rights as British citizens under the crown – and no maimed Parliament or corrupt Liberal government will take them away from us!'

He glared round the square at the hushed crowd, right hand

raised, his great jaw thrust out pugnaciously. A man would have to have a death wish to challenge him, Werner thought grimly. Carson's great fist swept down, and smashed expressively into the palm of his left hand.

'Not today, not tomorrow, not ever! All of us here have signed a solemn Covenant to say that we will never, under any circumstances, submit to Home Rule!'

He held his hands out in front of him and tapped the fingers of his right hand against his left wrist. 'I signed it in a silver pen, some of you cut your wrists and signed it in your own blood! 100,000 of us signed it! And there will be no backsliding, no shabby compromises with the words of that Covenant. Men like Colonel Cavendish and his fine soldiers in front of this platform will keep us from that. Their discipline and resolution has already called the bluff of this immoral, unprincipled government. We are prepared to take control of Ulster tomorrow and make no mistake, we will if we have to – and with your support we'll hold this province loyally for His Majesty the King, until this madness of his ministers has passed away for ever!'

Carson took a deep breath, filled his lungs, and raised his already powerful voice to a new crescendo of defiant thunder.

'The Liberal government has erected a boom between Ulster and the British people, as King James did before them at Londonderry. I promise you one thing, my friends! We will burst that boom just as our fathers did before us! There will be *No Surrender*!'

There was a brief, echoing silence. Then the mighty throb of the huge Lambeg drum signalled an explosion of cheers and applause.

All around Werner men were shouting, waving their caps in the air, cheering until their faces were red and the veins stood out on the side of their necks. Carson watched, impassive, his big hands thrust into the pockets of his coat. His face glowed with grim resolution and pride, accepting the burden of their trust.

It was magnificent, Werner thought, and quite terrifying. How could any government tolerate a man like this? But then, how could any government dare to arrest him?

Werner felt his crippled right hand shaking, and grasped it with his left to steady it. He thought of the plan on von Falkenhayn's desk and shivered at the lunacy of it. It was all very well to report on events, gather information about them, learn secrets about the background of some of those involved. It was quite another to try to use his knowledge to begin a war.

It's impossible, he thought. I wish I'd faced Falkenhayn down. Carson is far more frightening than von Falkenhayn could ever be. Not to mention his 100,000 bodyguards.

The trouble is, Moltke and von Falkenhayn were right in a way. Carson may be frightening but he is too intelligent to begin a civil war himself. All this talk of a Provisional government and the UVF fighting the British army is just a gigantic bluff. He won't start a war because he's not strong enough. He'd be bound to lose. He just wants it to seem as though he's ready to fight. So that the British government are afraid to attack him.

This could never happen in Germany. The government would simply arrest him. But in this country the government are too feeble, they're afraid to try. Anyway it would be too difficult.

Werner smiled to himself as he imagined, half a dozen policemen trying to push their way through the crowd and arrest Carson here. The idea was ludicrous. In a town like this, the crowd would wrench their limbs apart in seconds, and feed their fingers to the seagulls.

The smile stiffened on Werner's face, and his spine crawled as though a spider was on it. He remembered the three sailors von Falkenhayn was sending to meet him in Belfast ten days from now. I must have been drunk when I wrote that plan, he thought. It was a bad idea. I'll just turn the sailors round and tell them to go home.

If Carson were arrested or kidnapped, what tremendous, uncontrollable fury would be awakened! The whole province would run around like a bear with its eyes put out, smashing and rending anything it could find.

Including – and especially – the British Army.

There would be civil war.

Definitely. No question.

I don't want to have anything to do with this, Werner thought. I wish I'd never thought of it. It's impossible and far too dangerous and bound to go wrong. I'll stay here for a few weeks and then write another report to Falkenhayn. It's a bad idea that couldn't possibly work.

And I shall never become a Colonel.

I'll go back to Germany and become a small town reporter for the rest of my life. Much safer. Let the British organise their own civil war . . .

It's only the impossible that's really worth trying for, Werner's father had once said, when he was trying to encourage his son. Werner had scorned such talk then. After all, if it hadn't been for his father's foolish ambitions he might have had a sound arm and a full army career.

But if I fail . . .

There's that bastard on the horse over there, smiling calmly as though he owns the world. Charles Cavendish. He'll have beaten me again.

He watched as Carson got back into his coach, to loud music from the band and cheers from the crowd. As the coach left the square, the crowd began to follow, and Werner went with them, walking light-headedly, without seeing where he was going. He laughed, and the people around him smiled back, thinking he was as elated by the speech as they were. But his mind was far away.

There's only one good thing about an idea like mine, he thought.

No one would ever expect anyone to try it.

10

On the ferry, Deborah Cavendish leaned on the rail, staring out into the night. The ship was just beginning to rock slightly, as it came out of the shelter of the Belfast Lough and headed east across the Irish Sea, but it was not a rough night and she had come up onto the deck for a breath of fresh air.

She thought about Rankin, making a similar journey from Dublin to Holyhead the morning after she had left him. Had he stood on the deck like this and thought about her at all? Or was he glad to be rid of her? She had heard nothing from him since then, not even a single letter to tell her his address. Even if she looked for him in London it was not at all certain that she would find him.

But first she would have to visit Sarah, if she could. She wondered if she would be welcome. They had been close as children, but always on Sarah's terms and, in the past few years they had seen each other less. Sarah had become obsessed with the suffrage movement, and though Deborah sympathised with the aim, the methods of the militants terrified her. She could not imagine herself speaking in public, being barraged with tomatoes, starving herself in prison. But if her sister's health was in danger, Deborah had to help.

That was how they had always been, since childhood. Sarah would try to jump her pony over some impossible wall, and Deborah would bandage the bruises.

She wondered how long she would be away. She had said

nothing to Charles about this, and he had not seemed to want to know. He himself was used to being away for months, even years on end – probably he imagined this as a separation of at most a few weeks or a month, scarcely worth talking about. And yet how could she ever come back, with the baby beginning to show? She could never face that.

She thought of Tom leaving her that morning at school, and wondered if she would ever see him again. The memory was slightly blurred because there had been a film of tears in her eyes at the time. None in his, of course. He had been in a crowd of other boys, all eager to swap stories of their hols, desperate to be rid of the embarrassment of their mothers. He had endured her final, brief kiss on the forehead with a polite, pitying expression, and had waved perfunctorily as Simon drove her away. By the time she had looked back from the main gates, he was gone – just one amongst a horde of gawky, chattering, scuffling boys. All without mothers until halfterm.

If I go and live with Rankin now, that's the end, she thought. Charles will never allow me to see Tom again. But then, if I stay and he finds out I'm pregnant it will be the same. I've lost my son whatever happens . . .

She looked out over the dark sea towards the lights on the shore. That must be Holywood, behind them there – and Bangor, close at hand. The hills behind were black, silent, empty. This place is my home, she thought, but it gives me nothing. Not now. I have a husband who has spent half his life on the other side of the globe and yet is prepared to fight and even die for Ulster, but he cares nothing about me. He even seemed glad to see me go. Can he really have a mistress? I felt so sure this morning, with that odious young Simon Fletcher smirking at me, except that it's so hard to imagine Charles unbending with any woman. He's so prim, so correct, so cold. When I go to touch him he shies away as though I have some plague. Lord knows I don't expect him to be a wonderful sensitive lover like James but he is a handsome man for all that, and he *is* my husband. He ought to make love to me if only out of a sense of duty.

What's wrong with the man?

Perhaps Sarah's husband, Jonathan, will be able to help me.

At least he's a man who can talk. But that's foolish, he won't have time to think about me. Not with Sarah starving herself in prison until she can hardly walk. I used to think those two were so lucky, but now it seems there's tension there too. Oh, the world is full of miserable marriages.

The wind was quite strong now, as the ferry came out of the shelter of Belfast Lough, and turned south-east towards Liverpool. Deborah lifted her head to let her hair blow out behind her in the cold, damp breeze of the night. The coast was a distant, dark line, receding under the stars.

London will be a place of decision, she thought. What to do about Rankin, Sarah, Charles – most of all about the baby. I couldn't make any of these decisions here in Glenfee, alone. I wouldn't need to come back here ever again, if it wasn't for Tom.

I hope someone needs me in London. If I'm not wanted there, where on earth is there left for me to go?

Charles Cavendish rode his bay horse at a slow walk up the drive towards Glenfee. It was dark, but the animal knew its way, and whickered softly with pleasure. There was a gas light spluttering dimly at the corner of the stables. Harry the stable boy would be there, ready to rub the horse down and give it a warm bran mash and fresh hay.

No doubt cook will have a meal for me, too, Charles thought, but there will be no Tom. He had enjoyed his son's company over the past two weeks much more than he had expected. He was becoming a person at last – an identifiable individual with a taste for riding and cricket and the ability to maintain a conversation and listen to his father's stories. I will miss him, Charles thought. Deborah was right, I should make the effort to visit him at his school more often.

He thought how Tom would have enjoyed the parade at Carson's speech earlier that day. It had gone off well – his predecessor had drilled the UVF unit to an efficient, disciplined body of men, they had done him credit. And if only the guns could be landed safely from Germany, they would be well armed.

He had spent the last part of the day at a tempestuous,

anxious meeting of senior staff, discussing the landing of the guns. The ship carrying them, the *Fanny*, had been spotted leaving Bremerhaven two weeks ago, but since then it had disappeared. Frantic messengers had been sent east across England, and north to Scotland, to make contact with it, so far without success. Several officers had argued that a message should be sent to Crawford, the man in charge of the ship, to abandon the mission because it was too dangerous, but Charles and a number of others had argued forcefully that they should go ahead. And, thank God, Carson had supported them.

Without that man, Charles thought, we would be lost; and without guns, we can do nothing.

And if the Union is lost, the heart of the British Empire will be destroyed.

He thought back to the argument he had had with Deborah earlier that day, and realised that she would be on the ferry now, crossing the Irish Sea. It was unusual for her to be so determined – her sister's imprisonment must have affected her more than he had thought.

It was even more unusual for her to defy him openly. She was usually so quiet, compliant. Unlike her termagant sister.

As the horse picked its way past the windows of the great house and lengthened its stride towards the stables, Deborah's words came back to him clearly.

I don't give a fig for your Union.

Whatever could have possessed the woman?

The freshening wind drove Deborah in from the deck at last, but she couldn't sleep. Her cabin was small, comfortable, intimate; the rocking and creaking of the walls exciting. It was like being in a treehouse, she thought, as a child – or under the canvas awning of a small boat they had had once, on holiday. Places you could hide in, while voices searched for you, far away. Places that were safe for secrets.

She didn't want to go to bed. She sat in a chair in her cabin, enjoying the ship's motion. She watched the oil lamp overhead sway to and fro. The yellow light from the lamp moved on the wall opposite. Up and down, up . . . and down. It was pleasant, restful, dreamlike.

For a while she tried to think about Sarah, alone in her prison cell. Deborah had never been in a prison, but she imagined that, even there, Sarah would make her presence felt. Deborah had great respect for Sarah's forceful, impulsive character. Often it could solve problems, though equally often it could create them. As children, Sarah would always shout and try to bully their parents into giving her something because it was her *right*; whereas Deborah would smile and snuggle up to their father and try to wheedle things out of him because he loved her.

Which has got me into even worse trouble than her, Deborah thought. If only people knew, they might pity *me*, instead of always talking about my virago of a sister.

No, they wouldn't. They'd despise me as a whore.

She took a letter out of her bag.

Sarah was a poor correspondent, but Jonathan, her husband, wrote to Deborah several times a year. In part this was due to the increasing interest of the political events which both were on the fringes of, in their different ways, either side of the Irish Sea; but it was also, sadly, to do with a loneliness they had both come to feel. Deborah's husband was frequently abroad; Jonathan, it seemed, had a wife in whom it was sometimes hard to confide. So he wrote to her sister instead.

The letter had been written several weeks ago, long before Sarah had been arrested again. Part of it was about a debate Jonathan had attended in Parliament after the debacle of the Curragh Mutiny. Deborah only remembered those events vaguely. Charles had just returned home, and she had been at the height of her misery about Rankin. The British Army had been ordered to move into Ulster in force, occupying all major barracks and public buildings, in an attempt to overawe the UVF. The First Lord of the Admiralty, Winston Churchill, had sent ships of the channel fleet steaming north to Belfast to support the soldiers and the government was rumoured to have signed warrants for the arrest of 200 leading members of the UVF – Charles undoubtedly among them.

The operation had been meant to be secret, but Sir Edward Carson had learnt of it somehow. After denouncing the government in the Commons, he had hurried to Belfast, where Charles had been among those detailed to meet him at the docks and escort him to Craigavon. For three days Charles had been away, and Deborah had been almost sure he would be arrested. Then the news had broken that the cavalry officers in the Curragh, near Dublin, had refused to obey orders, and offered to resign rather than act against the UVF. The Minister of War and several senior generals had resigned, and the operation had blown up in the government's face.

Charles had returned home, triumphant, and Deborah had scarcely known whether to laugh or cry. Of course she was glad that Charles was safe, but she took no joy in the UVF's triumph. Neither, it seemed, did Jonathan.

> *My dear Debbie,*
> *What in the world has your husband been up to? You will not be surprised to hear that the UVF has been the talk of the town these past few days, the more so since Churchill's speech in Bradford when he called Carson and the UVF 'treacherous conspirators'. There was uproar in the House after that, as you can imagine – I couldn't hear a word that was said, sometimes for five minutes at a go! But all the time, Debbie, I was thinking of what all this must have been like for you. Alarums in the night, no doubt, and no knowing when Charles would be home at all, or indeed if . . .*

That was true enough, Deborah thought. But she had cared so little about it. Had been glad, even, that Charles was so busy. She skimmed down the letter, seeking the paragraphs she had found most interesting. The letter had been written after Sarah had been released from her second term in prison, and was supposedly convalescing at home, under constant danger of rearrest under the Cat and Mouse Act.

> *Like you I seem to be saddled with a marriage partner who is obsessed with something higher than her duty towards me. Your sister has talked and thought of nothing else, I believe, but the women's suffrage movement this past two years. If she is not actually in prison, starving herself, there are always meetings to attend, newspapers to sell, garlands and ribbons to adorn their stalls – the Good Lord alone knows what she does with her time! She is constantly with these women who seem to take a delight in excluding men. I know I can say this to you, Deborah, and trust to your discretion – for in my way I love her dearly*

but there is no contact any longer, none at all!

Of course you will say I encouraged her in this, in the early days. She and I used to share so much of our work together in the East End, producing surveys to show the squalor and poverty the poor wretched people lived in. I thought her so fine then, such a noble young woman taking on these great matters by my side, and I was proud to be a supporter of a Liberal government which was actually doing something about these things. But now she has abandoned all that for a single issue – and one that, if it does succeed, is likely to give the vote to women of property only – most of whom will vote Tory and bring back a Conservative government who will oppress the poor worse than ever, even! But she cannot see that. She even talks, God help me, of the nobility of smashing windows and setting fire to pillar-boxes – as if that will do anything but harm! If you had seen ladies, Deborah, as I have done – respectable women like yourself and Sarah – screaming and prodding at the Home Secretary outside Downing Street – one even kicked him! Can you believe that? To tell you the truth, Debbie, it filled me with laughter at first, but then anger and a terrible grief, mixed.

It is absurd, frightening, to know that my own wife has now twice been arrested for taking part in such a degrading pantomime. And then, when she is arrested, to find her starving herself until she looks gaunt and bony like the skeleton of the woman I once loved. She is at home just now, with a passable nurse – a Mrs Watson, a raging suffragette herself, I regret to say – and I have done a deal with the Home Secretary, McKenna, which I hope *will keep her out of prison if she behaves herself, but there are no guarantees.*

So you see, Deborah, when I sit alone and write to you like this I realise a little of what life must be like for you. The difference is that when Charles's UVF defy Parliament, it is seen by all the world as manly, respectable, dignified. He is threatening to plunge the nation into civil war – and why? To retain his hereditary right to oppress the poor Catholic Irish peasant! But if he is arrested, society won't make you feel ashamed, whereas with Sarah . . . Lord, Debbie, you are so lucky to have Tom. If only Sarah had not lost those babies, we should be a family like you, instead of two individuals who scarcely speak to each other for days on end. And if she had children she would surely never dare risk herself as she does. It is so sad. But perhaps when she is recovered . . .

The ship, meeting a freak wave, gave an unusual lurch, and Deborah stretched out a hand, automatically, to catch a glass of water before it slid off the table. She let Jonathan's letter fall into her lap. Now it has happened, she thought. Sarah has done something worse than even he feared. He will be destroyed by it.

But we are all destroying ourselves. If he knew about my child . . .

She stared at the pool of lamplight swaying across the opposite wall, lost in thought. I suppose I could have predicted this, she thought. Years ago when they got married . . .

When Jonathan first appeared in their house Deborah met him at the door. She was seventeen, he was twenty-seven. She saw a tall young man, rather gawky, with a short dark beard. He wore a blazer, straw boater, white trousers and shoes. He looked at her intensely with eyes that were a pleasant brown, alight with interest. Then he took off his hat, and smiled. The smile was quite dazzling. She felt her cheeks flush with the warmth of it. He said: 'You must be the younger sister.'

'Yes, that's right,' she said. 'I'm Debbie. Have you come to see . . .?'

'Sarah? Yes. We're going boating on the river. Why don't you come too?'

'Well, I'm not sure. I . . . '

'It's all right. We're not going to spoon or anything like that. We won't embarrass you.'

And so it was settled, quite simply, with a charm that Deborah found enchanting. The three of them spent the whole afternoon on the river, taking it in turns to row, and trail their hands in the water, tying the boat up at a little island to eat their picnic out of the hamper. He talked at times intently of the social conditions of the poor, and how he was studying to become a lawyer to help them remedy it. Then, when he saw Deborah was becoming bored, he laughed and recited comic poetry instead. They came home tired and happy in the late June evening to reassure their worried and hypochondriac mother that they had not drowned. It had been one of the finest summer days that Deborah could remember.

There had been other days like that, but not many. Deborah had made the mistake of speaking to Sarah about her enchantment with the young man, and Sarah had said she should not get silly ideas, she was just a child, he was only being polite to her because they needed a chaperone, that was all. Jonathan was a rising young lawyer from a good family, with aspirations to go into politics. Often he had taken Sarah out to political meetings, where people talked about trade unions and income tax, and Deborah had only been allowed to a few of those. But then there had been other excursions – walks or visits to concerts or bicycle rides – when Deborah was allowed to come along. Sarah tended to monopolise the conversation with Jonathan, but Deborah enjoyed the excursions nevertheless, even though the others often left her for an hour at a time to pack up the hamper or read by herself. Jonathan was always charming and full of fun when they returned, Sarah flushed and rather quiet.

Deborah could still remember the unusual embarrassment of one particular afternoon. They had found a picnic spot by the river, and she had been left to guard the bicycles while the other two went off to walk or spoon or recite poetry or whatever it was that young couples did. On the way out Jonathan had been unusually charming, and Deborah, lying on the grass by herself, had been trying to imagine what it would be like to be kissed by him. It must be strange to be kissed by a man with a beard, she thought. Perhaps it would scratch, you might get bits of moustache in your mouth. But perhaps it would be nice. Other young men's faces looked a little rough in the afternoon, she had noticed, like sandpaper with the bristles coming through. She began to experiment with a tuft of horsehair from her bicycle saddle, stroking her own cheeks with it gently. It *was* nice. She closed her eyes. 'My sweet darling,' she murmured, 'my sweet love.' Then suddenly she heard a giggle, and the crack of a stick.

She had opened her eyes, and to her horror, Sarah and Jonathan had been staring down at her.

Sarah asked: 'Debbie? What on earth are you doing?'

'Oh, nothing. Just reciting a poem I learnt at school. It's nothing really.' She felt her cheeks flush hot, but luckily Sarah was too full of her own news to be very interested.

'How strange. Well?'

'Well what?' If Deborah hadn't been so embarrassed she would have noticed that her sister, too, was blushing. She dropped the horsehair surreptitiously on the grass.

'Aren't you going to ask why we've been so long? Weren't you worried?'

'No, should I have been?' Deborah's daydream had been so intense, she had no idea how long the others had been gone.

Jonathan smiled – that radiant smile he had in those days which somehow warmed her all through. 'Debbie was too engrossed in her poetry to think about us, my dear,' he said. 'But I think . . . '

'No, let me tell her, Jonathan,' Sarah said, in her impulsive, forceful way. 'She's *my* little sister, not yours. What he is trying to tell you, Deborah dear, is that Jonathan and I are going to get married. And we would like you to be our bridesmaid.'

Deborah could never remember the rest of that afternoon. She knew that she had burst into tears, and that Sarah had looked shocked and a little angry, but whether she had recovered herself and congratulated them, she was not sure. Presumably she had, since her next memory was of following Sarah down the aisle. She had been holding Sarah's train, and feeling utterly hollow and desolate inside. When Jonathan had put the ring on Sarah's finger, Deborah drove her nails into the skin of her own ring finger so hard that the marks were still there the next day.

But that was all the fantasy of a girl of seventeen. Two years later, Deborah had a husband of her own, a handsome army officer whom she had known since she was twelve – just the kind of man Jonathan liked least. Jonathan had become a successful barrister and a Liberal Member of Parliament. The year after that Sarah had her first miscarriage, and Deborah gave birth to a son, in India. Even when she returned home, they lived on opposite sides of the Irish Sea, meeting once or twice a year at most. They were responsible married people.

So responsible that Sarah had just slashed a picture in the National Gallery, and Deborah was pregnant by an Irish trade union leader. And Jonathan sat up late at night in his house in Belgravia, writing to Deborah because he could not talk to his wife. At a time like this, Deborah thought – he might even be writing to me now!

She knew she would have to go and see Sarah, but somehow, the thought failed to touch her. Most likely she would receive a defiant lecture, find her offer of help despised. Instead, Deborah felt an intense yearning to talk to Jonathan. Part of it was protective, maternal almost – a desire to help him in his loneliness. But also it was a desire for understanding, comfort for herself. She wondered if she would have the courage to tell him about Rankin, and what he would say, if she did.

She smiled, and smoothed the letter gently against her dress, as though it were a child.

As for Charles, well, Jonathan is right. No doubt he will behave very well if he is arrested or has to fight. Young Tom will believe his father is a hero. And if anything happens to Charles he will have brought it on himself.

As, no doubt, Charles would say about me.

Deborah shivered suddenly, put the letter back in its envelope, and stood up to get ready for bed.

PART THREE

London

11

'London Euston!'

The train door slammed behind Deborah and she stood in a vast, grimy cathedral with iron vaults overhead, and pigeons flying through gouts of escaping steam. The shouts and whistles of guards and porters filled the air. A donkey, blinkered, pulled a line of Royal Mail trolleys along the platform.

'Carry your bags, lady?'

'Thank you, yes. These – and this one here.' An old man, bent, fifty, white moustache and broken veins all down his face, hurrying away at surprising speed with her bags, his gammy right leg swaying to the side and back again as he pushed the trolley. Gracious – he'd almost gone! Quickly, she wormed her way between a flag-waving guard and a bowler-hatted clerk, and saw him pushing through a crowd outside W.H. Smith's newspaper stall. People – so many people everywhere! She bumped into a portly man in a tweed coat and top-hat, dodged some boys larking by the hot-chestnut stand, and emerged, breathless, hat slightly awry, at the taxi rank.

'Belgrave Square, please.'

London overwhelmed her. After Glenfee it was so big, so crowded, so full of energy. She had always wondered how Sarah could bear to live here, but perhaps it suited her aggression, her impulsiveness. Deborah felt that if she stood still or hesitated she would be ignored, knocked over, pushed to one side. She felt at first panic, then exhilaration. It was a place where she didn't matter. Where she could do what she liked with no one to watch or complain.

Where she might solve the problem of her baby. Or find Rankin, and disappear. But then she would lose Tom for certain. Or was there a way around that, too?

Oh, there has to be!

But first, she had come to help her sister. And her brother-in-law too, if he needed it.

In the taxi she gazed curiously out at the fashions. Hats, she saw, were larger than ever – even quite ordinary-looking girls sported hats wide as bicycle wheels, laden with flowers and fruit and feathers. Several others, in Oxford Street especially, carried parasols. Nearly all the dresses she saw were gathered in with a belt or a sash at the waist, and those she liked most descended in several layers of frilly taffeta to the ankle. One or two women still wore the hobble skirt, tied with a bow just below the knee, but most, she was glad to see, had abandoned it. She had tried one once but thought it absurd. It was impossible to walk in it – she nearly fell over.

So much attention we women pay to the surface of things, she thought, while so much horror goes on underneath. And yet, if I had time, I would like to come back here and buy something for myself. Even bring Sarah with me. She might like that. It would take her mind off her militant protests, make her think of pleasing Jonathan, for a change.

But that's foolish. She won't be out for six months, unless she starves herself out, and then she'll be too weak to do anything except lie in bed for days. As for me, in a few months no fashionable clothes will fit me, whatever I buy.

Sarah's house was a four-storey terrace in a square in Belgravia. It was in a prosperous area; Jonathan was a successful barrister as well as a Liberal MP. As Deborah's taxi drew up outside it she saw a large, shiny limousine parked outside. Several other cars were parked haphazardly along the street, and a horsedrawn milkfloat was trying to edge past. The milkman was engaged in heated debate with the chauffeur of the limousine. Several men in cloth caps stood around with notebooks in their hands, watching the door.

Deborah got out and persuaded the taxi-driver to carry her

bags to the foot of the steps. As she was paying him, the front door opened and Jonathan came out.

She had not seen him for nearly a year, but he was little changed. Pale, perhaps, his face thinner under the beard, but she would have known him anywhere. Not as tall or as strong as Rankin but still a handsome man. To her he seemed scarcely to have changed from the smiling young man for whom she'd opened her mother's front door, all those years ago.

He did not notice her at first; and that was normal, too. He was as tall and wiry as ever; his face slightly more lined, perhaps, but not a trace of grey in the short black beard. He seemed to have cut himself, shaving perhaps – there was a small white plaster on one cheek. His eyes, even at this distance, were bright, intense. He wore a frock coat, pinstripe trousers, and had a top hat in his hand; and he was clearly in a hurry. He saw the reporters waiting at the foot of the steps, and stepped down quickly towards his chauffeur.

'Excuse me, Mr Becket, could you say a few words?'

'Have you heard anything from your wife, sir?'

'Is it true that you are going to resign from Parliament?'

He reached the car door and turned, his hand held up firmly. She remembered he had worn a wedding ring once. No longer. It chafed his skin, he had said.

'I'm sorry, gentlemen. I have nothing to say – no comment whatsoever. I am going to make a statement in the House – you can come and listen to me there.'

'Hello, Jonathan.'

'What?' He was within a yard of her now and had still noticed nothing. She had spoken so quietly, she thought her voice might have gone unheard. He glanced at her, almost irritably she thought – a strange woman among the reporters. Perhaps she shouldn't have come.

Then he recognised her and the smile transformed him. It was all right, he was pleased to see her. It was just as she remembered it. Radiant, warming her with its power. But she saw, too, the lines of strain around the eyes, the pallor under the skin.

'*Deborah*! Great Scot! How did you get here?'

'By train, of course, Johnny. How do you think?'

He bent forward and kissed her, gently, on the cheek. His beard brushed against her softly, like a wisp of horsehair. As though the reporters, the men around them, did not exist. A family reunion. His sister-in-law, come up to town.

'But why are you here now, of all times? Do you know what's happened? Sarah . . . '

'Is in prison again. I know. Jonathan. I have come to be of help, if I can.'

He took her hand in his and held her fingers lightly, without pressure. If only Charles could behave like this, she thought. But then, Jonathan had always had good manners, even as a young man.

'Thank you, Deborah, that's kind. How very like you. But, my dear, you must be tired. And I am off to speak in the House, about this wretched business.'

'About Sarah, you mean?'

'Yes.' She saw how drawn he looked, anxious, now that the smile had gone. 'Some members will laugh, no doubt, but mostly they will pity me, and that is the worst. But no matter, she has forced me into it. Some things have to be said. If you go inside my butler Reeves will take care of you.'

Deborah looked at the empty house, confused. She hadn't come all this way to hide in there, alone.

'No, let me come with you! Please, Jonathan – I am not tired and I would like to hear what you say!'

He was pleased, she could tell that. He thought for a moment, then stood back and handed her into the car. 'Yes, why not? I suppose I can get you into the Ladies' Gallery. Come, and welcome.'

It was a nightmare. No one could survive six months of this, Sarah thought. No one.

Lots of women have.

It was true. She remembered reading how Sylvia Pankhurst had been force-fed for five months, how dozens of other nameless women had endured it, how Emily Davison had thrown herself over the top balcony of a prison walkway in protest against forced feeding.

Emily Davison. She had been killed later, catching hold of the

King's horse in the Derby, in protest against the government's treatment of Mrs Pankhurst. She hadn't just endured, she'd *died* for the cause.

Up till now, Sarah knew, Mrs Pankhurst herself had not been forcibly fed. She had been tortured by the government's alternative, the Cat and Mouse Act. Sarah had thought that was what would happen to her, too, but perhaps government policy had changed. Perhaps Mrs Pankhurst was being forcibly fed here now, in the same prison as her.

Sarah had no way of knowing.

Sarah only knew that she had been force fed again, twice, and she had never felt so dirty or frightened or helpless in her life.

She had no way out. Only rarely was she allowed out of the cell, and she met no one. Her only exercise was to hobble from window to door, and back again. Her hands shook, her throat was scraped raw by the tube, her teeth battered by the gag, her dress stained by vomit.

And this could go on for six months.

She wondered if anyone outside knew, if even Jonathan knew what was happening to her. Probably not. Probably he was still blithely going to visit his whore. Could a man do that? Life is so unfair, she thought, it is a cruel joke. Not only is society organised to serve the needs of men, they are also born with a greater need for sex than us, and a lesser need for love. Perhaps they can divorce the two. How could God make a world like that?

Is that what my husband is really like?

He wasn't once. People said we were a handsome couple. Women admired him, not just because of his appearance but because he was kind, sympathetic, understanding. He used to listen to people, make them laugh. I remember once Mrs Watson said to me: you are a lucky woman, Mrs Becket, to have a husband like that, so distinguished and good-mannered. Who even votes for women's suffrage in Parliament. There are so many ladies whose husbands let them down and I have seen them destroyed by it . . .

And then I get a letter from a prostitute telling me to keep suffragetes away from Dr Armstrong because *my husband gets the same treatment as other men* and I see him going into

Armstrong's house and not come out. So I have the information to destroy this foul pimp and I daren't use it because it would destroy my fine distinguished well-mannered husband at the same time . . .

A terrible thought struck Sarah, so sudden and painful that she flushed, and got up to walk up and down the tiny cell to calm herself. *What if Mrs Watson and the other women in the movement knew all about Jonathan? If they knew, but didn't tell me, to spare my feelings because I am his wife?*

If that was true, she thought, then I would be an embarrassment to the whole movement. Perhaps they want to expose this Dr Armstrong and his wretched prostitution racket but are holding back because my husband is one of his customers. So they have done nothing about it and the evil goes on.

Would they do that?

They might. Mrs Watson is a kind sensitive woman and so are most of the others. They might easily hold back from something that might hurt me because they thought I was still weak from last time in prison, and they thought it might break my heart.

Oh God! Perhaps I have embarrassed them all.

The doctor and the wardresses came once a day with their trolley. Each time they asked her, before they began, if she would agree to eat. Each time she refused, as vehemently as she could. Today, for the first time, she experienced the torture as a punishment, as though it were in some way deserved for her own foolishness.

And yet it is Jonathan who is at fault, she thought later, as she lay sore and trembling on her vomit-stained bed. Why should I blame myself? That is just another wretched male trick. I shouldn't have just scratched him in those police cells, I should really have torn his eyes out.

Those pale blue eyes I used to love. I couldn't do that, I'm not a monster. *He* is. I wish he loved me. Why can't I think clearly any more?

If only I knew someone, she thought. If only I had a friend. Someone to talk to, who could help me get my thoughts in order. Once she had looked out of the window and seen other prisoners, subdued, walking in a ring. At least, she assumed that was what it was. The exercise yard was blocked from her view by a wing of the prison that jutted out, and she could only see a couple of square yards of gravel. Every few seconds a different woman in a grey, arrow-striped prison dress had shuffled into view, head bowed, hands clasped in front of her, and then disappeared. None had looked up. Sarah had been taken out for exercise like that once or twice in her first prison sentence, before she had begun her hunger strike. Women walked in a ring for the allotted time, in silence. No one was allowed to speak or look at the others.

Nonetheless, it was in the open air. This time, because Sarah refused to eat, she was denied even that.

'Slops out, now! Hurry it up!'

'What? I'm sorry, I don't . . .'

The heavy wooden cell door opened suddenly, almost striking Sarah in the face as she staggered on her endless walk to the window and back again. A wardress stood in the doorway, the same sturdy, slab-faced young woman who had bathed her on the first day. She had her hands on her hips and a big bunch of keys at her belt. The one whom Sarah had thought of as an underservant, a coalheaver. She scowled at Sarah.

'Time to slop out, yer ladyship! Pick up the bucket from under the loo, take it down the corridor and pour it away. You know the routine. This is a clean place, 'olloway!'

'Oh, yes, I know.' The intrusion, after so many hours of solitude, was devastating. Sarah felt herself sway, and hung on to the edge of the door to stop herself falling. Then she sat down, abruptly, on the edge of the bed.

The wardress waited a moment, then sighed, with something that might have been interpreted as sympathy. 'I see. A little bit tired are we, yer ladyship? You might not need yer mid-morning rest, my dear, if you was to see sense and eat the food provided for you. Or is it all pigswill, to a fine lady like you?'

Sarah's head suddenly hurt terribly, and red spots were moving to and fro before her eyes. She heard the exasperation in the woman's voice, and thought, of course, she probably eats things much worse than this prison food every day. She thinks I'm proud.

'It's not that,' she said. 'There's nothing wrong with the food, it's a protest . . . '

'D'yer think I don't know that? But you're wasting your time refusing the food, Becket. You're too much of a fineckity lady, you've not got the strength for it. Can't even lift a bucket yourself, can you?'

'Of course I can,' Sarah said. She thought, that's another thing I've learnt here. At home my maid takes the chamber pot out from under my bed every morning and thinks nothing of it. But why should I expect someone else to do it? 'It's just that – I've hardly used it, really.'

'I'm not interested in that. Regulations. It stinks the same, anyhow – even a little bit. Probably you can't smell it, but it does.'

'Yes, I'm sure. I'm sorry.' She dragged herself to her feet, fumbled under the wooden seat, and lugged out the bucket. There was a small amount of urine in the bottom. As she walked past the wardress in the doorway, she looked the woman in the face, and was gratified when the narrow disapproving eyes met hers. It was the first time any of the prison staff had looked at her, or talked to her directly, since she had come.

'Thank you. Miss Harkness, isn't it?'

'Down the corridor on the right. And no talking to other prisoners.'

'I wouldn't dream of it.'

For a moment Sarah felt almost happy. The freedom of the long corridor – nearly twenty, thirty paces without stopping or turning – that was a walk to be enjoyed! She went along it like a little girl swinging her bucket on the beach. There were half a dozen doors on either side of the corridor. She wondered if there were any other suffragettes in there. They must be in here somewhere – possibly even Mrs Pankhurst herself. But how could she find out?

She began to sing:

> *'And did those feet in ancient time*
> *Walk upon England's pastures green . . . '*

'That's enough of that!' The wardress behind her shouted, but Sarah took no notice. What can she do now, anyway, she thought. Anyhow I *like* singing. If only my voice was not so cracked and feeble!

'I shall not cease from mental fight
Nor shall my sword sleep in my hand . . .'

She stopped. Her throat hurt abominably, and the wardress's hand was on her shoulder. But as she stopped, another voice took up the refrain. A squeaky, defiant whisper from behind the doors of – the last cell on the right, wasn't it?

'Until Jerusalem is builded here
In England's green and pleasant land.'

At last! As she poured her bucket down the sluice and rinsed it, Sarah thought: I'm not alone, of course I'm not! There *are* other suffragettes here, probably dozens of them. It's part of our duty to keep in touch – that's how we'll survive!

And so, on her way back down the corridor, she sang again, and tried to stop outside the door of the cell which the singing had come from. But the wardress was ready, and grabbed her arm. All Sarah could do was shout out '*Votes for Women!*' once before she was dragged away.

The wardress pushed her back into her own cell, and stood in the doorway for a moment, glaring.

'You only make it worse for yourselves, you know. You break the rules, you don't behave like proper ladies, you lose people's sympathy. I'd like the vote with the rest of you, course I would – but you'll never get it like that!'

Amazed at the woman's admission, Sarah gazed at her for a second, open-mouthed. Then the great door slammed in her face. She lay back on the hard wooden bed, defiantly, smiling to herself for the first time that day.

'Oh yes we will, Miss Harkness,' she said. 'Oh yes, my dear, we will!'

Deborah had not been in the House of Commons before. She was curious, faintly amused at the pomp of it all. So this is what the men want to keep us out of, she thought. Where they deployed ranks of policemen to prevent Mrs Pankhurst presenting a petition to the Prime Minister. Yet if I go in dutifully on the arm of my brother, no one will stop us at all.

Jonathan escorted her past the Master-at-arms, who bowed with some deference but also with a touch, she thought, of suspicion – did he think she had a bomb in her bag? – and took her to the Ladies Gallery. He found her a seat in the front row.

'There was a metal grille here until recently,' he said. 'But some of Sarah's friends chained themselves to it and the police had to take it away, with the ladies still attached.' He laughed. 'It hasn't been replaced. Don't throw anything down on our heads, now, will you?'

Deborah smiled nervously and leaned forward to watch. The whole atmosphere of the place intimidated her. She could not imagine herself, or any woman, doing anything of the kind.

'Don't worry, Jonathan, I'm on my best behaviour.'

She found the story of the grille amusing. Why on earth had it been there in the first place? Had the men thought their female visitors were best kept locked up, behind bars, like concubines in some Middle Eastern seraglio?

Already about half the seats on the green benches below were taken. The members were lolling or chatting quietly to each other, only a few listening to the Minister who was answering questions at the Despatch Box. How casually they take it all, Deborah thought. It's like peeping down into a gentleman's club.

She noticed the gaps in the rail where the metal grille had been removed, and glanced round at the half dozen or so ladies who were in the gallery with her. One or two looked middle-aged and formidable, several others young and quite strikingly fashionable, but none looked at all violent. Just ordinary women like herself. Even without a grille, surely no woman in her right mind would dare to attack such a large gathering of men?

No woman in her right mind.

Perhaps it was true that Sarah and her friends were a little mad. Deborah did not like the thought, and pushed it away.

Jonathan had left her and, a moment later, she saw him enter the chamber below. It's a pity about the plaster on his cheek, she thought. Otherwise he looks truly handsome. As distinguished as any man there.

There was a murmur as he came in – mixed sympathy and jeering, as far as she could make out. But the moment passed quickly. The chamber was filling up. As Jonathan took his seat, she realised that the stolid, grey-haired man strolling in behind him must be Mr Asquith, the Prime Minister. Opposite him, picking his teeth nonchalantly as he waited, was Mr Bonar Law, the leader of the Conservative Opposition.

It is real, then, she thought, it is not just a theatre. They really do meet each other and argue here.

She had arrived just before Prime Minister's Questions, and for a quarter of an hour she watched one MP after another rise and put his question to Mr Asquith. Frequently there were shouts of anger or dismay from the Conservative side, while Asquith replied with heavy, imperturbable dignity. Throughout all this Jonathan sat quietly, very pale and still, on the front bench just below the gangway.

Then suddenly, his name was called.

'Statement by Mr Jonathan Becket!'

As Jonathan stood up, Deborah thought: I have never seen him so pale before. He looks nervous, defiant, like Daniel in the den of lions. She felt afraid and wanted to hold his hand and give him support.

It was clear, too, that what Jonathan had to say was of interest to most members of the House. Very few had left their seats, and the Prime Minister and Bonar Law were still there. Deborah noticed a rustle of dresses around her, too, and two women moved from the back of the gallery to the front bench, beside her.

'Mr Speaker, sir, I crave the indulgence of this House for the chance to address you on a certain regrettable incident which took place in the National Gallery this week.' Jonathan paused, his thumbs hooked into the fob pockets of his waistcoat. Deborah could not be sure at this distance, but she thought one of his fingers was shaking. No one was talking in the House – all attention was focused on him.

'As most members will know by now, my wife entered that building with a knife concealed in her muff, and deliberately slashed the painting known as the *Rokeby Venus*, leaving a number of gashes in the centre of it. I have been informed, to my great relief, that the damage, though serious, is not beyond repair. My wife has since appeared in court, and been sentenced to six months' imprisonment in the Third Division.'

A murmur of sympathy met this announcement. Encouraged, Jonathan threw back his head and continued in a slightly louder voice.

'My wife has for some time been a member of the Women's Social and Political Union, and she undertook this action for two reasons. Firstly, to demand votes for women; and secondly, to put pressure on the government to release the WSPU's leader, Mrs Emmeline Pankhurst, from prison.'

A considerably louder murmur met this statement. One or two shouts of approval, but many more jeers – and, to Deborah's annoyance but not surprise, some laughter. She thought – but could scarcely believe it – that someone below her had said: 'Hang Mrs Pankhurst on the wall, to replace the painting!' And the reply: 'That'd scare the art critics away!'

The women beside Deborah stirred indignantly, and Deborah glanced at them for the first time. A middle-aged matron and her daughter, both well-dressed, obviously prosperous. And another, rather smaller woman, with a yellow parasol.

Through the hubbub Jonathan was saying: 'I want to make it clear to this House that I myself was in no way connected with my wife's action. I had no knowledge of it beforehand; I do not approve of it; and I have already offered my sincerest apologies to the curators of the Gallery.'

Someone shouted: 'What about the painting?'

'I have offered to pay for repairs to the painting also, and the curator will be sending me the bill.'

Sarah may have ruined him then, Deborah thought. The cost of repairing that painting may be enormous. And he has disowned her here, in public. What a terrible thing for a man to have to do!

Jonathan had not finished his speech. He stood quite still, waiting for the noise to die down. Then he said: 'Mr Speaker, Honourable Members will also know that in the past I have spoken in support of votes for women. I have even voted for it –

as have many other members on both sides of this chamber.'

There were cries of approval at this, and also derision. Deborah noticed Asquith, the Prime Minister, staring stolidly straight ahead, more like a marble statue than a man. At least he was not smiling. But then, Jonathan is a Liberal, one of his own supporters. He must be furious about that.

Jonathan was having to shout now to make himself heard. Although he was facing the Speaker, Deborah was pleased to see that some of his anger at least was directed towards the Prime Minister, a few feet away on the front bench.

Sarah should be here to see this, she thought. Will he dare to defy them all, on her behalf? Speak up for the vote again, as she would like? That would be a fine thing to see.

'But I have to say to the House that although I understand the frustration which women feel when their demands are not immediately satisfied . . . '

At this point Jonathan had to stop, because the noise was too great. Someone, it seemed, had made a joke about Jonathan satisfying women, which had a number of members rolling in their seats with laughter. Others waved their order papers at them, either in anger or delight – it was hard to tell which.

Deborah thought: Do they behave like this all the time? They are like schoolboys. Drunks in a music-hall, baiting the singer.

The Speaker rose: 'Order! Order, I say. The Honourable Member is making a serious statement to the House. It is not a matter for levity.'

Jonathan resumed, red-faced, but grim, determined. ' . . . I say to the House that my ideas have changed. I would no longer vote for female suffrage if a Bill was introduced again. In common with many members of this House, I feel that these dreadful acts of violence and damage to property – including the destructive and misguided action which my wife performed last week – have irrevocably damaged their cause. I would therefore like to offer my support to my honourable friend the Prime Minister in his resolute resistance to these acts of female terrorism!'

There was a stunned silence, during which Jonathan hitched up his trousers and sat down.

Then the House erupted. Members on both sides of the

chamber stood up, shouted, and waved their order papers at each other. Some, it was clear, were cheering Jonathan; others seemed outraged. In the midst of it Deborah noticed, the Prime Minister, Asquith, met Jonathan's eye and inclined his head to him, with a calm smile.

Deborah felt sick. How could he do such a thing? She knew, from his letters, that he had grown increasingly suspicious of female suffrage because he feared it would bring the Conservatives to power, and that he had been badly hurt by Sarah's militant actions, but how could any man openly denounce his wife like this in the House of Commons? And this is the man I thought was charming, kind, understanding! What's the matter with him?

The smaller of the two middle-aged ladies beside Deborah seemed to feel the same. She had got to her feet and was shouting, furiously waving her yellow parasol at the men in the chamber below.

'Traitor!' she yelled. 'Scum! How dare you betray your wife like that?'

Hurriedly, two uniformed attendants ran down the steps towards her, seized her by the arms, and dragged her, protesting, away. Deborah and the woman with the young daughter watched, embarrassed.

As the hubbub declined, a number of MPs immediately rose to their feet, to catch the Speaker's eye. But the Speaker ignored them, calling out instead: 'The Home Secretary!'

So that was what Mr Reginald McKenna looked like, Deborah thought. The man who had introduced the dreadful Cat and Mouse Act, under which Mrs Pankhurst had been arrested six times for the same offence, of simply supporting protests for women's votes. She hadn't even broken a window herself. McKenna looked civilised, urbane enough. Standing relaxed beside Asquith at the Despatch Box, he looked pleased, as though Jonathan's statement had amused him. But Deborah was delighted to see that his very appearance seemed to excite renewed fury amongst some members of the House, who were still on their feet shouting and waving their fists.

He waited until the tumult died down and then spoke briefly and clearly. 'The Honourable gentleman has my deepest sympathy, and I thank him for his explanation, which I am sure must have caused him considerable pain and embarrassment. I am also most grateful for his unexpected and wholehearted statement in support of the policy of His Majesty's Government. With regard to this appalling act of vandalism . . . '

Again the noise was rising. Don't they ever stop this awful row? Deborah wondered. There seemed to be a number of members, on the opposite side of the chamber, to whom the very sight of Mr McKenna was an insult. Deborah wanted to weep. What chance did any woman have – even an impulsive mad-woman like her sister – when the country was in the hands of men like this?

' . . . furthermore, I can reassure the honourable gentleman that, on the question of giving women the vote, His Majesty's Government have not the slightest intention of giving way to threats of terrorism and vandalism of any kind. We shall consider the matter dispassionately on its merits alone, and I feel bound to say to him that actions such as his wife has committed make us even less likely to grant votes to women than before. If women want votes, they should show they are mature enough to deserve them!'

He sat down to a roar of mixed approval and anger, and again, a number of MPs rose to catch the Speaker's eye. But the speaker did not respond. Instead, he moved immediately ahead to other business, and to Deborah's surprise the subject was dropped.

Deborah turned to the only other woman who remained in the gallery with her daughter. She was a large, comfortable, motherly-looking woman, but Deborah thought she detected a slightly cynical, mischievous look in her eye.

'That was a dreadful performance, wasn't it, dear?' the woman said.

Ashamed for Jonathan's sake, Deborah muttered: 'Yes. I understand the militant suffragettes better now. Asquith's the main cause of it all, isn't he?'

'Him and half the others in the Cabinet, I've heard. Need their bottoms smacked, in my opinion. They're all terrified because their nannies knew best when they were babies. They think we'd make a better job of running the country than they did, if we got the chance. I think they're right, too!'

'Women Members of Parliament, you mean?' Deborah was generally in favour of the women's vote, but she was surprised to realise she had not thought much about this, the logical consequence.

The woman smiled. 'Why not? Don't you think you and I could make a better job of it than all those schoolboys down there? Even my Belinda here could. Oh dear, me. Talk of the devil.'

The woman's gaze travelled past her, in surprise and distaste. Jonathan had come into the gallery. He sat down beside Deborah.

'Well, that's done,' he said. 'What did you think?'

'I'd rather not say,' Deborah said coldly. She avoided his eyes.

'Oh come now, you don't think I've let Sarah down, do you? That was the best thing I could possibly have done to get her released.'

'Do you really think so?'

'Yes, of course. Now I'm in McKenna's good books, he's far more likely to listen favourably to any petition I put to him. It was pretty distasteful, I agree, but that's politics. Now you and I have got another call to make. Come, my dear.'

Deborah got to her feet automatically, and let him take her arm. She was horribly conscious of the eyes of the motherly woman burning into her back as they left the gallery. She felt ashamed. 'Where are we going?'

Jonathan smiled at her; that old, charming smile, which used to warm her so much.

'To see a friend of mine, a doctor who works in the prison. Chap called Martin Armstrong.'

12

'I'm sorry, Jonathan. Even I couldn't do that.'

'But surely you have influence?'

'Of course. A great deal.' Deborah thought she saw the man, Dr Armstrong, swell with self-importance as he spoke. He was already a very large man, with a round, fleshy, clean-shaven face. He had smiled at her briefly when she came in and then ignored her, addressing all his remarks to Jonathan, in the way that men often did. He sat behind his desk with big heavy hands clasped complacently over the expensive cloth of his waistcoat, wheezing slightly as though he were short of breath. She could tell Jonathan was getting angry, and wondered a little at the faith he had seemed to have in this man. On their way to this dreadful place he had spoken confidently of Dr Armstrong as the key that would unlock all doors. But it seemed it was one thing to get into the office of the Assistant Medical Officer at Holloway prison, and quite another to progress further and visit a prisoner in the cells.

The office itself was quite comfortable. Large desk, leather armchairs, bookcases, thick woollen carpet on the floor. And in the far corner, a shelf full of strange medical-looking items in glass jars. Through a door at the side she could see a bed, a sink, a screen, instruments – a room presumably for examining patients.

Dr Armstrong was explaining, portentously, 'You have my deepest sympathy, Jonathan. The first time your wife was imprisoned here I felt it my duty to stay uninvolved, so as to cause you the least embarrassment, but this time, since you insist . . . '

'I do.' A muscle twitched at the side of Jonathan's jaw, and Debbie noticed a slight flush on his scarred cheek.

'Then of course I shall do what I can. But I regret to say that my orders are quite clear. The Governor had them from the Home Secretary McKenna himself, and he took particular pains to stress them to me. From now on there is to be no exception to prison regulations for any suffragette, specifically including your wife, and Mrs Pankhurst as well for that matter.'

'Even after my assurance in the House today?'

'I have heard nothing about that, I'm afraid.'

'No, well. Perhaps it's too soon.' Jonathan drummed his fingers impatiently on the edge of his chair. 'Then I cannot see her?'

'No, I'm afraid not. No visits, no letters. Not even if her charming sister comes all the way over from Ireland.'

'It is not a matter for joking, Dr Armstrong.' It was unusual for Deborah to interrupt a male conversation, but there was something about the man's thick-lipped, ingratiating smile which deeply irritated her. And after this afternoon, she felt that men alone would never protect her sister. She glared at him, shaking slightly. Dr Armstrong looked offended.

'No, of course not, madam. I didn't mean that at all. But you have to understand that your sister has committed a most serious criminal offence.'

'I know that, Doctor. But she needs help and comfort too. According to my brother-in-law she was not at all a healthy woman when she was arrested.'

He nodded sagely. 'That may well be so. It is my belief, in fact, that many of these crimes may be connected with an undiagnosed medical condition. But in any case that is what I am here for. I have not had the pleasure of meeting your wife so far since her arrest, Jonathan, but I shall certainly make it my business to examine her as soon as possible, and convey your concern to her also. I have been away for the past three days, but I understand that so far she has refused to eat, as she did before.'

'I was afraid of that.' As Jonathan spoke. Deborah noticed one of his hands playing nervously with the arm of his chair. 'So she will already be in a feeble condition, I imagine. I suppose it might have affected her mind. Can't you arrange for her release as soon as possible, Martin, without her having to go through all this wretched charade of damaging her health first? I had an agreement with McKenna before that if she stayed at home without making speeches or involving herslf actively in the movement she would not be rearrested.'

'An agreement he regards as broken now, I suppose?'

'Of course.' Jonathan waved his hand dismissively, although there was something of anxiety in the gesture too. 'But he can't keep her in until she dies, can he? That is the nub of the whole dilemma these women confront the government with, you know that. The women cannot be allowed to die in prison, so they have to be released sooner or later. All I am asking of you is that you help me make it sooner. I've done you some service, after all . . . '

'And I you.'

'Yes, I know.' There was a slight, infinitesimal pause, and, although neither of them looked her way, Deborah had the impression that both men had simultaneously become highly aware that she was present and wished she was not. But it was only for a second; then they both hurried on, as though concerned that the pause itself should not be noticed.

'All I can say, Jonathan old chap, is that of course I'll give her an examination and do my very best to get her out as soon as I can. If I certify that her health is likely to be damaged by further exposure to prison conditions then that's it, no question. I can't do it tonight because I'm leaving here in half an hour and if I barge in over the heads of the other medics the governor will smell a rat and say it's political pressure – but first thing tomorrow morning, all right? I'll let you know what I find. Can't say fairer than that, now can I?'

Jonathan stood up. 'You're very kind.' He held out his hand and as he did so Deborah had the impression of great tension throughout his body, as though he might start to shake or tremble or scream at any moment.

'Not at all.' Dr Armstrong took Jonathan's hand in his, and

shook it, and as he stood up Deborah realised he was not a tall man, just bulky. He took up more space than most men, breathed more heavily. He held out his arms to shepherd them out of his office and escort them to the main gate.

As they crossed the quadrangle Deborah glanced over her shoulder at the solid, gloomy building they were leaving. Everywhere tiny windows crisscrossed with iron bars. Which one was Sarah's? None of them had a face behind it – perhaps they were too high up in the wall for the prisoners to look out? The building must be full of women but no noise came from it at all – the only sound was the pigeons cooing overhead, and the clatter of the traffic beyond the walls. It is like a great catacomb in the middle of the city, where people are buried alive, she thought. How can anyone stand it? It is worse than death.

And Sarah has come here twice before. She *knew* what it would be like before she slashed the picture. Perhaps Dr Armstrong is right, it *is* something to do with a strange medical condition. Perhaps her mind is affected.

Either that, or she is a very brave woman indeed.

By evening, Deborah was exhausted. She had travelled for two days, she had been to Parliament, and visited Holloway prison. She had seen her brother-in-law publicly disassociate himself from her sister in Parliament. And beneath that, like a whale just below the surface of her mind, was the constant question of the baby inside her, and what she was going to do about it.

When they returned to Belgrave Square, Jonathan's housekeeper had already unpacked her bags in the guest bedroom, on the same floor as the separate suites that Jonathan and Sarah shared. Gratefully, she undressed, drew the curtains, took a teaspoonful of laudanum, and slept.

In her dreams she was looking for Rankin. She was standing in a crowd in Dublin, and she saw him speaking to a sea of people. Really a sea, for, as he spoke to them, the heads of the crowd rose and fell rhythmically as waves passed through them. Then a huge wave upset the cart and she was struggling on the ground with men and boots and sticks all around her. If only I could get up, she thought, I could find him and then everything would be all right. But each time she stumbled to her feet she was knocked down again and her belly was bigger and rounder and heavier, and the boots of the men ran faster and faster in every direction, kicking her and jumping over her until suddenly there was no one left . . . she was all alone, huge and pregnant like a beached whale, lying on the cobbles in the middle of an empty street, while the mounted police rode slowly down the street towards her, their long batons swinging in their hands. In front of them, smiling coolly down at her from his tall bay horse, rode her husband, Charles.

She awoke, sweating and uncomfortable, to the sound of movement in the room. A maid was there, with a candle. She hovered uncertainly at the foot of the bed, the light illuminating her white pinafore dress and frilled cap, but leaving her face dark, ghostly.

'What is it?'

'Oh, excuse me, my lady. Mr Jonathan sent to see if you were awake, and if you were, dinner will be served in quarter of an hour, but if you are not, or are indisposed and would prefer to have it served in your room, it's all up to you, just as you wish. I'm sorry, ma'am, I didn't mean to wake you.'

'It's quite all right,' Deborah smiled at the girl's confusion. It might have been tempting to stay in her room, but not after a dream like that. The best way to clear her mind of her own troubles would be to talk to Jonathan, see what comfort he could offer her. If he could be trusted, after this afternoon.

But then, who else is there?

'Tell my brother-in-law I shall be down to dinner. And light the gas, would you please, before you go?'

Jonathan was undoubtedly pleased to see her. He stood with his back to the dining room fire, waiting, alone in full evening dress. The beautiful cut of the black clothes suited him, making him more distinguished than ever. He had removed the plaster from his cheek and there were two red scratches there, nearly healed.

Deborah had put on a pale green satin evening gown, one of the few she had that made the best of her colouring, even when, as today, there were dark lines of weariness under her eyes.

'Come in, Deborah. I know it is late by your country

standards but I think we both need our strength restored. Can I offer you a drink?'

'Yes. A small sherry, please.' The hovering butler brought it to her and she walked up to the fire and stood near him. The long polished table with its silver and candlesticks gleamed in front of them. There were only two places laid. She glanced at it and said: 'If you think it is all right for us to drink after what Sarah is going through now . . . And what you said in Parliament this afternoon.'

Jonathan's dark brown eyes watched her, twinkling, as the butler lit the candles. 'I know, it seems callous. But remember what I told you. It was done for the best, although the ways of politics are not always straightforward. My words may even help Sarah, you know.'

'Help her? How?'

'By making it clear to McKenna that I, at least, do not support her senseless action. That might make it possible, in time, for him to exercise clemency on her behalf.'

'In time?'

'Yes. I am afraid there is nothing more either of us can do today. Unless you want to go out yourself, and throw a stone through a window, to join her?'

Deborah shook her head, reprovingly, irritated by his flippant manner. 'Don't be silly, Johnny, that's unkind. You know I don't approve of the militants. But . . . '

'But you wish she were here, and so do I. But if Sarah were here, you know, she would either ignore me, or give us both the most monstrous lecture, I'm afraid. And you and I would look at each other, and sigh, and think, how did it ever come to this?'

'Perhaps.' Deborah glanced, embarrassed, at the butler, who was waiting to serve the soup. Did Jonathan always talk in front of the servants like this?

'It's all right,' he said, noticing her glance. 'Reeves knows things in this house are not – quite as they should be. Both he and I have been engaged for some time in an attempt to make things appear normal when they are not – isn't that right, Reeves?'

'Indeed, sir.' The butler avoided her eyes, discreetly, and Deborah thought, oh dear, Jonathan's been drinking before I came down.

Throughout the soup and the fish and the main course, while the servants were present, she managed to steer him away from any discussion of Sarah. They talked of the possibilities of Asquith's sending troops against the UVF – small, in Jonathan's view; of his duties in the House and how he managed to combine them with his flourishing legal practice; of the fogs and the difficulties of getting around London; and the threat of war from Germany.

'No one thinks it's a joke, I assure you,' Jonathan said. 'It's not at all that long since the First Lord, Churchill, sent out a twenty-page detailed memo to all the Cabinet and Chiefs of staff detailing a German landing in East Anglia. His idea was they would put ashore a fully equipped army corps able to march south and attack London, and thus prevent any embarcation of a British Expeditionary Force to the Continent in support of the French. Shook them all up, I can tell you. Especially when no one could satisfy him that sufficient measures could be taken to prevent it.'

Deborah smiled, and her disapproval of Jonathan began to fade away. She had always liked him when he was like this. It was the sort of conversation she missed, living with Charles in Glenfee, or managing alone for long periods when he was on service abroad. Perhaps Jonathan had been drinking a little but it had only loosened his tongue, and what was revealed was an intelligent, articulate man with his finger on the pulse of most of the important issues in the capital. A man who, one day – if Sarah had not ruined it now – might be in the Cabinet. A man who, unlike Charles, actually talked to her. Who appeared to care what she thought.

She began to relax, and forgive him for this afternoon.

After the meal they went into the library. It was a large, comfortable room with a blazing fire. Books lined the walls, there was a desk in each corner, card and chess tables near the windows, and two comfortable armchairs and a sofa. Thick, brown velvet curtains were drawn against the night, and the fire and a heavy wooden standard lamp by the mantlepiece provided the only illumination. It was curiously comforting, intimate.

Jonathan lit a cigar and offered her a glass of brandy. She

smiled. It was a gesture Charles would never have made.

'What I'd really like, if you don't mind, is a cup of hot cocoa.'

'But of course.' He rang the bell for Reeves and shortly afterwards it came, in a bone china cup on a silver tray. Reeves bowed himself out and left them in peace.

'That's what I like about having my sister-in-law to stay,' Jonathan said. 'No need to be concerned with appearances.'

He drew on his cigar and looked at her, and she thought, this is what it might have been like if I'd married him, instead of Charles. What it *was* like for a short time with Rankin. Just a man and a woman in companionable friendship, either side of the fire. None of that awful tension, that loneliness I sense in Charles.

But I'm deceiving myself. Remember what Jonathan did to Sarah in the Commons this afternoon. Because she had broken the code, done what a woman should not. Would Jonathan talk to me at all, if I dared tell him what *I* have done?'

I would be the lonely one then.

Jonathan blew a smoke ring and smiled. 'Penny for them.'

'What?'

'Your thoughts. I've been sitting here watching you all withdrawn into yourself. Do you know you get a little crinkle in your brow just here when you think?' He gestured to his forehead with his thumb. 'What were you thinking?'

She sipped her cocoa thoughtfully, gazing into the rosy firelight. 'Just memory. Wondering if we can bring back the past.'

'Explain.'

She sighed. 'Just that – what you wrote in your letters about Sarah doing something wild. Well, now she has done it. I heard what you said in the Commons, and I understand what you said about trying to please the Home Secretary, but . . . you're angry with Sarah, aren't you?'

'Always the deep questions. Yes, I suppose I am.'

'Will you forgive her?'

There was a silence. Abruptly, he jabbed the cigar down into the ashtray, and stood up. He tapped his fist nervously against the mantelpiece. She waited.

'I don't know, Deborah. Truly I don't. Of course it is the

Christian thing to do, and I don't want her in that damn prison, but . . . when I get her out, I don't know. Things can go so far, sometimes, between a man and a wife, and then they reach a point – where it is very painful, Deborah.'

She sighed, and said: 'I know, Johnny. I know that only too well.'

He looked down at her. 'You too, then? I had guessed something of the sort from what you say in your letters. And what you don't say. Things are not so well between you and Charles, either, are they?'

'No.'

He sat down on a stool beside her and took her hand.

It was the comfort she wanted, that she had come all this way to get. She put down the cocoa and took his hand in hers, silently, and she thought, it is so sad, to marry with all that ceremony and commit your lives together and have it all go wrong. But, if there is no love, it is all wasted. Perhaps I should tell Jonathan what I have done now, and ask his advice.

But she dared not. Her dream had brought into her mind what she knew she had to do. Rankin was here in London somewhere; she had to find him. He is the only man I love, she thought, no matter what the law says, and it is his baby. When I find him and tell him I have come all this way, and why, he will take me in. Then I will write to Charles and explain. If I am very lucky, he'll let me see Tom sometimes, and try to understand.

Jonathan said: 'Sometimes I think I chose the wrong sister.'

'What?' It had been a thought that she had had too, long ago, but it was irrelevant now. Anyway, it was one thing to think such thoughts and entirely another to hear them said. She looked into Jonathan's eyes and saw something she did not entirely like. She tried to withdraw her hand but he was stroking it, gently.

'I don't understand you, Jonathan.'

'Don't you? Oh come, my dear, I'm sure you do. When I married Sarah I was in love with her but I always knew . . . that you and I could be . . . friends, too. As has been proved over the years, in our correspondence. And things do not always work out as one expects, over the years. There are things that should be in every marriage which Sarah – does not like any more. And

I am a man like other men, just as you are a beautiful woman . . . '

'Jonathan, don't!' She snatched her hand away quite forcefully now, and stood up, not knowing quite where to go. She turned to face him. 'Please, don't talk to me like that. It's not decent . . . '

'No, of course it's not. But we are grown people, you and I. I doubt if Charles values you as he should, and anyway he will never know.' He took a step towards her, put his arms on her shoulders, with that charming, insincere smile.

'*No*!' She took two steps back, banged her knees against the arm of a chair, sat down, stood up again immediately, and walked towards the door like a flustered girl. 'Please, Jonathan, stop it at once!'

'I'm sorry.' He hurried after her so that she had to turn and face him before she could reach the door. 'I see I have frightened you and that is unforgiveable. Please . . . ' He stood before her, just blocking the easy way to the door, serious, polite, making no attempt to touch her any more. Again the charming smile. ' . . . forgive me, if you can. It is only that I have admired you for so long, and sometimes the life we are given can be so disappointing. I really did not mean to offend you. Take it as a compliment, if you can.' He reached out a hand, tentatively, to touch her face. 'Debbie? Are we friends?'

She put the hand away, softly, with her own. 'I am very tired, Jonathan, and I have come a long way. Please let me go to bed now. In the morning I will try to forget everything that was said – and you would be wise to forget it too, if you can.'

'If I can.'

He made no effort to prevent her going but instead stood by the door, watching her, as she climbed the stairs. When she got to her room she hunted about for a key to the door but there was none, so she thought about jamming a chair against the door then told herself she was being absurd. Hysterical. After all, the house was full of servants and there was a thick, blue bell-pull hanging next to the bedhead if she needed to summon anyone.

Which of course she would not.

He's just a little drunk and upset because of what happened

to Sarah and what he had to do in the Commons today. No gentleman would dare to break into my room in the night, surely? After all, I have stayed in this house dozens of times.

When Sarah was here . . .

Oh, poor Sarah! You tried to tell me that men could not be trusted when father died and I wouldn't listen, I didn't want to believe you. And now when you're starving in prison your charming, handsome husband does *this*!

To me, your pregnant little sister.

Why did he choose *me*? Perhaps it is because I wanted more satisfaction from a man than any woman has a right to have, and actually dared to have it, too, with Rankin. Perhaps that's changed me too, and this is what I'll inspire in men from now on.

Or perhaps it's something I inherited from Papa.

A while later she heard Jonathan's footsteps go upstairs to his own room, with only the slightest pause outside her door. But long after that she lay awake, listening to the unfamiliar night sounds of the city, and thinking about Rankin, and his baby growing inside her.

And her sister, alone and starving in her cold stone cell.

13

Footsteps in the corridor. The jangle of keys. Sarah shrank back into the furthest corner of her cell, her knees hunched up to her chin. Was there the sound of wheels, the rattle of the trolley? Surely it wasn't the right time! They weren't varying the time, were they?

Perhaps the young doctor had to go off duty early to visit the theatre. So he would force-feed his patients earlier, *oh please God let it not be that not now it's too early in the day I'm not ready I . . .*

The door crashed open. A wardress came in and a man. Not the young doctor. An older man not in a white coat. This man was big, burly, in a respectable suit. His bulk filled the doorway. A heavy, fleshy man, with a solid, portentous face, heavy jowls, slightly receding brown wavy hair, cold grey piercing eyes.

There was no trolley behind him. *Thank God!*

The man watched her, mocking, eyebrows raised. Thick sensual lips slightly redder than most men's, smiling. Look at me, woman, I am important, his pose said. He stood just inside the doorway, posed, pompous, watching for the effect of his presence.

She looked and thought, oh my God I know him!

Martin Armstrong.

The man she had last seen striding briskly away from his consulting rooms in Kensington. Her husband's pimp.

'What are you doing here?' Her voice a whisper, faint, like an old lady's.

His flesh, all that pompous self-assured bulk of it, made her squirm. The smile, his teeth between the thick lips, was worse. As though she could not fail to be delighted to see him.

He said: 'I should ask *you* that, perhaps, if it were not in all the newspapers. But I have an appointment as Assistant Medical Officer to this prison, and when the Senior Medical Officer is away on holiday as he is now I replace him entirely. Didn't you know?'

'Know? Of course not, how should I?'

'I thought perhaps your husband might have said.' The smile was still there, enjoying her discomfiture. A hand – thick spatulate fingers – strayed to his waistcoat pocket, unconsciously patting his belly.

My husband? Does the man think I know, and don't care? A fog began to swirl in Sarah's head, and she thought, I'm too weak, I can't cope with this. 'Why should my husband speak of you?'

'He and I were at college together, you know that. You surely remember the night I came to dinner with you, last autumn? We spoke of the work I do amongst the destitute families of prisoners? The hostels I work in – for orphans and the children of prisoners? They have been most favourably spoken of in Liberal circles. Your husband has even visited a few, and praised them most kindly. It is charitable work, that brings its own rewards.'

She thought: so Jonathan actively helps this man! Praises him for work he does with young children. Oh God – what if those hostels are where the girls came from! The woman in the collecting cell said something about that, didn't she? It's too dreadful.

'And so when I read of your case in the papers I was interested, and when your husband asked me to visit you I was happy to do so.'

'My husband asked *you* to . . . '

'To visit you, Mrs Becket, yes. In my official capacity, of course. Though I hope I may be of some help to you if I can, for old acquaintanceship's sake.' He sat down, on the foot of the bed, his heavy trousers an inch from her feet. Smiling, as though enjoying the power he had over her. She shrank away from him, her hands pressed flat against the hard surface of the bed beside her, to still their trembling. *Did Jonathan send this monster here?*

'May I feel your pulse?'

'Why?' She kept her arms where they were.

'I am a doctor, Mrs Becket. I have come to examine you.'

'Why do I need to be examined?'

'You have refused food and my colleague has prescribed treatment for that. Your husband is very concerned. Naturally, I need to know what the results of that treatment are, and if you are capable of withstanding some more.'

'Treatment! Is that what you call it?' She had meant to scream, but her throat was so dry with shame and fear it came out as a croak.

'Treatment, yes. Give me your wrist.' He took it. She snatched it back. 'Really, Mrs Becket, I cannot act as your medical adviser if . . . '

'Don't you dare touch me!'

The smile faded, the thick lips pursed together disapprovingly in the round fleshy face.

'Really, Mrs Becket, I assure you . . . '

'Save your assurances for the wretched little girls you molest in the house where you have your consulting rooms!'

'I – I beg your pardon?'

'You heard.'

To her surprise, he had gone quite white. If she had not been so afraid she would have noticed it more, but even in her rage she saw that his normally ruddy face had gone sickly white, as though he were suddenly afflicted with nausea. The wardress saw it too. It was the young one – the one built like a coalheaver, Miss Harkness. Sarah saw her glance at him with horror. She took a deep breath, drawing in courage.

'You know what I mean! You're not a doctor at all. Martin Armstrong, you're a sham! I know about the brothel you keep above your consulting rooms in Kensington, the high-class prostitutes and whores you keep there for men like my husband! And you take little children in there, too, don't you – girls of fourteen and fifteen! Where do you get them from – your brothels in Hackney? Or those charitable hostels you talk about? You introduce them to prostitution, don't you? Or do you abuse them yourself first?'

He gazed at her, appalled. Sarah was aware of the watching eyes of the wardress, over his shoulder.

'That – is a monstrous allegation, Mrs Becket!'

'Is it? I don't care, it's true! You are a liar and a procurer and a hater of women. It is *you* who should be locked up, not me! When I get out of here I shall make it my business to bring round a party of suffragettes to your consulting rooms and we shall see for ourselves! We shall rescue those poor girls there and the children you torment, and print the story in our newspaper. I shall destroy your reputation altogether, even if I ruin my own husband's in the process! Tell him *that*, when you see him, will you?'

Martin Armstrong sat quite still. A little of the colour had come back into his face, but his big fleshy hands were opening and closing unconsciously on his lap, as though they wanted to squeeze something. He glanced briefly at the wardress, as though for support. Then he said: 'That is the most ridiculous outburst I have heard in my life. I can only think you are affected by a form of collective insanity, like most suffragettes. It is a form of hysteria to which the female mind is uniquely susceptible.'

'Nonsense!' Sarah suddenly felt how trapped she was, helpless, quite unable to walk out and slam the door or call her servants and ask him to leave as she would at home. She had to listen to everything he said until he decided to leave. She was utterly in his power.

'It is not nonsense. I am a medical man and I know. Your wild accusations prove it. I also know that if you continue to refuse to eat, you will suffer serious physical damage. Your brain will be starved of nourishment and may deteriorate further. It is my duty to ensure that your treatment continues while you remain in my care. So I must continue my examination. Give me your wrist.'

'No!'

Every vestige of his ingratiating smile had gone now. Instead, there was a frown, dark brows scowling together, a slight flush on the heavy jowls. Why did men have to be so *big*! she thought. It's because of that, as much as anything else, that they bully us.

He beckoned to the wardress. For a moment Sarah thought the

girl would take her side, but after a slight hesitation she obeyed. She stepped forward, sat on Sarah's legs and gripped her arms so tight Sarah thought they would bruise. The man felt her pulse.

'A trifle fast, but normal in the circumstances. Let me listen to your heart.'

Oh God, Sarah thought, Jonathan sent this man and now he is going to force feed me. How could any husband treat his wife like this?

Martin Armstrong took a stethoscope out of his pocket. Miss Harkness pulled down the front of Sarah's dress, roughly, and he listened through her slip. She saw the slightly balding head bent in concentration, and thought, shall I spit? But her mouth was too dry with fear. If I had sharper teeth I could tear his skin like a tigress . . .

'Fine sturdy heart. Good pair of lungs too. I congratulate you, Mrs Becket. Your mind may be deranged, but you are in excellent physical health, and if we continue with the treatment there is no reason why it should fail.'

He says that when he can look at my arm and nearly see through the skin, it is so transparent! Sarah's heart was beating so fast now that she could feel it pounding in her throat. Any minute now the trolley would come. To spin things out she said: 'What do you mean, treatment?'

'The forcible feeding, of course.'

This man is my husband's friend, she thought. He is savage, inhuman, a torturer. He is *smiling*, damn him! What is it that's wrong in men's brains?

She stared him straight in the eyes and said: 'You are a devil! A murderer!'

'Quite the opposite, Mrs Becket, I assure you. Your life is in my hands.'

He turned his back on her, and suddenly he was gone, his wide leather shoes scrunching heavily on the stone floor of the corridor outside. For a moment the young wardress, Miss Harkness, stared down at Sarah, shaking. Only a second, and Sarah thought the girl was about to hit her.

Then she, too, was gone.

The door crashed shut. The key clanked in the lock.

Sarah slumped onto the end of her bed, and drew her knees up, trembling, to her chin. She thought: I thought I had a happy life before I came to prison but I was wrong. It was all a sham, an illusion. I thought I had married a gentleman but he turned out to be a monster, a grub who sent his slimy friends to feed off me as though I were a living corpse. It's only in here that I've learnt what he's really like.

She waited, listening, to the clanks and howls and rattles of prison life.

Waiting. For the clatter of the trolley in the corridor outside . . .

Martin Armstrong prided himself on his ability to look calm at all times. Calm, avuncular, masterful – that was the image he aimed at. It was useful to him not only as a doctor, but in his other dealings with women. He was a big man and he used his size to dominate others, physically and morally. Most people were in awe of him. Patients especially, of course – they were worried about their illness, often tearful, nervous, afraid. His calm reassured them. Prostitutes were similar – often flighty, overtired, skittish, drunk, hysterically excited one minute and depressed the next. Martin was able to control them by his calm, his stolidity, and, occasionally, by his strength.

Most women were a little afraid of him, and Martin liked it that way.

He regarded women as basically inferior creatures. They could not control their emotions because of their monthly cycles. They were physically weaker and less intelligent than men. They were obsessively interested in foolish frippery, things like clothes and music and novels and flowers.

Some, of course, like his own wife, had to be treated with respect. He kept her in a pleasant house, with beautiful furniture and clothes and a piano and a nice garden to occupy her mind. She spent her time supervising the servants, playing with their two young children, going to bridge parties and coffee mornings and the theatre, and visiting her friends to talk about babies. He bought her presents, and she smiled at him like a happy child living in a doll's house.

He made love to her regularly, once or twice a week, but it

was very boring. She lay on her back and thought, he supposed, of having children, while he tried to get as much enjoyment as he could without crushing her with his bulk. It never lasted long. Occasionally she became ill and then he treated her for a disease which he understood very well, and she didn't.

Gonorrhea. He didn't get it very often because he examined all the girls he let rooms to in his brothels, but even he could make mistakes. He fucked most of the girls he employed but usually only once or twice, because to establish any kind of closer relationship with them would undermine his authority.

He couldn't afford that. They were the other kind of women in Martin's world. Their own marketable asset was their ability to fornicate in all kinds of exciting and interesting ways, which respectable women like his wife would never believe, even if they heard about it. From this asset they made money, and he helped them. London was full of rich, respectable men who found making love to their wives excruciatingly dull. They wanted excitement, but needed discretion.

Martin provided the discretion and the premises, and the girls provided the excitement.

Apart from that he had no relationship at all with the girls. In fact, he despised them. They were like horses in a stable which he rode once to see if they provided a good ride, and then hired out. When his customers got bored with them he got rid of them. Presumably most of them in the end got married, or set up in business on their own, or found work in a shop or as servants or in a factory. Martin neither knew nor cared.

Suffragettes had no place in Martin's view of the world. They seemed to be interested in neither sex nor marriage; indeed, they did not behave like females at all. They neglected their homes, and ran around like screaming savages in skirts throwing stones and breaking windows and setting fire to things. Many of them, like Sarah Becket, appeared to actually hate men so much they could not bear to be touched. It seemed to him like a form of hysterical madness.

It was also very dangerous.

As he strode along the corridor in Holloway he appeared outwardly calm as always, but inside he was shaking with anger. That appalling woman Sarah Becket – he had not wanted to help her, but because of her husband he had tried, and she had more or less spat in his face. In front of the wardress too – God knows what gossip she would make out of this, in their grubby little common room downstairs. And the worst of it was, everything she said was true.

He marched into his office, slammed the door behind him, and paced furiously up and down the carpet. This was where he had agreed to help her husband Jonathan, against his better judgement – and now look what had happened! She and her wretched suffragette friends must have followed Jonathan to his consulting rooms; or spied on him somehow, and now they knew exactly what went on.

He was in no doubt what would happen. Even if Sarah only wrote about it in *The Suffragette*, enough respectable people would read it for questions to be asked, and if the police became involved other newspapers would follow the story up. He would almost certainly lose his job at the prison, and more importantly, a lot of his patients would probably leave him as well. Some of them, like Jonathan, knew exactly what went on in the rooms in Kensington, but others would be appalled if they found out.

Including his wife. This would make things very difficult at home.

But it was worse than that. The girls in Hackney and Kensington paid him a very high rent for their rooms, and if the police asked them they would probably cheerfully admit that many of their clients came to them through Martin. Living off immoral earnings was a crime. Particularly if some of the girls, as at present, were under sixteen.

I could go to prison, Martin thought. I could be shut in a cell like the ones here. All day behind a locked door and four stone walls. With filthy clothes and foul food and a bucket under the window.

He sat down at his desk abruptly. Sweat was prickling his forehead. He pulled a handkerchief out of his pocket and thought, what shall I do?

The woman, Sarah Becket, was clearly demented, even if she was not clinically insane. Crazed, perhaps, by jealousy of her husband, or by the suffragette ideology. Perhaps I could make an appeal to her, explain the damage she would do to her own husband if she exposed him.

That's no good. She's too emotional to understand logic. All women are like that. Even if she grasped the point at first it would be swept away in a flood of jealous rage the next.

So as soon as she gets out, I'm in trouble. And so is Jonathan.

How long is she in for? Six months. But she'll never stay in that long because she's refusing to eat. If I do as Jonathan asks and stop the forced feeding, she'll continue to starve herself and be free in a couple of days.

And if I don't do as he says, and keep on forcibly feeding her, and Jonathan finds out, he will kick up the most appalling row. There'll be questions asked in Parliament. The stupid man is still fond of her – I could see that when he came here yesterday.

So I'm damned if I feed her, damned if I don't.

What the devil am I going to do?

For a moment Martin's habitual calm deserted him. He sat at his desk in the large, comfortable office, sweating, staring with unseeing eyes out of the window across the grey slate roofs of Holloway. In one hand was a handkerchief, which he crumpled between his fingers and used occasionally to mop his brow.

The thick, hairy fingers of the other hand drummed on the desk in front of him, moving restlessly back and forth like an angry, tethered tarantula.

Deborah's arrival had complicated things for Jonathan. He was glad to see her, of course, but . . . she added another dimension to the sense he had that his life was becoming a series of roles, which had to be played out with care and caution. There was the successful lawyer, the astute, up and coming Member of Parliament on the one hand; and the wounded, hard-done-by, tolerant husband of a militant virago on the other. The husband who did, however, know where to draw the line in the end, as he had done yesterday in Parliament. He hoped he had gained respect for that, at least from the people who mattered.

There were other roles in his life, though, and Deborah's arrival had focussed on some of these.

He had always been genuinely fond of her and, over the years, had enjoyed meeting her and writing to her. He had used his letters to explain almost all his difficulties and, in doing so, he had created a persona, almost as though he were writing a diary. The frank, honest brother-in-law who bares his heart and tells his sister-in-law everything . . .

Almost everything.

He had not expected to try to seduce her. Until recently, he would not even have dreamt of it. But over the past two years his relationship with Sarah had deteriorated so badly that he had found himself taking up a completely different role – a despicable, wicked, *wonderful* role – that gave him a quite new attitude to women. All women – even respectable married ladies like his own sister-in-law.

It was something he could never admit to publicly. Something that terrified him whenever he thought of it. Something that ran up and down his spine like thin streaks of red and orange lightning while all the rest of him was grey and sober and black.

It was the real reason he had come to Kensington this afternoon.

The ostensible, obvious reason was to find out about Sarah. That was what he had told Deborah this morning at breakfast. He had been relieved, and also slightly amused, to find that, although she appeared slightly wary of him, she appeared to bear him no grudge.

'I have some business in chambers this morning, and then I am going straight on to meet Dr Armstrong this afternoon. He will have seen her today – he *must* – and he will be able to tell me how she is and when she is likely to come out. If she is refusing food it cannot be long now. We'll have her home within the week.' He hesitated, stirring sugar thoughtfully into his tea. 'I, er, I'm not quite sure what time I'll be there, though, so it might be a touch tricky for us to meet.'

'Where, Johnny? At Holloway?'

'No, at his consulting rooms in town. You can come if you want, of course, but as I say . . . '

'I'd be in the way? That's what you mean, isn't it?'

'Of course you wouldn't, Debbie! It's only the timing, really. I can't guarantee it. And . . . '

She smiled. It was a strange, rather enigmatic smile, he thought much later, when he came to reflect on it. As though she were somehow very distant from him and his concerns. And at the same time tense, full of excitement, like a woman in a dream, almost. At the time he thought it had to do with last night.

She said: 'It doesn't matter, Johnny, I'm sure you can deal with the man on your own. He looked to me as though he hates women, anyway. And I've got some shopping to do, I'll be all right. You'll tell me all about it when you get back, though, won't you?'

'Oh yes. Yes, of course,' he lied.

It was a lie, not because of what he hoped to learn about Sarah, but because of the place he was going to before. Jonathan was very regular and organised in his infidelity. He made appointments days, sometimes weeks ahead, and wrote them in his diary. Often they were like the notes Sarah had found: *Dr Armstrong, 6 p.m.*, but there were others too. *Dentist 2.30.* Or *Visit tailors for first fitting.* All very drab, uninteresting to anyone who might pick the book up. But to Jonathan, the entries glowed with secret meaning.

When he walked up the steps and rang the bell outside the quiet, respectable house in Kensington, a maid opened the door. She smiled demurely, took his top hat, coat, and gloves, and showed him up the pink-carpeted stairs into a small sitting room. Everything here was furnished in comfortable bourgeois taste. There was a thick soft blue carpet, net curtains on the windows, pale pink and yellow flowery overstuffed armchairs, a piano, standard lamps with tasselled fringes, expensive china dogs on the mantelpiece, a comfortable warm fire burning in a black-leaded grate.

The maid smiled at him. It was a friendly smile, not in the least inappropriate to their surroundings. Unless one counted the way her gaze held his for a little too long, as though she were measuring, assessing what he would be like.

'If you will wait a moment, sir, I'll tell Mrs Burgoyne that you're here.'

'Thank you.' Jonathan sat down, feeling the excitement spark up and down his spine. Of course he should not be here now, with Sarah in prison, but the appointment had been made over a week ago. What difference could he make to her in the next hour or two? Anyway, if it had not been for Sarah, he would never have been here at all.

And he would have missed so much.

He had been married to Sarah for eleven years now, and for the first nine of those years he had not been unfaithful to her once. Indeed, he had not even considered it. He knew how much she had been hurt, as a child, by the death of her father. The cause of that death – syphilis – seemed to him, as to her, a dreadful, terrifying scourge. At first he thought it a punishment of God on the wicked – a cruel Old Testament punishment which afflicted not only the man who sinned, but also his family. A man could infect his own wife, his children could grow up riddled with the disease, die of it. Sarah and Deborah were lucky not to have inherited it from their own father. Jonathan had promised Sarah it would never, ever, happen to their children because of him.

But they had had no children. Three times Sarah had miscarried. That, Jonathan felt sure, was why everything had gone wrong.

In the early years of their marriage there had been no question of unfaithfulness. Aware of her fears about sex, he had been kind and caring and gentle in bed, and she had responded more than he had hoped. He had been helplessly in love with her – with her long dark chestnut hair and her smooth soft skin and the way she responded to his kisses and caresses. At first she had been shy, skittish, trembling like a young deer. Then, after a few weeks, she had nestled into his arms more trustingly, purring softly like a cat. Finally, as the months went by, she had come to respond to him with a passion that was equal to or greater than his own, wrapping her long, slender legs round him and pulling him down on to her while her hands roved up and down his back and she covered his face with kisses and then arched her back and moaned . . .

Jonathan had thought God must have singled him out to be especially blessed among men.

Then Sarah had become pregnant. He had watched her body change and bloom as their child grew inside her. He shared the excitement of laying his palm on her stomach to feel the first kicks, and he had worshipped her more than before. She had wanted him to make love to her more than before, too, and they had found ways to do it which seemed safe and gave her greater satisfaction than ever before, and then . . .

The baby had been born dead.

Sarah had descended into a sudden, black depression. Jonathan tried to help her but it was as though she was in a deep pit with smooth sides and no way out, and she was deaf as well so she did not hear what he said. She rejected him because she felt he was part of the cause. I should never have allowed you to make love to me like that, she said, we killed our baby with our lust. One doctor they visited said this was nonsense, but another one, a portentous man with a long beard and rheumatic eyes and horrible pickled things in jars on shelves behind his head, said it might indeed be possible. And he was the one Sarah believed.

So when she had become pregnant the second time she had resisted all Jonathan's advances, and he had kept away from her and slept in his own room. But once or twice this abstinence was too much for him, and he persuaded her to relent. He came into her room to feel her stomach reverently and cup her ripening breasts, and she allowed him to slide gently into her once again.

The day after the third time they did this, her waters broke and her nurse helped her to deliver a six-months' child in great agony on the floor of the bathroom, in blood and screams and bitter, bitter, tears.

Jonathan had been delivering his maiden speech in the House of Commons. When he left the Chamber, to warm handshakes and pats on the back from his fellow Liberals, he was handed a note by his secretary.

After that it had been as though the child's open grave lay in bed between them. It had been two years before she conceived again. During those two years Jonathan had been as gentle and kind as he could, but it made no difference. Sarah appeared to feel that God had cursed her for her earlier wanton passion. He spent more and more time away from home, in court or in the House. When they did make love it was an embarrassing parody of their former passion, which left them hot, irritable, and ashamed.

Nonetheless, she became pregnant a third time. Praying that the baby would bring them together again, Jonathan moved out of her room entirely, and did not come near her bed once.

Perhaps because of this, she did not miscarry until the eighth month.

Since then they had lived in the same house for three years, but she had not let him touch her. They had tried to discuss the matter, but neither could see any way forward. She could not bear the pain and disappointment again, and he did not want to inflict it on her. So they slept apart.

Their marriage became a matter of respect and politeness and regret, for something beautiful that was dead. Sarah was silent, bitter, aloof. It was like sharing a house with a ghost. Jonathan found more to occupy him in Parliament and in court, and there were long, empty absences. He was aware of her suffrage activities and, at first, he supported the women's vote in the House, but the issue did not move him as it did her. It was one of many issues of social justice. It would not bring back their love.

There were times when he was very depressed. He knew that many men of his social standing had quite open affairs with other men's wives but he found the idea contemptible, cruel. He knew that it would not take long for news of such an affair to get back to Sarah – and that would destroy her. Besides, she was his wife, he did not need another one. He still liked and admired her from a distance. He had no desire to court some other man's wife, buy her flowers or jewellery or spend time going to the theatre with her. All that would just provide material for gossip which would hurt and destroy everyone involved, in the end.

But he was lonely and restless in bed.

One day he sat up late in his club with his friend, Martin Armstrong, and somehow the conversation made its way from the headaches he had been suffering to sex. Martin explained to him, man to man, that in his view this was a medical matter. Men were different to women: to maintain a satisfactory state of health they needed regular sexual intercourse. It was a common problem, Martin said. There were ways it could be solved. He understood absolutely the need for total discretion.

That was why, now, Jonathan was here in this living room in

Kensington. Martin had been right, up to a point, he thought. Over the past two years his sex life had become almost as interesting, as exciting, as it had been in the early days of his marriage. With this crucial difference – he hardly ever made love to the same woman twice.

This made for tremendous, tearing excitement beforehand, and also avoided the slightest possibility that Jonathan might fall in love with anyone else. Emotionally, Jonathan was still married to Sarah. But sexually, his needs were taken care of by others.

There was a slight danger of disease, but Martin assured him that all the girls were regularly checked by him personally. This, and the constant turnover, made it very expensive, but Jonathan could afford it.

It was a pleasure that had entered his bloodstream now. He did not want to give it up. He had made love to so many women that he now looked upon all of them – shop assistants, waitresses, typists, actresses, servants, fashionable housewives, debutantes, even his own sister-in-law Deborah – in an entirely different way.

Mrs Burgoyne came into the room.

Mavis Burgoyne was the lady who looked after the girls for Martin. A rather blowsy middle-aged woman, in a flowery pink dress that went with the furniture and wallpaper. Very feminine – a little too much powder and frills perhaps for his taste, but then she was well past her prime. An ordinary face; nothing hard even about the eyes. Certainly nothing lewd or suggestive. Everyone's maiden aunt.

'Tea, Mr Becket? With perhaps a little something, to take out the chill?'

'Please.'

She smiled and pulled a scarlet bellrope behind her.

'A busy week in court?'

'So-so.' For a few moments he entertained her with an edited version of a recent, rather amusing case, and then the maid brought in the tea. It was on an elegant wooden tray, with a single red rose in a jar and bone china tea service. Mrs Burgoyne poured, adding a slight dash of whisky from a silver flask beside the milk jug. She sipped, her little finger crooked elegantly.

'So now, to business. The young lady whom I told you about has arrived, and is waiting to meet you. I will send her down in a moment. In the meantime, perhaps you would like to consult the book for your next appointment. It is fully up to date. Here.'

She put her cup down, and took a thick, leather-bound volume from a shelf behind her. It was one of the few things in this feminine, chintzy room that looked out of place. Like a lawbook, perhaps, or a volume of Parliamentary reports.

'Have a look through. I'll be back in a moment.'

She handed him the book and went out. Jonathan put down his teacup and lifted the book on to his knee. His hand was trembling slightly with suppressed excitement. So foolish, he thought. Such wicked fun.

Inside, the book was more like a photograph album. On every page there was the photograph of a young woman. Some of them Jonathan recognised, others he had not seen before. Most wore skimpy, suggestive dresses. One or two wore nothing at all. Besides each photograph was a brief biography, and a description of the things each girl, apparently, liked doing.

All the things were shocking. Some of the things were very shocking indeed. Jonathan thought he might like doing them all.

He leafed his way slowly through the book. One or two of the girls were extremely young, he noticed. At first he had felt qualms of conscience about these, but then one day he had tried one, and found a strange pleasure in it. The child had been young, skittish, afraid, anxious to please – it was not necessary to be cruel, just gentle and firm. It was like breaking in a young horse; there was a pleasure in bending the creature to your will. And, after all, these were girls born to the life, who would profit by it. They could become richer this way than in any other that was open to them, and most of them knew it.

Bernard Shaw had a play on in London this year, called *Pygmalion*. It was about a gentleman – a professor – who picks up a girl from the streets, and takes her to his house to teach her the King's English, so that she can enter high society. Jonathan had gone to see it, and laughed all the way through with the rest of the audience. But all the time he had been thinking: of course there are plenty of girls from poor backgrounds who rise in society this way. But it is not by opening their *mouths* that they do it.

Mrs Burgoyne came back in, and Jonathan gave her the book, open at the photograph of a young woman of about eighteen. She had dark curly hair, a mouth with soft pouting lips, and a very generous bosom indeed.

Mrs Burgoyne glanced at the book and put it back on the bookshelf behind her.

'Certainly, Mr Becket,' she said. 'Next Friday, at six-thirty, as usual?'

Jonathan nodded.

Mrs Burgoyne smiled. 'I'll note it down, then,' she said. 'Now I must leave you to finish your tea in peace.'

Again she left the room, tugging the long red bellrope as she went. For a moment Jonathan sat there, feeling the blood course through him. He did not feel guilty. He had got into the trick of leaving thoughts like that behind him like an umbrella at the door. In this place he was a different man.

A maid came in to collect the tea tray. It was a different maid, but, like the last one, she wore a frilly mob cap and a starched white pinafore. The pinafore looped over her neck and was tied with ribbons behind her waist.

But under the pinafore, Jonathan noticed as she smiled at him, she had no other clothes on at all . . .

'I have seen her, Jonathan, yes.'

Martin Armstrong sat back behind his desk in his thick, leather swivel armchair. He hoped he did not look as nervous as he felt. He thought he had found a way of dealing with the danger Sarah Becket presented. He did not like it, but it was better than the alternative. Prison, exposure, disgrace.

Jonathan isn't going to like this either, Martin thought. But then he isn't going to find out all the details straight away. I shall have to lie to him. When he finds out about that our relationship will be over for good.

But then it's his own fault. If the bloody man could control his own wife none of this would have happened at all!

As he leaned back in the chair the expensive leather creaked, and Martin's thick, capable hands were clasped comfortably over his ample stomach and watch chain. The look on his face was benign, mellow, comforting. Like a doctor about to reassure a difficult, anxious patient.

'You have seen her? Good! And?' Jonathan was impatient for him to go on.

'And I am pleased to tell you she is well.'

'Oh! Really? Thank God for that.'

For a man who has spent the last two hours in the rooms upstairs, he gives a good impression of concern, Martin thought. But then, lust is one thing, concern for wife and reputation, another. He smiled reassuringly.

'Not only well, but she is eating normally. In fact, after my little talk with her she is co-operating with the prison authorities in every way.'

'Good heavens!' Jonathan stared at him, temporarily speechless. 'What on earth did you say to her, man?'

Martin's smile broadened. 'What do you think? I told her of your concern, and explained to her as a medical man that if she did not eat she would do herself irreparable damage, and that that would be no good to anyone at all. I told her that she had already struck her blow by slashing the picture. It was in all the newspapers, she need do nothing more to help her movement. And I explained to her that if she ate now and completed her sentence then you, as her husband, would take full care of her when she came out. I hope that was not going too far?'

Martin frowned and peered at Jonathan over the desk. There was just the faintest hint of a conspiratorial twitch at the corner of his mouth.

'No, of course not. Not at all. Do you mean she made no attempt whatsoever to starve herself?'

'Oh yes, she did at first. For two days in fact. But I think it was giving her some pain and my visit . . . persuaded her.'

Martin smiled, his thick lips peeling back briefly to reveal strong teeth only slightly yellowed by tobacco.

'Then – if she is obeying prison regulations, can I see her?'

'I'm afraid not.' This was the difficult part. Any communication between husband and wife at this point would expose his lie straight away. Martin shook his head sorrowfully.

'Not for the first month, at least. I tried to persuade the governor but he is adamant. You can try to put pressure on from above, but I think it would be unwise. If . . . I don't pretend to fully understand the female psyche but I get the impression that if Mrs Becket believed she was being granted special treatment she might well begin to starve herself again in some perverted form of protest. I grant it is a strange way of thinking but that is what we have to suffer these days, it seems.'

He watched Jonathan carefully across his desk, the professional frown still thoughtfully in place. There was a slight throbbing pulse in Martin's neck which betrayed his anxiety, but he judged correctly that only he himself was aware of it. If Jonathan accepted this, it would be all right. No suspicions would be aroused; there would be time for the next step. If Sarah *could* be kept in prison for even part of her six month sentence, he would have time to cover up every trace of what he was doing in the rooms upstairs. Then she could shout her head off all she liked. No one would believe her.

Jonathan hesitated. 'Well, if you're sure . . . '

'Believe me. In my profession, even more than yours, one gets to see more than one type of human behaviour, and what you and I might consider logic is . . . not universally accepted. But if we play it her way I am convinced Mrs Becket will come round without harming herself further. And that is what you want, Jonathan, is it not?'

'Of course I do, man. She is my wife.'

'Yes, I know.' Martin relapsed into silence, guessing the conflicting tides of emotion that were coursing through Jonathan's mind. Jonathan had come to him because his marriage was in trouble, but that did not mean that he was not still fond of the woman, however oddly she behaved. And he was fonder still of the institution of marriage – and his own reputation. He did not want that destroyed, whatever he did with the girls upstairs. So far, Martin believed, Jonathan saw him as a confidant, a helper. But the relationship could easily turn the other way. And now, above all times, he could not afford to let that happen.

'You will see her again?' Jonathan asked.

'Of course. Frequently. Every day almost, until the Senior

Medical Officer returns from holiday.'

'You will take care of her, won't you?'

'Oh yes, of course. To the best of my ability. Your feelings do you credit, Jonathan. Especially when I know the strain she has put you under this past year.'

The two men looked at each other over the table. It was very quiet in the consulting room for a moment, and Jonathan could hear the ticking of a large case clock somewhere outside in the hall. Outside there in the hall, too, were the rich pink hangings of the wallpaper, he knew, the soft pink carpet leading away upstairs. It was a path he had trodden often, over the past year. A long staircase, over a carpet deliberately, luxuriously soft. He had come down it only a quarter of an hour ago, after the most delicious time in bed with the maid, who had removed her apron to reveal the most perfect pair of smooth, elegant breasts, their nipples slightly rouged with lipstick. No one knew he went up there but Martin – and Martin would never tell. After all, it was a medical matter, in a way, and no doctor would betray a confidence.

'Yes,' he said. 'Life is not always straightforward, but when we married it was for better or worse, I promised her that. And with your help, Martin, I shall be able to keep that promise without losing my sanity. At least this way there are no strings, no ties, no emotional complications. A healthy mind in a healthy body, what?'

'Quite so.' Martin smiled, waited a little, and then stood up to indicate that the interview was over. He escorted Jonathan to the door, watched as he took his coat, umbrella and hat from the stand. 'Don't worry about your wife. I shall see that her health is taken care of.'

And you will probably want to murder me when you find out how I am doing it, he thought, as he watched Jonathan walk briskly away down the pavement.

14

The routine was the same every morning. At about half past five a terrible grinding, crashing noise would come from the depths of the prison. Sarah never found out what it was – it sounded as if a giant iron fireplace was being dragged from the wall, smashed with sledgehammers, and lugged from one end of the building to the other. For what purpose, other than to wake the prisoners, she could not imagine.

Then heavy cell doors would begin to open and close, keys would rattle and clank, trolleys would clatter along corridors. The harsh voices of the wardresses would shout orders – 'Come orn, slop aht!' 'Rise and shine, dress yersel – you've two floors to scrub and the loos to clean afore breakfast!' 'Jump to it, there! This ain't no workhouse or rest 'ome!' ''Olloway's a clean prison!'

Sarah lay on her cold hard bed and listened to the clanking and the rattles and the voices. Despite her discomfort she was glad they were so loud. All night she lay in cold isolation, drifting in and out of dreams and memories. Once she had believed Jonathan was there in the cell with her, and she had reached out to touch him, only to find her hand waving feebly through cold, shadowy air. She had screamed abuse at him and had thought she heard a male voice answering back, not Jonathan's voice, but her father's . . .

But none of her night voices were nearly as loud or as real or as inescapably human as the harsh screech of the wardresses.

They woke Sarah up with a start, to the gritty reality of the cold stone cell, the grey light of dawn, the clank and crash of buckets and the hard wooden slats under her back.

She lay and listened. Each voice had a different tone; the words and the volume were much the same but the personality each revealed was different. Some, she was sure, really meant what they said. They hated and despised the prisoners, they were truly obsessed with the cleanliness of the prison. Perhaps it had to be kept clean, Sarah thought, because that is the only way to wash away the defiling touch of the criminals. Some of these wardresses think we are a disease, so they force us to scrub away every dirty mark we make. Then there were others who varied their tone, according to which prisoner they spoke to. That seemed especially cruel, Sarah thought. A wardress would be hearty, jovial with one woman, and then address the prisoner in the cell next door with virulent hatred. So that the second prisoner was denied even the small hint of human sympathy that had been shown to her neighbour.

No one came into Sarah's cell until nearly seven. There was no point. Though she was a third division prisoner she refused to do any duties, and there was no way they could make her, so they left her alone. She supposed it was tacitly assumed that the forced feeding was punishment enough. But they insisted her cell was tidy, and she agreed to that herself. It gave her a touch of self-respect and a sense of a new day begun. So at six every morning she got up, folded her bedclothes neatly, dusted the table and chairs and bedhead with a little cloth they had left her, and combed her hair.

The comb was her greatest luxury. It was a small bone comb which she had been allowed to keep. It had been in the pocket of her skirt when she had been arrested. It was the one bit of civilisation that she had retained, the one link with her dressing room at home. So every morning when she had folded the grey blankets on her wooden bed, she sat at the scarred wooden table and combed her hair, slowly, diligently, luxuriously. As though there were a gilt mirror in front of her, and ivory-backed hairbrushes and pots of face cream and makeup and phials of scent scattered around the dressing table in front of her, instead of . . .

'Porridge, yer ladyship.'

The young wardress stood in the cell door, a mocking smile on her face. She was the big, sturdy young woman, Ruth Harkness, the one Sarah thought of as a coalheaver because of her build and the strength of her forearms. Her face was heavy, with wide eyes, solid flat features and a skin that was usually pale and unhealthy. Because of spending so much time in the dank, foetid air of a prison, Sarah thought. The wardress glared at Sarah with an intent, sullen malevolence. Damn you, Sarah thought. What's the matter with the girl, is she jealous because I have this wonderful room to myself?

She ignored the wardress for a moment, continuing to comb her hair and gaze at the wall as though it were a fine, inlaid mirror. Then she sighed and indicated the table in front of her. 'Thank you. You may put it down there for a moment if you must, and take it away again when you are ready.'

The young woman scowled. 'Right then.' She dumped the steaming bowl of porridge in the middle of the table, rather closer to Sarah than Sarah had intended, and plonked a spoon beside it. Then she stood back and watched, arms folded, with a deliberate, hostile glare.

The draught from the door sent the steam from the porridge into Sarah's face. The scent of it was, as usual, delectable. Sarah sat quite still and took a deep, nourishing breath. Then a second and a third. Then, very carefully, she began to comb her hair again.

The wardress stared for several minutes without speaking. Sarah glanced at her once then ignored her. She combed all the right side of her head very thoroughly, then the back, then the left. When she was beginning on her fringe the wardress said: 'You're a stupid, bloody-minded madwoman, Becket. Do you know that?'

Surprised, Sarah glanced at her, and smiled ironically.

'Well, Miss Harkness, how kind. That is really the nicest thing anyone has said to me all week.'

The wardress scowled once more. 'I didn't mean it kind. I meant it's stupid, to turn up your nose at good healthy food like that, when you know that later in the day the doctors'll be shoving tubes down your throat again, and like as not I'll have to help them. It don't get you nowhere, so why bother?'

Sarah combed her fringe carefully before she answered. Her pause was not meant as a snub; it was because she was so unused to having a real conversation – even an argument – with anyone, that she found the words did not come straight away. At least it was a sign that this woman cared, for her to break the rules and speak to her at all.

'What would *you* do then?' she said at last.

'Me? What do you mean?'

'If you were in my position. You know why I'm here, you've seen how I'm treated. You're a woman too, Miss Harkness. What would you do?'

'I wouldn't *be* in your position, would I? I don't break the law.'

'No, but imagine for a moment if you did. Not to steal or hurt anyone or to be unkind, but the way I did it, to help other women. And then if you had decided not to eat as a protest against the injustice of the law. Would you give in just because doctors came and tortured you with the loathsome tube?'

'Well, I . . . ' The young wardress hesitated. Sarah saw the confusion drift across her face and thought, now she'll walk out because she can't answer and anyway she isn't supposed to talk to prisoners at all.

But to her surprise Miss Harkness stayed. And said: ' . . . I wouldn't let no man do that to me, never. I'd punch his face and kick him where it hurts if I could. That'd stop him!' She laughed. 'I'm strong, see. Men don't mess with me!'

'Maybe not. But if the man brought in four or five strong women like yourself to hold you down, as you held me?'

'That ain't the point. I'm not daft like you, I don't break no laws. Listen, Becket.' She stepped forward, and Sarah realised, by the intensity of the look in her eyes, the low, earnest voice, that this was what Miss Harkness had really come to say. 'That ain't true what you told Dr Armstrong the other day. You're wrong about it and you're daft to say it, too. The doctors here are respectable, decent men. They wouldn't have this job if they weren't! Holloway's a clean prison!'

Sarah stared at her, astonished. There was definitely a flush in the girl's pallid cheeks, and her solid arms and bosom were trembling with emotion. She had the impression the young woman might hit her at any moment, or scream or break down in tears.

Sarah put down her comb and said, very carefully: 'That's very interesting. Why are you so sure?'

'Sure about what?'

'Sure that what I said was untrue.'

'Well, because . . . it's obvious, ain't it? I mean, a man like that, he's a respectable doctor, he's got his name, his reputation to think of. He wouldn't never do a thing like that. Even if there was money in it, he'd be daft to take the risks.'

Silence. The clang of buckets in the corridor. Sarah's mind was racing. There's something strange here, she thought, something very odd. And I have only a couple of minutes to find out what it is, because wardresses never stay to talk, they're not allowed. *Why does this one want to?*

'So you think there's money in it, do you?'

Miss Harkness laughed scornfully. ''Course there is! You la-di-dah fancy suffragettes, you don't understand nothing, do yer? Best way for a girl to earn a few bob – most of the East End does it, given 'alf a chance. Not for posh hoity-toity ladies like you, you wouldn't understand. But girls who can only get a job shoving bristles into brushes fifteen hours a day in some cellar, or fishing rubbish out the sewers to sell for a few coppers – 'course they go on the game if they can. Good luck to 'em I say. I might have, too, if I'd 'ad the looks. And if my old man hadn't brought me up proper. To know what's right and what's a sin.'

'Children too?'

'Maybe.' Miss Harkness glanced over her shoulder, then said bitterly: ''Course that's a sin, that's disgustin', that is. But it happens.'

'And people don't mind?'

'They do, yeah. Me, I think it's sick. But they ain't got no religion, people like that. They're not respectable, like you an' me – they don't understand that it's a sin you can be damned for. They just think it's better'n starving, most of 'em. After all, some of 'em ain't got no dad an' their mum's inside. An' the mums encourage 'em, so's they get clothes on their backs an' food in their gobs, poor little mites.'

So it *does* happen, Sarah thought. And this girl knows it does. Very quietly and calmly, she said: 'But you must understand, that sort of dreadful choice is exactly the sort of thing we suffragettes are fighting against. Mrs Pankhurst is not rich, you know – she has worked among poor women all her life, and so has her daughter Sylvia and hundreds of others. And we *do* think it's wrong – very wrong – for women and young girls to be exploited in this way or any other. It's all part of men's inhumanity to women. Of course there should be decent work and proper wages so women don't starve. But the only way for us to get that is to get the vote.'

'Well, you won't get it by telling lies about Dr Armstrong! He's respectable, he *couldn't* be involved in wicked things like that. He says you're a madwoman, now, and I believe he's right!'

'Do you really think I'm mad?'

'If he says so. Yes, 'course I do.' The wardress's eyes bored into Sarah's with hatred and distrust, then looked away hurriedly above her head at the wall, as she had been trained to do. But she had also been trained not to talk to prisoners at all.

Sarah took a deep breath, pressing her fingertips on the table in front of her until they went white. She felt anger rising in her and struggled to control it.

'All right. I understand that you respect Dr Armstrong, and I suppose your loyalty does you credit. But what if I were to tell you that I had definite evidence that he *is* involved in prostitution?'

'You couldn't.'

'Couldn't I? Just you listen. I had a letter, a threatening letter, telling me to stop suffragettes bothering Dr Armstrong because he was a good friend to prostitutes and my own husband was involved. I didn't believe it, so I stood outside your precious Dr Armstrong's consulting rooms in Kensington and saw my husband go in with my own eyes – *and stay in there after the doctor had come out!* Then I saw another man go in with a woman who was painted and dressed and behaved in a way that could only mean that she was a prostitute. Those rooms were directly above Dr Armstrong's surgery – he must know what goes on there!'

'Doesn't prove nothing!' Ruth Harkness looked uneasy, but her heavy face remained set, stubborn. 'You're making it up, Becket. You're seeing things that ain't there. You're just so upset about your husband that you've imagined all the rest.'

'No I haven't. And when I was in the collecting cell at the police station before I came here, I heard two women talking about putting one of their daughters – "on the game", is that what it's called? And one of them actually told the other to take the girl to a house in Red Lion Street, Hackney, which was owned by a doctor called Armstrong. What more proof do you want? If he can be connected with prostitution in one place, why can't he be connected with it in another?'

'Because he's a decent respectable Holloway doctor, that's why! We don't do things like that here!'

'Oh no? You just torture suffragettes, is it? Is that the clean, decent work you're so proud of? Torturing innocent women who tell the truth?'

Sarah had risen to her feet. For a moment the two women faced each other, and Ruth Harkness felt her hands itching with an urge to seize the slender, skeletal woman in front of her and shake her until she saw sense. Instead she said: 'You're wrong – you must be! The lack of food's gone to your head. If you carry on telling those lies he'll carry on force feeding you and he'll be right to do it. And I shall have to help him.'

'That's your choice, Miss Harkness. But I believe I am telling the truth and I cut the picture in the National Gallery precisely to draw attention to the monstrous evils that men inflict on women both inside prison and out of it. Only when we get the vote will we get decent treatment for all women, and put men like Martin Armstrong behind bars instead of me. If my death were to make that happen it would be worth it, Miss Harkness, don't you think?'

For a long moment Ruth Harkness stared at the thin, intense woman in front of her, without speaking. The pale, almost translucent skin on Sarah Becket's face made her dark eyes unnaturally large, haunting; and there was a seriousness in them which made it difficult to look away once one had looked into them. Ruth shuddered as she thought of the thick, heavy frame of Martin Armstrong scrunching along the corridor towards his office in his wide leather shoes, and the way he had intoned with relish to anyone within earshot: 'Insane, definitely. I shall certify the woman as clinically mad, suffering from delusions brought on by self-inflicted absence of food. Never seen a clearer case in all my days, or a better justication for continuing forced feeding in the patient's own interests.' And she wondered what her conscience would make her do if for one moment she believed what the prisoner Becket had said. And what would happen to her if she did it.

She snatched up the porridge bowl and opened the cell door.

'Like I told you, Mrs Becket,' she said. 'You're a stupid, bloody-minded madwoman. And you deserve anything you're going to get.'

But that doesn't mean I don't know courage too, when I see it, she thought to herself bitterly, as she strode furiously away along the corridor.

15

Deborah was glad that Jonathan had left her on her own that morning. If he had not, she would have had to find some excuse to be rid of him.

All night she had been unable to sleep. Confused images kept drifting through her mind – of Sarah, with a knife in her hand, of Holloway with its high rows of tiny, barred windows and that dreadful pompous doctor, of Jonathan coming to her bed with that dreadful charming smile, of her husband drilling an army of soldiers with wooden guns, of her son Tom riding up to Charles on his grey Connemara pony with the light of hero worship in his eyes, of herself rocking a cradle in the nursery at Glenfee . . .

And of James Rankin.

The baby in the cradle, if there ever was one, would have thick dark hair and twinkling green eyes like Rankin. It would not look like her husband Charles at all. Charles would look at it with that glacial, superior face of his and throw her out of the house. She would be on the road like a gypsy, with her baby and the clothes she stood up in and nowhere in the world to go.

No, that was wrong! Charles would throw her out long before the baby was born. As soon as he realised she was pregnant with a child that could not possibly be his.

She had wondered if she should tell Jonathan about this but she had not dared. Especially not now. There was only one person to whom she could go for help. The child's father, James Rankin.

He was in London but she didn't know where. He had not written to her or left an address. All she knew was that there was some kind of dispute among the dock workers, and he had come to be part of it.

So I will have to go to the docks, she thought. And what then? The docks in London must be huge, I can't expect to just bump into him by walking about.

If there's a union it must have a headquarters somewhere, a place where the leaders meet. He'll have gone there. But if he's not there when I arrive, will anyone know who he is?

A big black-haired Irishman with a green silk scarf round his throat, who can make some of the most electrifying speeches I've ever heard?

They'll know him all right. If Rankin's there, they can't possibly have missed him.

Cheered by this thought, Deborah waited until Jonathan had gone, then went up to her room to dress. It was difficult to decide what to wear. She was going to the docks, so she did not want to dress too well, or she would look out of place. On the other hand, she had to look attractive to Rankin. The whole purpose of going was to appeal to him to care for her, take her back. He wouldn't do that if she looked a fright.

In the end she put on a long pale cream skirt, with a white blouse buttoned up to her neck, and a waist-length navy blue jacket over the top. She wore a small round hat with two silk roses in it. The effect was smart, attractive without being unnecessarily feminine. There's no point trying to look like a working-class woman because I'm not that, she thought. I look like a pleasant, self-contained middle-class lady who won't stand any nonsense and knows her own mind.

Oh but I don't, she thought. *I don't know what I want at all. I want James to help me but he's right, I don't want to live in a slum.*

As she went downstairs Jonathan's butler, Reeves, looked at her with respect and approval.

'Would you call me a cab, Reeves,' she said. 'I'll wait in the morning room.'

'Yes, of course, madam.'

That's the trouble, she thought. I belong in houses like this.

The only thing that doesn't belong is the way I behave. And my baby, which belongs to Rankin . . .

She did not find him until the evening. All day she had searched from one dock to another – she had not realised London had so many. St Katherine's Dock, Rotherhithe, Princess Elizabeth Dock, Albert Dock, Grosvenor Wharf, Battersea, Wapping, the Isle of Dogs; in each one she visited someone had heard of Rankin, or a man that sounded like her description of him, but he was not here today. He was always in another dock, further along the river, upstream or down; and when she got to that place he was not there either, but someone *thought* he had been seen in yet another dock, a further weary distance away.

She travelled by cab at first, then tram, then hired a waterman to row her on the river. The hem of her cream skirt became splashed with mud, the seat stained with tar from the boat. In the morning she felt hot as the sun blazed down out of a clear sky. In the afternoon a spring storm blew up and she huddled in doorways as sleet lashed the streets. When the storm had passed she shivered as an east wind blew cold across the muddy Thames water, and swirled grit into her eyes.

The docks themselves were busy, loud, dirty places, full of huge ships and cranes and coal and iron and timber and crates and carts and lorries and big, dirty men in heavy boots and dusty work shirts with tattoos on their massive forearms. They stared at her in surprise. Several whistled or laughed or turned their backs but most, thank God, were decent and polite to her. They could see she was a lady, too old to tempt the young lads, too plainly dressed and straightforward to have come here to lord it over them as a shipowner's wife might do. They directed her to the union office or their gaffer, the foreman, and here mostly a man would take his flat cap off his head, scratch thoughtfully with thick dirty fingers at the greasy hair behind his ear, and say 'Rankin, eh? Yes, lady, that rings a bell now. Wot's 'e look like? Tall, dark, 'andsome, Irish, wiv a green silk scarf round 'is throat? Yeah, I seen 'im, but not in this dock. Try Rotherhithe.' Or Queen Elizabeth's, Angel Wharf, St Katharine's . . .

She found him at last at five o'clock that evening. He was in a little street outside St Katharine's Dock, standing on a soapbox, talking to a crowd of about fifty men. Others streamed past on their way home from work. A few were curious, standing for a moment to listen before carrying on. One or two shouted catcalls. Most marched stolidly past, weighed down with weariness, casting a curious eye in her direction before hurrying on to home or pub.

Deborah stood at the back of the crowd, quietly watching. There were maybe three or four other women in the whole crowd, all in drab black or brown dresses, their faces heavy with weariness and work. Each seemed to know some man in the crowd and one, with a baby on her arm and two youngsters tugging at her skirts, was obviously trying to persuade her man to leave the meeting and come home. He ignored her at first, then pushed her away and when she would not go, smacked her back-handed around the face. She walked out of reach, weeping, but stood defiantly in the doorway of a nearby pub, waiting until the meeting should be over.

Rankin's eloquence, Deborah saw, was as compelling as ever. He had already been speaking for some time when she arrived, and the crowd was quiet, fascinated, entranced. He was talking of the struggle they had had in Dublin, the poverty of families there and how it had been reflected in his own childhood. Of the way that, if they all combined, they would have the strength to make things better for the next generation of children . . .

Then he saw Deborah.

She was standing on a doorstep to see over the heads of the big men in front of her. His eyes, constantly roving through the crowd in front of him to compell their attention, suddenly caught hers. He faltered in mid-sentence, stopped, repeated himself, and continued to stare at her over the heads of the crowd as though he had completely forgotten what he was saying or where he was.

One or two men looked back over their shoulders, puzzled. They saw a strange middle-class lady, in a stained cream skirt, blue jacket and flowered hat, standing silently on a doorstep, watching. They nodded knowingly, muttered among themselves, and nudged their friends. More men turned to look.

With an effort, Rankin dragged his eyes from hers and

refocused his mind on his speech. But the fire had gone from it. He stumbled to a lame, mechanical conclusion. Men had started to leave before he finished speaking. As they walked away up the road, their boots sparking on the cobbles, they glanced at her appraisingly. Several laughed or whistled. Two tall young lads began to sing: '*When Irish eyes are smiling . . .* '

'Deborah! Dear Lord, is it really you?'

He was there, in front of her. The same lean, dark gypsy face that she had loved. The sparkling green eyes searched hers and he flicked a long black lock of hair away from his forehead. He was looking slightly up at her because she was above him on the doorstep. She longed to lean forwards and fling her arms around his neck. But she dared not, because of the eyes that were watching them.

'Still the same James,' she said softly. She reached out and fumbled with the green silk scarf, setting it more neatly in place inside the worn cloth jacket. It was an oddly domestic, wifely gesture.

'Why have you come?' Was there pain in his voice, she wondered, or was he just embarrassed, because she had spoilt his meeting?

'I couldn't stay away. You're a hard man to find, though.'

'Am I? I thought all of London knew where I was by now. I must try harder.'

'I'm sorry I spoilt your speech.'

'What does that matter?' He glanced over his shoulder, where the remaining dockers were leaving in dribs and drabs, watching them curiously. 'Half of them have heard it already and, if they haven't, they'll hear it again. It doesn't change so much.'

'Still the same old agitator, then?'

'Surely. You know me.'

He looked at her quietly and she thought, for a moment, he's going to reach up and kiss me now. But instead he stepped back and offered his arm as a gentleman might.

'Well, now you're here, will you take a walk with me at least? I don't know about you, but my belly's cleaving to my backbone. Can I find you a bite to eat?'

'You can indeed.'

She stepped down off the doorstep and took his arm. How courteous he can be when he wants to, she thought. When I am on his arm like this I feel honoured . . .

What will he say when I tell him?

That will have to wait, she decided. Just for the moment she felt so proud, like a young girl again, walking along this grubby London street on the arm of her handsome Irish lover. I wish I had been born poor, she thought, then I could have had a man like this of my own, without having to give up anything.

But that's nonsense. Poverty's not a blessing, it's a curse. Look at those men pouring into that pub to drink away their wages. Think of the blow that man gave his wife in the meeting a minute ago. Remember all the miserable abandoned girls I saw in my work for the Irish Women's Guild. My problems with Charles are nothing to theirs.

To me they're overwhelming.

'Where do you live, James?'

'Me? In a terrace in Battersea, just now.'

'Take me there.'

'What? No, darlin', that's not a place for you. There's four of us fellers in it. Dirty plates and washing everywhere, no carpets or wallpaper and rats sifting through the rubbish in the back garden.'

'But I want to see it.'

'What? *No*, I tell you. Holy Mary, are you trying to make me ashamed?'

She felt the tension in his arm, and she wondered if he would pull away from her. She did not cling on, but he relaxed and they continued up the street, arm in arm like man and wife or lovers.

Almost.

His other hand was fumbling in his jacket pocket. She heard the clink of coins. He said: 'There's a fish restaurant in a little street behind the Tower. It's cheap but it's better than anything round here. I'll take you there, shall I?'

'All right. Don't worry about the money, James. I can pay.'

'I said *I'd* take *you*, madam. Act like a lady, now.'

'I am. An independent one, James. Have you forgotten that?'

'I've forgotten nothing.'

He stopped for a minute at the corner of the street, and turned her to face him. His eyes searched hers, unsmiling. She looked back at him. It might have been seconds, or half an hour, she did not know. All those nights in Mrs McCafferty's, the long walks along the quays beside the Liffey. The passion, the beauty of him – my Gaelic prince. And the laughter.

Hesitantly, she tried a smile. He shook his head, in wonder.

'My fine English lady, Deborah – why did you come?'

'To see you, my lover. What else?'

'And your husband? The Unionist soldier. You were to go back to him?'

'I did. But I missed you. And – there were other things. It's a long story. Come on. You said you were starving.'

'I am that.'

They crossed the road, went down a few side streets, found the restaurant. He was right, it *was* cheap. Run, as far as she could tell, by a family of Greeks, whose chubby brown children played around a handcart on the pavement. An older boy, eleven perhaps, came to take their order. He had smooth olive skin, serious dark eyes, and a sudden gleaming smile when Rankin made him laugh.

Perhaps my child will look like that, she thought, with a pang of keen sadness. So dark and beautiful. So utterly unlike Charles . . .

At least the place was private. No dockers, no union men, no one he seemed to know. There were a few single men, eating quietly at plain wooden tables. Most had a book or a newspaper open in front of them. Probably he chose it for the privacy, she thought. Is that a good thing? Does it mean he wants to spend time alone with me? Or to keep me separate from the rest of his life? She wasn't sure.

They were both hungry and ate ravenously when the food came. He began to relax. She told him of her travels round various docks during the day, and he laughed and related odd anecdotes about the places she had been.

'I was lost more than once myself, when I first came here,' he said. 'But you've not told me how you come to be in the big city at all. I pictured you at that fine country house of yours in Ulster. What do you call it now?'

'Glenfee.'

'That's the one.'

'Oh, I went there, James, of course I did.' But he has never been there, she thought. How remote our lives are from each other. There was bread and butter with the fish, and tea. She rolled the bread into little pellets between her fingers and ate it thoughtfully, between sips of hot, strong tea, while she wondered how to begin. Should she tell him now? She was so afraid of what he would say. He looked less tense than he had, but still not . . . entirely pleased to see her. 'It's partly because of my sister that I came.'

'Why?'

She told the story of Sarah. It was true, it was safe, it was interesting. She could see him relax as he became absorbed. Amused at what Sarah had done, angry at her sentence, concerned at the way she might have been treated in prison. Thoughtful, too, about Jonathan's response.

'You say he disowned her in Parliament?'

'More or less, yes. He didn't just say he disagreed with what she had done, he said he wouldn't even vote for female suffrage any more. Not if women did things like that.'

'So he rejects the end because he doesn't like the means?'

'In a way. Even I don't believe in smashing windows, James. You know that. But I can't just denounce my own sister.'

'No.' He sipped his tea, his elbows on the table, gazing at her thoughtfully over the cup. 'Always the lady bountiful.'

She didn't like that. 'I don't mind getting my hands dirty, you know that. Working among the poor, taking their children to my home. I'm not afraid, there's no need to sneer. I just don't think violence makes things better, that's all.'

'All right, all right, I know.' He held a hand before his face, as though to defend himself from the vehemence of her response. 'But she must be a powerful woman, your sister, to pick up a meat cleaver and slash a painting like that.'

There was a twinkle of amusement in his eyes; whether at the thought of what Sarah had done, or herself, Deborah was not sure. She frowned. It did not seem funny to her.

'Sarah's not big or strong, if that's what you mean. Just passionate and impulsive, I suppose. And rather unhappy, too, I think.'

'That must run in the family, then. The passion, at least . . . '

And not the unhappiness? 'What do you mean, James?'

He put his teacup down, smiled. 'Well now, I seem to remember, in Dublin . . . '

It was that beguiling, entrancing smile she remembered so well. Impulsively, she reached across the table and seized one of his hands in hers. There would never be a better time to tell him than now.

'James. Listen to me, my dear. I came to tell you something.'

'Is that a fact now?' He glanced at his hand, surprised. She was gripping it tight, imprisoning it in her own. 'Sure you'd best spit it out then.'

'I am . . . ' His eyes were fixed on hers, quiet, waiting. She glanced over her shoulder, around the little dining room. The other customers were eating, reading. Three men near the door were talking quietly. No one seemed to be listening.

'I'm pregnant, James.'

Some animals have a little membrane that can move across their eyes, to clear them from dust or an outside intrusion they do not want. When they do this for a moment the eye appears clouded, opaque. Something similar happened to Rankin's eyes as she watched them anxiously for his response. The sparkle faded. The pupils widened slightly and he seemed to go away from her inside himself. Into a dark pool of thought.

Only for a second. Then a smile returned to his lips.

'Well now. Congratulations.' His left hand moved across the table, to stroke her hands which clung tightly on to his. 'A new son to ride in the hunt at Glenfee. Or a daughter perhaps. Your husband must be pleased.'

'I haven't told him, James.'

'Not told him? You came all this way across the water to tell me, and you haven't told your husband?'

Oh come on, James – don't mock me now!

'I *can't* tell him, James.'

'Why ever not? The man will be delighted, surely!'

'Because . . . ' She glanced hurriedly round the room. The beautiful, olive-skinned boy was carrying a tray from the kitchen to the three men at the door. This is a mistake, I shouldn't have told him here. She lowered her voice to an intense, nervous whisper. 'Because he won't sleep with me, James. He hasn't once, not since he came back. It's your baby and when I tell him about it he'll *know*!'

Rankin was silent. His left hand stroked hers absently while she gripped the fingers of his other hand tight and stared at him, beseechingly. He saw the pain in her face, the intensity, the ugly tense lines that go with anxiety and fear. It's as though she is drowning, he thought, and clinging to me to save her.

But I can't swim.

'How do you know it's mine?'

'Don't be silly! There's no one else.'

'No. Of course not.' He took a deep breath. 'So what are you going to do?'

'What *can* I do, James? I've come to you. You're the father!'

'What do you think *I* can do, then?'

'Help me! Take me in, find me a home. There's nowhere else – I can't go to the workhouse!'

'Would you like any more, sir? Madam?' The young waiter was standing by the table, looking at them with his beautiful, impassive eyes.

'What? No, no, that's all. Here, son, we've finished. Let me pay now.'

He freed his hand from her grip, delved into his pocket, gave the boy some coins. When he had got his change, he stood up, pushed his chair in, and said: 'This is a rotten place to talk. Come on, let's go for a walk outside.'

She had her little blue jacket but not a coat, and it was dark and cold in the street. She shivered, but he did not put his jacket round her as she had hoped. They set off, walking quickly towards the river and the Tower.

'I told you, I haven't got a place here. Only a filthy men's lodgings which I'd be ashamed to let you see.'

'But you're the father, James! You've got to help. There's no one else!'

They stopped under a gas lamp by the walls of the Tower of London. Fifty yards to their right, the black waters of the Thames flowed dark and silently downstream. The gas lamp hissed above their heads, the wind blew cold around them. Deborah looked up into his face and saw not love or compassion but fear, anger, irritation.

'How *can* I help, woman? Think now for a minute, will you! We discussed all this in Dublin, and you said you wanted to leave me then.'

'Yes, but then I didn't know . . . '

'You understand the laws of nature – you knew it was possible, surely! But it's not just the laws of nature you have to understand, it's the laws of society. You're a different class to me, Deborah. You could never live as I do. If you left your husband and came to me you'd lose all your money, your house, your son – and you'd live in one room with no carpets, and spend your day scrubbing cockroaches out of the bed. You couldn't do it, woman! And, even if you could, I wouldn't want you to. If that's my son in your belly I'd rather he grew up rich, with a decent house, warm clothes, and a good education, not shivering in a slum as I did! And another thing . . . '

'No more, James, please!' She stared at him stunned, shaking. But he wasn't listening to her. Perhaps he never had.

'If I took in a woman like you my work in the union would be over. Half the workers in the union would call me a fornicator and throw me out, especially the Catholic Irish. Look what happened to Parnell!'

'James, you're not Parnell, nor anything like him!' She turned to walk away from him, towards the river, but he snatched her arm and held her back.

'No, but the principle's the same. Anyway, Deborah, I know it sounds harsh, but what I'm telling you is for the best in the long run, believe me! Go back to Glenfee, go back to your husband and *make* him sleep with you – you can do that surely, a pretty woman like you? Then he'll think the child is his and bring it up with a silver spoon in its mouth, and maybe I'll come over and see it some time. And we can meet . . . '

'Why should we want to meet?'

The words, to her, sounded bleak, cold as the unfeeling black river flowing silently past the embankment. To him, too, they sounded strange. He stopped for a moment, puzzled.

'Why? Well, for old times' sake, of course. And if your husband is as bad as you say . . . I thought you loved me.'

'I thought so too, once, James Rankin.' It was hard to get the words up, she was so choked with the tears that would have to come, soon, when she left him. But first – a vast flow of anger began to surge through her.

'I don't think you know the meaning of the word love, really, James, do you? It was all lust with you, wasn't it – fornication, as your union colleagues would say! And they'd be right, too, if they said it now, when you *won't* take me in. Because the difference between love and lust is whether you care for the other person, and the results of the time you spend together in bed! You don't give a fig for that, do you – not even for your own child!'

She snatched her arms out of his, and went away, half-walking, half-running, along the embankment, feeling the tears well up inside her. A policeman stopped and watched her go, but did nothing. After fifty yards she turned once and looked back, hoping perhaps that even now Rankin would change his mind and come after her. But he had not moved. He was still there, with his flat cap and warm jacket, under the gas light, watching. He had his hands in his pockets. The green silk scarf, which she had adjusted so maternally earlier when they had met, was fluttering loose in the cold wind.

They watched each other for a long, cold moment.

Then, very deliberately, he turned, hands still in his pockets, and walked slowly away . . .

16

Fingers. Drumming on the desk. Thick, strong fingers with virile black hair growing on the backs of them. Fingers that were stronger than most men's, twice as large as any woman's. Martin Armstrong remembered how he had once bent back the fingers of a cheeky little whore who had dared to argue with him. It had been so easy. He had used perhaps a quarter of his strength, and almost at once her sinews had cracked and she had screamed with pain and agreed to do what he asked. He remembered how, afterwards, she had shuddered in terror as his powerful hands kneaded her breasts – his groin warmed at the thought of it.

Now those same fingers drummed irritably on the desk in front of him, for once he wished they were smooth, soft, well-manicured, hairless like most men's.

My trouble comes from too much respectability, he thought. That, and greed.

He had come from a family with little money and had studied hard to become a doctor. He had never been very successful in his profession. Although he had a private practice in Kensington he had few patients. So he had been forced to take a second post as Assistant Medical Officer in Holloway Prison. And here he had come into contact with prostitutes. And then he had hit upon the idea of opening a second, smaller surgery in Hackney, and specialising in the treatment of venereal diseases. For the first time in his life, he had begun to make money.

He studied the market and discovered two things. Firstly, that the pimps and bawds – those who made the contacts and provided the premises – often made more money than the girls themselves. And secondly, that some men had distinctly peculiar tastes.

He began to make use of both of these pieces of knowledge.

Firstly, he made introductions. Men – sometimes patients, sometimes respectable married men whom he met in his club or through his wife – were secretly eager to meet the better class of whore but did not know how to go about it. For a price, Martin helped them. For a higher price, he made contacts for those who had unusual tastes. Bondage. Sado-masochism. The seduction of virgins.

The desire for the last of these seemed to be confined largely to middle-aged men. It did not appeal particularly to Martin, but it was highly profitable – and a stroke of luck made him well-placed to supply the demand. He had recently been appointed Medical Officer to a number of charitable children's hostels. The children in these places were there either because they had been abandoned by their parents, because they had run away from home, or, in some cases, because their parents were in prison. The girls were, therefore, from immoral backgrounds in the first place, and almost certain to lose their virginity before they knew they had it.

But they had something unique to sell, and Martin knew men who wanted to buy it. So a deal was struck, and everyone profited.

It all depended, Martin thought, on the gap between respectability and desire. Respectable women, it seemed to him, were unable to satisfy men's sexual desire, and normally felt none of their own. Less respectable women – those from the backstreets, the gutter, servant girls, the criminal classes – apparently could, and did. It was strange, but true. There was something about respectability that created a demand for prostitution.

And since respectable men had money, those who met that demand could grow rich.

Martin had calculated that in a year, if all went well, he would be able to give up his post in the prison entirely. In two years like this, he thought, he would earn more than in ten years of respectable employment. In five years he might be rich enough to retire to the South of France . . .

Greed, however, made him take risks. It had been tempting, but foolish, to take the expensive flats above his consulting rooms and use them to supply very rich, highly respectable customers. Men like Jonathan Becket, MP. But then, very respectable clients needed discreet and apparently respectable premises. How was he to know that the wretched man's suffragette wife was to come snooping outside?

Martin drummed his fingers on the desk again in frustration. The whole thing was a nightmare. Suffragettes, in his opinion, were the enemy of male freedom. They were the army of female respectability. They were puritans – they wanted all women to be respectable, frigid, and all men to be chaste, too. Christabel Pankhurst had said so, in a dreadful pamphlet she had written called *The Great Scourge*. Prostitution led to venereal disease, she said – over two thirds of all men contracted these diseases at one time or another. It was a war waged by men against women. The only solution was chastity for men, as well as women. Prostitution, lust, infidelity must be stamped out.

Martin had read the pamphlet with fascinated horror. If these women got their way, his livelihood would be destroyed. It was true that venereal disease was widespread – he was a specialist in treating it. It was also true, in his opinion, that men needed sexual freedom precisely *because* respectable women were unable to satisfy them. In that case, men should stand up for *their* rights. It was feeble liberals, like Jonathan Becket, whom he most despised. The man had once voted for women's suffrage in Parliament, and yet he was happy to use the services of a whore. Not only that, but he had come to Martin to plead for special treatment for his suffragette wife.

The woman who would destroy them both, if she were set free . . . Out of self-righteousness and jealousy, nothing more.

Martin drummed his fingers on the desk and tried to think clearly. What were his options?

It all depends how long I can keep her in prison, he thought. Out of touch with her husband. And how much she really knows.

Last time he had spoken to her he had been too shocked and angry to interrogate her carefully. He had been hugely embarrassed that a wardress had heard what she had said. Well, he would have to deal with that. But first I have to talk to Sarah Becket on my own, he thought.

Without the wardress being present.

The fingers on the desk stopped drumming. He sighed, pushed back his leather chair, and walked grimly towards the door . . .

'Good morning, Mrs Becket.'

'What? Oh no, not you! Get out, please. Leave me alone!'

She was shocked, as Martin had expected, but at least she did not scream. That was a good sign. She had been sitting hunched at one end of her bed, shivering in the coarse serge prison dress with the arrows on it. Her hair was neatly combed but her face was pale, drawn. Shivering, he knew, was one of the consequences of starvation and inactivity.

He sat down on the end of the bed, as far away from her as the cell allowed. I must try not to get her hysterical, he thought. If it is possible to have a rational conversation with this woman, that is what I want. He leant forward, folding his hands between his knees, and forced a smile.

'I haven't come to hurt you.'

'Oh no? What about last night?'

'That was the medical treatment. I warned you about it. So long as you continue to starve yourself it has to be applied.'

It had been a grim business all the same. When he had come back to force feed her the wardresses had been, it seemed to him, unusually reluctant, and Sarah had screamed and tried to claw his face. Afterwards, she had vomited up almost as much as he had poured into her stomach so the whole thing had been pointless, except as punishment.

'Treatment!' she said. 'You're a torturer. You live in the Middle Ages.'

Martin tried to keep the smile on his face. 'It is that I have come to see you about. None of us like having to treat prisoners like that. If you would only co-operate it wouldn't be necessary.'

'Co-operate? With you?' Sarah tried to laugh, but her throat hurt too much where the tube had rubbed it raw. Instead she stood up and turned to face the wall, with her back to him.

Martin sighed. He felt an urge to seize the silly woman and shake her until her teeth rattled, but that would do no good. He said, as reasonably as he could: 'If you would eat, you wouldn't have to be fed.'

'If men would treat women as human beings, I wouldn't need to be in here at all!'

This was not what Martin had come to talk about. He waited for a moment, collecting his thoughts. There was a clatter outside in the corridor as a wardress went past with a trolley.

'Yesterday, Mrs Becket, you made a number of accusations against me. I have come to talk about those.'

Silence. She did not turn round.

'In the first place, you appear to believe I keep a – what is the word? – a brothel in the flats above my consulting rooms. Is that right? Did I understand you correctly?'

She turned round to face him. Arms folded, she leaned against the wall under the high barred window. Her hair was hidden under the regulation mob cap and there was a mocking, sardonic smile on her bruised lips.

'You understand perfectly, Dr Armstrong, because it's true.'

'And what proof do you imagine you have?'

'I saw my husband go into your consulting rooms and stay there when you came out. Later, I saw another man go in with a prostitute on his arm.'

Martin laughed. It was a fairly good effort, he thought. He hoped it shook her confidence.

'Then you did not understand what you saw. Whatever woman went into the flats she could not have been a prostitute. And your husband often stays behind after I have left. He receives . . . therapy and medical advice from a young colleague of mine.'

'For three hours?'

Sarah watched Dr Armstrong's eyes and saw a shadow of fear flicker in them. In fact she had no idea how long she had waited outside the consulting rooms. It might have been three hours, or one, or five. The pain of the discovery had made it seem interminable. But Martin did not know how long she had been there, either.

'The place also has a back door. Perhaps he left by that.'

'I shall ask him then, when I get out. Jonathan is an even worse liar than you are.'

Martin coughed, awkwardly, and his hands squeezed each other between his knees. He wanted to slap the wretched woman's face but it would not do. The point of this interview was to gather information, not lose his temper.

'Please do – ask him whatever you like. Though you will have to wait a while, I fear. But you made another accusation, a rather worse one. You seem to believe that I own yet more houses of ill repute. In different areas. What possible proof can you have of that?'

Annoyance flitted across Sarah's face. The women in the collecting cell; they would probably deny everything, even if I could find them – I never knew their names. The only other real proof I have is the letter warning me to stay away from Dr Armstrong because even my husband visited his prostitutes. I stuffed it into the back of my desk, but it's no use telling this man that. For all I know he might tell Jonathan to get it out and burn it. Oh Jonathan, Jonathan!

How could you?

She confronted the smug ugly slob of a man in front of her – *Jonathan's friend*! – and said: 'I'm not going to tell you what proof I have. You can wait and find out later. But I know it's not just ordinary prostitutes you rent those rooms to. You take children there too, don't you? Little girls thirteen or fourteen years old, for men to deflower. You make me ill!'

Martin stood up. The strain of sitting quietly was too much for him. Sarah saw the big, hairy hands flexing by his sides and flinched. But he did not touch her.

With an effort, he kept his voice calm. 'You have no proof because these things don't happen. You are suffering from a mental delusion. But, just out of interest, Mrs Becket, let us pursue this line a little further. When you have completed your six months' sentence in here . . . '

'I shall be out before that!'

'. . . what do you propose to do with this supposed information about my activities?'

It was the crucial question. Sarah savoured it. For the first time in Holloway, she felt that the balance of power had swung in her direction. She said, sweetly: 'You will just have to wait and see, won't you, Dr Armstrong? But I imagine that the press will be interested. And the police too, perhaps. Doctors who abuse women and young girls do not usually rise to the summit of their profession, do they?'

'And your husband, Mrs Becket? Will you drag him down in the mire as well? His reputation and career will be ruined, if you make these accusations. Even if they are untrue.'

Sarah's sense of triumph faded. Rage flared in its place. *Jonathan did this!* He betrayed me – he sent this man here to taunt me. On his own head be it! Beneath the rage burned a grim, hard determination. I owe this to all women – the children, the young women who are exploited, the suffragettes who are tortured in here with me. Whatever the consequences, this man is evil. I have to expose him!

'My husband can look after himself. My concern is the rights of women, Dr Armstrong.'

Martin stared at her impotently. Such a slender, pale creature in the drab shapeless prison dress. The cheekbones seemed unnaturally high in the sunken hungry face, the eyes unusually bright. A martyr, he thought, with that cut-glass high society accent of frigid respectability. No wonder Jonathan Becket had to go to a whore; her thighs must be sharp as razors!

With an effort, he raised an eyebrow superciliously.

'In that case, you will make fools of both him and yourself, Mrs Becket, when you discover that your accusations are untrue. But in the meantime, if you will not eat, I regret that your treatment for self-inflicted starvation must continue.'

The fear in her eyes pleased him. He turned to open the door, and to avoid too many more kicking and screaming matches like we had last night, he thought, the woman had better be drugged. I will feed her a measure of bromide tonight, before her meal. That way, she'll keep more of it down.

He strode away along the corridor, smiling grimly to himself. From what Sarah Becket had said, he didn't believe she had much proof. It was a nuisance, but long before she was released from Holloway, he would have closed all the flats down and moved the girls on to other, more secret premises. If the police raided the addresses she knew of, they would find nothing.

But that was all in the future. For the moment she was safe here in Holloway. She could have no visitors at all for a month, not even her feeble husband. So until then, the girls and Mrs Burgoyne could continue to make money for him.

Every day. Every night. Greed profiting from respectability.

Ruth Harkness had not planned to become a prison wardress. As a child she had shown some promise at school and her father, an enterprising man with his own hansom cab, had expressed hopes that she might get a job in an office operating one of the new modern typewriting machines. If she did very well, she might even become a teacher. But when Ruth was nine her father was stabbed by a drunken passenger late at night. All hopes she and her sisters had had of higher education were buried with him in a graveyard in Hackney.

She left school at fourteen to work for four years in her uncle's bakery in the East End. Every morning at half past two she had to get up to clean out the ash from the big coal ovens and light fresh fires in them, and then make hundreds of little bread rolls for people to buy on the way to work. She stood in the shop, then, until four or five o'clock in the afternoon, when nearly everything was sold. Then she was free to help her mother with her younger sisters until they all fell asleep exhausted in the single back room they shared above a tailor's shop.

In 1911, her uncle had a heart attack early one morning. He fell face forward into a stack of loaves in the oven which he was unloading, and by the time Ruth pulled him out he was dead, one side of his face singed raw by the oven wall. The bakery passed to a cousin who planned to run it with his wife, and Ruth was out of a job.

For a year she had various unsuccessful jobs as an office cleaner, scullery maid, and shop assistant, all of which she hated; and then one night, in a public house in Putney, she met a man who was to change her life. His name was George Smith.

George was an unusually tall and broad-shouldered young man with a face like a wrestler. He looked down expressionlessly on even the tallest men in the pub, whose heads only came up to his chin, and they all showed him respect. Women gazed up at him in awe, as though he were a giant out of a childhood story book. But Ruth was considerably larger and stronger than most girls, and she found, to her surprise, that this seemed to attract George almost as much as it had previously put off other men. He walked her home that night and they arranged to meet again. By the end of the month they were courting.

George was a police constable. He came from a poor family not unlike Ruth's and most of his wages went to support his widowed mother and his younger brothers and sisters. He had only recently joined the force and was determined to do well in it. To Ruth's surprise, his stolid, taciturn manner hid a relatively acute brain. As well as being determined, he was ambitious.

'I couldn't offer a girl marriage at this stage, Ruthie,' he confided to her solemnly one Sunday afternoon as they sat listening to a band playing in Hyde Park. 'I couldn't afford to do it properly yet, it would just drag us both down. When I marry I want to have a decent house, security. A home I can be proud to bring up kids in. So I'll have to wait, and work, and save. I'd want a wife who knew how to work and save, too.'

It was then that they fell to discussing Ruth's string of unsatisfactory jobs, and how she loathed them and had always hoped for something better. George considered this gravely for a few minutes, and then suggested the prison service.

It had never occurred to Ruth that such jobs existed for women. And yet, the more she thought, the more sense it made. A prison wardress had a proper, relatively well-paid job, with regular wages and meals and a uniform – and none of the drawbacks of going into service. Perhaps because of her father's early ambitions for her, Ruth had always hated the idea of becoming a servant, all day at the beck and call of people who were richer than her by mere chance and no ability. She found it hard enough taking orders in shops from owners who were less intelligent than she was. But in a women's prison, she thought, the situation would be almost entirely reversed. The criminals would be there to receive orders from *her*!

George told her how to apply for the job and to her surprise she was accepted. From the beginning the work appealed to her. For the first time she had a position with some of the status her father had led her to hope for. The job was respectable, the rules were clear, and *she* was in charge of others. And since the criminals had not only been wicked enough to commit crimes but also stupid enough to get caught, it was clear that they richly deserved their fate.

After a month she was able to open a small account in a bank – the first savings she had ever had. And George's respect for her grew. After twelve months they became engaged.

She was thinking about this as she walked towards Holloway at five o'clock one morning. The streets were still grey in the early dawn, but already they were busy – barrow-boys heading towards Covent Garden to collect vegetables for the market, fishmongers going towards Billingsgate, street-cleaners and crossing-sweepers and lamplighters dowsing the gas lamps. Already I earn more than most of these people, she thought, and I am only twenty-two and the only woman going to work so early. What would father say if he could see me now? It was not what he planned but he would not be ashamed, either. He always taught me to earn my living and to know right from wrong, and that is what my work and George's is all about. Without us the city would be torn to shreds by criminals and anarchists.

She entered the great gloomy stone portals of Holloway, and gazed across the courtyard for a moment. Every window of the huge brick building in front of her was blockaded by iron bars. It was like a medieval castle, a fortress to contain evil and misery and to punish it.

Ruth knew there was misery as well as evil in those cells. But she had learnt early on to harden her heart to the sob stories the prisoners tried to tell. She nearly always cut them off automatically now before they had even begun. That was an important part of prison discipline, anyway – the rule that said prisoners should not speak unless spoken to. Prisoners should obey instructions instantly, and wardresses should never look them in the eye. It was a good, effective rule, Ruth thought; cruel on the surface but merciful after a while. It made the boundaries clear and did not create expectations. If that was part of the punishment, all well and good.

The one group of prisoners who troubled her were the suffragettes. Not because she agreed with them; she was quite definite about that. A crime was a crime whatever its motive. The problem was the women themselves. They were often well-educated, articulate, independent – the sort of woman Ruth had hoped to become herself. *And they would not accept the rules.* They spoke when they were not spoken to, refused to eat, sang, protested, argued, blockaded themselves in their cells, and endlessly asked questions. *We are political prisoners*, they said, *we are not criminals, these rules were not meant for us at all.* And so, to refute this argument and enforce the rules, Ruth and all other wardresses had to treat them more harshly than anyone else. By forcible feeding. Confinement to the punishment block. Leaving them manacled sometimes all night in their cells.

Ruth hated it. It made her unhappy in a job she was proud of. She hated it even more when George seemed to sympathise with them. He told her how sensible, even grateful, the suffragettes often were when arrested. He thought they had spirit and accepted that they would win the vote in the end. He had carried a little grandmother of about seventy all the way across Parliament Square in a suffragette demonstration one day. She had slapped his face to ensure she was arrested for assault and breach of the peace – and then complimented him for giving her the best piggy-back ride since her father took her to the wedding of Queen Victoria!

So why can't they behave decently in prison? Ruth thought. She scowled as she climbed the dark stone stairs inside the prison. Today she would have to deal with that woman Becket again. And Sarah Becket was the worst of all, because Ruth had begun to believe her . . .

Ruth was not sorry for the woman. The fact that Sarah Becket was rich and well-connected did not matter to her at all. Indeed, she rather enjoyed the fact that such women had to be washed and shampooed for nits like the others, carry their own slop buckets to the sluice, even be forcibly fed if necessary. That was common justice – proof that no one was above the law, wherever they were born.

But . . . Dr Armstrong said that Sarah Becket was insane. And while Ruth Harkness was not medically qualified, she did not believe that. She had met several madwomen in prison. One had claimed to be Mary, Mother of God; another had persisted in lifting her skirt and showing her drawers to anyone who opened the door of her cell; a third had screamed all night because she could see her dead child floating in the air in front of her; a fourth had sat, totally silent, with her face to the wall for three days.

Sarah Becket had done nothing like this. She had simply stated, in a clear, forceful, upper-class accent, that Dr Armstrong was a pimp.

Put baldly like that, Ruth admitted to herself, it did sound mad. Dr Armstrong was a respectable, prosperous doctor, a figure of authority in the prison; Sarah Becket was a convicted criminal, so unbalanced that she thought she could influence Parliament by slashing a famous picture with a meat knife. That was why Ruth had not yet voiced her suspicions to George. But . . .

Ruth had *been* there. She had seen the conviction with which Becket spoke, the shock, almost guilt, on the face of Dr Armstrong. And then, she had worked beside Dr Armstrong for some months . . .

It was irrational to feel revolted by a man who was always perfectly polite and professional, but . . . Ruth always kept as far away from him in a cell as she could. As though those great, stubby fingers of his might suddenly grab *her* instead of palpating the chest of a patient; as though the thick black hairs on the backs of his wrists could come alive like spiders, and crawl out of his sleeves in dozens.

She shuddered, as she hung up her coat and hat in the locker-room and put on her regulation apron. Of course such thoughts were nonsense, but – what if the story Becket told her was true? If this doctor, those *hands*, were really leading little girls out of the safety of a charitable institution into a life of prostitution, where men would pay to paw them before they were even old enough to . . . it did not bear thinking about! Ruth Harkness buckled a bunch of keys on to her belt and set off down the long grey corridor to her first duties of the day.

But it *had* to be thought about.

If what Becket said was true, then Dr Armstrong was not just a criminal but a serious, monstrous one. A bluebeard of a man who should be locked away for far longer than most women here. One of the fundamental beliefs that Ruth shared with her fiancé George was that the police and prison service were the soldiers of right in a war against wrong. They prayed, every night, that god would guide their hands in the cleansing of society, the crusade against evil. If she, Ruth, suspected Dr Armstrong of such a crime and did nothing about it she would be a traitor to God.

But if she did something about it and it proved to be untrue, she would almost certainly lose her job.

All morning Ruth Harkness went about her duties in a foul mood. She cursed Sarah Becket for ever coming to Holloway at all, and she cursed herself for listening to the woman and getting drawn into a discussion with her. She was still angry when, at two o'clock, she received a summons to go to Dr Armstrong's consulting room.

Surprised, she left the main cell block, climbed two flights of stairs, and knocked on his door.

'Come!'

She entered, and strode quietly into the centre of the room. It was peaceful here, civilised in comparison to the rest of the prison. A carpet on the floor, a fire in the grate, no bars in the windows. Dr Armstrong sat with his back to the window, writing at a large wooden desk. He had a pipe in his mouth and, as he wrote, he puffed and grunted to himself. After a moment he blotted the paper, sat back in his chair, and smiled.

'Ah. Miss – er – Harkness, is it not?'

'Yes, Doctor. You sent for me.'

'I did indeed. It was good of you to come.' He hesitated, and the ingratiating smile faded, to be replaced by a frown of portentous solemnity. 'It was, er, about an unfortunate scene that you were forced to witness the other day. I realise that you must witness very many unpleasant things in the course of your job, but I thought perhaps that this event was peculiarly . . . distressing.'

'What scene was that then, Doctor?' Ruth kept her face wooden, to force him to say it. Already she felt anxious, thinking how easy it would be to lose her job, how important it was to her. And there was something else, less tangible, to do with the man himself. He folded his fleshy fingers under his chin.

'Surely you remember, Miss Harkness? The outburst of the prisoner Becket, when only you and I were in her cell. She made some most distressing and slanderous allegations. You remember that?'

'Yeah.' He glanced at her sharply, as though suspecting insolence in the flat monosyllabic answer.

'Well, Mrs Becket is a distinguished lady of a certain social class that we would not normally expect to find in Holloway, and I appreciate how hard it must be for yourself and your colleagues to control such women. Particularly when they make appalling allegations that you might be tempted to believe. So . . . '

He hesitated, cold grey eyes watching her carefully from under thick bushy eyebrows. The fingers writhed thoughtfully under the chin.

' . . . so I have decided to take the unusual step of reassuring you about the nature of her illness. Mrs Becket is, I regret to say, suffering from a depressive illness which can lead to paranoid delusions about those who care for her. I am acquainted with her family doctor and am told that she has suffered from this for some time. It leads to precisely the sort of fantastic outburst we heard yesterday, which can be most upsetting for all who have to deal with her. Including her husband, poor man, from what I hear.'

'You mean she's mad?'

'If you wish to put it that baldly, yes. But it is a form of madness in which the patient can appear perfectly normal for most of the time. She may appear so to you, I don't know?'

Again the smile, ingratiating, pleasant, the fat lips in the heavy, solid face. Like a concerned family doctor inquiring about how you felt.

'Yes, she does.' Ruth answered bluntly, without thinking. She regretted it almost immediately. Yet it was the truth, and if she challenged him with that, perhaps she would see what he really meant. After all, if he *was* lying . . .

The smile faded. The thick fingers picked up the pipe, enveloped it, struck a match. 'Well, that's natural enough. Have you seen many madwomen, Miss Harkness?'

'A few. An' they was proper loonies, not like her. Seems to me she talks a lot of sense most of the time. Wrong-headed o' course, bein' a suffragette, but sense all the same. Not madness.'

He sighed heavily. 'Well, that's just what I said. It is a form of lunacy in which the patient can appear sane for most of the time, until suddenly her outbursts become so fantastic as to burst the boundaries of sense. I have considerable experience of it, I can assure you. And Mrs Becket's behaviour – first in slashing that painting, and then in making those absurd allegations – are classic symptoms of the disease.'

Silence. Ruth stared at him, thinking. A coal fell in the fire and a puff of smoke drifted out into the room. The lines of a kindly understanding smile lingered on his face, but the message of the steely grey eyes was: *there it is, young woman. Believe me or lose your job.*

Ruth remembered the prayers she made, every night, and the young ragged girls she sometimes saw, begging in the streets. Rescued, if Sarah Becket was to be believed, not by the Salvation Army, but to be whores for dirty old men.

She said: 'If she's mad, like what you say, she ought to be treated for it, not punished. Why ain't she being released?'

The smile returned, but it was an effort, Ruth could see that. The eyes were grey as winter.

'A good question. I can see we have recruited some intelligent wardresses this last year. But since you are so intelligent you will understand when I say there are two – no, three – prongs to the answer. Will you bear with me while I go through them?'

'All right.'

'Good. Well, the first point is, Mrs Becket was imprisoned for a crime which she claimed was a political protest, and she made no defence of illness or insanity. So she is still guilty, and it is clearly in the interests of justice that she serves her sentence if at all possible. Are you with me so far?'

'Yes.'

'Excellent! The second point – and you will please keep this absolutely confidential, because you must appreciate that I should not normally be discussing it with you at all – the second point is that treatment for this form of insanity is, in any case, to confine the patient in a quiet room, which is precisely what happens here in Holloway. As it happens, I am unusually well qualified to carry out this treatment, so Mrs Becket is actually lucky to be here. She should be kept well fed – and we are trying to arrange that also – and in addition I intend to treat her with bromide, which will calm her down and clear her mind.'

'Bromide?'

'Yes. Surely you have come across it before? It is a mild sedative, that's all. It brings calm and comfort to people of troubled mind. That was my third point. So you will see, although we cannot release her, she is receiving the best possible treatment where she is.'

Ruth did not know what to think. On the face of it, the doctor's arguments made sense, but if the situation was as clear as he said it was, why did he have to explain?

As if reading the doubt in her face, he said: 'I understand what you are thinking, young woman, believe me. You are wondering why I am telling you all this. Well, let me be honest with you. Mrs Becket made some very serious and unpleasant allegations about me personally the other day, and I would take it very seriously indeed if anyone repeated them. Indeed, I would sue that person for malicious slander, do I make myself clear? As I would sue Mrs Becket, if she were not my patient. But as I am an honest man, I would also like to convince you, as the only other person who heard these allegations, that they are, in fact, untrue. I have no connection with any impropriety whatsoever.'

'You don't think . . . ' Ruth hesitated. The man's candour had captured her. Despite her personal dislike of him she almost believed him now. He seemed truly to want to explain, and he was a doctor, after all. Nonetheless, in her life in the East End she had met too many liars to take everything she heard at face value. Since he had asked her here, she had one more question.

'Come on, out with it, Miss Harkness. If you have any more questions let's hear them.'

'Well . . . ' Ruth swallowed. ''Course it was crazy what Mrs Becket said about you corruptin' young girls an' orphans an' all – anyone could see that . . . '

'I'm glad you think so.'

'But what if not everything she said was true? If she's got 'old of the wrong end of the stick, like. If what she said *does* 'appen to some o' them young girls in the orphanage where you work, and you don't know nuffink about it. If it was 'appening, as you say, it would be a pretty nasty business, like, and someone ought to look into it. Even if she is a few farthings short of a penny she might 'ave 'eard something from someone else.'

There was a silence. Maybe it lasted less than a minute, but to Ruth it seemed like ten. Somewhere far away in the prison a door clanged shut, and the wind rattled at the windows of the consulting room. Martin Armstrong tapped his pipe thoughtfully on an ashtray.

'I suppose it's possible. But hardly likely. After all, I can hardly trouble the police about the ravings of a madwoman.'

'I could 'elp, sir.'

'I beg your pardon?' Behind the look of amusement and surprise there was definitely a sense of alarm, Ruth thought. Quickly hidden. She pressed on.

'I could give you a bit of 'elp. Just to sort of check the story out, like.'

Another silence. The grey eyes watched her, thinking. If he refuses, then maybe he's got something to hide, she thought. But if he accepts and there *is* some truth in it – then what?

'What help were you thinking of, Miss Harkness, exactly?' The fat fingers toyed unconsciously with the pipe, reflecting the turmoil of the man's thoughts.

She swallowed again. Why had she said this? 'To keep an eye on them girls and wardens in the 'omes, maybe. It would be easier for me to talk to 'em than for you. An' I know how girls like that fink.'

'Oh you do, do you?'

Up until then she had almost believed him, but those five words changed her mind. Not the words, but the way he said them. Being a big girl, powerfully built, Ruth had very seldom been looked at in quite that way by men, but she had seen it happen often enough to other girls, and been at once jealous and disgusted. Now, suddenly, there was an unmistakable knowing leer in Dr Armstrong's eyes, a cynical smile on those puffy lips that made her shiver. She felt as though her apron and thick serge dress were not there any more, and he, the Doctor, could see her standing in front of him as naked as when she washed herself alone in the morning. She watched his eyes and the hairy backs of his hands, carefully, ready to run or fight if he got up and came near her.

She heard her voice answer: 'Oh yes, I think I understand girls like that. When you're poor an' come from a criminal background you could be tempted to do almost anyfink for money. But it's a dreadful sin, o' course. Mrs Becket's dead right about that. That may be why she got so terrible upset, like.'

'Quite the young philosopher, I see.'

'You learn to think a bit, in this job.'

'No doubt. Well, Miss – er – Harkness, you may have a point after all. I see I am dealing with an intelligent young woman, and I understand your concern. It does you credit. Though as far as I am aware the homes are run in a most proper and excellent fashion.'

'Yes, but . . . '

'But maybe there is, as you say, a grain of truth in Mrs Becket's ravings. A very small grain, I hope. Nonetheless, I shall reflect upon your suggestions about how to investigate them. And also whether to take up your offer of help. Since you have shown such concern I shall let you know what I propose to do in a day or so. Is that fair?'

'Yes. Thank you, sir.'

'Good. In the meantime, I hope you will accept the truth of what I have told you about Mrs Becket's medical condition, and treat that knowledge in the strictest confidence. She is, I repeat, suffering from paranoid delusions, which is a form of insanity. And this condition will only worsen with shortage of food, so the forcible feeding must continue. I trust you have no objection to that?'

'Oh no, sir. It's her own choice not to eat.'

'Quite. I'm glad you see it so clearly. So, Miss Harkness, if that is all . . . '

He rose to his feet, pressing his hands on the top of his desk, and Ruth took an involuntary step backwards. But he had only got up to escort her to the door, like a valued patient. All the way across the room, Ruth wondered how she would disguise the shudder, if he were to be so polite and patronising as to put his arm across her shoulder . . .

17

'It's very quiet, sir, isn't it?' Simon Fletcher said.

Charles Cavendish glanced at his young ADC. As usual, the boy looked trim, smooth, unruffled. Simon was one of a minority of the UVF who had so far managed to procure an acceptable military uniform, and he wore it with style, the battledress blouse neatly pressed, the Sam Browne belt gleaming with polish, the cap, with its distinctive badge, tilted slightly to the side of his head. Charles smiled, reassured for the moment by his presence.

'It's always quiet in Bangor, lad,' he said. 'Especially at eleven o'clock at night.'

But he knew what Simon meant. As they paced slowly along the promenade, the sound of their boots echoed eerily back at them from the silent boarding-houses on the other side of the road. There were hardly any lights on in the houses, and almost no other sound at all. Just the swish of the sea on the beach to their right, and the rattle of a broken gas lamp in the thin drizzling wind that blew in out of the darkness across Belfast Lough. And the occasional murmur of the other men as they waited, smoking and talking quietly, in small detachments where Charles had posted them around the quay.

'Do you think anyone knows we're here?' Simon asked.

Charles glanced at him sharply. It was a question that had begun to gnaw at his mind, now that all the arrangements had been made, and every picket posted. Certainly, no one from the outside world was supposed to know they were there. So far as Charles knew, the entire town of Bangor was sealed off, and had been for the past three hours. The telephone exchange had been occupied, and all the lines earthed; every road in and out of the town was blocked by a detachment of UVF soldiers; no boats could leave the harbour. The police and coastguard stations were surrounded, and such RIC policemen as continued to patrol the streets were accompanied everywhere by a superior force of Charles's men. Charles had planned meticulously, and he believed he had done everything necessary. And still no one, even in the force of nearly a thousand UVF men who occupied the little seaside town, knew for certain what the purpose of the exercise was.

No one, that is, except himself, his three company commanders – and Simon.

Simon, who a few days ago had threatened to betray everything to a foreign journalist, if Charles ever talked of ending their affair again.

Simon saw, by the look on Charles's face, that his casual remark had been misunderstood. It had been a nasty moment, that afternoon, when he had come into Charles's room to find his wife there. Since then, Deborah Cavendish had gone to London, but Charles had remained unusually cold, aloof. Simon regretted the threat he had made, and wanted to make amends.

He laughed lightly. 'I was only wondering about the old ladies in the boarding houses,' he said, waving his hand casually at the darkened windows. 'I mean, do you think the old biddies turned their lights out so that they could stare at us out of their darkened windows, or do you think they are all tucked up with a hot water bottle and not a care in the world?'

'The latter, I hope,' Charles grunted. Despite the silence, he was not in the mood for idle chatter. He had always found waiting the most arduous part of soldiering. It was the time when there was nothing to do but think, and hope, and worry about what you had forgotten. It was always bad, but tonight it was worse, because so much responsibility rested on him. If anything went wrong in Bangor, he would be blamed, and his position in the UVF, on which he had staked so much, would be lost.

But more than his personal reputation, that of the UVF itself was at stake tonight. So far, everything they had done to resist the extension of Home Rule to Ulster had been an enormous bluff. The rallies at Craigavon, with the dozens of speakers and the biggest Union Flag ever made; the hundreds of thousands who had signed the Covenant, many in their own blood; the parades and drilling and military operations in which they had practised, over and over again, occupying towns like Bangor – all these had been, fundamentally, a bluff, simply because nine out of ten UVF soldiers had no arms to fight with. They drilled with pick-handles and wooden staves, not rifles.

Tonight, they were here to get those rifles.

While Charles paced along the silent promenade at Bangor, other elements of Operation Lion, the most important task the UVF had ever undertaken, were falling into place along the coast of North Down, Belfast, and South Antrim.

In Larne, about now, Charles hoped, the steamer *Clydevalley*, with 20,000 of the most modern Austrian Mauser and Mannlicher rifles, and 3 million rounds of ammunition, was about to arrive. A convoy of cars and motor lorries from the UVF motor division – the first such convoy ever organised in military history – should be there, waiting to take them off. Most of the rifles were to be loaded into the cars, but smaller consignments were to be loaded into the smaller ships *Roma* and *Inismurray*. They were to be taken by the *Roma* into Belfast, and by the *Inismurray* south to Donaghadee, on the North Down coast, where a detachment of men similar to Charles's was waiting to take them off. The last consignment was to be left on board the *Clydevalley*, so that it could bring them across the mouth of the Belfast Lough to Bangor, where Charles and his men were waiting.

At the same time, in the centre of Belfast itself, a decoy steamer, the *Balmarino*, was arriving, carrying a perfectly legal cargo of coal. A large UVF detachment was ostentatiously on parade in the centre of Belfast Docks to welcome the *Balmarino*, and ensure her arrival did not go unnoticed. Both the UVF men and the steamer's crew had orders to be as unco-operative as possible towards the police and Customs officials. On no account were they to be allowed to inspect the *Balmarino*'s hold until late tomorrow morning, by which time the real guns should be speeding away far inland, in hundreds of cars taking them to their future owners.

In theory, then, everything had been thought of. But then, in theory, only twelve men in the entire UVF had these details clear in their minds. And Charles knew that was not true.

In the silence, a sound began to bother him. Beyond the swish of the sea and the click of their boots, there was the roar of a motor-cycle engine, somewhere near the edge of the town. Charles glanced past the peak of Simon's cap, and saw a single headlight, and then another, flash into sight at the end of the promenade, and rush towards him.

As they drew nearer, the shattering roar of the motorbike engines re-echoed from the walls of the boarding houses, and Charles felt a twinge of pity for the old ladies asleep inside. Then the first rider spotted him and drew up in a swirl of gravel.

As he killed the engine and saluted, the words came rushing out. 'Sir, a detachment of troops left Holywood Barracks, sir, half an hour gone, maybe . . . didn't see them on the road but we had to run to fetch our bikes first, sorry sir but we hid them in a wood while keeping watch, or we'd have been here sooner . . . '

'Wait! Control yourself, man! Start again!' In the roar of the second bike's arrival Charles had missed half of what the man was saying, but in a couple of minutes he had the picture clear. The two motor-cyclists had been set to watch the army barracks at Holywood, five miles towards Belfast along the coast road. At 10.40 they had seen a detachment of British Army troops march out.

'Were they armed, man!'

'Yes, sir, fully equipped in marching order.'

'How many?'

'About company strength, sir.'

'But you didn't pass them on your way here?'

'No, sir.'

Charles considered the man. Young, but short, square, confident. Cullen, he thought his name was; had served in India as a sergeant before leaving to join the UVF. He would know what he was talking about.

'All right, I want to have a look at this. Come back with me. Simon, get the car!'

As they followed Cullen's motor-bike along the promenade and up, out of the town, there was a strained silence in the car. Simon drove, his goggles masking his face against the stream of cold air that blew in over the Lancia's low windshield. Charles sat beside him, sunk in thought, gazing out over the dark waters of Belfast Lough, searching the road ahead for the first sign of troops.

'What will you do if they come?' Simon asked.

'God knows.' Once Charles had encouraged the boy's familiarity; it had been a comfort to him. Now it had begun to grate horribly. The question was too near the bone. He couldn't resist armed, determined soldiers – Simon knew that. If tonight went wrong, the whole bloody cause would probably be lost, forever. Sir Edward Carson would be arrested and imprisoned, and the rest of the UVF High Command would look like a bunch of incompetent idiots. Perhaps because of him.

Bitterly, his voice deliberately hard and cold and clear above the noise of the engine, he said: 'If they come, I shall ask them exactly how they knew.'

But, for all his anger, as soon as the words were out he wished them unsaid.

Simon drove on for a while, unspeaking. He clashed the gears horribly as he changed them at the foot of a hill. As the car strained slowly upwards, he said: 'I mean what I say, you know. I've kept my word to you so far. You had no call to say that.'

'I'll say what I bloody well like! Stop here.'

As the car reached the top of the hill, Charles got out and walked a few paces away down the road, taking his binoculars from their case. It was the highest point on the route; they could see down into Holywood one way, with the distant gas lights of Belfast twinkling beyond; and behind, back into Bangor. In the Lough were the navigation lights of a few ships, moving mysteriously over the coal-black sea. Charles ignored them. He stood beside Cullen and his motorbike, peering down the empty road towards Holywood, listening for the slightest sound of advancing troops. As the sound of the engines died, it became very quiet. Only a damp, insistent breeze gusted around them.

Simon sat very still in the car, his gloved hands clenched tight around the steering wheel. He had never felt hate for Charles so far, but he was coming very close to it now. This had happened to him several times before. It was the pattern of his life . . . His first lover, when he was eight, had been his father. They had made love when his mother was out at work, and Simon had thought, for a while, that this was how he would get all the love he needed in life. It brought him presents, a secret companionship, a father who no longer scowled but sighed and looked relaxed and happy because of what Simon could do for him. What Simon was happy to do for him.

Then one day Simon's father left home, without warning, for another *woman*! Simon's life had fallen apart. His father returned, occasionally, but after a few months Simon refused to have anything to do with him. Then, one day, he found out where the woman lived. He locked the doors and set fire to the house when she and his father were in it. To his astonishment no one suspected him. Indeed, so far from being found out and punished for what he had done, he was actually *rewarded*, in a way. For it turned out his father had more money than anyone suspected – enough money to enable Simon's mother to send him to a minor public school, and for him to qualify as an officer in the merchant navy.

As he travelled the world he met other lovers, and a pattern began to repeat itself.

An affair began with the thrill of discovery, the chase, the secret beddings. Always with the adrenalin-surging fear of detection, the excitement of the utterly illegal. Then, sometimes, there was affection, companionship, something that might be called love, on one side or the other. At first on Simon's side but increasingly, as he grew harder, on the other. Never, in his experience, on both. And then always, sooner or later, the relationship was corroded by fear, guilt, and the desire of one or other party to escape.

And when that happened, particularly to mature, established men, they began to realise how seriously, and absolutely, they had put themselves in Simon's power. And how great was his desire for revenge.

With Charles Cavendish, this process had only just begun. Part of Simon's mind still thought of him as a kind, generous man, a father like the one he would always have liked to have. A considerate, if not particularly exciting, lover. A man who had trusted Simon and given him a position of respect in the eyes of society.

But he was about to take it all away, as they all did in the end. Because of a woman – Deborah, Charles's wife. Simon gazed out over the dark waters of Belfast Lough, and realised suddenly that one of the ships – the one far out in the middle, with passenger lights all down its sides – was probably the ferry that Deborah Cavendish had taken to England yesterday. Simon gazed down at it with venom, wishing it had sunk or caught fire. With her on it.

But it hadn't, of course. Things like that could be made to happen, but you have to do more than just wish it . . . Simon thought about that for a while. Then he turned his eyes away from the ship, and gazed instead at the tall man in the long Ulster raincoat and military cap, who was still peering anxiously down the road towards Holywood. It was a man he had loved more than many before. Now that love was stained at the edges, with a growing mould of hatred and distrust. Soon it would be disfigured beyond recall.

Simon knew he would have to plan his own revenge . . .

'Coffee, sir?'

'What? Yes, thank you, Simon.' Charles took the cup gratefully, wrapping his hands around it for the warmth, before he sipped. It might be April but it was cold, here on the end of the quay at 3 a.m. Cold, and, for the moment, quiet. Just the wash and suck of the rising tide on the harbour walls outside, and the buzz of the gas mantle in the harbour light above his head. Waiting.

'Sergeant says 47 cars all arrived and in position, sir. Engines off and lamps doused as you said. Those with the furthest to go, for Banbridge and Donacloney, are at the front of the line, ready to be loaded first.'

'Good. No reports of the phantom army?'

'Not yet, sir, no. They must have marched down a hole in the ground somewhere.'

'I wish them joy of it.'

Charles favoured his young ADC with a brief smile, then

retreated into the haven of his own thoughts. There was no rancour now; for the moment that was behind them. Just the anticipation, the shared worry of what might happen, what might go wrong.

His main concern was that the company of British troops – the 'phantom army' as he had come to think of them – would reappear. Bangor could be so easily cut off. There were only two main roads to the west, both of which passed within a few miles of Holywood Barracks. If they were blocked, Charles would have no way of sending his guns to the UVF units who needed them, inland in North and South Down. He could only keep them here or send them south, into the trap of the Ards peninsular. Either that, or fight his way out.

But so far, there was no sign of the phantom army. Charles had stayed on the hill outside town for over half an hour and then sent two sections of scouts out to trace them, all without result. All roads were clear, so far. Either the commander in Holywood was cleverer than he had thought, or his men were on a night training exercise on their own, marching off into oblivion somewhere inland.

Since that time Charles had been round all his pickets twice, organised a load of thirty tons of coal and water to be ready for the *Clydevalley* on the quay, and supervised the arrival of his convoy of cars. Now there was a lull. The sleeping town was occupied by over a thousand tense, expectant men. All ready.

And no *Clydevalley*.

'Sir! Sir! Colonel Cavendish, sir!'

A sentry called, running out of the little harbourmaster's office at the side of the quay. The nails in his boots sent red-hot sparks leaping into the air from the cobbles as he sprinted through the dark. 'Sir! Message on the phone from Larne, sir!'

'Right, I'll come!' Leaving his coffee steaming on the harbour wall, Charles hurried to the phone, the one vital line that his engineers had left connected in the whole town.

'Cavendish here, sir!'

'Ah, good! *Karnal, yahãa sab thiik-thaak hai. Jahaaz aa gayaa hai aur hamtog saamaan utaar rahe haĩ. Puliis kii taraf se koii pareshaanii nahĩi hai.*'

Charles smiled. It was the old trick, which had been perfected in the Boer War and carried over into the UVF, of communicating crucial messages over doubtful phone lines in Hindustani. Certainly it had foxed the Boers, but in an operation in Ulster against their old comrades in arms it was a little more problematic. But still, any RIC officers or telephone operators who were listening would have had to have served in India to have a hope of understanding it. Charles had been brought up in Simla as a boy, and served again for two years in the Punjab after fighting the Boers.

'*Bahut acchaa! Jahaaz hamlogõ ke paas kitne baje pahücegaa?*'

The smile faded as his question was answered. The *Clydevalley* was late. She was still unloading in Larne and could not be expected to arrive in Bangor before 5 am at the earliest. The fact that her crew had also renamed her *Mountjoy*, in memory of the ship that had first broken the boom at the siege of Derry in 1689, impressed Charles considerably less than the fact that it would be well after daylight before he could hope to finish unloading.

And in daylight, sooner or later, someone was going to get across the fields to Holywood Barracks and give them away.

Charles put down the phone thoughtfully, and strolled out into the night. At the end of the quay the long line of cars stood, silently waiting. Their paintwork glistened dimly under the gas streetlights, and little red spots in the gloom showed along the promenade where their drivers stood patiently, smoking. Charles walked down to his company commander at the end of the line to pass on the message.

The man, a short, burly Canadian with a bristling moustache, shrugged his shoulders and grinned reassuringly.

'So? We'll have more light to see what we're doing. Should make the job quicker, eh?'

'Maybe. Just make sure the noble officers of the law don't get in the way.'

'Them?' The Canadian glanced at the little group of RIC officers standing round their Inspector on the other side of the road, loosely guarded by half a dozen UVF men. 'Not a chance. They'll be as happy to see the guns as we are.'

Charles had already spoken to the Inspector, and he thought

he agreed. There had been only the mildest protest, and the RIC presence throughout the night was probably only a matter of form, rather than real concern. A lot of RIC men had relatives in the UVF, and sympathised with its objectives. On the other hand, they had their careers to think of. If it could be proved they had at least tried to prevent the operation, their consciences would be clear. But then it only needed one, more zealous than the rest, to bring the troops down on them.

Charles wondered what he would feel if that happened. Angry, undoubtedly, if the operation failed. But if the guns were landed, and he and his men had to fight their way out, that would be a different matter. He had spent a lot of time in the last few months, training his men to combat readiness. But playacting was one thing, the stimulus of real battle another. If the gunrunning ended in a real, victorious skirmish, his men's morale would be sky-high. And, as far as Charles was concerned, the political message it would send to the Liberal government in London would be long overdue.

He had had nothing but contempt for politicians most of his life, and this last attempt to destroy the country by breaking the Union at the heart of the Empire filled him with scorn. Surely a blind fool could see that that was the one thing, the Union, that mattered above all else?

It was then, as he walked slowly back along the quay, his hands clasped behind his back, watching the dark water flowing between the hulls of the moored fishing boats, that Charles remembered again what Deborah had said. Over the past few days the words had faded from his mind, but now, in the empty waiting of the night, they came back to haunt him.

I don't care a fig for your Union.

She had seemed almost shocked herself when she said it. It was such a strange thing for her to say, she was usually so mild and unassertive.

I wonder where she is now, he thought, and whether she has come to her senses. Perhaps I will write, and persuade her to come home . . .

Charles was tired, and the old lady worried him. She must have been about seventy, and she wore a very long blue coat which was buttoned up to her neck against the cold. She also wore a wide-brimmed hat with a considerable number of flowers on it, and carried a folded pink umbrella. In her other hand, she held a dog-lead, with two long-haired dachshunds tugging eagerly at the end of it.

She walked in a deliberate, stately fashion along the promenade, with the two dachshunds whining and scrabbling ahead of her at the end of their leash.

Charles watched her with a horrible fascination. He was sure she was the first of many. It was 6 a.m. now, and the early morning sun was sparkling on the water, bathing the facades of the seafront boarding houses with exhilarating light, piercing the curtains and calling on the inhabitants to get up! come out! breathe deeply and enjoy the delights of another wonderful day!

Any moment now, these houses were going to disgorge hordes of ancient ladies and gentlemen, exercising their poodles, taking a morning constitutional, stripped to their bathing costumes for an early morning dip in the briny.

And the entire promenade looked like a hideout for car thieves.

Everywhere, the road was choked with frowsty, weary UVF men, huddled in their greatcoats, many smoking, their cheeks bristling with stubble, standing around the most comprehensive collection of motor vehicles Bangor had ever seen.

Already this was dawning on the old lady. At first she walked quickly, sniffing the crisp air. Then more slowly. She began to look around her. Finally, ten feet from some steps down to the beach, she stopped altogether. The dachshunds began to scrabble at the pavement, beside themselves with frustration. Charles walked up to her.

'Good morning, Madam. Fine day.'

'Yes.' The old lady's mouth was half open, her eyes darting this way and that with suspicion. 'Who are you?'

'Colonel Charles Cavendish, Madam, UVF. These are my men – we're here on an operation. There's no cause for concern.'

'No cause? This place – this beach is usually completely empty at this time of day.'

'I'm sure it is, Madam. But all these men are under military discipline, they won't disturb you in any way. Please feel free to exercise your dogs exactly as normal.'

'And the police? Do they know of this?'

'Oh yes, Madam. They are kept fully informed. You see the Inspector over there?' Charles pointed to where a weary RIC Inspector stood with four constables, still surrounded by a dozen UVF soldiers. He wondered why the man had not given up and gone to bed.

'I see.' The old lady drew herself up to her full height. 'Then I think I shall just go over and have a word with him.'

'Er – not just now, Madam, if you please. The Inspector is very busy and it would interfere with the duties of my men. Please just exercise your dogs as you usually do.'

The old lady thought for a moment, then, with great dignity, walked the ten yards to the steps, unleashed her dachshunds, and proceeded to walk, slowly and stiffly, after them along the beach.

Charles sighed, and a cheerful laugh met him as he walked back onto the quay.

'Having trouble, sir?' Simon said. 'I think she was expecting you to requisition the dogs!'

Charles scowled. He noticed an old gentleman of about sixty emerging from a boarding house further along. He was wearing a dressing gown and had a towel under his arm. The old man observed the car parked outside his door with extreme suspicion.

'It's no joke, Simon. The whole place is going to be cluttered up with these people in a moment and we'll be involved in crowd control. And still no sign of this damned ship!'

'Yes, sir.' A voice came from the harbourmaster's hut, where one of Charles's company commanders was peering carefully through a telescope. 'I think we've got her! There, coming round the headland! I'm almost sure that's her!'

'Where?' Charles looked for himself. The sun was on the side of the ship, and she was head-on to him, but he could see the funnel, the upperworks of a coaster, coming across the channel from Larne. It had to be, surely!

'Right. Good.' Charles spoke calmly, already regretting his brief outburst of irritation. It was bad form for a commander to lose his nerve, even for a second. 'She should be here in twenty minutes then. At least we've had plenty of time to get everything in place.'

They had been ready all night, but they went through the details once again. As they talked, the ship grew in size, from a chance to a certainty, and then she was alongside, a white sheet draped along her dark sides covering the name *Clydevalley* and proclaiming her new name – *Mountjoy!*

The sailors swung their cranes into operation. As the first car drew up alongside, a small man in civilian clothes, tired, but still vibrant with energy, ran down the gangplank.

'Colonel Cavendish?'

'Yes. Mr Crawford, sir – delighted to see you!' Charles saluted, then shook Crawford's hand. Of all UVF men, this was the one he most admired – the little determined gun-runner who had managed, against so much cautious advice, to actually hire the ships, buy the rifles in Germany, and bring them here now, running the gauntlet of the whole British Channel Fleet to do it.

But Crawford was in no mood for smalltalk. 'Same here. You got my message? Where's the coal?'

'There.' Charles waved to his left, where a platoon of men were already heaving coalsacks out of a lorry and standing ready to run up the after gangplank with them as it was lowered.

'Good. I hope it's better quality than the muck we had last night – that's what slowed us. And the water?'

'Over there.'

'Good. Listen, Cavendish, these rifles you've got: I've had 'em all wrapped ready for use. Each rifle's got a hundred rounds of ammunition with it in its pack, and they're bundled in sets of five. So if your men meet any opposition they can take them out and use them straight away. I suppose they know how to shoot?'

Charles stiffened. He had always taken any insult to his troops as reflecting on him personally. Even from Crawford he would not take that.

'Half of my men are ex-army anyway, sir, and every single one has had firearms practice, despite the lack of ordnance. This isn't the boy scouts, you know.'

A faint grin flickered briefly across Crawford's tired face. 'Glad to hear it, Colonel. I haven't come all this way to throw these guns away on fools or halfwits. They're here to be used, if need be.'

The two men's eyes met, and each saw the same hard

resolution in the other. It's really going to work, Charles thought. With men like this on our side, we can do it! Just get these guns out of Bangor to their units in the country, and the Liberal government will never be able to use the army against us without the most almighty bloodbath. And the Liberals haven't got the stomach for that. Only we have.

The next hour was one of the proudest of Charles's military career. The operation, so carefully planned, moved ahead like a parade at the Coronation. Each car, shuddering and gleaming in the morning sunlight, came up to the ship in turn, was loaded with its bundles of rifles, and moved off, to be replaced by the next. Gradually the line grew shorter, as the cars trundled away off the quay, along the promenade, and out of sight.

The first coal lorry was replaced by a second and a third, while the coalsacks were heaved into the ship in a never-ending stream. Gallons of water were pumped into the ship through a snaking hose. And all the time, Charles's men moved smoothly, knowing exactly what to do and knowing the urgency of doing it right, first time, straight away.

Inevitably, there were hiccups. Two car engines stalled, but Charles had anticipated that. The reserve mechanic section immediately pulled them out of line, and had them running again within ten minutes. A coal lorry drove over the water hose and burst it, but a second was found in five minutes. Worst of all, when a message came through from the UVF's efficient spy system that a Royal Navy destroyer had been seen steaming south from Lamlash in south-west Scotland, Crawford's engine room crew refused to sail, stating that he had paid them to come this far and no further. But within quarter of an hour Charles had found qualified replacements from within the UVF.

Charles's Lancia was the last car to be loaded. There was no time for ceremony. He shook Crawford's hand and watched, for a few minutes, as the ship steamed out again into the bay. There was no sign of the destroyer yet, but already Crawford had his crew busily altering the paintwork on the funnels, and taking in the sheet with *Mountjoy* on it, so that the *Clydevalley* had her own name back again. Under Crawford's orders, the ship sailed north, *towards* the rumoured destroyer – playing the part of an innocent coaster with nothing to hide. Charles got into the car beside Simon, and laughed.

'What's the joke?' Simon asked. He let in the clutch, and moved the car smoothly down the quay, past the dispersing UVF footsoldiers towards the small, astonished crowd of nervous Bangor residents watching from the promenade.

'No joke. I was just thinking, what a pleasure it is, to do something perfectly right for once.'

For a while Simon did not answer. He steered the car carefully past the crowd of elderly onlookers, and began the climb up the hill towards Holywood, where they had been earlier in the night. To Charles's great relief, there had been no further messages from his scouts about the 'phantom army', and motor-cycle riders had come in to tell him that the first cars had already cleared all possible bottlenecks and were away safely into the country.

Simon said: 'Morally right, do you mean, or good organisation?'

Charles glanced at him. There was something a little cold about the question, he thought, unnecessarily analytical at this time of the morning.

'Both, of course. Why do you ask?'

'No reason. I just like to know what you are thinking.' Simon flashed his dazzling smile at Charles, a little too early, a little gratuitously to create the reassurance he wanted. 'Of course, it was a brilliant piece of organisation. Crawford was hugely impressed, I could see that.'

'Good. So he should be.' Despite his pleasure, the conversation made Charles feel slightly uncomfortable. It was too important to him, to look well in the eyes of UVF High Command. It was the thing he wanted more than any other – a reputation that would take him to the top because men trusted and admired him. But it was a weakness, too, not a thing he liked others to notice. Simon knew him a little too well . . .

But Simon had no intention of being unpleasant. Charles had been successful and he hoped that the good mood that had engendered would bring to an end the unpleasantness of the last few days. He did not want to think of Charles in the way he had thought of his father, before he died. Not yet, at least. Perhaps never. He said: 'If we do have to fight with these rifles, I shall be right beside you. I would be fighting *because* of you. You know that, don't you, Charles?'

'Of course.' Charles glanced at the young man, surprised. The eyes, behind the driving goggles, were obscured, but the slightly nervous smile on the thin lips were perfectly pleasant, charming, sincere. 'I never had any doubt of it.' Even as he said it, he realised the young man had had no actual experience of soldiering, except over the past few months in the UVF. He thought, that is not the sort of thing a soldier would say. Would ever even think of saying.

'Why would *you* be fighting, Charles?' Simon asked. 'I mean, apart from believing in the cause, being against Home Rule, and all that. What would be your personal reason for going out to fight?'

'I don't know what you mean,' Charles said. He was tired. He leant back in his seat and gazed out at the hedges and fields flashing by. No police, no soldiers, no roadblocks. A perfect operation. 'I joined up because of the Union, after all. Personal ambition doesn't come into it.' But even as he had said it he was aware the words were not strictly true. He did want to be successful – if it came to a fight he hoped he would gain fame and respect from his peers. And why was that? What did he need that for?

They passed a river, with a light mist hanging over it. A heron, startled, flew up from beneath a willow with long, dignified beats of its wings. Red cattle gazed at them through the mist, with the blue hills behind. Charles thought how often he had seen this sight, how the countryside belonged to him and people like him, and how he never wanted it to change. Suddenly it came to him.

'I suppose it's because of my son,' he said, half to himself. 'Yes, that's it. I'll fight for the Union if I have to – because of Tom.'

Satisfied, he closed his eyes for a moment, and thought of the little boy cantering his pony through the fields at Glenfee beside him. The mudspattered delight on the small boy's face as he had jumped a three-foot hedge had filled Charles's heart with joy. Yes, I would die for Tom, he thought, if I had to. He'll be starting going into the classroom at St Andrew's for today's first lesson, in an hour or so. I hope the term goes well for him. Perhaps if I have time in the next few days, I'll write to him and tell him what we did today. A boy should be proud of his father.

Absorbed in the thought, he did not notice the slight tightening of Simon's lips, or the tense silence with which the young man drove for the rest of the journey. So it never occurred to Charles for a moment, that the question had been important to Simon.

Or that he had asked it, in the hope of a very different answer . . .

PART FOUR

Holloway

18

Deborah's return to Belgrave Square from the embankment by the Tower of London was a nightmare in itself. It was cold – increasingly cold, she realised, as she walked along shivering in the darkness by the river. She had been very foolish to come out in the morning with only a short blue jacket; but it had been sunny then. She tried to order a cab near London Bridge, but none would stop for her. Either they were all full, or she did not look respectable enough – her skirt was stained with mud and tar, and her face streaked with tears because she could not stop crying. Two men offered to help her but she saw instantly that the sort of help they were thinking of would be no good at all. She marched off briskly, frightened, towards Cannon Street, looking for a policeman, but there were none to be found. Then it began to rain. The men who had been following her disappeared, but she became soaking wet. At last, in a street not far from St Paul's, she managed to persuade the driver of a dilapidated hansom cab to take her home, and spent the best part of another hour sitting cold, wet, and shivering as the horse plodded slowly in front of her through the night.

When at last she reached Belgrave Square she went straight upstairs to have a hot bath, ordered a tray of soup and toast in her bedroom, and crept miserably into bed, resting her feet gratefully on the stone hot water bottle. The butler, Reeves, looked concerned, but said nothing, and luckily Jonathan was dining out, so she did not have to explain why she was so late.

But she could not sleep. The noise of the traffic kept her awake. She had her bedroom window open and all night long there was the clatter of horses' hooves, the rumble of motor cars, taxis and omnibuses. Even in the middle of the night it seemed to continue – the good-natured shouts and laughter of people returning from theatres and dinner-parties gave way to the growl and clatter of lorries and carts bringing in produce from the country for the early morning markets; and then, as the birds began to sing in the trees in the square, there were milkmen, postmen, and the first omnibuses and trams grinding their way to work.

She wondered how Londoners bore it. She remembered her mother once telling her how people spread straw in the road outside their house when she was ill, to deaden the sound of hooves and wheels, and she wished someone would do that now. But that was foolish. She was not ill. Just tense, muddled, frightened. Pregnant . . .

I am carrying a child that no one wants, she thought. I am twenty-eight years old, a married woman with a son, a fine house in Ireland, a brother-in-law who is an MP, and I am as terrified as any sixteen-year-old chit of a servant girl would be!

More, perhaps, because I have more to lose.

No, that's not right. A servant girl would have everything to lose, just as I have. It's just that my everything is bigger.

Towards morning she dozed, and dreamed of Charles. In her dream she told him about the baby and he slapped her hard across the face. Then he took a knife in his hand and walked up to a photograph on the wall. The photograph was like the big wedding photograph of the two of them in the church porch, except that in the one in her dream she was in her bridal dress but hugely, grotesquely pregnant, and she thought *Dear God, no! He's going to slash the picture of me and tear the baby out of my stomach!* But he didn't.

He slashed the picture of himself in the photograph instead.

Deborah screamed and woke up and thought, why did he do that?

It's just like what Sarah did. Turned the knife on herself, slashed a picture of a woman. But why?

Towards morning she found herself thinking more and more

of the knife that Sarah had used. She wondered how big it was, what it would feel like in her hands. She imagined Sarah going down the steps in this house, creeping into the kitchen before cook was awake – how early would that be? – taking the knife, hiding it. If it was a big knife, how would she carry it in her clothes? What would it feel like, to walk along the street with a carving knife hidden under your coat, ready to take it out and slash a picture with it?

A beautiful picture of a sensual woman. Naked, lovely – the way she herself must have appeared to Rankin.

It seemed to her an image of madness, of nightmare. Like something out of that horrible play *Macbeth* she had once seen. But even then, surely, the men had wielded the knives. And the women had gone mad . . .

When at last she fell properly asleep she did not wake up until ten o'clock, and when she rang for breakfast, a maid brought the *Observer* in with her breakfast tray.

She turned to the centre pages and saw the headlines.

THE ARMING OF ULSTER
Volunteers' Night Surprise

Stunned, she read the reports. The Ulster Volunteer Force, it seemed, had successfully landed some 20,000 rifles and three million rounds of ammunition. The police had been completely fooled, and had apparently spent most of the night trying to gain entry to the holds of a ship which contained only coal. The British Army had done nothing.

Charles, she thought. *He* has done this. There will be war.

She got up, agitated, and dressed herself without eating breakfast. I must do something, she thought, but what? There isn't anything really for me to do. He won't want me there now, especially not with the news I have to tell him. But he might be killed . . .

She was astonished to find that she actually cared. After all, he had been away so many years, and might have been shot at any time in some battle in the far side of the globe. But this was different, somehow. If there was war in Ulster it might involve her home, Glenfee, and her son Tom – he would be in the middle of it too. Even with the horrible, nagging guilt of the baby inside her she felt she belonged there, not here.

But first there was Sarah . . . After all, she had come to help her.

She went downstairs and was relieved to find Jonathan working quietly at his desk in the library. He got up as she came in.

'Ah, good morning. You have seen the news, I take it?'

'Yes. Astonishing, isn't it?'

'Indeed. Your husband has really excelled himself this time.'

There was a hint of sarcasm in Jonathan's tone which she did not like. Once, it would have attracted her – it went with the pose of the suave, successful lawyer and politician, the man who was at the heart of things and could afford to despise the uncouth efforts of soldiers and colonials. But her view of him had changed. However much of an arrogant fool Charles is, she thought, at least he is not afraid to act for what he believes in. And he is still my husband. For a few more weeks at least.

However, Jonathan was more likely to know what would be in the government's mind. 'Do you think there will be war?' she asked.

He frowned, sat down, lit a cigar. 'It is certainly a great deal more likely than it was a couple of days ago,' he said. 'I can't imagine what your husband's friends are thinking of. To an extent, the Unionists have had the public's sympathy so far, but this is hardly likely to increase that. Landing guns bought in Germany, of all places, to threaten civil war!'

'But would Asquith dare to send in troops against the UVF?'

Jonathan blew a smoke ring, still scowling. 'He's a cautious man. He will be angry, of course, but he will want to solve it by talks if he can. And there is the question of whether the troops would go if he sent them.'

'So Charles may have called his bluff?'

'Hardly! I would have thought the boot is on the other foot. It is the Unionists who are bluffing. A handful of men like that cannot expect to hold the rest of the country to ransom, however many guns they have. After all they are only rifles, not machine guns or artillery.'

'They have some of those already,' Deborah said, softly. As she spoke she felt the hairs rise slightly at the back of her neck, as they had when she had first seen the newspaper. She had known, of course, that there was a possibility of civil war for some time. The papers were full of it. But, like Jonathan, she had thought it was all hot air, a bluff, until today. Now she realised it was not. The whole province of Ulster could become a battlefield overnight, with smoking, shattered houses, maimed bodies, homeless children . . .

Charles is a soldier, he won't shrink from it. I should go home, to try to persuade him to take care.

She had a vision of his lean, patrician face looking down at her coldly, as he had done that day in his bedroom. In front of that smooth unpleasant young man Simon Fletcher. Why should I expect him to listen to me, she thought. He won't even treat me like a wife!

Jonathan got up and strolled elegantly across the room to rest his elbow on the mantelpiece above the fire. He smiled.

'Anyway, I have other news that may interest you. Good news this time.'

'Oh? what's that?'

'I met Martin Armstrong yesterday. You know, the doctor I introduced you to at Holloway. He has seen Sarah.'

Deborah shuddered as she remembered that man. There had been something . . . gross, overbearingly smug about him somehow. If she had been ill he would have been the last person she would have allowed to touch her. She wondered why Jonathan liked him.

'Thank goodness! How is she?'

'Quite well, apparently. The great thing is, Martin had a talk with her, and persuaded her to give up her hunger strike. Sarah's started eating!'

'Oh!' Deborah was amazed. There were many things she did not agree with Sarah about, but she had always respected her sister's determination. And she was not opposed to the hunger strike in the same way that she opposed Sarah's other militant activities. After all, it was non-violent, and it embarrassed men. In her present mood she thought there was something almost attractive, appealing about it. A form of self-denial, a way of punishing yourself and furthering the cause at the same time. Like a hair shirt.

If I starved myself, would that makes Charles forgive me?

It might kill the child – oh God, I don't want to do that!

But Jonathan seemed pleased with this news about Sarah. After all, Deborah thought, it would mean she was in less pain.

'So it is good news, then?' she said.

'Yes. Yes, in many ways I suppose it is. Of course it is good news.'

Deborah observed her brother-in-law curiously. He turned casually, and flicked some ash from his cigar into the flames of the fire behind him. He seemed a little anxious, guilty almost, as though he wished she were not there.

'Sarah is eating and co-operating with the authorities,' he said. 'That *is* good news, marvellous news. Though I agree, it is strangely out of character.'

He laughed softly to himself, in a way that she remembered from when she had first met him. She had liked that laugh then. It had seemed to suggest he found the world amusing, and knew a number of fascinating secrets about it which he might share, if he chose. Now she found it merely irritating.

'Yes,' she said. 'Sarah has never been one to give in easily.'

'No. But Martin – Dr Armstrong – said that he had persuaded her she was injuring herself to no purpose. He must have a silver tongue, that man.'

'Do you trust him, Johnny?' After yesterday's meeting with Rankin, Deborah thought there was no man left in the world whom she could trust. Except possibly Charles. At least he was straightforward, and predictable. And about as sensitive as a stone.

'Trust him?' Jonathan glanced at her in surprise, then looked away, into the fire. 'Yes, of course. Why should I not?'

'Oh, I don't know. He's not – exactly my sort of man. Too full of himself, I thought.'

'That's just his manner. I've known him quite a while now. He's a doctor, he understands – what people need.' Jonathan glanced at her again, searchingly this time, as though trying to read her mind. Then he stood up abruptly and crossed the room to pour himself a drink.

'So when can we see her, Jonathan?'

'We can't. That's the worst of it. Not until she's been inside a month, Martin says. Prison regulations.'

'But that's monstrous! You mean she can't have any visitors at all for a *month*?'

'Not if she's confined in the third division. She'll probably have to work, too, cleaning floors and so on. I can't see Sarah doing that willingly, can you?'

'Certainly not!' Deborah stood up, and walked across the room distractedly. She pressed her forehead against one of the cool windowpanes, thinking. She had so many troubles of her own, now. She had not known life could be so difficult. Last night she had thought she might as well die, just throw herself into the Thames. But she couldn't do that, because of her baby. A few minutes ago she had thought she should go back to Ireland, to be with Tom, and Charles, in this time of danger. But she had come to London, after all, to be with her sister. And there was something very strange in this news about Sarah.

'Jonathan, I can't believe this. It's all wrong from beginning to end. I can't understand it!'

'What can't you understand, Debbie? It's simple enough, isn't it? My good wife took it into her head to slash a famous painting with a carving knife, and as a result the courts of this country sentenced her to prison for six months in the third division. After a brief flirtation with self-starvation she has come to her senses enough to eat and obey the prison regulations, and as a result she will learn how to clean floors and wash dishes or whatever else they do. In just under a month I shall be able to go to see her. Meanwhile I have to arrange to see that odious little jack-in-office at the National Gallery to pay for the repairs to his painting. That's all there is to it. End of story.'

He tossed back his brandy and turned away to pour himself another. How bitter he is, Deborah thought. Suave. Self-assured, like all men. But bitter. Even callous.

Callous?

'Johnny, you can't mean that!'

'Can't mean that?' He held the brandy between himself and the fire, admiring the morning sunlight through the glass. It's very early in the day to be drinking, she thought. She crossed the room towards him.

'You can't mean that this is the end of the story! That you're not going to do any more to help her.'

'What else *can* I do?' Jonathan looked at her in surprise, one eyebrow raised, mocking. 'Do you want me to break down the gates of Holloway with a hammer? Lead a march of suffragettes to storm the place like the Bastille?'

'No, of course not, but . . . '

'But you would like to do just that, wouldn't you?'

'Don't be silly. I'm not a suffragette. But Johnny . . . '

'Yes?'

'I would like you to *care*!'

'Oh.'

Jonathan stepped away from her very deliberately, and stood with his back to the fire. There was still a trace of that charming, elegant smile on his face. But his voice was harsh, bitter.

'You think because I face facts that I don't care, do you? That because I accept that Sarah is a responsible woman who has brought all this upon herself that I somehow don't love her, is that it?'

'I didn't . . . '

'You haven't had to live with her, Deborah! You haven't had to put up with being constantly ignored, blamed for any and every illness or setback that she and all other women have suffered. You haven't had your advice scorned, your help thrown back in your face. Damn it, I even voted for the female suffrage once! Never again. Anyway for Sarah it wasn't nearly enough. Because they don't get the vote straight away, because the Prime Minister has to take other matters into account – there *are* other issues in politics, you know – she has to turn everything against me. She blames all men, it seems to me. She actually enjoys throwing herself into prison by committing these outrages which are the very opposite of peaceful democratic persuasion. Why can't she see that?'

'Johnny, I . . . '

'And even that's not the worst! When I offered her sympathy and love she turned against me – do you realise she believes the miscarriages were my fault? She's said that, you know – she even turned me out of her bed! I'm only a man, Deborah – I'm only human!'

As I saw the other night, Deborah thought coldly. She watched as he slammed the brandy glass down on the mantelpiece, and thought, this is another play for my sympathy. I might have fallen for it once. Not any more.

She said: 'She wanted those children desperately, Jonathan. Perhaps, when she had the miscarriages, it hurt her more than you know.'

Jonathan shook his head, bewildered. 'I *know* it hurt her, of course it did. It hurt me too. But that's no reason to reject me in that way. You're not saying she took up all this militancy because of the miscarriages, are you?'

'No. I don't know, Johnny, how can I know? I've never talked to her about it. But it is a terrible thing to do, to take up a knife like that and slash a painting – a painting of a woman! I think . . . I sometimes think that our minds are not always in our own control, you know, especially for us women. Giving birth is such a hugely emotional matter that when you want it and it doesn't happen . . . '

Jonathan laughed, mockingly. 'That is the most convincing argument for not giving women the vote that I have ever heard!'

Deborah flushed. 'Well, perhaps it is. I don't care. I only meant that – maybe that is one reason why Sarah has turned against you. She wanted babies and couldn't have them, so maybe she put all her energies into getting the vote instead. That doesn't mean it isn't a good idea for women to vote – it's just the reason why Sarah is so passionate about it, perhaps.'

'It's hardly the same thing though, is it? Babies and the vote?'

'No, but – women aren't always entirely rational, are they? And before you say it, *men* aren't either. I expect even you do things sometimes for reasons you don't fully understand, don't you? Like the other night.'

Jonathan was silent for a moment. A log fell in the fire and as he bent to pick it up with the tongs she saw again those lines by his eyes that she had noticed on her first day in London. Without looking at her he said: 'Yes, perhaps. I've already said I'm sorry for that. I suppose I do.'

'Well, then. You must be patient with her. Even more than you have been already.'

He picked up the poker and jabbed viciously at the logs,

sending a shower of sparks up the chimney.

'I tell you I *have* been patient with her, Debbie. More than you can know. A lot of men in my position . . . ' He hesitated, then seemed to change his mind. 'Well, anyway, patience is what I was talking about at the beginning, wasn't it? The prison authorities have said Sarah cannot receive any visitors for a month, and so far as I can see, there is nothing whatsoever that I can do about that *except* be patient, as you suggest. So that is what I intend to do. What else do you want?'

'I don't know.' Deborah took a deep breath. 'But whatever happens, I intend to stay here until I can get into that prison to see her. She's my sister, after all, I owe her that. And I hope that you can help me.'

Jonathan raised an eyebrow. She had the impression that he was surprised, perhaps, to see her so determined. Surprised, and also a little uncomfortable. As though he would prefer she were not there.

'Well, yes, of course. If you can find a way past the prison authorities where I have not, then good luck to you. But I warn you, it may mean that you will have to spend the rest of the month in this house. So long as you can put up with my company that long, you are welcome.'

19

Two days later Deborah came down to the breakfast room and noticed a letter propped in the middle of the table, with her name on it. She helped herself to some bacon, eggs, and mushrooms from a silver tureen on the sideboard, warmed by a small spirit lamp, and opened it.

It was from Charles.

Glenfee
Monday 27 April

My dear Deborah,
I felt I should write to you because you will surely have read in the newspapers of the highly successful landing of guns here, and will want to know that all went well with the men under my command. I am happy to tell you that they could not have behaved better. On the night of the 24th April . . .

There followed a long, detailed account of the gun-running at Bangor. Deborah read it with surprise and intense interest. Many of the facts she had already gleaned from the newspapers, but the pride and excitement with which Charles told them gave them new life. It could so easily have gone wrong, she realised. It still could, if all this leads to a real shooting war.

The letter ended:

It will be a fine tale to tell Tom when I see him next weekend, as I hope. A soldier's life really can sometimes be a matter of secret codes and midnight assignments as the storybooks tell! I hope that you too, my dear, will forgive me if I seemed a trifle abrupt at our last meeting. You and I are going through choppy waters at the moment but so long as we keep our chins up and pull together we shall not go under!

Yours as ever,
Charles

'A fresh pot of tea, madam?'

'I beg your pardon?' Deborah looked up to see Reeves, Jonathan's butler, hovering near the table with a tray in his hand. To her surprise her eyes were full of tears, whether of surprise or laughter she could not tell. She brushed them away with her sleeve, and smiled.

'Oh yes, please, if you would. And could I have a couple of slices of toast?'

'Certainly, madam.'

As Reeves disappeared, Deborah read the last paragraph again, with astonishment and – hope? What had come over the man? Did he really miss her, care even a little?

It was so like Charles to see his exploits in the UVF as an exciting schoolboy's game, something to boast about to his son. But that he should apologise to her, even briefly, was almost unheard of. Even if it was in such ridiculous boy scout language. *Choppy water, chins up and pull together* – did the silly man think their marriage was some sort of boat trip? If so, she thought, he doesn't imagine me in the stern sheets cradling a gypsy child in my arms, surely?

But he does care. He realises there's something wrong and he wants to put it right. Even if he doesn't know how wrong.

Maybe there *is* a faint hope.

What shall I do? Write back to him and put it all in a letter?

I must write something back. She picked up a pen and wrote:

My dear Charles,
I was pleased and touched to receive your letter this morning. With all the difficulty and danger of landing so many guns it must have been hard for you to find time to write . . .

And harder still to find the words, she thought sardonically. That had never been Charles's strong point. But then, it's the same for me. What in the world can I say to him of what has been happening to me, and to Sarah and Jonathan? Nothing of that.

> *I had an uneventful journey over and Jonathan is well . . .*

It was absurd. Her hand shook as she wrote the word Jonathan, and her eyes misted over with humiliation. If Charles knew how Jonathan had behaved towards her . . .

'Excuse me, madam.'

'Yes, what is it?' Reeves was in the room again, waiting discreetly for her response.

'There is a Mrs Watson at the door. She has heard, apparently, that you are here and has asked to see you.'

Not now, for heaven's sake! 'Mrs Watson? Who is she?'

'She is a friend of Mrs Becket's – her nurse, in fact. She was here most days during the past month to look after Mrs Becket during her convalescence. She is herself a member of the women's suffrage movement.'

Reeves was a butler of the highest order; he might have approved of Mrs Watson or loathed her, it was impossible to tell which from his manner. Deborah hesitated a moment. She wanted to be alone, to think about her baby and Charles. But, after all, she had come to London to help Jonathan and Sarah too, if she could.

'Of course! Show her into the front drawing room. I will be there directly.'

Mrs Watson proved to be a small, bespectacled, grey-haired woman of about fifty. She wore a long olive-green dress and matching short jacket over a cream-coloured blouse, and a small round hat with a single rose in it. On her lapel was the badge of the WSPU. She had been sitting on a chair by the window, but when Deborah came in she stood up and held out her hand.

'Good morning! I am sorry to trouble you, Mrs Cavendish, but I am instructed by the officers of the union to find out if you have any more information about the imprisonment of our colleague, Mrs Becket.'

'Oh, I see.' Deborah was taken aback by the directness of the woman's manner. 'Well, of course I am pleased to see you. Won't you sit down?'

They sat together on two upright chairs by a small table in the window, where the early morning sunlight streamed in through the leaves of the trees in the square outside. The window was open at the top, and Deborah thought how much quieter the hum of the traffic seemed in the daytime, when one was awake. She offered Mrs Watson coffee, but she refused. So this is an English militant suffragette, she thought, the first one I have ever spoken to. She seemed quite normal except rather brusque, somehow. Forceful and direct.

'Well,' Deborah said calmly. 'I don't know a great deal, I'm afraid. She was arrested last week for slashing a picture and . . . '

'Yes, of course, we know all that. I wondered if you had visited her?'

'Well no. We tried, her husband and I, but we were refused access. It seems she can have no visitors for a month . . . '

Mrs Watson smiled, and shook her head. 'She will hardly be in Holloway that long, if I know Sarah.'

The use of Sarah's first name surprised Deborah. It was not that it was wrong, exactly, but Mrs Watson was hardly the sort of woman to be on first-name terms with anyone of their class. Perhaps suffragettes regarded all women as sisters, or something.

'Well, I – I'm not sure about that,' she said slowly. 'You see, she has agreed to eat.'

'What?' The small brown eyes stared at her from behind the spectacles. Deborah repeated what she had said, and explained what Jonathan had told her last night. Mrs Watson shook her head in real surprise this time.

'I would never have thought it of her. I don't believe it!'

'Do you mean you expect her to starve herself to death?'

'To death?' Mrs Watson looked at her scornfully. 'No, of course not, not to death. It is a hard cruel business but one only has to put up with it for a few days, a week at most, then they let you out. Unless of course she is being force-fed.'

'Oh no, I don't think so. Dr Armstrong told Jonathan nothing about that. They would never do anything so dreadful to a woman like her, anyway, would they?' Deborah flushed. 'I mean, from what I have heard about these things in Ireland, I thought they only did that sort of thing to poor women.'

'You're lucky in Ireland. They've only force-fed two women there.' Mrs Watson's eyes fixed themselves on Deborah's face, thoughtfully. 'And we thought they had given up forced-feeding in England, too, in favour of this Cat and Mouse business, until a month or so ago. Then it started again, in one or two cases. There seems to be no rhyme or reason, just chance and spite . . . Dr Armstrong, you say?'

'Yes. He's a friend of Jonathan's. He works in Holloway prison sometimes. Indeed, we met him there.'

There was a silence. Mrs Watson continued looking at Deborah, and Deborah had the uncomfortable impression that she was being measured by someone who did not entirely approve of what she saw. When she had finished staring, Mrs Watson stood up abruptly and walked across the room to the fireplace. Then she turned and came back and said: 'Are you very fond of your sister, Mrs Cavendish?'

Deborah flushed. It was an insolent question and she resented it. 'Well yes, of course. I came over from Ireland especially to help her, if I can.'

'But you are not a suffragette?'

'No. I think women should have the vote but I don't believe that throwing stones or slashing pictures is the way to go about getting it, that's all. It just puts men's backs up.'

Whereas if you're nice and reasonable to them they smile at you and speak kindly to you and get you pregnant and then abandon you, a bitter dissident voice hissed in her mind. If you'd been Sarah you would have just picked up a knife months ago and cut Rankin's throat with it and slashed everything in sight and then . . .

Don't be silly! Your own stupid misfortune is nothing to do with Sarah or politics.

It's the only thing that's important, though, isn't it? *What am I going to do?*

'How would you get the vote, then?'

Deborah frowned at the woman, collecting her thoughts with

an effort. This is going badly, she thought. I agreed to see her because I thought she would tell me more about Sarah, but all that happens is that *she* interrogates *me*

'Well, by persuasion, peaceful, rational argument. Convincing men of the logic of our case, I suppose.'

'Do you think we haven't tried that?' Mrs Watson smiled ironically. 'Men are not logical rational beings, my dear – surely you've found that out for yourself by now?'

The remark was meant, probably, as a joke, but it stung Deborah too sharply to be funny. First Charles, then Rankin – now even Jonathan had let her down. Tears sprang unwanted to her eyes.

Mrs Watson noticed, surprised. Clearly this woman was softer, less forceful than her sister. In a gentler voice she said: 'I beg your pardon, my dear, I have no right to come here and browbeat you. But I had hoped you might have more news.'

It was even worse to be pitied by a stranger than interrogated by one. In a high, sharp voice Deborah said: 'I told you! No one is harming her at all. Jonathan has heard from the prison doctor and she has agreed to eat and obey the regulations and is serving out her sentence as best she can.'

'Yes. I know that is what you said.' Mrs Watson glanced away from her, out of the window. She drummed her fingers thoughtfully on the table, and for a moment Deborah thought she was about to get up. Then she changed her mind and said: 'Is that the picture you have of your sister, then? An obedient woman, sweeping the floor in prison?'

Deborah stared at her, and saw that behind the thin face and tight lips there was a glint of humour.

'No,' she smiled. 'I suppose not. People have said many things about Sarah but I have never heard anyone call her *obedient*!'

'Exactly. That is what worries me. What can they have done to her in there, to change her so suddenly?'

Deborah shuddered. She had read of women being beaten, kicked, hosed down with cold water in prison. Surely not Sarah? She pushed the vision away and said: 'They didn't do anything. Dr Armstrong persuaded her, that's all. He told Jonathan.'

'Dr Armstrong, yes.' Mrs Watson looked at her again,

carefully. Deborah had the impression she was making up her mind about something. 'You've met the man, you say. What did you make of him, Mrs Cavendish?'

Deborah thought. 'Well, I suppose I would call him pompous, to tell you the truth. A big, heavy, rather fat man, short of breath. Very full of himself.'

'The sort of man your sister would take to easily?'

'I shouldn't think so, no.'

'Then how did he persuade her to obey orders and eat?'

'I don't know!' The conversation was beginning to make Deborah feel ill. She had a vision of that big fat man with his thick fingers leaning over Sarah in a prison cell, doing – what exactly?

But Jonathan knew the man and trusted him. Feebly, she said: 'Jonathan said he persuaded her that she was only harming herself to no purpose.'

Mrs Watson took a deep breath. 'Mrs Cavendish, I am going to tell you something about your Dr Armstrong. Something that is known already to several women in the WSPU, though I believe not to Sarah. I have only just found out about it myself. I am afraid it is not pleasant.'

Deborah said nothing. She waited, sitting at the little round table in the window of her sister's house, transfixed by this forceful, businesslike woman who had walked into her life just a few minutes before. She had a feeling that maybe she should get up and leave the room because what she was going to hear was something she was going to regret, but she did not move. She had so many tragedies in her life, one more could not matter.

She heard the clock on the mantelpiece tick and the voice of Reeves giving instructions to a maid somewhere outside in the corridor, and still Mrs Watson's eyes watched her, as though gauging for the last time whether it was wise to speak.

Then she said: 'Three days ago we received a complaint, at the WSPU, from a woman who had been imprisoned in Holloway. The woman was not a suffragette, she was a criminal, a petty thief. She had been imprisoned for stealing children's clothes.'

'From a shop, you mean?'

'No, from the children themselves. She and her partner, a man, would lure the children away from their nannies, in Green Park or Kensington Gardens or other places like that. They would offer the child a sweet or something and then, when the child was out of sight of the nurse, they would strip it and run off, leaving the child half-naked. Then they would cut all labels out of the clothes, dye them, and sell them in the market.'

Deborah shook her head, puzzled. 'How awful! But – what has this to do with Dr Armstrong?'

'Nothing, directly. But this was not the first time this woman had been convicted and she was sent to prison for some time. Her man was imprisoned too. And the problem was that the pair had three children – three girls. The eldest was not yet twelve, and so, of course, when the parents were imprisoned the children were unable to care for themselves. This is where Dr Armstrong came into the picture.'

'How?'

'Well, he is a doctor at Holloway and he is also on the board of a charitable institution for the children of prisoners. So apparently, when the mother arrived in Holloway, he arranged for her three daughters to be taken there.'

'So – what is wrong with that?'

'Nothing, of course – but wait. Remember, the mother was sent to prison for four years, and we did not hear of this story until she was released a few days ago. She went to collect her children – and it was because of the state she found them in that the poor woman came to us.'

'Why? Were they badly fed or clothed? They could not expect all that much, after all, I suppose, from a charitable children's home. I have cared for the poor myself, Mrs Watson. I have seen these places.'

'I see.' Mrs Watson looked at her with increased respect. 'Well, then, you will understand that these children had not been used to much, Mrs Cavendish. They were children of the streets, after all, and their mother was a criminal. But, in fact, they were well clothed and fed; that was not the problem. The problem was that while they were living in the institution they had been going out in the evenings to work, to earn that food and clothing. And the work they did . . . ' Mrs Watson sighed, and looked down at her hands a moment, before saying: 'They had been earning their living with their bodies, you see. They went to a house where they were visited by men, most evenings, and these little girls had been taught to – well, you can imagine, I suppose. It seems that there are men – quite a number of men – who will pay a lot of money to deflower and – abuse young girls in this way. By the time the mother found them her daughters were quite used to this; they were proud of it, even, because of the money they earned. The eldest was fifteen by this time, the youngest – eleven.'

Mrs Watson paused, and again Deborah was aware of the silence in the room. Occasional sounds – the ticking of the mantelpiece clock, the clop of a horse's hooves outside – oppressed her. And there was something else: a singing in her ears, the pounding of her own blood in a pulse at her neck. She knew these things happened, of course – so why was she blushing? *I* am like these girls, she thought. They could have been me!

'And you say that . . . Dr Armstrong arranged this?'

'It is possible. We are not quite sure. He is a careful man, he covers his tracks well. But since we heard this story some of our ladies have investigated this charitable institution and it is clear that such stories are not uncommon. He is the doctor there and has treated some of the girls for venereal disease. They wrote a report for our files, which I have just read. It is hard to imagine he does not know exactly what goes on.'

'My God!' And Jonathan knows this man – he introduced me to him, he calls him his friend. He has asked *him* to talk to Sarah! 'Have the police been told?'

'Not yet, no. It is a difficult matter, you see. The complainant, the girl's mother, is a convicted thief, and the girls themselves want nothing to do with her. They seem to like their work, that is the worst of it. They did not want to go home with her. They said they could earn more money by themselves. That is the cunning of it, you see – many of the girls in this place are the daughters of convicted women who have very loose morals anyway, so the parents are usually *pleased* because of the money the children bring in. This is the first time any parent has dared to object.'

'But this is a scandal! It's monstrous!'

'Yes, of course.' Mrs Watson looked at Deborah quite simply across the table. She did not look pleased or triumphant, nor did she apologise for the appalling story she had told. Her lined, resolute face looked quite calm, composed. Thin lips pressed closely together, grey hair, brown quiet bespectacled eyes watching curiously for Deborah's reaction. Her expression said: this is the truth, lady, this is what life is like. How are you going to face it?

'But why are you telling me? I mean – did Sarah know this?' Deborah suddenly thought of the knife again. If Sarah had known about something like this, that knife would begin to make sense. If I myself had a knife, Deborah thought, and that Dr Armstrong were here now . . . but I wouldn't know what to do, I wouldn't have the strength or courage. Anyway they weren't my children. If they had been . . .

'Well, I am not sure.' Mrs Watson looked suddenly embarrassed, hesitant. 'Certainly, she knew nothing of the story I have just told you. She couldn't have. We only learnt about it after she was arrested. But nonetheless,on the last day I saw her – Monday – she did ask me about this suffragette investigation. She must have heard something about it, I suppose, so I told her what I knew. It was all in fairly general terms because I hadn't read the files properly then. But now I think of it, she went very quiet. I didn't think anything of it at the time. But since then I have consulted the files more closely, and the name of this Dr Armstrong you mentioned was in there. Under suspicion, no more.'

Thoughts were crowding into Deborah's head, too quickly for her to make sense of them all. She said: 'And two days later she took that meat-knife and slashed the picture?'

'Yes, she did. But that was a political act, it had nothing to do with . . . '

'Are you sure?'

'Yes, of course.'

Silence. Why does this woman look so cool, as though she knows everything and feels nothing, Deborah wondered. Why did she tell me this story, anyway? Oh God, Jonathan. *What did he know?*

The blood singing in her ears was worse now. To calm

herself, Deborah got up and walked across the room, twisting a little piece of her skirt unconsciously between her fingers. She felt her horror and disgust turn to anger suddenly – it was a blessed relief. She turned and almost shouted at Mrs Watson.

'You were supposed to be looking after my sister, weren't you, Mrs Watson? As a sort of paid nurse? And you knew she was still weak from her last stay in prison. But you told her this horrible story about children being prostituted by this monster Armstrong who is a friend of her husband's—'

'I didn't say that! Please, Mrs Cavendish, credit me with some sense!'

'I beg your pardon?'

'I only answered her questions in the most general terms because she asked me, that's all. I didn't even know the name Armstrong at the time and I certainly had no idea that he was a friend of her husband. Of course, if I had known that, I would have been much more careful about what I told Sarah, given her state of health and knowing that she is, well . . . '

'She is what?'

'An impulsive, strong-minded woman, given to dramatic, forceful action on behalf of the movement.'

'Exactly!'

The two women stared at each other. The anger was still trembling in Deborah and she had an ominous feeling that there was more to this, more than Mrs Watson had already told her. Why are all men so foul, she thought. And why is this woman so calm? There are more threads to this story than I can follow yet. *Where does Jonathan fit in?*

'You don't think my brother-in-law knew anything of this? You're not saying that, are you? It would be terrible!'

'No.' Still that infuriating calm. And something else – almost *pity* in the older woman's expression. 'I have no reason to think that. Mrs Cavendish, I am sorry if I have shocked you.'

'Then why did you tell me this?'

'Why? Because of your brother-in-law's faith in Dr Armstrong, Mrs Cavendish. He said, if you remember, that Armstrong had spoken to your sister and persuaded her to abandon her hunger-strike. And you implied that your brother-in-law believed this because he trusted Dr Armstrong. I had to make it clear to you why I do *not* believe it. Your brother-in-law has nothing to do with this story, as far as we know.'

As far as we know, Deborah thought bleakly. But it's not impossible, either. I could believe anything after the way he behaved the other night. She felt herself trembling, and clutched the back of a chair for support. Mrs Watson watched her, choosing her words carefully.

'As I said, I had no idea before I came into this room that Mr Becket even knew Dr Armstrong. But when you told me he did, I felt it was my duty to make it clear that this friend of your brother-in-law's is not a trustworthy character. Especially since he claims to have persuaded Sarah to give up her hunger-strike. Added to which we both agree that it seems strange that Sarah should give up her hunger-strike for no apparent reason. That's all. I don't know why she's given it up, if she has. I'm just saying that I don't understand it and I'm not sure I believe it. And, since she's your sister, I believe you should know.'

'Yes, of course. But . . . ' Once, when she was young and on holiday in Ulster, Deborah had gone for a swim in what she had thought was a calm mill-pond, only to go too near the leat and be caught in the swirl and rush of conflicting currents which swung her this way and that and threatened to suck her under and drown her. The same sense of shock and panic seethed in her now. Charles had thrown her a rope to rescue her then, it was the first year she had met him. But this time . . . 'Why should Dr Armstrong lie to Jonathan? Even if he is a scoundrel as you say he has no reason to do that. This business of these poor abused girls has nothing directly to do with my brother-in-law or Sarah, has it?'

'Not so far as we know, no. But I wish now that I had not told Sarah about it. I assure you I would never have done so if I had thought there had been any connection with anyone she knew.'

'I see.' Deborah wandered distractedly up and down the room for a moment longer, then sat down abruptly at the little table by the window opposite Mrs Watson. 'No, I'm sure you wouldn't. I'm sorry. You meant well, I'm sure.' She passed her hand distractedly across her brow. 'But if you're saying Sarah hasn't given up her hunger-strike, then that means she'll be released soon, doesn't it? Otherwise she'll die.'

'It does. And, to do men credit, they have not so far been barbaric enough to let any woman starve herself to death.'

'So if I stay in London for a few more days I may see her after all. And then I can ask her if she knew anything about this dreadful business of Dr Armstrong – that is, if she is strong enough . . . '

'Yes, perhaps.' A slight frown creased Mrs Watson's forehead. 'Unless, of course . . . '

'What?'

'Unless of course she *has* given up her hunger-strike. That's what worries me. Not because Dr Armstrong talked to her, but for some other reason. In which case your brother-in-law is quite right, she will stay in prison and no one will know what is happening to her for at least a month. And she was not a strong woman when she went in.'

Deborah searched the dark brown bespectacled eyes of the older woman for reassurance, but found only, beneath the surface calm, a reflection of her own anxiety and confusion. I shall have to find out more about this, she thought, before I go home to Charles.

'Oh dear,' she said at last. 'Perhaps I will come to the WSPU offices with you, if I may. I should like to have a look in those files.'

20

Light began to filter through the curtains. As it did so, it caught the colours of the material, and patterns of orange, green, yellow and blue appeared on the ceiling. Faintly at first, then more strongly as the sun came up. Sparrows began their relentless chirp outside, and dustbins clattered as the cooks in the hotel across the yard began their morning's work.

Five o'clock. Ruth Harkness sighed, and sat up in bed. It was Wednesday, her day off. She had hoped to sleep in until six, but in fact she had scarcely closed her eyes all night. If only George were back, she thought. He would know what to do. But her fiancé was visiting his sick mother in Berkshire, so he would not be back until Monday. Ruth had to decide on her own.

She gazed at the swirling patterns on the ceiling. The curtains were the first things she had made when she moved into her own two-room flat, and she had bought the best material she could afford from the market. When she had discovered the way the sunlight glowed through them and filled the room with colour, she had been delighted. The colours were a symbol of everything the flat meant to her – security, prosperity, a good job, the hope of a happy marriage in the future. Her own private rainbow . . .

Now all that was in danger, because of this wretched suffragette, Sarah Becket. For the hundredth time Ruth went over the interview with Dr Armstrong in her mind. She wanted to believe him. It was enormously tempting. He was a man, a doctor, a figure of authority. All you have to do is believe me, young woman, his voice said in her mind. Say nothing, and nothing will happen to you. You will keep your job. I may even put in a word to help you get promotion. You will have your happy home, your security, your marriage.

Founded on a lie.

The sun outside was obscured by a cloud, and the colours in Ruth's bedroom faded. She saw the damp stains discolouring the ceiling, the peeling wallpaper in the corner which she had tried to paste back a dozen times and which always came loose. So much work to do, so much money to save before she could really afford somewhere decent. And there, on the wall, the framed and embroidered text which George had given her for her birthday. '*He that putteth his trust in The Lord, shall never be confounded.*'

If I keep my mouth shut and do nothing, I shall be damned, Ruth thought. Perhaps nothing will happen and I shall marry and be prosperous but I shall know, all my life, that I turned and passed by on the other side of the road. I will have ignored, not an injured Samaritan, but little orphan girls who are being corrupted and abused, and a woman who is being forcibly fed.

But she's a madwoman, the doctor's voice inside her said. A liar, a slanderer, a sufferer from paranoid delusions. A woman who could perfectly well eat if she chose to. A militant suffragette – *Oh, leave me alone! I don't know which is right! What am I going to do?*

Ruth flung the bedclothes aside, got out of bed, poured some water into a basin from a jug beside her bed, and began to wash herself briskly. The cold water revived her. For a moment she felt fresh and healthy and forgot all about the torments in her mind. Then as she was soaping her neck and under her arms she caught sight of her breasts in the little cracked mirror and thought: Oh no. This is what the doctor was thinking of when he looked at me that time. He thought of me as a naked woman to exploit as he does those poor little girls.

It's because of that look that I *know* he's not telling the truth. It's not proof, any more than Sarah Becket has clear proof. I just *know*.

As she does.

Ruth got dressed and had breakfast and did her housework and went shopping – and still the dilemma was there. What to do. Who to approach for help. Which choice was the right one.

She boiled herself an egg at lunchtime but she could not eat it because it was slightly underdone and the white reminded her of the bile that had come out of Sarah Becket's mouth after the forcible feeding last night. Sarah had continued retching long after all the soup had come up. That woman will die of it if we go on, Ruth thought. Bromide treatment or not. She is being tortured. And I am one of the torturers.

At one o'clock she got up, put on her coat and a long scarf over her head like a factory girl, went out into the street and caught a tram. Half an hour later she was in Clements Inn. She walked up and down it for another half hour.

Each time she came near number 4, she screwed up her courage to go in, and failed. It was a double-fronted shop entrance with plate glass windows either side and a large clock projecting out into the street above the heads of the shoppers. The window frames and doors were painted blue and slightly tattered, as though they had been damaged by vandals. On the face of the clock, in place of the numbers and across the middle, were the letters VOTES FOR WOMEN. And in the shop window were dozens of posters, books, leaflets and newspapers, all proclaiming more or less the same message. There were also hats, scarves and handkerchiefs in the suffragette colours of purple, white and green.

As Ruth went past she saw a number of women going in and out. A few were well-dressed, but most, she saw with relief, wore quite ordinary, even dowdy clothes. There were a number of young girls who looked more like shop assistants or factory workers than anything else, as well as middle-aged matrons and the sort of women who might well have been running a small hospital or giving orders to half a dozen servants in their own homes. The distinguishing feature, Ruth thought, was the business-like, purposeful air they all had. A cheerful energy which suggested that there were a dozen vital things that had to be done and they all had to be finished *now*.

Ruth felt superfluous and embarrassed. I don't belong in there, she thought, I'm not like them at all. I might agree with their aim but certainly not with their methods. Most of them are militants – criminals, for heaven's sake!

They don't abuse children, though . . .

The fifth time she walked past, she turned and went in.

The door did not have a bell that rang when it opened, and nobody looked up when she came in. The inside of the shop was filled with a number of tables, piled high with books, newspapers, pamphlets, leaflets and clothes. Around and behind the tables women were writing, typing, reading or talking busily. They all seemed to belong and know exactly what they were doing.

Ruth almost walked straight out again.

'Ah, good. Lucy Shaldon?'

'Sorry?'

Ruth turned and looked into the face of a cheerful, fair-haired young woman of about twenty. There was a welcoming smile on her face and she was holding out a large bundle of copies of a newspaper called *The Suffragette*. She smiled and said: 'These are yours.'

'Why?' Ruth stared at the newspapers in confusion.

'To sell, of course.' The young woman frowned. 'I'm sorry, you *are* Lucy Shaldon, aren't you?'

'No. No, I'm not.'

'Oh, I do apologise. I've been waiting for her for twenty minutes and I was told she was tall, like you, so I just assumed . . . ' She laughed, a friendly, happy laugh that reassured Ruth despite her embarrassment. 'You must think I'm a fool. I haven't seen you here before, that's all. Can I help you?'

'Yes. I want . . . ' What did she want, really? Ruth had spent so much of her energy just deciding to walk through the door that she had not worked out exactly what she would say when she got in. She flushed and said: 'I want to talk to someone about Sarah Becket.'

'Oh.' It was the young woman's turn to look surprised. 'But I'm afraid you can't, you see. She's in prison.'

'I know. I've seen her there. That's what I want to talk about.'

'You've seen her in *prison*? Good heavens, I didn't realise. When did you get out?'

'I didn't, exactly. I mean, I work there. Look, can I talk to someone – I mean, someone who knows her? It's very important.'

'Yes. Yes, of course. Just stay there.'

The young woman disappeared into the depths of the shop, and Ruth stood awkwardly beside the table with the pile of newspapers on it. All around her the women continued to talk and work energetically. Ruth glanced at the newspaper and saw the banner headline CABINET OF TORTURERS printed above a number of small photographs of the Prime Minister, Asquith, with Churchill and Lloyd George and his other government colleagues. She shuddered, and glanced away through the window. Two police constables were strolling along the pavement, observing the suffragette shop with considerable interest.

Those are my people, she thought desperately. What am I doing in here? This is all wrong.

Her feet began to edge their way towards the door. Then, when she had almost reached it, the cheerful fair-haired young woman reappeared, marching briskly towards her. Behind her was a middle-aged lady with glasses, and another woman. All three of them looked anxious and excited.

'There she is, Mrs Watson,' the young woman said. 'Over there by the door!'

'You say you saw her yesterday evening?'

'Yes. I told you once already.'

'At what time?'

'Four o'clock, about. When we force fed her.'

Alice Watson shuddered and, beside her, Deborah Cavendish's eyes misted over with tears. The conversation was extraordinary, but so, from Deborah's point of view, was the entire day. She had begun the day thinking about her letter from Charles, and spent most of the rest of it in the WSPU headquarters with Alice Watson, looking through their files on prostitution. The evidence, she thought, was depressing, but lacking in precise, relevant details. The name of Dr Armstrong cropped up once or twice, but there was nothing definite, nothing completely damning that would have held up in court. She began to wonder if Mrs Watson was blaming the man unjustly.

She had come to the suffragette headquarters with Mrs

Watson expecting long tiresome arguments about the rightness of militant tactics, and had prepared what she thought were clear reasons why burning post boxes, smashing windows, and pouring weedkiller on golf courses – not to mention slashing the *Rokeby Venus* – were bad ideas. But none of that had been necessary. The women she had met had been friendly, open, talkative – but also brisk, extremely busy, and unnervingly sure of themselves. Since she was Sarah's sister, and had come with Alice Watson, they assumed that she supported their cause. In any case, to them, the necessity for militant action was so transparently obvious that it was not worth discussing. More important were the day's press, the points they were going to make in speeches that afternoon, and the most cogent articles from *The Suffragette*.

When she had read everything Alice Watson had to show her, Deborah sat for a while in an upstairs room, staring into space and thinking. She supposed she ought to be thinking about Sarah. Clearly Sarah was in a terrible position if this Martin Armstrong was as bad as Mrs Watson thought. But Deborah didn't see what *she* could do about it, other than warn Jonathan. And then what? The problem kept drifting away into the distance, and Deborah thought instead about Rankin walking away from her with his hands in his pockets, and the baby, growing inside her.

I am surrounded by women who might help, she thought despairingly, but I daren't say a word. I don't know any of them well enough and anyway, they might despise me. None of them would be so foolish or immoral as to do what I've done and get found out. And what help could they offer except tea and sympathy and gossip later behind my back?

I'm on my own.

No, you're not. There's me.

For the first time ever she thought of the baby inside her as the person it would become. It would have blue eyes at first and black hair, and then maybe the hair would stay black and the eyes shade to green. The skin would be sallow and smooth like Rankin's – and, whatever I've done, it will love me.

We're on our own, my baby. You and me against the world. *Oh God what will Charles say when I tell him?*

Suddenly, a young fair-haired woman, Mary Lemprier, to whom she'd been introduced earlier, burst into the room. She was bubbling with astounding news. A prison wardress from Holloway was actually *downstairs*, and she had seen Sarah Becket! Deborah gazed at her vaguely, and then dragged herself back into the present. This is what it is like, she thought, I remember with Tom. The longer the pregnancy goes on the more distant everything around you becomes. Of course it's very important that someone has news of Sarah but I can't feel it.

A few minutes later she found herself sitting with Mrs Watson in a little gloomy office at the back of the building, staring at the newcomer.

The girl did not fill Deborah with confidence. She sat on the edge of her chair as though she were about to leave. She wore a long black coat and had a scarf over her head. She looked unusually big, almost mannish, with a slightly stooped back that conveyed an air of embarrassment. But she also seemed pathetically anxious to speak; and, if her story was true, her embarrassment was hardly surprising.

Mrs Watson asked: 'Why did you do that?'

'Do what?'

'Forcibly feed Sarah Becket.'

'Why? 'Cause she refused food, o' course. And because it's doctor's orders.'

'Doctor's orders?'

'That's what I come to tell you about.'

Slowly, hesitantly, Ruth Harkness told her story. Of the two women in front of her she preferred the older lady, the woman in the green dress with the round glasses and grey hair. She had a manner like an old-fashioned schoolteacher, Ruth thought; she would stand no nonsense but you knew where you were with her, you could trust her. The other one, the fair-haired lady in the fine grey dress, upset her. She had been introduced to Ruth as Sarah Becket's sister, but she was as unlike the defiant woman in prison as she could be. She thought of Sarah Becket as slim, haggard, with a pale suffering face and haunting dark eyes that could flash and mock and make you tremble; this woman opposite her now seemed quiet, anxious, almost afraid of what Ruth had to say.

Ruth described the forced feeding, and told them what Sarah

had said to Dr Armstrong about her husband, and what she had heard from the women in the collecting cell about the house in Red Lion Street, Hackney; and how she had followed her husband to his premises in Kensington and seen Dr Armstrong come out and Jonathan stay in.

'But why did she go there?' Mrs Watson asked. 'I mean, what led her to suspect him in the first place?'

'She said she got a letter, ma'am, from some prostitute. Warnin' 'er to keep you suffragettes away from Dr Armstrong because her husband was involved.'

'Dear God,' Deborah breathed. 'The poor thing!'

'Did she say where that letter is now?' Mrs Watson asked.

'No, ma'am. Didn't mention it.'

'Pity,' Mrs Watson said. 'Nevertheless, that explains it.' She glanced at Deborah.

'Explains what?'

'Why she didn't tell me what she was planning to do. Why she slashed the picture and got herself arrested instead of talking to me first. If we could have exposed the person who was running these bawdy houses it would have had enormous political impact and done far more for our cause than slashing the painting. But if – God forbid – Sarah believed her husband was involved in any of this, then of course she would have been shocked. Emotionally disturbed, perhaps. She wouldn't have been able to control what she was doing.'

'Dear God!' Deborah sat down, stunned. She didn't want to believe it but it was too likely, too inescapably true. All men betrayed their women, in the end. Even Jonathan. Poor, foolish Sarah. No wonder she had taken up the knife. She must have been so shocked she couldn't think what else to do.

'That's what the doctor says, too.'

'What?'

Ruth's flat tones dragged their attention back to her. 'Dr Armstrong. He says she's emotionally disturbed. Suffering from paranoid delusions, he calls it. It's his way of saying her whole story's a pack of lies. That's why he says she's insane.'

As Ruth explained Dr Armstrong's diagnosis, and the subsequent conversation she had had with him about it. Deborah leaned forward slowly on the table, resting her head in her hands. Tears were trickling down her cheeks but she made no effort to wipe them away. Her eyes were still fixed on Ruth.

'It's monstrous,' Mrs Watson said. 'If Sarah *is* mentally ill he should release her immediately!'

'He's got an explanation for that, too,' Ruth said. She explained about the bromide treatment.

'But that – bromide?' Deborah said. 'Surely that's not a treatment for mental illness?'

'Dr Armstrong says it is. It calms 'er down, he says. Stops her being hysterical, like.'

'But I remember – a woman was driven mad by it recently. I read it in *The Times*. She was being treated with bromide for something and she became delirious because she was given too much. Her husband thought she was losing her mind. It's poison – she might have died if they hadn't stopped.'

'I don't know nothing about that,' Ruth said. 'I think Armstrong gives it to 'er so that she don't kick so much when 'e shoves the tube in to force feed her. But it didn't do 'er much good last night, because she sicked it all up again.'

'Oh my God!' Deborah was on her feet again. 'He may have damaged her already, for all we know! The man's trying to poison her!'

'We don't know that for certain, Mrs Cavendish,' Mrs Watson said. 'But it is a possibility. He might do that, if he is truly guilty of introducing these children to brothels, and afraid that he will be found out.' She turned to Ruth. 'Does he think that only Sarah knows about this?'

'That's what she told 'im, yeah. Only 'im and me 'eard what she said. And he's explained to me that it's all her madness, her paranoid delusion, 'e calls it.' Ruth paused, and looked at the two women in front of her cautiously. 'I come 'ere today because I didn't really believe that, and although I don't approve of militant suffragettes, I think child prostitution is worse. What I want to know is, do you think this story is true, or is Sarah Becket mad, like what 'e says she is?'

'Of course she's not mad!' Mrs Watson said. 'And I can assure you, young woman, that this story of the child prostitutes is absolutely true. Some of us have been investigating it for some weeks. Only definite evidence to link Dr Armstrong with some of the premises was missing – and now it seems we have it. I am deeply grateful to you.'

Ruth nodded. She looked at Deborah carefully. 'I'm sorry, Mrs Cavendish. I know it sounds dreadful, like, but it's true.'

'It's more than dreadful!' Deborah said. 'Her husband, an MP – to do that with a child!'

There was a long silence. There was the sound of typing, busy discussion, and laughter from the rooms all around them. The three women looked at each other, and shared Deborah's grief.

At last Mrs Watson said: 'There is only one way to find out the truth of this, and that is to get Sarah out of prison. And if she is being force-fed and possibly poisoned as well, as you say, then the sooner we do that the better.'

'But we can't!' Deborah said. 'You heard this girl, she's a prison wardress and she ought to know. Sarah's being kept in for six months! And we aren't even allowed to visit her, let alone get her out!'

'We'll run a campaign,' said Mrs Watson. 'We'll tell this story on the front page of *The Suffragette*. We'll have mass demonstrations and a march on Holloway. They'll *have* to let her out!'

'She'll be dead by then.' Ruth's hard, flat voice brought them up short.

'What do you mean?'

'I've seen 'er. She's fainting away already, with the strain of it. She can't keep any food down. Any other doctor would let her out, but not Armstrong, not if this story's true, as you tell me it is. He'd rather have 'er die, wouldn't 'e, and then the evidence is gone. And without the evidence, your story in *The Suffragette* would be all lies and no proof, wouldn't it? Libel they calls it – he could sue you for thousands. And *I* can't tell yer if her story is true or not, I can only tell yer what she told me. If she's dead, 'e'll just say she was mad, and sign a paper to prove it.'

'So what do we *do*, then?' Deborah asked. 'Even if she is a little mad, even if part of her story is wrong. Sarah's in terrible danger. Surely there's some way we can get her out?'

'From 'Olloway?' Ruth shook her head, slowly. 'You ain't never been a prisoner, 'ave yer, Mrs Cavendish? I've been over every inch of that building and I can assure you there's ain't no way anyone can escape. No way at all.'

'Well, I don't know about that,' Mrs Watson said, slowly.

They both turned and looked at the small, governessy woman in surprise. There was a small, grim smile on her face.

'You may not realise it, Miss Harkness, but militant suffragettes are extremely resourceful people. Some of us have got into the House of Commons, and 10 Downing Street, and even Buckingham Palace before now. And we have put quite a lot of thought into how to get out of prisons, as well as into them. It *is* difficult, I grant you, but then we have never before had the advantage of a prison wardress on our side.'

She paused. The little beady eyes behind the round glasses weighed up the younger woman carefully. Watching her, Ruth Harkness had the feeling that she was back at school, in her headmistress's study.

Except that her headmistress had never had quite the same glint of mischief behind her spectacles.

'If you *are* on our side, that is, Miss Harkness,' Alice Watson went on. 'I am asking you to risk your job. But it is, after all, a case of saving a woman's life.'

21

Suffer . . .

It was so hard to write, now. It had taken Sarah most of the morning to mix the paste. First she had to collect the dirt from her cell floor with bare hands – and there was very little of that because every day she was made to sweep out her cell with a dustpan and brush. She had to scrabble with cracked fingernails around the feet of the bed, and in the corner where there was a crack between the flagstones and the woodlice lived, to find any. Then, when she made a little pile, she scooped it into a hollow in the flagstones, and crumbled bits of the grey gritty prison soap on top of it. Then she took the metal cup which was chained to the wall and poured water into her palm.

Water . . .

Her eyes focused on it, yearned for it. Her tongue, which had begun to swell in her mouth, touched her dry cracked lips and her hand moved towards her mouth.

She stopped. Deliberately, she knocked the cup over.

She had begun the thirst strike last night and this was her first crisis.

She watched the water trickle down the walls and flow over the floor and she bent down on her hands and knees and did not lick it up. Instead, she brushed it away from the hollow in the floor where her pile of soap and dirt was, and only added a few drops at a time from her finger ends to mix the paste.

Damp, black, sticky – it would do.

She dipped her slate pencil in the ink and wrote on the wall.

Suffer . . . the little . . . children . . . to come . . . unto Me.

It was hard work. The paste had not quite run out when she finished so at the end she scrawled a little cross. Then her head started swimming so she had to sit down. There were spots dancing in front of her eyes and her pulse was beating so strongly through her head and neck and chest that she felt her skin was quite transparent.

She lay on her bed, waiting for the attack to pass, and thought, this is what it is like, this is what I have to suffer to win. I have to win for the children.

In the long cold echoing nights she had thought a lot about the children. She began to daydream about them now. They were all girls, the children of the brothels, with half-formed breasts and cheap gaudy clothes and hard staring eyes that she imagined were too frightened to weep. In her dreams she opened the door of the brothels and took them away and they were with her in the garden of a beautiful house in the country, walking across a lawn with daffodils around the edge, and one of them laughed and called her Mother. And she wondered if any of them were her own children, the ones who had miscarried. Then a man came out of the house, a tall handsome man in black, and she turned her back and grabbed the girls by the hands and ran.

I will never be anyone's mother, she thought. Not now. If Jonathan comes near me ever again I'll kill him.

The cell door crashed open. A wardress stood there. Big, burly, pasty faced. Ruth Harkness, my friendly torturer. Sarah stared, and said nothing. Prisoners were supposed to stand up, but she couldn't be bothered. Anyway, she felt too weak.

Ruth closed the door behind her. She looks nervous, Sarah thought. Am I so frightening, even now?

Ruth looked at the floor, noticed it was wet, saw the empty cup.

'Clumsy,' she said. 'I'll get you some more water.'

'No need.'

'Why not? It's no bother.'

'I'm not drinking.'

'Oh no.' Ruth shook her head firmly. 'Don't start that

nonsense now! Believe me, Mrs Becket, you've got more important things to think about. Not drinking ain't going to do no good at all.'

'That's what you think.' It's not fair, Sarah thought. When you're so hungry, rage takes you over so suddenly and completely that you shake all over, and yet your body's too weak to do anything about it. Even your voice hurts, so that it's a pain to speak. Nonetheless, she got to her feet, and turned her back to stare at the wall.

'Oh, come on now, Becket, I've got something important to say to you.'

'Torturer! Get out.'

'I went to the Women's Social and Political Union. I talked to 'em about you. They want to rescue you.'

Sarah's shaking stopped. She turned round. Stars swam briefly in front of her eyes and she thought: hallucinations already? I thought my mind was stronger than this.

'What did you say?'

Ruth repeated herself. Her voice was low, urgent, just above a whisper. 'I saw a Mrs Watson and another one, calls herself your sister, Mrs Cavendish. I told 'em what you said to Dr Armstrong and they believed it. They want me to get you out.'

Sarah laughed. She felt quite light-headed. 'You can't, silly. This is a prison.'

'There may be a way, though.'

'What? Tell me.'

Ruth hesitated. She was used to wild swings of mood amongst prisoners, but Sarah Becket seemed to have deteriorated drastically since she last saw her forty-eight hours ago. Was this the effect of the bromide, or the thirst strike? Whichever it was, it made the woman less reliable, dangerous even.

'I can't tell you now. But when the time comes, you've got to trust me – do exactly what I say. It can't be for a day or two, anyway. Just keep yer mouth shut, for heaven's sake – and trust me.'

Sarah felt dizzy standing up and her mind was hazy too. Perhaps what this wardress was saying was important but she seemed immeasurably distant somehow, irrelevant. With an effort, Sarah tried to focus her attention. Surely the girl must be lying, sent to deceive her.

'How did you get to the WSPU?'

'I walked, didn't I? Went up to the front door and walked straight in. Why?'

'Who did you see first?'

'A young woman. Fair-haired, shortish. I don't know what 'er name was. She was giving out newspapers, like.'

'And then you met Alice Watson and my sister, Mrs Cavendish, you say?'

'That's right, yes.'

'I don't believe you! My sister lives in Glenfee, in Ulster. She never comes to London. And she's not a suffragette, anyway.'

'Well, I can't help that. I met her. She was there.'

'So what did she say?'

'Say? Nothing at first. Then, when I told 'er what you'd said about Dr Armstrong and your husband, she cried.'

'Oh my God.' Sarah turned round feebly and leaned against the wall. 'Surely to God you didn't tell Deborah that? You couldn't have!'

'Why ever not? She was there, wasn't she? She had to know. Listen, Mrs Becket, I ain't got much time . . .'

'Don't you understand? Look, this is between me and my husband, no one else! What right have you to go round telling everyone things that are shameful and private . . .'

'They're not private, they're important! Look, why d'yer think I went to the WSPU, risking my job? Not because I approve of your silly suffragette crimes. I don't! But because what you say Dr Armstrong's doing is much worse. It's got to be stopped, ain't it? And if your husband's part of it then he should be stopped, too. Whoever he is.'

Sarah shook her head, desperately, and ran her hands through her hair. She had a headache and spots before her eyes and she wanted to lie down and go to sleep. It was all too much. Hours of private torment and then sudden, bitter argument and decisions.

'Not Jonathan,' she said. 'I can't do that to him. I should never have told you.'

'Why? Ain't it true?'

'I don't know! He's my *husband*, damn you!'

I hate him, I'll tear his eyes out. But on my own!

'Why don't you leave me alone?'

'If I leave you alone here, you'll die.'

'What?' Sarah stared at the young wardress, bewildered. Again the stars in front of her eyes. She put one hand against the wall, to steady herself.

'You ain't eating, and now you've stopped drinking. He'll carry on force feeding you but you puke half of it up anyway, so that don't do much good. You'll get weaker and weaker an' in the end you'll die.'

Sarah wanted to sit down because of the trembling in her legs but she ignored it. 'You just don't understand, do you,' she said. 'The pain of starving yourself is something we all have to face up to before we come in. Of course we get weaker, and of course it hurts, but that's what forces the authorities to let us out. They daren't let us die in here. It would look too bad.'

'Normally it might.'

'What do you mean?'

There was a clatter of pails along the corridor and the sound of another wardress opening a cell door and ordering a prisoner out. Ruth Harkness glanced nervously over her shoulder to ensure that she was standing with her back to the little judas spyhole in the door, so that no one could see in.

'Listen to me, Mrs Becket, please. I didn't want to get mixed up in your troubles but I am, and if I get this wrong I won't just lose my job, I'll end up locked in 'ere like what you are now. So do me a favour and trust me and try to think straight, will yer? Mrs Watson wants to send a party of suffragettes round to expose what goes on in these 'ouses of Armstrong's but she daren't, not while you're in here.'

'Why not? She doesn't know where they are, does she?'

'Yes, well, they know something, it seems. I didn't understand it all. But if anything goes wrong they want a signed statement, sworn before a lawyer, and the only person who can do that is you, right? About what was in that letter you got sent, what you 'eard from them women in the cell at the police station, what you saw outside 'is consulting rooms in Kensington. And Armstrong knows that too. So he ain't going to let you out no matter how much you starve yourself, is he, eh? If you die there won't be no proof. He might even be glad if the world thought you'd starved yourself to death. Can't you see that?'

'But if I died in prison there'd be a scandal . . .'

''Course. But he'd survive it, don't kid yourself, Mrs Becket. You may think force feeding's wrong, but there's plenty of others what don't. I seen dozens of letters in the papers saying as 'ow suffragettes orter be left to die, or be made outlaws an' lose all their property, or be sent to a desert island, like. Chances are if you die, Dr Armstrong'll become a public hero. Anyhow it's a risk he's got to take, rather than let you out to tell the world about those poor kids in them brothels.'

Sarah slumped down on her bed. She was too weak to stand up. Spots were swirling in front of her eyes and her legs were shaking uncontrollably.

'What can I do then?'

'I've got a plan. I ain't going to tell you what it is but it can't happen till Monday. Today's Friday. So you've got to get through the weekend without getting any weaker or dying. You've got to start drinking again, and I suggest you give up your 'unger strike as well.'

'Don't be silly. I can't do that now!'

'Look, I ain't going to carry you out of 'ere. You'll need yer strength. Anyhow, 'ave you thought he might poison you with that soup what he pours down that tube? He's already feeding you bromide.'

'Feeding me – what?'

Ruth explained. 'Ain't you noticed yourself feeling weaker? I look in 'ere and you can 'ardly stand 'alf the time.'

'But bromide's a poison.'

'It's a sedative, that's what 'e calls it. But it might be worse than that if 'e gave you too much. He's a doctor. He could poison you with anything he liked and you'd never know.'

'Even the food *you* bring me.' Sarah shivered. The cell seemed suddenly icy cold.

'Maybe. But we get ordinary cooked food sent up straight from the kitchens, don't we. He prepares the forced feeding soup himself. There could be anything in it. Look, Mrs Becket –

eat, won't you? Think of me, if no one else. I've got to feed yer, later today. D'you think I like it?'

It was the wrong thing to say. In the riptide of bewildering emotions that were surging through Sarah there was no place, at the moment, for gratitude to the young wardress. She looked at the cross she had scrawled on the wall this morning, and remembered suddenly the story of Christ, who had fasted forty days and forty nights. At the end of that time the devil had taken him up onto a high mountain, and shown him the world spread out below. What had he said? 'All this can be yours, if you will but abandon your fast and listen to me.' Wasn't this the same temptation?

'How do I know you're not lying to me? Torturer! You're on his side, aren't you – a devil sent to tempt me!'

'Oh, for God's sake! Think, woman, can't yer?' The two women stared at each other, in desperate incomprehension. Then, abruptly, Ruth heard something outside. Had anyone heard them? She was not supposed to talk to prisoners about anything at all, let alone about escaping. Hurriedly, she shouted: 'Pick up that pot now and take it to the sluice! This cell's a disgrace. 'Ow many times 'ave I told yer? 'Olloway's a clean prison!'

While Ruth opened the door, Sarah stumbled off her bed and picked up the toilet bucket. Then the two of them went out into the corridor. As they passed another prisoner and one of Ruth's colleagues on the same errand, Ruth thought: Please God, don't let her say anything now!

And a little later: Perhaps she is mad, just like Dr Armstrong said. In which case I'm about to commit a crime and risk my job for nothing.

Deborah paced up and down in Jonathan and Sarah's library, thinking. Such an impressive house, so comfortable, so deceitful. She stopped for a moment in front of Jonathan's writing desk. It was a large, luxurious desk, with a number of little pigeonholes for paper, envelopes, ink, nibs and so on. The surface was made of richly engraved red and brown leather, which she knew his butler, Reeves, polished carefully several times a week. It was a desk which Jonathan was immensely proud of.

It was just the sort of thing he would like, she thought. All beautiful colours and glossy surfaces. Probably he looked at women in the same way. He liked the ones with fancy clothes and feathered hats and too much lipstick . . .

And little children.

Oh God, what am I saying? My sister's husband! He couldn't do that, could he?

Why not? He even tried to seduce *me*!

Deborah picked up an elaborately engraved paper knife and pressed it into her palm, hard, without realising what she was doing. *How could he*? Were Alice Watson and Ruth Harkness both mistaken? No – it all made too much sense. Sarah's sudden, surprise action, apparently unauthorised by the movement. Even she had to have a reason for it. Deborah knew that the women in the WSPU were usually highly organised, well disciplined. Christabel Pankhurst, their general, master-minded the whole thing from Paris and disliked spontaneous actions like Sarah's. They happened, all the same – but why would Sarah go out and do such a dreadful thing, so suddenly, unless some violent inner urge had compelled her?

Unless she had found out that she had been betrayed by her husband.

In such a dreadful way too. With whores. Perhaps with young children.

She put down the paper knife and went to the window. Outside, in the square, there were new leaves on the trees. A nanny was taking two young children for a walk, a servant was pushing an old lady in a bath chair. A motor taxi drove into the square and stopped. A man got out – a prosperous gentleman of about forty in top hat, tailcoat, striped trousers. He paid the fare, swung a silver-topped cane jauntily in his hand, turned and ran up the steps to one of the houses.

One of Jonathan's neighbours. *He* is like that, Deborah thought. Prosperous, successful, urbane, civilised. *How could he possibly . . .*?

Look at me. I did.

Not for money, though. I didn't pay anyone or take a child to my bed. What I did was quite different, it was all done for love.

So?

The world won't see it like that. The man's world. The world of prosperous, urbane gentlemen who were educated in the Inns of Court and sit in Parliament and live in Belgrave Square. What was it Jonathan told me the other night? The law allows a man to divorce his wife for one single instance of adultery, but she cannot divorce him unless his adultery is aggravated by something more serious such as – what was it? Cruelty, desertion, sodomy.

Nothing about paying to go to a whore, or seducing under-age children. That's normal, civilised, male behaviour, then? If I have a baby girl she'll grow up in a world like this.

Poor, poor Sarah. Deborah clutched the curtains so tight, she felt her fingernails coming through the thick damask cloth into her palm. That's why she slashed the picture, I'm sure. She probably stood all alone in this room just like this, knowing what I know about her own husband.

With a letter in her hand from a prostitute. That's what that Miss Harkness said, wasn't it? Sarah had received some kind of blackmail letter from a prostitute, telling her that her husband wasn't going to Dr Armstrong because he was ill, but because he was morally sick. She probably stood right here in this room and read it.

If I had that letter it would be conclusive proof, Deborah thought suddenly. What did she *do* with it? What would I do?

Deborah glanced around the room. Sarah's writing desk was at the far side of the room, in a corner next to a side window and a small table cluttered with books and pamphlets. Deborah went over and started to rummage curiously through the clutter on the table. Old copies of *The Suffragette*, pamphlets about sweatshops and socialism and suffrage in New Zealand . . . No letters though – they would be in Sarah's desk. It was a roll-top desk, closed, but the key was still in the lock. Deborah opened it. It was fairly tidy inside, with everything stuffed into its little pigeon-hole or drawer. Writing paper, envelopes, ink, nibs, stamps, paper clips, postcards, blotting paper . . . She felt a little like a thief, rifling through someone's private possessions. But there was nothing here, no secrets.

She sighed, moved her elbow clumsily, and knocked the blotter on the floor.

When she bent to pick it up, she saw the corner of a letter sticking out from under the blotting paper. She took it out and read it.

> *Dear Mrs Becket,*
> *I suppose you know that your friends in the WSPU have recently been poking their noses into things which concern them even less than the vote. They have been troubling several of us young ladies and asking for the names of our gentlemen friends, which is none of their business at all, especially when they stand outside the house where we live and work and try to put men off, so we have to move house. This does no one any good and makes us all poorer. In particular, they have been troubling Dr Armstrong too, who is a decent man and a good help to us.*
> *Well, all this has got to stop. Tell your friends to stay away from our houses and Dr Armstrong or you will be sorry. Your husband gets the same treatment as other men and whose fault is that? If you don't want to read about him in all the newspapers tell your friends to STAY AWAY. That's all.*

Deborah shuddered. It was what she had expected but it still made her feel ill. She held the letter a little away from her, between finger and thumb, as though it might contaminate her.

'Ahem.'

'What?' She whirled round and saw Reeves, standing discreetly just inside the door. How long had he been there? She had been so busy with her thoughts, it could have been ages. He was such a quiet, unobtrusive man.

'Yes, Reeves, what is it?'

'A letter has arrived, madam. From Mr Jonathan.'

She saw he had a silver tray in his hand. 'I see. Thank you.'

She took the note, waited until the man had padded noiselessly out of the door, then walked across to Jonathan's desk to pick up the engraved paperknife to open it. It was on House of Commons notepaper, with a small portcullis at the top.

> *My dear Debbie,*
> *A quick note in haste. A trial in which I am defending has come to the boil more quickly than I had anticipated, and I shall have to spend most of tomorrow in Lewes*

sorting matters out, so I am taking the train down to Sussex tonight. It is only a brief matter but it concerns a promise made to an old friend of mine. I had thought of inviting you but in all likelihood it will be a tedious round of dull business and the womenfolk are dreary, so I hope you will forgive me for deserting you. I will probably stay over on Sunday but hope to see you some time Monday.
Yours,
Jonathan.

She read it twice, incredulously, and then crumpled it slowly in her hand. So he could just walk away for the weekend like that, could he, while his wife was being force fed in prison? Does he really have a court case so pressing it had to be discussed over the weekend, or has he got some whore down there that he doesn't want his wife's sister to meet?

And not a word in the letter about Sarah.

How *could* he?

Quite deliberately, she picked up the paper knife and jabbed it into the polished leather surface of Jonathan's writing desk. Then, fiercely, she dragged it sideways, six inches, a foot, two. The leather parted with a steady ripping sound, like the opening of a wound. Reeves isn't going to like this, she thought. He'll probably want to mend it before his master comes home on Monday. To make that harder she took the knife out and jabbed it in at the opposite corner, tearing across the surface of the desk again until it was split by a cross.

There, Johnny, she thought.

I am a savage too, beneath the surface.

Perhaps we all are . . .

' 'Ere. Go on, read it.'

'Get out! I don't want to see you!'

'I'll go when you've read this. Not before. You owe me that at least.'

'I owe you nothing. Leave me alone!'

Sarah had her back turned to Ruth. Her arms were folded and she was staring at the corner of her cell. Like a child who had been punished in school, Ruth thought. But this woman is punishing herself. Refusing deliberately to see what has to be done. She looked at the short dark hair, the thin, determined shoulders under the grey arrow-striped prison dress, and said: 'I'm riskin' my job for you, you know.'

'Go away!'

Ruth sighed. I should shake her, she thought. I should pick her up and shake her until her teeth chatter, to bring her to her senses. Instead she said: 'All right. I'll leave the note on the table 'ere and come back in five minutes. If you've read it and want to change yer mind, fine. Otherwise I'm giving this up. The children can stay in them brothels for all I care.'

She went out and closed the heavy door. When she had gone Sarah stood for a long time unmoving, staring unseeing at the wall. I hope you die, Ruth Harkness, she thought. I hope you trip at the top of the stone stairs and fall and smash your head and the brains come out and . . . *Stop it!*

Stop this, for heaven's sake, and come to your senses, woman!

She turned round abruptly and sat on her bed and began to cry. Harsh dry sobs that shook her frame and brought no tears. They didn't last long; they hurt too much. Her throat was raw from the forced feeding and the inside of her mouth had ulcers everywhere and her tongue was swollen and her lips cracked, but that wasn't the worst. There was an ache deep inside her ribs that never let up, and whenever she moved too quickly it stopped her dead with a jab that brought bile into her mouth. She'd had it for two days now. She was sure they had put too much tube into her stomach, too roughly and fast – and it was that Ruth Harkness who did it. She held the tube while Dr Armstrong shoved it in through the gag with his big butcher's hands. And he'll do it again today . . .

I wish I was dead!

If I was dead they couldn't do it again. Then I wouldn't have exposed Martin or Jonathan but I would be a martyr to the cause and they would have a huge funeral like they had for Emily Wilding Davison, and my death would make them stop the forced feeding and set Mrs Pankhurst free and give women the vote. And then the exploitation of children would stop with everything else. We'd have the vote. That would be worth giving my life for.

Maybe that's what Emily Davison thought when she seized the reins of the King's horse at Ascot and it killed her.

Nothing happened, though. They just said she was mad.

Like me.

Sarah looked at the folded piece of paper on the table. She took a deep breath. Maybe I *am* going mad. I've never had emotions as violent as this before. They sweep through me like flash floods and I can't control them at all. It must be the starvation or maybe I'm being poisoned or perhaps it's Jonathan – *you bastard, Jonathan, if I ever see you again I'll rip your eyes out and suck the blood from their sockets . . .*

No, don't. Please don't. Not again.

Why not look? It can't do any harm.

Very quietly she stretched out her hand and picked up the piece of paper and looked. She held it in her hand a little distant from her, by one corner, as though she could drop it at any time if it displeased her.

It said:

> *Dear Sarah,*
> *Please trust the bearer of this absolutely. She is taking a great risk to bring it to you. I understand your doubts and that it is hard for you to abandon your fast but you must do that. It is an order from the WSPU committee. We will be waiting for you on the outside.*
> *With all my love and admiration,*
> *Alice Watson.*

And underneath, in another hand:

Deborah Cavendish.

Sarah's hand started shaking and she let the note flutter to the floor. It lay there, upside down. But she could still read it. She considered it thoughtfully.

It was definitely Alice Watson's writing. She had seen that too many hundreds of times to be in any doubt. And almost definitely her sister's signature . . .

WSPU headed notepaper too.

The cell door opened. Ruth Harkness came in and closed it behind her. She stood carefully with her back blocking the judas hole. She saw the letter on the floor and frowned.

'Well?'

'I'm . . . sorry.' Sarah looked up.

Ruth's frown remained. 'What d'yer mean, you're sorry?'

'Sorry . . .' Sarah sighed, and tears started unbidden to her eyes. 'Sorry I disbelieved you.'

Ruth took a long, deep breath. She had come into the cell angry, more than half prepared to give up the whole escape plan. It would be so easy, so safe. To pass by on the other side. To keep your conscience quiet and pretend that you had not seen, or could do nothing. Now everything would be harder.

'You're quite sure you believe me now?'

'Yes. Quite sure. You couldn't have forged that letter.'

'No.'

'What must I do, then? If I am to get out it must be soon – I can't bear this place. It's like hell, full of monsters!'

'Ssssh! Calm yerself, Mrs Becket, please. I can't work miracles.'

'Can't you? But I'm told to obey your orders, trust you absolutely. What are you going to do?'

If this woman's not insane she's on the edge of it, Ruth thought. The strain has been too much for her. But then what do I know of what she's going through? If I get this wrong I may find out. I'll be locked in, too.

'The first thing, Mrs Becket, is to eat the food I'll bring you at twelve. You don't 'ave to eat all of it if there's too much, just so long as you eat some. Then I can announce your 'unger strike's off and you won't 'ave to be forcibly fed.'

'And then? What will Dr Armstrong do?'

'I don't know. I don't see what 'e can do at first. Just make sure you don't eat nothing unless I bring it to you. But eat as much as you can to get yer strength up.'

'For what? Do you want me to climb the walls or something?'

''Course not. But the other thing is you got to obey normal prison rules. Do third division work, scrub the floors and take out laundry when I order you. That's important, you'll need your strength for that. And with luck you'll be allowed into the yard for exercise.'

'Exercise!' Sarah thought ruefully of miserable women walking in circles round the prison yard, heads bowed, forbidden even to speak to each other. Oddly, she felt afraid of it. It would be so strange after this cell.

'When do I get out?'

'On Monday, I 'ope.'

'How?'

'That . . . I ain't going to tell you yet. For two reasons – *please*, Mrs Becket, listen and trust me.' Ruth saw with alarm the light of combat leap into Sarah's eyes, saw how quickly emotion could engulf her. She ploughed on, determined. 'In the first place I don't know yet, exactly, not all the details. And in the second, you got to admit you're in a highly emotional state just now. You might let slip something without meaning to, and give us both away. But if you don't know, you can't. Just trust me, please. And do what I say.'

Sarah stared at her blindly for a moment. She hardly saw the girl, so intent was she on fighting down the flood of resentful memories within herself. The filthy bath Ruth had forced her into when she first arrived; carrying the slop-bucket to the sluice, the brutal feeding. And now she was asked to trust and obey a girl who had done all that to her. A servant who had held her down while men thrust a tube into her body. A torturess . . .

'All right.'

'Good.' Ruth picked up the letter from the floor and put it into her purse. 'Don't want no one to find this now, do we?' Then she looked at Sarah for a long moment. 'You're a brave woman, Mrs Becket. Maybe I should have said that before but it's hard, when you're in my position. If we get out of 'ere I might even come and join you in that suffragette shop. If they'll 'ave me.'

There was a brief twitch on Sarah's face that might have been meant for a smile. She herself felt it chiefly as pain, from muscles unused for too long.

'Don't worry,' she said. 'We take all sorts, you know!'

'Mmmmm!'

'Tastes good, does it?'

Sarah did not reply. She was overwhelmed by the number of tastes, memories, and textures that could co-exist in a single spoonful of chicken broth. For the first time in nine days her salivary glands responded willingly to food; the sensation was exquisite. For several minutes she savoured it; then took another spoonful. A third.

'Don't overdo it, now.'

Sarah nodded. After the fifth spoonful she felt bloated, obese. She pushed the bowl away and shot an anxious glance at Ruth.

'That's all right, Mrs Becket. You've started, that's the main thing. You'll manage some more tomorrow.'

By the next morning Sarah's body was beginning to return to normal. She had slept a little better; she managed to eat most of a bowl of porridge. Ruth let her rest for three hours, then put her on light duties, cleaning the corridors.

It was odd, not to be supervised the whole time. True, there were always wardresses around, appearing from one place or another every few minutes; but no one stood over her continually. She could rest, as she needed to, for long minutes at a time, without being scolded. She could choose where to go, which areas to sweep next. It felt like freedom.

It was also exhausting. In the afternoon she was allowed outdoors for the first time, to exercise. It was as she had expected – slow silent circles round a restricted tarmac quadrangle, a regulation three yards from the other prisoners. She could not talk to them, but she could exchange glances – curious, silent glances of sympathy – which were themselves a thrilling form of human contact, after so many days alone with four walls.

And then there was the sun. She had forgotten what it was like, that unexpected caress of heat on your neck and face and arms. To bathe in warm air, breathe in light. To hear the sounds of the city all around you, even if distant, over high walls topped with jagged glass. Sarah spread her arms to embrace the luxury of it all – and because Ruth was supervising the exercise, was not rebuked, the first time.

Afterwards, in her cell, she slept. At five o'clock, when the rattle of the feeding trolley had previously made her break out in cold sweat, she was sleeping the deep refreshing sleep of a child. The trolley did not come. Dr Armstrong did not disturb her.

Sunday was the same, but better. Sarah felt a little more

strength return. She could sweep the floor and walk the yard for a moment or two longer without pausing. And she felt, too, a return of impatience.

When Ruth brought her evening meal she said: 'Tomorrow's the day, isn't it?'

Ruth nodded. Sarah's decision to eat had brought a welcome interlude of calmness, of rational obedience, to her behaviour; but Ruth was acutely aware that this could change at any moment, if she said the wrong thing. And she herself had scarcely slept last night, worrying over every detail of her plan.

'Aren't you going to tell me what I've got to do? I need to know something, or I may get it wrong.'

'Yes, you do.' Ruth spoke softly, her voice scarcely a murmur above the busy hum of the prison. But she had decided for herself that Sarah needed to be prepared. 'Listen. Tomorrow morning I ain't going to ask you to do no sweeping. You've got to strip beds and carry laundry. Are you strong enough for that?'

'Up to a point. I'm not Hercules yet, you know.'

'Well, you got to do your best. You'll be taking dirty clothes and sheets down to the laundry room. Most third division prisoners will be doing it. I'll only give you one load, two at the most. When you're there you stuff 'em into baskets, and when the baskets are full, the laundry company takes them away.'

The thin whisper of a smile flickered across Sarah's lips. 'That sounds exciting.'

'It will be for you.' Ruth watched her carefully. This was the first crucial point. She thought of Sarah as a courageous woman but people could be bold in one way and finicky in others. 'You're going out in one of them baskets.'

Sarah's eyes sparkled. She drank a spoonful of soup and rested her elbows on the table, staring at Ruth.

'In a basket. How amusing! But how?'

'Exactly 'ow, you'll 'ave to leave to me. When one of the baskets is fairly full and there's no one around, you hop in and I'll fasten it down. Make yerself a space to breathe somewhere near the top, I should. Then keep mum until you reach the laundry.'

'But what then? They'll find me there, won't they? I'll come back washed and ironed.'

'Not if your Mrs Watson can do what she promises. She tells

me most of them women what work in that laundry are suffragettes. They've been urging her to try this trick for some time.'

Sarah thought for a moment. 'How long shall I be in the basket, do you think?'

'An hour or two, probably. No more. We usually pack the baskets before ten and the wagon comes at 'alf past.'

'And if I can't breathe?'

'Don't worry about that. I'll check you can before I close the lid.'

'It'll be a triumph if it comes off.' There was a definite smile on that haggard, intense face now. I could like her, like this, Ruth thought. Then Sarah frowned. 'What about you?'

'How do you mean?'

'When I'm gone, won't they suspect you? If you were in charge and you've lost me?'

'If I'm lucky, they won't know.'

'What on earth do you mean, they won't know? We're counted all the time in here, like coins in a bank.'

'Yes, but I do the counting on this floor, don't I? Mostly. So before we start we'll bring some of the laundry in 'ere, and make it up into a roll to look like you're lying in your bed. If anyone asks I'll say you're tired and resting after straining yourself with the unaccustomed work. Them bundles of sheets can be 'eavy, you know. Specially for fine ladies what ain't used to work, and prefer starving theirselves instead.'

Sarah ignored the jibe and frowned thoughtfully. 'I'm not sure I like that part of the plan so much. I mean, any wardress can come in here at any time. And if they find out you're lying . . .'

'That's for me to worry about, Mrs Becket. I've said I'll get you out and I'll do it, but I ain't about to get meself caught either if . . .'

The cell door crashed open behind Ruth, catching her between the shoulder blades. As she stumbled forwards and turned she saw a man in the doorway. Big, burly, in respectable tweed suit. Heavy jowls, thick sensual lips, a solid fleshy face.

Martin Armstrong.

Behind him, an older wardress, carrying a tray. On the tray a jug, a glass with a spoon in it, and a glass jar.

When both of them had come into the room there was scarcely room to move.

Martin Armstrong smiled. It was a confident, patronising, avuncular smile. The sort of smile many doctors affect when going from bed to bed in hospital. But the smile did not quite reach the cold grey eyes in the flabby overfed face. There was a ghost of fear in them, Sarah thought. Fear and hatred. Or was that just a reflection of her own eyes in his?

'So, I am pleased to see our patient eating at last. It was a wise decision, Mrs Becket, very wise. I am sure you will find that your mental faculties return to you soon, if you persevere with this course.'

As soon as he had come in, Sarah had stood up, with her back to the wall beside her small table. She grasped her spoon in her right hand like a weapon.

'There is nothing wrong with my mind, Dr Armstrong, as you very well know.'

'You will allow *me* to be the judge of that, madam.' He turned away from her and took the tray from the wardress who had come in with him. He put it down on Sarah's table by the bowl of soup. 'Thank you, Mrs Canning. Since Miss Harkness is here I think I can manage. We can hardly move with the four of us.'

As the older woman left, Sarah said: 'I suppose you ask her to go so she won't hear my description of your abysmal character. Of how you pimp to middle-aged lechers and supply them with poor under-aged girls from charity homes for children.'

Despite herself she found she was trembling. I thought I had stopped the violence of these emotions, she thought. The spoon rattled against the wall beside her as she gripped it in her hand.

'No one wants to hear that sort of thing, Mrs Becket. But your fantastic accusations prove my point about your mental state. Now, I have brought you some medicine which may help to put these matters right.'

He spooned some reddish-brown powder from the jar on the tray into the glass, mixed it with water, and held the glass critically up to the light.

'I won't take it! I don't have to – I've had enough of your poison!'

She swiped at the glass with her spoon, but Martin Armstrong was too quick for her. He swung the glass out of reach with one hand and caught her wrist with the other, laughing deep in his chest.

'Temper, temper, my fine lady! Every move you make proves your own lack of mental balance. Hold her arms, will you, Miss Harkness?'

From the moment the man had spooned the powder into the glass Ruth had been frozen with horror. What was it? What was he going to do? If she stopped him, if she refused to help, there would be a tremendous row and she would probably be dismissed at once. So there would be no escape, no hope for Sarah. But if she let him give Sarah the medicine, the woman might be dead by morning.

'Come on, girl, help me, don't hang about!'

Sarah, at least, had no doubts about what she should do. She was reaching for the glass desperately with her free left hand, trying to grab it or knock it over. Dr Armstrong held her away by twisting her right wrist across her throat, so that Sarah had to either turn left away from him or be half throttled by her own forearm. Wildly, she began to scream and kick his shins.

'Miss Harkness, quick! Before I spill the damn stuff!'

Ruth made up her mind. Feeling her arms like lead, she grabbed first Sarah's free left arm, and then the other, and twisted them both behind her. Then she swung Sarah round to the right, so that she couldn't kick the doctor because the table was in the way. She pushed Sarah forwards against it.

'Let me go, you pig! I shan't take any – ooooooh!'

Armstrong shoved his hand across her face and forced her forehead back with the palm of his hand, so that she was staring upwards into the great meaty fingers across her eyes. At the same time he pinched her nose between finger and thumb, so that she couldn't breathe. For a minute the three of them swayed backwards and forwards, but Sarah couldn't kick the wretched man because of the table and she couldn't bite him because his hand was too high up her face and she couldn't hit him because Ruth held her arms behind her and worst of all she couldn't *breathe* . . .

She opened her mouth to suck in air and as she did so he

poured the medicine down her throat.

She choked and spewed half of it back. He caught most of it in the glass and when she breathed in again he poured it back into her mouth. Then he put the glass down and jammed his free hand under her jaw so that her head was tilted back even further and her mouth was closed.

After another long minute she swallowed.

He took his hands from her face.

'All right, Miss Harkness. You can let her go now.'

Ruth guided Sarah towards the bed so that she collapsed onto that rather than the floor. For a moment she slumped face down, ignoring them both. Martin Armstrong picked up the tray with the glass and jug and jar on it. Ruth gazed at him expressionlessly. He glanced down at the crumpled figure sprawled on the bed.

'If you didn't resist, everything would be much easier, Mrs Becket,' Dr Armstrong said. 'Take my word for it, I only give you medicine for your own good.'

Sarah was sobbing, gasping for breath. She moved her head slightly and gazed up at him from the bed, speechless. There was blood on her chin from her lips and also a rust-coloured smear, from the medicine she had spat out.

Dr Armstrong opened the cell door. He glanced at the table where there was some soup, some of it miraculously still in the bowl.

'I should feed that to her if you can, Miss Harkness. It all helps to build up her strength, you know.'

Then he was gone. Slowly, Sarah's eyes focused on Ruth.

Just survive until tomorrow morning, Ruth thought. Please, lady, don't die on me now. She bent down and hissed: 'Stick yer fingers down yer throat! Quick – you've got to puke it up!'

As she touched Sarah's chin Sarah jerked her head up convulsively and spat in her face.

Then she turned her back and hunched into a ball on her bed, her head as close into the far corner as she could get.

'Please, Mrs Becket! It may be poison. You've got to get it out if you can!'

'I don't want your help! Ever! Leave me alone!'

For a long time Ruth stood watching her sob, but she could

think of no more to say. To force the woman to vomit now, after what she had helped the doctor to do, was impossible. Also, she could not remember if she had heard Dr Armstrong's footsteps going away down the corridor, and she was obsessed by a fear that he might be outside . . .

She mopped up the spilt soup on the table with her handkerchief, picked up the bowl, opened the door, and went out. There was no one there. She locked the door behind her, and walked away down the empty corridor.

22

When Ruth came on duty in the morning she did not know what she would find. Maybe an empty cell with Mrs Becket moved to the hospital wing. Under the intensive care of Dr Armstrong. Or an unfortunate death in the night. An inquest – who had last seen the prisoner, what state was she in, why had the doctor not been called?

Lies to write on an official form. Collusion with Dr Armstrong. What could she say that would not implicate herself as well as him? But surely he would not use a poison that could be easily traced back to him? Surely – unless he were in such a panic about what Becket might say that he would do anything . . .

And then what could she tell Mrs Watson? I helped poison her, you see. I had to, to keep our plan secret. To save my own skin.

She opened the cell door and went in.

Sarah Becket sat on the bed and looked at her.

White-faced, pale as a ghost with wide dark haunting eyes. Dazed, a little sleepy, hazy-looking. But a firmness too around the mouth, a grim smile that no ghost ever had. She stood up shakily, steadied herself with one hand behind her against the wall.

'You're all right then?'

'Yes.' Sarah nodded towards the bucket in the corner. 'I took your advice. Some of it's in there at least. If it was poison at all.'

'How do you feel?'

'Strange. As though my legs don't belong. But they work – look.' She took a bold stride away from the wall towards the table, another – then sat down abruptly, hard on the stool. She swayed, clutched at the wall to steady herself, and started to giggle. 'They don't work very well, do they? It's just that they seem so far away, and the floor is too . . . unsteady. I'm sorry.'

'Don't be. Just concentrate, you've got to walk downstairs somehow.'

'Yes.' Sarah stopped giggling abruptly and propped her head in her hands. 'Don't worry. I'll manage.'

'You'll have to. We won't get another chance.' A cocktail of relief and fear flooded into Ruth's veins, making her hand tremble. So she hasn't changed her mind, she thought. She plonked the bowl of porridge down on the table.

' 'Ere. Eat this if you can. To give you strength. It may mop up what's left of that medicine, too.'

Listlessly, Sarah spooned some into her mouth. Then spluttered and choked. 'Quick – water!'

' 'Ere.'

Ruth held the mug while she drank. Then Sarah's hand came up and took it from her. Gently, but firmly. It was hard for her to grip it but she forced herself. Sipped, deliberately, then looked up. Not a kind look.

'About yesterday,' Ruth said. 'I'm sorry, but I had to do it. You do realise that, don't you?'

A nod. As though the matter was acknowledged, dismissed for the moment. Then Sarah said: 'I spat at you, too. That was unforgiveable.'

Ruth flushed. 'It don't matter. I've had worse.'

'Nonetheless, I'm sorry.' Grimly, Sarah fed herself a second spoonful of porridge, swallowed. A third, and a fourth. Half the bowl.

'When do we begin?'

'When you've eaten and slopped out. Take your time.'

All around them was the noise and clatter of prison, the slamming of doors and shouting. Anxiously, Ruth listened for the rattle of keys that would mean another wardress on the corridor outside. She was shaking with nerves and the need for hurry, but at the same time acutely aware that the woman in front of her looked scarcely able to carry herself, let alone a bucket or a bundle of linen. But it *had* to be done.

Sarah finished her porridge and stood up, swaying slightly. To Ruth's surprise she did not sit down again. She nodded towards the corner of the cell.

'All right, I'm ready. Pass me the bucket, will you?'

For a wardress to perform such a task was unheard of, but Ruth did it. It was a gesture of respect to the woman's bravery, her determination to go through with the scheme after all. A recognition that they were in it together.

It took a long time for Sarah to carry the bucket to the sluice, empty it, and return, but not quite so long, Ruth thought, as to attract attention. It was not unknown, after all, for prisoners to dawdle out of spite, or sullenness. And, on the corridors and landings around them, others were busy with their own duties. When they returned to the cell, Ruth recovered her normal loud assertive bawl.

'Now, roll up the linen from your own bed first, and make a decent job of it. 'Olloway don't send things out all scrumpled up and ragged, whatever the men's prisons do. We teach respect 'ere! When you've done that yer can carry it down. Jump to it, Becket, if yer wants to go out and exercise later!'

Sarah managed to get out into the corridor with her bundle of dirty sheets. She swayed and put one hand against the wall, but Ruth dared not help her. There were other wardresses and prisoners in sight – such a gesture would be bound to excite comment. Slowly, Sarah walked along the landing and down the metal stairs.

I came this way yesterday, she told herself. It's not so far. And if I fall I can just hold these sheets in front of my face and they'll form a lovely soft pillow and I can sleep for a week, right here on the floor . . .

'Becket! Stand up straight and stop dawdling! We 'aven't got all day!'

Ruth's harsh wardress' voice awoke her. Just in time. Sarah realised she had been drifting off into a dream. She managed the rest of the stairs without mishap, concentrating on the clank of her heavy prison shoes on the metal staircase. I am a condemned woman going to execution, she thought. Mary Queen of Scots perhaps . . .

For God's sake pay attention! This is real, it's important, you'll never get another chance to escape. Don't let your mind drift now.

The laundry room was down a short passage at the foot of the steps. There were a dozen large wicker baskets in it. Eight of them were already full, four stood half empty. Sarah entered the room behind another prisoner in a grey arrow-striped dress, who threw a large bundle of sheets into the basket furthest from the door. Then she turned, glanced briefly at Sarah, and went out.

Ruth came in behind her. There was no one else in the room.

'Quick – there!' Ruth hissed. She nodded at the further basket, which was now three-quarters full. 'I'll stand by the door.'

Sarah walked to the basket, dropped her bundle of sheets in, and then clutched the side with her hands. She swayed, bowed her head.

Ruth watched her, appalled. 'What the 'ell are you doing? Get in, woman – quick!' She could hear footsteps clanging down the metal stairs at the end of the corridor.

'I can't!' Sarah turned to her, a silly, desperate smile on her face. 'It's . . . too high, you see. The sides, I mean. We didn't think of that.'

'Great God Almighty!' Ruth left the door and strode swiftly across the room. It was true. The woman was so weak and dazed with bromide or whatever it was that the side of a three foot wicker basket seemed like a wall to her, impossible to climb. She reached Sarah's side and put her hand on her sleeve.

'Bit slow on your landing this morning, aren't they, Miss Harkness?'

'What – beg pardon?'

Ruth swung round as though she had been stung. Mrs Canning, her supervisor, stood in the door – a short stocky woman with iron-grey hair and forearms like legs of lamb. Panic-stricken, Ruth thought: she knows – she knew all along, she's come here on purpose to trap us!

'Oh. Yes, ma'am – it's this suffragette 'ere, coming off hunger strike. She's still weak, can't move so fast. I thought she was going to fall.'

Mrs Canning glanced dismissively at Sarah and then glared at Ruth as though she were being deliberately obtuse.

'Nonsense, girl. You're not trying to mollycoddle 'em, are you? If they've still got legs, they can walk. Bit of hard work'll do 'em good.'

Behind her, two other prisoners came in. The first threw her sheets into a basket, turned, and went out. The second was slower, dawdling as though even the small liberty of the laundry room was a refreshing change to her.

So we've failed, Sarah thought. I can't even climb into the basket and anyway the room is full of people. She sighed, and began to move dispiritedly back towards the door.

A loud noise echoed outside, from somewhere up on one of the landings. One of the usual appalling prison noises, which echoed in the vast central hall, Sarah thought. As though someone was banging a metal bucket, deliberately, as loud as she could. Not just one person, but several. And women screaming, chanting.

'Just a minute.'

Mrs Canning pushed past her, strode out into the corridor. Sarah could make out some of the words from upstairs now. They were like a song of joy to her.

'Votes for Women!'

'Justice!'

'Free Mrs Pankhurst!'

'Down with the Cabinet of Torturers!'

And then the banging of buckets became more rhythmical, the accompaniment to a song:

'I shall not cease from mental fight
Nor shall my sword sleep in my hand
Til we have built . . . Jerusalem
In England's green and pleasant land.'

'What is it?' Sarah glanced at Ruth and the other prisoner, stunned, then stepped towards the door. It was like a dream. Perhaps she would not need to escape anyway. Suffragettes were taking over the prison!

'Just a minute, Becket,' Ruth said. Her voice was loud, overbearing. 'Ignore that row, whatever it is. Just get over there and 'elp fasten these down, will you?'

'But it's . . . suffragettes . . .'

'I said ignore it, Becket!' Ruth stared at Sarah insistently, forcing her to meet her eyes. 'Just get over 'ere now and 'elp me, will yer? Now!'

The other prisoner in the room, a young, healthy girl with a pinched, disrespectful face, glanced at Sarah, clicked her tongue, and rolled her eyes upwards to indicate how deeply stupid any order from a wardress was. Then she made a movement as though to help Ruth herself. Ruth scowled.

'Is your name Becket?'

'No, but I thought . . .'

'You ain't in 'Olloway to think, Raikes, you're in 'ere to do what yer told and be punished. Now git off up them stairs smartish!'

'Charmed, I'm sure!'

The young woman ducked the ghost of a curtsey, then flounced briskly out of the door before anything could happen. Ruth glanced out after her. Several wardresses were hurrying towards the landing where the noise was still going on. Mrs Canning was striding determinedly in the same direction, keys clanking at her hip. There was another prisoner at the top of another flight of stairs with a bundle of linen in her arms, but she was staring open-mouthed at the row, with no sign of moving. Ruth turned briskly back into the room and took Sarah firmly by the arm.

'All clear. This one – now!'

'But what is it? What's that noise?'

Ruth grinned. 'Your friends, isn't it? That Mrs Watson of yours gave me a note to take to 'em, telling 'em to make a hell of a row at nine-thirty this morning, and by God they have! She promised 'em if they did they'd have something to crow about later, so we'd better make sure that's right, 'adn't we? Come on, get in, quick!'

The laundry baskets were large, about five feet long by three feet wide, and three feet deep, too – that was Sarah's problem. The one they had chosen was about three-quarters full, with its lid propped open against the wall behind. But this time Sarah had more energy. She leaned against Ruth with one arm round her neck, lifted one leg over, then stopped. The long prison skirt impeded her. Something caught, held her back. The song on the landing ended. There were shouts, screams.

'What's the matter?'

'It's my skirt – I can't move.'

'Hold still. It's snagged on this buckle.' Conscious all the time of the need for haste, Ruth wrenched, ripped it free. 'There! Get in now. Bury yourself under them clothes!'

'But if I can't breathe?'

'Make a place for your head. *Hurry*!'

Ruth snatched a sheet from another basket and flung it on top of Sarah. Then another, while Sarah hunched herself into a ball, her arms around her face to hold the clothes back. Wide, scared eyes – footsteps on the stairs outside. Ruth seized the lid, dragged it swiftly down, ignoring the hand that Sarah raised feebly to prevent her . . .

'Wait!'

But there was no time. Ruth had the lid down, one leather strap through the buckle, heaving it tight against the creak of the wickerwork. She looked round, a fine mist of sweat prickling on her forehead, under her arms.

No one.

The row upstairs was still going on. Cell doors were slamming, buckets clattering, women screaming. She could hear Mrs Canning's loud voice shouting orders. I must get up there and help before it's over, Ruth thought. People must remember I was up there, not down here.

She fastened the second strap. A prisoner walked in with a bundle of sheets in her arms. Without looking at Ruth, she marched straight to the last empty basket and threw them in. Ruth hurried past her, ran along the corridor and up the landing towards the noise of screams and bangs.

As she went, she glanced at the big clock on the wall in the hall.

Nine thirty-six.

In another quarter of an hour, if all went well, the laundry van would arrive. If Sarah's departure hadn't been noticed by then, the van men would come, carry her out, and she would be free.

And, with luck, they won't discover there's just a rolled-up blanket on that bed in her cell for another two hours. By which time she'll be out of the laundry.

But if they find out I was alone with her down in the laundry room while this riot was going on, it won't be just a rolled-up blanket that takes her place in that cell.

It'll be me.

If I can't breathe . . .

For the first few minutes in the basket Sarah thought of nothing else. Her pulse raced, her breath came short and fast, there was a singing in her ears. She writhed and twisted among the linen, trying to get her head in a freer position where she could see light through the wickerwork, ignoring the creak of the basket around her. She moved her hand to try to push the lid, and a fold of old smelly sheet came with it, wrapping itself over her nose and mouth like seaweed. *Dear God, I will die in here!* She dragged her hand free and shoved hard against the lid but nothing moved, the straps outside held it firm. Sarah thought she would scream.

'Over there, and be quick about it. The van'll be 'ere soon, and this lot's not 'alf full.'

A strange wardress's voice came to her and somehow in a moment the panic was gone. The calm bullying certainty of it – I don't want to return to that, she thought. That and the foul medicine of that doctor. I have to take this chance – if Ruth Harkness is right, I'm lucky to be still alive.

Further away, she could hear shouting and banging from the landing upstairs and she thought those brave women will be punished for this if I call out now and the escape is discovered. And Ruth Harkness will be locked up, too. I will have betrayed someone who's risked everything for me – and let down all those who are waiting outside, just because I can't bear half an hour or so in a basket. Look, I *can* breathe, it's easy. There's air coming through these gaps. I can even see a little – is that dark shape a woman's dress?

For a moment she stared but she could see nothing distinct,

and it made her eyes ache, so she gave up and closed them. It was not uncomfortable here, among the bundled sheets and dresses, when she got used to it and wriggled free from the hard lumps that one or two had tangled themselves into. Her legs were bent awkwardly, but she had her arms in front of her, humping a bundle of cloth under her head like a pillow. For a while she listened intently, taking in every nuance of sound from outside. The noise upstairs carried on for a while, grew louder and then stopped. A couple more prisoners came into the room – she heard the slither and slop of their ill-fitting shoes across the floor, the flop of the sheets as they threw them into the other baskets, the creak as those baskets were closed and strapped tight. Then silence.

She was alone.

Sarah was so tired . . . The laundry room was warmer than any she had been in for days, the sheets softer than her bed at home. Without intending to or even realising it, she fell asleep . . .

It was the longest morning of Ruth's life.

The riot on the upper landing went on for nearly quarter of an hour. Ruth had passed Mrs Watson's message to only two suffragette prisoners, but they – bless them, she thought now – had managed to pass it on to three more. These five women, all of whose cells were open for the change of linen, had seized sluice buckets, cups, brooms and mops, and marched up and down the landing banging and shouting out songs and slogans as loud as they could. The other prisoners, startled and amused, egged them on, and Mrs Canning and her warders found their way obstructed by women carrying piles of linen and offering to help in the most useless way possible.

When Ruth arrived on the landing, the five suffragettes had not only linked arms across the corridor, but thrust two broom handles behind their backs, which they gripped with their elbows while they clasped hands in front. This had the effect of making them into a completely solid straight line which stretched right across the corridor. No one woman could be moved in any direction unless all the other five went that way, too – and this they resolutely refused to do.

Singing and chanting slogans all the way, they backed slowly along the corridor towards the sluice, and jammed themselves across its doorway. All the wardresses were in front of them; there was only one elderly prisoner behind in the sluice itself, and she sat there on an upturned bucket, cackling helplessly with laughter.

Eventually, by dint of much pushing and slapping and punching, the five women were disentangled and locked into their cells. Ruth was quite prominent in the struggle, and frogmarched one of the ringleaders, Mary Lethwaite, along the corridor past Mrs Canning, who was outraged.

'Shameless baggage!' Mrs Canning yelled. 'You ain't fit to be in a decent prison like Holloway. You ought to be whipped!'

'Votes for Women!' Mary Lethwaite yelled back. 'Set us free, then, if you don't like us here. We'll get out anyway, so save yourself the trouble! Wait till this afternoon, fat cow!'

For a terrible moment Ruth thought that Mary, carried away by the excitement, might give the game away. Ruth swung her roughly by the arm so that she cried out with pain, and then, when she had slammed the door behind them in Mary's cell, said breathlessly: 'Sorry if I 'urt you. Thanks. It was magnificent!'

Mary rubbed her arm, grinning ruefully. 'It was fun! But did it work? Did she get out?'

'Don't know yet. Keep your trap shut for another couple of hours, whatever you do. Then you can claim it was all your own work.'

'Without knowing how we did it, eh?' Mary said.

'Yes. Best way.' Ruth turned quickly, went out of the door and locked it. Mary and the other woman had been asked to make a disturbance to cover Sarah's escape, but they had not been told how she was going to get out. It was best like that, Ruth thought, and Alice Watson had agreed. She and Mrs Watson had discussed the plan two nights ago, slowly and painstakingly going through every detail. Now they would see if those plans would work out.

On the landing Mrs Canning was hot, red-faced, angry.

'Shut the whole lot of them up in their cells for an hour and let them cool down. Blasted suffragettes!' she muttered furiously. 'Has that laundry gone yet?'

That was what Ruth wanted to know, but she dared not go down to find out. Instead, she went across to her own landing, where Sarah's cell lay quiet, the door closed, one blanket rolled into a sausage with another spread over it, in the hope that a casual observer might think the prisoner was asleep. She locked the door and went along the corridor to where a window looked out towards the main gates. They were just closing. Did that mean the laundry van had just gone out? She couldn't see, but she hoped so.

For the next half hour nothing unusual happened. Ruth let out one or two of her trusty prisoners and set them to cleaning the floor. The noise in the prison died down. Ruth began to breathe more easily.

It was Alice Watson who convinced me to do this, she thought. I was impressed by Sarah Becket, of course I was, but I wouldn't have done it for her alone. That Mrs Watson has persuaded me to change my life.

She had sat with Alice Watson for hours in the little upstairs office in Clements Inn, and afterwards had accompanied her home. Mrs Watson lived in a small top-floor flat in Blackfriars. It was neat, comfortable, unpretentious, with soft green curtains, faded brown carpets, and photographs on the walls of groups of young women in white dresses and pinafores with high white bonnets with badges on. In the middle of each group sat a proud, younger version of Alice Watson.

Ruth had been nearly right when she thought Mrs Watson was a headmistress. In fact she had once trained nurses in hospital. She had probably been very good at it, Ruth thought. Certainly she found the woman easier to talk to than any other middle-aged lady she had met for years.

To her surprise, Ruth learned that Alice Watson had come from an unpretentious lower middle-class background, little better than her own. Her parents had not wanted her to become a nurse; that had been a struggle. But, like Ruth, she had a strong sense of right and wrong.

'They used to think nurses were prostitutes, too – do you know that?' she had said, as they sat drinking tea at the little table in her window, looking down on the tops of trams and drays in the street below. 'Men thought they could do what they liked with them, especially the doctors. That's why the uniform was so important. It marked us out, made it clear we were doing something decent and clean for society. I can understand you felt something of the same for the prison service.'

'Not any more.' Ruth had told her of her childhood struggle to get a decent job, the pride she felt in her own little flat, her hopes of a decent life with her fiancé, George Smith. 'If I help you now,' she said. 'I'll lose all that.'

'It's possible, certainly,' Alice said. 'And I've no right to ask you to take that risk. I'm just grateful for what you've done already. If you decided to do no more, I couldn't complain.' She paused, looking at Ruth calmly through her round spectacles. Waiting perhaps for me to get up and walk out, Ruth thought later.

But she hadn't. So Alice had poured her some more tea and said: 'If you go on, then of course we'd welcome you and there'd be a lot of companionship. But it's not easy. You should be clear in your mind that what you're doing is right.'

That, for Ruth, was the crux of the matter. She was a very moral young woman. She had gone into the prison service not just because it was a secure, respectable job, but because she had believed she would be on the side of right against wrong. Of Christian against Apollyon. Now, with a man like Martin Armstrong in authority over her, she felt that was not true. Either she kept her job and served the devil, or left it, and served God.

Alice Watson had listened to her explanation, and smiled. Then she reached out and patted Ruth's hand.

'You are a brave young woman,' she said. 'I am proud to have met you. It is not easy, what you are doing, but let us not despair too soon. If everything we have planned works out as I hope, there will be no reason for anyone to point a finger at you. They will blame the suffragette movement, which is too big to arrest and imprison all at once, however hard they try.'

Ruth remembered that conversation now as she stood in the upper corridor of Holloway, a few yards away from Sarah Becket's empty cell. Certainly they had planned carefully, and it had gone well enough so far. Alice Watson had been in Holloway herself, twice in the past five years, and that had been invaluable. But, as a prisoner, she remembered long empty stretches of utter boredom, when she was left in her cell to think or starve or watch a sunbeam crawl slowly across the floor. To her it seemed quite likely that no one would notice Sarah's absence for two hours.

To Ruth, now, feeling the sweat prickle on the back of her neck, it seemed almost impossible.

Prison, to a wardress, was a busy place, with countless duties to get through in the course of a day. Not the least of these was keeping an eye on the prisoners. Spying on them through the judas hole as you went down the corridor, just to see what they were doing.

Any wardress could do that, on any landing. Any time.

They had decided on two hours for a number of reasons. They had hoped to get Sarah in the basket between nine-thirty and nine forty-five, ready for the van which usually arrived and began to load at about ten to ten. It then took the best part of an hour, perhaps longer, to splutter its way through the traffic to High Holborn and stack the baskets in the large shed beside the laundry for the laundresses to empty. That was the most frightening part, Ruth thought. There would be little enough air in those baskets as it was, and the men might easily stack one or even two baskets on top of the one Sarah was in.

Then the drivers usually stopped for a cup of tea and a chat in the laundry. They were not part of the plot, nor were all of the laundresses. So it would take at least another half an hour, maybe more, before Ruth could be reasonably certain that Sarah was out of her basket, and free.

Then she could sound the alarm. They had agreed that if Ruth herself found that Sarah was missing, it would point less suspicion at her. Providing I can act well enough, Ruth thought.

I'll blush, my hands will shake, sweat will pour down my face. I was brought up to never tell lies . . .

She walked out onto the landing to look at the clock in the main hall. Five to eleven. Another forty minutes. Then she would be safe.

Safe?

'Where is the girl, damn it? Miss Harkness? Ah, there she is. Come here, girl. I need you.'

Oh my God. Ruth turned, feeling her mouth dry, sweat damp in her palms. Dr Armstrong, climbing the iron staircase towards her. Control your face, girl. Don't show any nerves now.

'Yes, doctor?'

'Just doing my rounds on your landing. Thought I'd call in on that blasted suffragette of yours. What's her name – Bucket?'

If it was meant as a joke even he did not seem to think it was a good one. Of course he knew her name, very well – as she knew his. Ruth looked at him and saw that behind the bluff, confident authority of his face there was something . . . what was it? Fear? Anxiety? Guilt? The eyes seemed smaller, darker, more sunken than she remembered. He was not examining her, quite the reverse. His gaze shifted away. *He* was sweating!

Ruth's mind worked fast. Five to eleven, it was too early. Sarah was still in the basket, she might be caught. Why is Armstrong sweating like that?

Because of that medicine he gave her last night? Perhaps it was too much. *He thinks she may be dead*!

'Becket? She's asleep, Dr Armstrong.'

'What's that you say, girl? Asleep, at this time of day? What is this, a rest home? Don't you get the damn convicts up?'

Not when they've been murdered, no. We leave them to lie until the doctors find them.

I was right. He's sweating more now. I've never seen guilt written so plain on a man's face. Murderer!

'Well, we'd better go along and wake her up. Got your keys?'

'Yes, of course, Doctor.'

Ruth turned and led the way along the corridor. But as she walked, she thought, this is no good. I've aroused his suspicions when I shouldn't have. He has to go in now because there's something unusual. And it's too early!

She stopped outside the cell door, glanced through, and said: 'She's still asleep, Doctor. It seems a pity to wake her. She was up early this morning, carrying the linen downstairs. I expect that tired her. She's only just started eating again, as you know.'

Dr Armstrong hesitated. 'Up early this morning, you say?' *Is that disappointment on his face*? 'What was she like then?'

'Oh, a bit tired, I would say. Not very strong, but all right in her mind. I expect the exercise was too much for her. That's probably why she's sleeping now.'

'What do you know about what's all right in her mind?' Dr Armstrong took a deep breath, staring at the cell door as though coming to a decision.

Go away, please! Let him come back in an hour and it won't matter, please God. Ruth prayed, her hands clasped demurely by her belt where she thought Armstrong wouldn't notice. *Our Father, who art in heaven . . .*

'Open the door, girl.'

'You're going to wake her up?'

'Yes, of course. I haven't got time to fool about. It's a medical matter. Come on, you've got your keys, haven't you? Hurry up!'

'Yes, Doctor.'

Ruth sighed, unclasped her hands, and slipped the key into the lock. As she did so a vision of the clock in the main hall came into her mind. Forty minutes too soon, she thought.

Eleven o'clock . . .

When Sarah awoke it was because the basket was moving, swaying abruptly and violent up and then down again, sideways, being carried somewhere at a slant so that she slid down towards her own feet and felt sure she would break through the wicker walls entirely at any moment. There were men's voices, grunting softly with the effort, swearing. Then without any warning the basket seemed to fly through the air and land with a crash on an echoing wooden floor.

It was dark. Cautiously, she stretched so that she was no longer bundled into a ball around her own feet, and moved until her head once again came into contact with the basket wall at the far end. It was less comfortable than before. The sheets had tangled themselves in a perverse way around and under her and for a moment she had a second panic attack. This time she would really not be able to breathe, and would have to scream . . . Another basket was heaved on top of hers, so that the wicker lid bent down, inwards, touching her head. Sarah could hear the men outside and stuffed a sheet into her own mouth so if she did scream she would not be heard. Then they were gone.

When they came again more baskets were slammed in behind

and around hers, and with the noise that they made she knew that the men were so distant and so busy that they would not hear her anyway unless she really yelled out loud, and she was not going to do that. Not now. She was going to escape!

It was really hot and close in the basket by now and she did have trouble breathing, but for a while she felt too elated to care. There was panic again when the van doors closed but then joy when the engine started and the van began to move – she actually sang for a moment and then felt suddenly, horribly sick with the jolting and the smell and the close, stale air. But she could still breathe. She took shallow, careful breaths with the top of her lungs only and thought, irrelevantly, this is how the midwife told me I should breathe when my baby was born, only it never was born. Not alive. Perhaps this is my delivery instead. *I* am being delivered. I am delivering myself.

The van stopped with the engine running and men talked outside for ages and ages. Sarah thought, miserably, they've discovered I'm missing and they've sent someone to search all the baskets and I'll be found and dragged out and . . . The van started.

This time it drove quite steadily with only brief stops here and there in the traffic for a long time and in the hot close air Sarah began to sweat and then doze again, so that she had no idea how long it was before the engine was switched off and there was a crash of doors opening. A little grey light seeped into the basket which let her see the weave of the lid. Then she heard grunting from the men again and the van bounced upwards on its springs as the first baskets were lifted out and there was more light. The basket came off the top of Sarah's lid and it was her turn; she felt herself dragged along the floor of the van and then lifted swooping into the air, with what seemed a louder grunt and curse from the porters.

Like a queen, she thought. Cleopatra wrapped in a carpet. She smiled to herself, enjoying the unpredictable jolting motion, and then panic came again – *who opens these baskets*?

If these men open them they'll take me straight back to Holloway and it'll all have been for nothing, all wasted. So I must – her basket was slammed down to the floor so suddenly that she banged her head on the lid and the bile came into her mouth and she thought nothing, nothing at all for a long moment until she came to and realised that the men had gone away.

Then no one came for quite a long time. Slowly, all the joy and anticipation drained out of her and a small voice began to whisper: *it's all a mistake, no one knows you're in here and you'll have to wait for hours and hours, perhaps they don't even open the baskets to begin the washing until tomorrow and by then you'll be too cramped to move, and also . . .*

A door opened. Footsteps, a rustling noise, skirts, women's voices, furtive, excited whispers.

'Sarah?'

Should she call out? Somehow the pressure of keeping hidden for so long kept her mouth shut. It was like a child's game of hide and seek – just because the others call you don't give your hiding place away. Anyhow, could she trust them?

The creak of a basket opening. Cries of disappointment. 'Sarah, where are you? Tell us, quick – are you all right?'

'Yes, here.' Her mouth was so dry it sounded like nothing to her. She shouted again and banged her hand feebly against the lid. A woman called out: 'Alice! This one!'

The straps loosened, the lid was pulled back and there was sudden, glaring light. And there above her was Alice Watson. Round spectacles on the lined face, grey hair as ever pulled back into a severe bun, thin lips pursed with anxious determination. Like a nanny with a naughty child. Sarah began to laugh. She could not help it. And with the laughter, tears, so that she could not see well. She tried to get up, failed, flopped back.

Hands came down to help, untangling her from the sheets, beginning to lift her. Many hands, many women. Her sisters in the movement. Laughing, anxious, triumphant.

'There now,' Alice Watson said. 'Put her down on her feet, gently, the poor dear lady. She weighs less than a ten-year-old child!'

23

When she was out of the basket, she could not stand. Her legs crumpled under her. But there were arms all around – to hold her, support her, carry her gently to a chair in the corner of the big laundry store room. Women all around – tears, laughter, kisses, celebration, and a lady doctor testing her pulse, peering quickly into her eyes, her sore mouth, asking how she felt.

'Wonderful!'

Sarah's first word led to smiles, laughter, applause even. But Alice Watson had no time for that.

'Then you must get out of that prison dress as quickly as you can. Here, I've brought one of your own. I'll help you put it on. The others will turn their backs if you wish.'

'What? No, no need. I'm not modest any more, I've nothing to hide.'

Indeed she had not, Alice thought, as she and the doctor bundled the dirty prison smock over Sarah's head and saw the thin arms and legs, the narrow sinewy neck, beneath. She had been thin enough before she slashed the picture; since then, Alice thought, she could scarcely have kept a mouthful down at all. Hunger is an illness when it looks like this.

But the cure is freedom – and joy.

As Sarah stood, tottering slightly, in her own long blue woollen dress with little white stars around collar and cuffs – one that Deborah had chosen from Sarah's wardrobe – Alice thought she understood, once again, what a striking figure

Sarah must have made as a young bride. The beautiful society girl who had married the elegant rising young bachelor and prospective MP, Jonathan Becket. Someone combed her hair for her, and with a smile of relief on her face and a sparkle in her eyes, she looked radiant. Her bones were good – only one did not expect to see them quite so clearly, in such a starved, emaciated face.

She will look like that when she is old, Alice thought. When she looks back and remembers these days.

Sarah smiled, overjoyed at her reception. She tried a few steps in her dress, swayed, and sat down rather too abruptly on a hard wooden chair.

'But how did you get this, Alice? It's perfect – it's my own!'

'Deborah sent it.' Alice Watson glanced up from a sack into which she was hurriedly stuffing Sarah's heavy shoes and grey, arrow-striped prison dress.

'Deborah? But how could she?' Sarah asked, confused. 'She's in Glenfee!'

'No. That's where you're going. Soon.' Mrs Watson stood up, the sack in one hand, and smiled down at her friend quietly. Ruth had been right. Sarah's mind was wandering. The bromide, perhaps. 'Didn't you get our letter?' she asked gently.

'Letter? Oh yes.' Memory came back, slowly. Everything in the prison seemed so distant, already. A dream. Another country.

But Alice Watson was full of bustle and orders. She handed the sack to one of the laundry women, with orders to burn it immediately. Then she bent down, put one of Sarah's arms gently round her neck, and raised her to her feet. The doctor, Rachel Camperdowne, took Sarah's other arm, and they walked her quickly out through a small door at the back of the building. Then down an alleyway between some dustbins.

'Where are we going?'

'To a car, I hope.'

A car was waiting in a back street at the end of the alleyway. A gleaming yellow 6-cylinder Noiseless Napier, with a young woman in plus fours and a motoring helmet holding the door ready for them to get in, and a crowd of street urchins in flat caps and oversize jackets clustered around to gape.

'Not perhaps as discreet as I could wish, but we'll change to a taxi cab before we get to the hotel,' Mrs Watson said. 'The chief thing now is speed, and young Miranda here makes a speciality of that! I don't want to have the air sucked out of my lungs or see any dogs run over, now, miss. We've an invalid aboard.'

What little they could see of the face of the young lady chauffeur grinned, and a gauntleted hand saluted. Then she walked round to the front to crank a handle, leapt aboard, and the car set off with an unfortunate jerk which dislodged three of the most curious street urchins from the back mudguard.

As they turned out into Holborn High Street, swerving between bicycles and grocers' drays at twenty and sometimes even thirty miles an hour, Sarah sat back in her seat and laughed in sheer exhilaration at the sudden extraordinariness of it all.

'Where are we going?'

'To meet your sister, Deborah Cavendish,' Mrs Watson said. 'She's in a hotel run by one of our sympathisers near Euston.'

'But – why not home?' Sarah asked. 'I have to meet Jonathan sometime. It may as well be soon.' At the thought of what she would have to say, all the joy went out of the unaccustomed sunlight, and a pulse began to beat unpleasantly in her neck. Alice Watson glanced at her oddly.

'Well, you can't meet him in Belgrave Square. Use your wits, dear – you've just escaped from Holloway, in open defiance of His Imperial Majesty's government. The first place the police are bound to look for you is your home, so you can't possibly go there. We hope they won't realise for some time just how you got out, but the chances are they will, so we had to leave the laundry as fast as we could. Not every woman there sympathises with us, or has the sense to keep her mouth shut.'

'But you said I was going to Glenfee – didn't you?'

'Yes. It seems the safest place. Deborah will tell you about it, later.' She leaned forward to tap their young chauffeur on the arm. 'This is it, Miranda. We get out here.'

The yellow car pulled up in a side street near Euston station. The three women got out and the car drove away quickly. They walked round the corner into the main road and Sarah suddenly felt dreadfully vulnerable, like a ten-year-old English child suddenly abandoned in Timbuctoo. The street was crowded with strangers, who understood nothing of how she felt. Her legs were shaky, and she could hardly stand, but she realised that to lean too obviously on Alice's arm would attract unwelcome attention.

There was a policeman in the street, further down – she could see him, calmly strolling along with his hands behind his back, occasionally catching sight of himself in a shop window and preening his moustache. Everyone in the street – men, women, children – was a potential enemy, who could betray her without even meaning to. Would it be in the newspapers that she had escaped yet? Surely not. But still, any attention attracted to her was dangerous.

The doctor, Rachel Camperdowne, left them to go along to the station and hire a taxi. She disappeared in the crowd and Sarah felt even more dreadfully alone.

'Why didn't we just drive there?' she asked irritably. 'This is stupid, Alice – I can't stand!'

'Lean on me. Look, if you do it like this it's not so obvious.' She stood very close to Sarah, holding her hand at waist level, shoulders touching. 'She'll be back in a minute. There are always taxis at Euston.'

'But why didn't we just drive there?'

'That yellow car of young Miranda's is too conspicuous. She was the only one I could trust to take us from the laundry but I don't want anyone to remember where we've gone. Look, there's Rachel already. You'll be all right, Sarah.'

To Sarah's vast relief the taxi arrived, and they got in. She sank back in the seat, exhausted. Her own weakness frightened her. Rachel Camperdowne felt her pulse anxiously, then pulled back the skin of her eyelids and looked underneath. Alice pulled the window across, so that they could talk without the taxi driver hearing. 'When did you last eat?'

'This morning. I think it was then. I had porridge.'

'And before that?'

'The day before. It was . . . difficult.' Haltingly, Sarah answered the woman's questions about her time in prison. Her fast, the forced feeding. The number of times she had vomited it all up. The bromide. Dr Camperdowne listened, appalled.

'The man should be struck off the register!'

'He will be, Rachel. Don't worry,' Alice Watson said. 'But not for any of that. That was just government policy.'

'Well, it's a good bowl of beef broth for you, Mrs Becket,' Rachel said. 'And then bed. A long quiet sleep, I should think, with just a few friends and no emotional strain.'

'You're very kind,' Sarah said. 'But I don't think I can. You see, there's something . . .'

'This is the place. Set us down outside that door, driver, would you?'

Sarah got out of the taxi carefully, and looked around. They were in a quiet side street with a motley terrace of tall buildings behind iron railings on either side. Directly in front of her was a tall narrow four-storey building sandwiched between two larger ones. The house was not very imposing. It had three small steps up to a brown door with a brass knocker and a fanlight above, in the glass of which she could see the letters Anglesey Hotel. There were net curtains in the windows, and colourful flower boxes on the sills outside. It looked clean and neat and comforting and feminine.

They walked up the steps and knocked on the door.

'You last saw her when?'

Ten forty-six. 'I couldn't say when exactly, sir.'

Ruth stood on the carpet in front of the prison governor's desk. It was a large room, comfortably furnished with a desk, fireplace, books, leather armchairs and a collection of pictures on the walls. The pictures were of ships on the Thames, sea battles, and bearded former holders of the governor's office. The present governor, a small man with luxuriant side-whiskers and moustache over a pink bristly chin, sat upright in the large leather chair behind his desk, glaring at Ruth. Beside him, on either side, stood Martin Armstrong and the head wardress, Mrs Canning. Both looked furious but, underneath that, a little anxious too. Ruth wondered at that. Were they afraid? Why was that?

She was too afraid herself to pursue the thought. This is my whole career at stake – my *liberty*, in fact. If they find out what I've done I'll be locked up straight away. Of course they'll find out – how can they fail?

'When *more or less* did you last see her, then, young woman,' the governor said with heavy sarcasm. 'Try to be as accurate about the time as you can.'

Ruth frowned. 'Well, it was between ten and eleven, I suppose, sir. You see, we were getting the cells cleaned out and taking the linen down, and then there was that riot on C landing. I was up there trying to quieten the suffragettes. Nearly all of us were.'

That was true at least, she thought. Nearly all the wardresses had been there. Ruth had played as prominent a part in quelling the riot as she could, so that everyone would remember her presence. Presumably the other wardresses who had been summoned into this office before her had already testified to that.

At least that was a point of faint hope. If the governor had been certain Ruth had been involved in Sarah's escape he wouldn't have bothered interviewing anyone else. She squared her shoulders and waited for his next question.

'When did you find out Mrs Becket was gone?'

'When Dr Armstrong came to see her, sir. I unlocked her cell door and went in and there was just a blanket rolled up on the bed. It was about – eleven o'clock, I think.'

And now it is twelve thirty-four, she thought, as she glanced at the clock on the wall behind Mrs Canning's scowling face. Joy burst in her like sunrise. Three hours since I fastened Sarah in the basket, two and a half since the laundry van went out of the main gates. If Alice Watson hasn't got her out safe and free by now she never will. And still the governor doesn't know how it happened!

Or are these three just playing with me?

'You are smiling, Miss Harkness. You find something funny about this, perhaps?'

The smile drained from Ruth's face. 'No sir, of course not.'

'Then why were you smiling?'

'It . . . er . . . I was just thinking, sir, how odd it was to see those blankets there on Mrs Becket's bed,' she said lamely. And how very much odder it had been to see the face of Dr Armstrong in the cell. She had thought the man would have a seizure. He had snatched the blankets from the bed in his great hairy hands and flung them aside as though he thought he would find Sarah Becket hidden beneath them. Stupid man – all he saw was a cockroach. Then he had turned on Ruth. His face had been as white as a ghost and he was sweating, great big droplets of it standing out on that fat forehead, running down his heavy jowls.

'Where is she, girl?' he had roared. He had even seized her shoulders and shaken them, beside himself with shock.

But that was all it had been. Only shock. He had not suspected Ruth at all, so far as she could see. He blamed Sarah – he seemed to think she had somehow escaped all by herself. And now – that man Armstrong is longing to be elsewhere, Ruth thought. She stole a swift, nervous glance at him. He was fidgeting, shifting anxiously from one foot to the other, gazing everywhere around the room but never particularly at her.

The governor was the real danger. And Mrs Canning.

'Try to think back, Miss Harkness,' the governor said. 'Did you take Mrs Becket out of her cell this morning?'

'Yes.'

'For what purpose?'

'To empty the sluice bucket as we always do. And then to change the linen.'

'Did she carry her own bucket and linen?'

'She did, sir. Yes.'

'And then you took her back to her cell?'

Ruth hesitated. Only for an instant, but it was a fateful one.

'Yes, sir. I did.'

The governor's eyes met Ruth's. She was aware that the other two were watching her intently too but she ignored them. Just kept her eyes cold and steady on the governor's while she trembled and shook inside.

'You took her back to her cell and locked her in? Are you sure?'

'Yes, sir. Quite sure.'

Dear God, Father in Heaven, don't let me blush now. Please if you have ever loved me don't let that happen. I have never told a lie in my life before – *why on earth did I tell this one*?

She had not planned it. The idea had come into her mind out of nowhere. A gift from God perhaps. Or the devil . . .

Mrs Canning stared at her fiercely. 'You were with her in the linen room, weren't you, Miss Harkness? You are saying you took her back up to her cell and locked her in *before* you came on to help to quell the . . . nonsense with the suffragettes?'

'Yes, Mrs Canning. I did it for her own safety, you see. She was weak after her hunger strike, and I thought she might get hurt, so I locked her in. I think she lay straight down on her bed. Then I came on to C landing to help you.'

'And you didn't check up on her afterwards?'

'Only through the judas, ma'am. She was asleep on her bed, or at least I thought she was, so I saw no reason to disturb her, like.'

This is it, then. Condemned out of my own mouth. They must know I'm lying, surely. Why did I do it?

To Ruth's surprise the governor and Mrs Canning began to confer in front of her.

'It must have been to do with the suffragettes' demonstration then, Mrs Canning. I'm sure of it. They started it deliberately to distract you and your staff. Then, when it was in full flight, one of them would have slipped over to D landing to unlock Mrs Becket's cell door . . .'

'But what with, sir? They wouldn't have a key.'

'A skeleton key or a copy, Mrs Canning. It's been done before. These women are educated and determined. They have connections outside.'

'But even if they got her out of her cell, sir, how could she leave the building?'

'Over the wall, perhaps with a rope ladder? That disturbance of yours took some time to quell, I fear.'

'It's possible, sir, but unlikely. If one could get out, why didn't they all go?'

The governor shook his head sagely. 'Ah that, Mrs Canning, is a political question, the answer to which may only become apparent with time. It depends on what advantages in publicity they believe they can make out of this wretched affair. What the devil?'

Ruth looked over her shoulder, away from her inquisitors, who seemed for the moment to be ignoring her. A wardress stood in the doorway. She looked upset and shocked.

'Excuse me, gentlemen, Mrs Canning. But there seems to be another suffragette demonstration. The prisoners on C landing are singing again and can't be stopped.'

The truth of what she said was obvious. Even at this distance the sound of singing came clearly through the open door. Mrs Canning reacted quickly.

'Right, then. I'll put an end to that straight away! If you'll excuse me, sir.' She strode across the room. 'Come on, Harkness. Come with me. It's time those fancy bitches learnt a proper respect for Holloway – and they can start right now!'

So I'm still regarded as part of the staff, Ruth thought with amazement. She followed the stocky figure of Mrs Canning out of the governor's room and down the corridor. At least, I'm a member of staff until I choose to resign. If they haven't worked out how I was involved by tonight, I can walk out of here and never come back. Take up that job Mrs Watson said she'd find for me. And by then Sarah Becket will be miles away.

The only problem will be to stop myself laughing. And singing. Singing the same song those women are singing right now on C landing.

As they came nearer, the words reached her more clearly. The whole landing was singing.

'Sarah Becket's body went a-marching through the wall!
Sarah Becket's body went a-marching through the wall!
Sarah Becket's body went a-marching through the wall!
And her cell is empty now!

Glory, glory halleluia!
Glory, glory halleluia!
Glory, glory halleluia!
Her cell is empty now!'

'Debbie!'

Sarah stood quite still in the doorway, swaying lightly. Deborah stepped forward, hoping that the smile on her face hid her shock at the gaunt face, the painfully thin hands her sister reached out to her.

'Welcome, my dear. I've been expecting you . . .' But her voice broke, she couldn't go on. For a moment the two embraced, and Deborah thought: how light she is, just a skeleton in a coat.

They drew apart and looked at each other through a film of tears.

'Same old Debbie. Always here when I need you,' Sarah said. 'But why . . .?'

'Never mind all that now.' Deborah took her sister's arm and led her forward. 'Come on in and sit down, poor thing. You need rest.'

'She does indeed,' said Rachel Camperdowne. 'I suggest this lady goes straight to bed. You can save any talking until she is comfortable there.'

Sarah said: 'Oh, don't fuss, please.' But she swayed as she said it. Deborah took her arm.

'It's all ready for you, dear. Come through here. I've brought clean nightclothes, everything.'

She led the way through a pleasant sitting room, furnished with soft carpets, comfortable chintz armchairs, and light, cheerful wallpaper, to an equally pleasant bedroom. The afternoon sunlight poured in through a window that looked out over a quiet mews and there was a large double bed with clean, crisp sheets turned back. On the dressing table were her own combs, hairbrushes and makeup case from home, a basin with a jug and ewer, and a small fire crackled in the grate. Tears came into Sarah's eyes.

'Is this my cell? It's like a dream!'

'Let me help you undress.' Deborah smiled, and began to unbutton the fastenings of Sarah's dress. It was an effort to keep the cheerfulness in her voice. She had known her sister would look thin, but not this skeletal. She wondered if she had been wise to plan the journey to Glenfee. And the other thing . . . But they could talk about that later.

Sarah climbed into bed and lay back with a sigh on the soft clean pillows. Deborah sat down beside her, took her hand.

'Now, our landlady, Mrs Stewart, has a particularly sustaining beef broth on the stove downstairs, with her own home-baked rolls and cheese. Do you think you could manage those?'

'Just a little, perhaps.' Sarah frowned, torn between laughter and a sudden, overwhelming desire for sleep. 'Debbie, what are you doing here?'

Deborah hesitated. Too much truth would be painful for both of them; she was not sure that Sarah was ready for it. But then, part of the truth could be a reassurance, she thought. She said: 'I heard you took a dislike to a picture, and so I came over to offer my help. I confess that at first I thought Jonathan might need my support too, but since then I have met Alice Watson here and learnt some things that . . . have made me change my mind. Oh Sarah, I am so sorry!'

'About Jonathan, you mean? Don't be. It's not your fault.'

'I used to like him, Sarah. I believed in him!'

'So did I, once. Debbie, I want to see him.'

'No!' They both turned to see Alice Watson glaring at them through her round spectacles, looking more than ever like a headmistress. 'It would be far too much risk for Sarah to go anywhere near her husband, either at her home or at his office. You have to appreciate that the police will be searching for you, my dear. It is your duty to stay out of sight. That is why Deborah and I have agreed that it would be best for all concerned if you were to get on the train tomorrow morning and go to her house in Ulster. No one will be looking for you there and you can rest in peace and comfort.'

'I see you have it all planned,' Sarah said. 'Glenfee would be wonderful. But, sooner or later, I have to see Jonathan. I could confront him at the House of Commons, Alice – why not? That would cook the man's goose – and the government's too. *Escaped Suffragette Raids Parliament – MP husband exposed as whoremonger* – wouldn't that look fine in the newspapers?'

She began to laugh, but then the tears took over. She turned away from them all, staring out of the window into the useless sunlight.

'You will do no such thing,' Mrs Watson said gently. 'Dr Armstrong is the main villain in this affair, not your husband, and, now that you are free, I will take care of him. If I can do it without causing a scandal to Mr Becket I will, for your sake. When you are safely settled in Glenfee I will write and let you know whether it is necessary to arrange for a lawyer to take a detailed statement of all you know about Dr Armstrong, but it may not be. We already have that letter you received, and there are one or two other things in the WSPU files about that wretched man which you may not have guessed at. So for the moment you need do nothing. Your duty is to obey orders, stay out of sight, look after yourself and get well. Do you understand me now?'

'Oh yes, I understand you.' Sarah wiped her eyes with the handkerchief Deborah had given her, and stared bleakly at the three women watching her. 'But life is not as easy as you think, Alice. You are a widow, but my husband is still alive, and marriage is for life, whatever happens. Whatever he has done, I loved him once, you know.'

There was a silence. Deborah watched and thought: marriage is for life. That is the cruellest thing she could have said, for either of us. What will Charles say, when we arrive together in Glenfee? God forgive me, but he will have to do exactly what I ask, for once in his life. At least as far as looking after Sarah is concerned. Then, when she is stronger, I will tell him about the baby.

And Sarah will be able to help me.

Not until Sarah had finished her beef broth, and Mrs Watson and Rachel Campderdowne had left, did Deborah say: 'It may have been very wrong of me, my dear, but I left a note for Jonathan before I came away. Asking him to meet me here in this hotel, tonight.'

For Martin Armstrong, the rolled-up blanket in Sarah Becket's bed had been like the sight of his own grave. He was a large man, overweight, addicted to good food and drink, and, when he had first seen that roll of hairy cloth where the woman's head should have been, he had thought his heart would drown in its own blood. There had been an intense pain in his chest and he remembered clutching the wardress, sweating, screaming something at her.

What he had said did not matter. It couldn't be her fault, surely. She was tough, stupid, unimaginative – she had helped him force-feed the woman every time he had done it. It had to be something to do with the other suffragettes in the prison, as the governor seemed to think. They had got her out while the wardresses were trying to control the demonstration.

Oh, what did it matter *how* the woman escaped or who

organised it? The point was that she was out, free, and within a day at most she would be telling her story to all and sundry. His life would be in ruins!

Twice he had tried to leave the governor's office, pleading that he had important appointments to keep with patients, but the governor had insisted that he send notes cancelling them. Not until three o'clock, when the songs of the suffragettes on C landing had been quelled, and several of them had been interviewed with no result, was he able to leave. He made immediately for his consulting rooms in Kensington.

As he sat in the cab on the way across town he totted up in his mind the list of dreadful things that were likely to happen, and what he could do about them.

First, Sarah Becket would tell her husband that she had been forcibly fed. And so Jonathan Becket, KC, MP, would know that he had lied to him. He would undoubtedly be furious. But what could he do about it, Martin wondered. Complain in Parliament, ask questions of the Home Secretary? Perhaps, but complaints had been made in Parliament about forcible feeding many times before. Public opinion was divided about it – many people would support the government. Particularly since this woman had destroyed an irreplaceable work of art, and then escaped from prison. Publicly. McKenna would be bound to stand firm and support Martin. There was no problem there.

Martin thought carefully. Jonathan might say that he asked me for help, though, and I lied to him, he realised. That wouldn't look so good. I could stop him from doing that by threatening to reveal that he visits prostitutes – that would shut his mouth. But then, if I actually *did* reveal that, he could tell the world that I rent rooms to these same prostitutes, which would ruin us both. That's no good, then. Damn.

The worst aspect of all, however, was that Sarah Becket knew, or appeared to know, a great deal about the brothels and prostitutes which Martin profited from. Ever since she had confronted him with this in her cell at Holloway – when he had gone in at the request of her husband to *help* the wretched woman, damn her to hell! – Martin had been wondering what to do about it. He would have to close the brothels down, he could see that. Move the girls to a different address where they could not be traced, and let the rooms to a respectable married couple, or a few elderly widows, or something. But such things took time, and he had been earning good money every day by leaving things as they were. So long as Sarah Becket had remained isolated in prison, nothing could have happened.

He had promised himself that he would begin the moves next week. He had already broached the subject with Mrs Burgoyne and received such a poor response that it had terrified him.

'Maybe *you'll* be sent down for a good long time, Doctor,' she had said. 'But I won't, and neither will the girls. A couple of months in the first division, at most. It's not such a crime or a scandal for us. If the Home Office start getting too harsh I shall threaten to name names in open court, and that'll stop 'em. Prominent lawyers with their members waving in the air and their pinstriped trousers round their ankles – won't look good in the columns of *The Times*, will it now?'

If she was forced to move at short notice from the rooms in Kensington, she said, she would have to cut down the amount of money she paid him. He already took far too large a cut for doing next to nothing.

It was after that conversation that he had returned to Holloway to find that Sarah Becket had decided to give up her fast and begin eating again. A decision which had enraged him so much with its pure wilfulness and perversity that he had lost his temper entirely and gone into her cell with a dose of bromide so large that it might easily kill her.

It had not done so and in a way he was glad, because the post mortem would have shown him to be incompetent at the least. But on the other hand, a dead suffragette could tell no tales. He would have been able to keep the girls and Mrs Burgoyne in the rooms where they were . . .

Now they would have to go. Today. Otherwise his career would be in ruins. He would be struck off the medical register. He would lose his posts in Holloway and the charitable children's home, and be unable to practise privately. He would be imprisoned. His wife would desert him.

He got out of the hansom cab outside his consulting rooms in Kensington and looked at the brass plate by the door and the rich curtains in the rooms upstairs. I was too greedy, he thought. Too confident. I thought that no one would suspect anything because this is such a respectable neighbourhood, with a doctor's plate downstairs. No one would think this could possibly be a brothel, and so rich, respectable men like Jonathan Becket would be happy to come here and pay ten times the normal fee.

God, I should never have pandered to a man with such a damned puritan killjoy for a wife!

But that's why they all come.

Damn! Damn! Damn!

He strode through the door and up the stairs. This deep pink stair carpet cost me nearly forty pounds, he thought bitterly, only a month ago. All wasted. On the stairs he met an eminent lawyer with a satisfied smirk on his face. Martin strode past him without a word.

Two hours later, after an extremely bitter and wounding conversation. Mrs Burgoyne and all the girls currently in residence had packed their bags and gone. Where they had gone, Martin did not, for the moment, know. They had not gone quietly, either. Not only had they made some extremely cutting remarks about his personal sexual abilities, they had flounced down into the street in their most conspicuous feathered hats and striking dresses, and sang and shouted at passers-by on the pavement while Mrs Burgoyne dithered around trying to hail a taxi. When Martin had gone down to check that they had finally left for good, he had noticed several neighbours staring openly at him from across the street.

Then, when he turned to go in, he saw that one of the girls had taken a penknife and scratched the words *Cunt for sale* underneath his name on the brass plate. Appalled, he dashed indoors, found a large screwdriver, and wrenched the thing bodily off the wall.

He spent another desperate three quarters of an hour clearing the place of anything that might be seen as incriminating evidence if the police should visit, or which might put off the seventy-year-old widows he hoped to introduce as new respectable tenants. In one cupboard he found a collection of dildoes and fancy underwear, in another a selection of young girl's dresses, in a third some ropes, straps, handcuffs, boots and riding whips. He took all these down into the kitchen and fed as many as he could into the fire. The rest went into a dustbin in the back yard.

The two things he kept were the large, leather-bound book in the front sitting room, with the photographs of girls and descriptions of their interests; and Mrs Burgoyne's book of accounts. She was a meticulous woman, well organised, and he was amazed she had left them. Probably she had forgotten in all the hysteria and the fun of mocking his sexual prowess.

He put them into his briefcase, thinking they would be useful when everything had calmed down and he was trying to set up a network again. Then he had a final look around, went outside, and hailed a cab for Hackney.

'How d'ye do. Reeves. Fine morning. Is my sister-in-law at home?'

'No sir, I'm afraid she is not.'

'Oh really? That's a surprise. She's usually here at midday.' Jonathan handed his top hat and gloves to his butler and began to shrug his way out of his coat. Reeves hung up the hat, dropped the gloves on the hall stand, and then moved behind Jonathan to help him off with his coat. There was something in the man's manner, Jonathan thought, which was slightly odd.

'Anything up, Reeves?'

Jonathan hoped not. It was a fine, breezy spring morning. His business in Sussex had gone well, and he had returned on the train to London in cheerful, expansive mood. He had thought quite a lot about his sister-in-law on the way, and realised he had been a bit precipitate that first night when she had arrived. After all she leads a sheltered life over in Ulster with that dreadful prig Charles. Of course she is fond of me but it will take time to make any progress.

He had hoped to find her here waiting for him in Belgrave Square. They could have had lunch together and gone out for a walk in the park, and he would have been charming and urbane and impressed her with his knowledge of the world. Then, perhaps a few days later . . .

He glanced at Reeves again. The man had not answered and there was definitely something odd, uneasy, in the expression on his face.

'Come on, man. Out with it! What's up!'

'It is . . . a little hard to say, sir. Perhaps . . . it would help if you came into the library.'

'The library? Why – is there a visitor?'

'No, sir.' Reeves opened the double doors of the hall, and stood back. 'On your desk, sir.'

Jonathan walked to the writing desk. It was a piece of furniture he was exquisitely proud of. It had been given to him in part settlement of a fee in his first really prestigious case. There was a letter lying on it. He reached out a hand to pick it up and then stopped, stunned.

'My God! What the devil is this?'

'I think perhaps the letter will explain, sir. It is from Mrs Cavendish.'

'Yes, but my God! The desk – it's slashed to ribbons!'

'Indeed, sir.'

Jonathan stretched out his hand across the ragged edges of ripped leather and picked up the envelope. The paper knife was there on the desk beside it. He slit the envelope.

Jonathan,

I will not write 'dear' because you are not that any longer. You will see from your desk that I have become a vandal, like Sarah. I believe it is from the same cause. What that may be is for your conscience to discover. I hope one day you repent of your perversion and become the brother-in-law I once knew. Until then, the damage I have done to your desk is as nothing to what you deserve.

Don't expect to find me here because I cannot bear to spend another night under your roof. I am going back to Glenfee.

Deborah.

Underneath was another sentence in a slightly different shade of ink, as though it might have been written later.

PS. It may be that you think you deserve a fuller explanation of this. If you think you do, meet me at the Anglesey Hotel, near Waterloo Station, between four and five.

He read the letter twice, astonished. Then he realised that Reeves was still standing deferentially, watching him. He had a sudden overwhelming desire to be alone.

'Yes, I see. That will be all, Reeves. You may go.'

'Sir.' The man inclined his head and left, his polished shoes clicking quietly across the floor. When he had gone, Jonathan stood for a moment in a daze, the letter crumpled in his hand. Then he sank abruptly into the chair in front of the desk and fingered the torn leather.

My God, he thought. Debbie did this! What the devil has she found out?

I hope one day you may repent of your perversion.

I go away for two nights and my wife's sister believes I have become a monster. Has all the world gone mad?

Sarah had not slept after all, that afternoon. Deborah felt guilty about it. Sarah looked far paler and weaker and thinner than she had expected. Twice she had insisted on leaving the room but each time Sarah had called her back, like a fractious child.

'I've been alone in a cell so long,' she said. 'You can't understand what a joy it is to have company. Don't go, please.'

So Deborah stayed and they talked. First, about life in prison, and how she had escaped. Then, innocuously, about Charles in Ireland. Sarah had not heard about the gun-running. She was intrigued, but not afraid, at all. She agreed with Deborah that, even if there was a conflict, women and children would be safe, and the fact of the troubles would mean that Ulster police would be too busy to search for missing suffragettes. But Deborah wondered if Sarah was strong enough to travel.

Sarah laughed. A rather strained, hoarse laugh from her scarred throat, but a laugh for all that.

'Don't worry – I may look thin but I'm not dead yet. This is the essential me you see before you, Debbie, bereft of all unnecessary fat. I think it's a wonderful idea going to Glenfee.'

'At least you will be safe from the London police.'

'Yes. I may have been a martyr for week, but I have no desire at all to go back to prison. The further we can get from Holloway the better.'

For a while they talked about Tom. Deborah was determined

to keep all news of her own problems from Sarah until she was stronger. Or at least until they were on the train.

Then, inevitably, they talked about Jonathan. Quietly, bitterly, Sarah told her sister the story of what she had discovered that day before she slashed the picture. And the role Martin Armstrong had played. It was as Deborah had suspected. Anxiously, she asked: 'Was I right to invite Jonathan here? If you don't want to see him, I can go downstairs and see him myself, or ask Mrs Stewart to send him away. He doesn't even know you're here, and he'll never suspect it.'

Sarah thought for a minute. She stared quietly out of the window into the sunlight over the mews, the bones over her sunken face clear and proud as those of a Spanish aristocrat. Then she said, very quietly: 'No. Send him up. I want to see him.'

'I shall be with you all the time. You mustn't let him tire you too much.'

A faint, bitter smile flickered on Sarah's face. 'It will be exhausting, of course. But it has to be done. You were right to arrange it. What time will he be here?'

'Between four and five, I said.'

'Then I must be up and dressed by then. I don't want to meet him like an invalid.'

'You should rest before then.'

'I'll try, if you stay beside me. You don't have to talk. Just be here.'

And so Deborah drew the curtains and sat quietly in an armchair by the fire, her hands clasped softly on her stomach, thinking, while Sarah lay in her bed and dozed. Both of them, from time to time, glanced at the clock on the mantelpiece and watched the way its hands gradually swept on towards four . . .

'Your visitor, Mrs Cavendish. In here, sir, if you please.'

'Hello, Debbie.'

'Jonathan. So you came?'

'As you see.'

Mrs Stewart closed the door softly behind him. Jonathan stood in the pleasant sitting room, taking in the flowery, overstuffed armchairs, the light cheerful wallpaper, the pictures of country scenes on the walls. The rigid, unsmiling pose of his sister-in-law standing in front of him.

'May I sit down?' Jonathan had left his hat and coat downstairs. He felt awkward, standing like this in a modest hotel room. It reminded him a little of the rooms above Martin Armstrong's consulting rooms. *Don't think of that now.*

'I think I would rather say what I have to say to you standing, Jonathan.'

She knows then, he thought. How on earth did she find out? He held out his hands, took a pace towards her.

'Debbie, what is all this? Why on earth are you here?'

'Partly, Jonathan, because I couldn't bear to stay in your house any longer. Oh Johnny, do I have to spell it out to you? Not only have you betrayed your own wife and lied to me – you put her life at risk by what you did!'

'Her life? Sarah's you mean? What in the world are you talking about, Debbie? I tried to help her – you know I did!'

'By sending in Martin Armstrong?'

'Yes. Of course. You know that – you were there.'

Deborah stared at him. Her own husband, she thought. Sarah could have been *killed* if Ruth had not rescued her. Does he really not know?

'Listen, Johnny. We know all about the . . . the women you went to see above Martin Armstrong's flat. We know about the little girls he takes there and the money men pay to seduce them. And about the house in Hackney – *and you know all this too*! So how could you possibly take me to see such a man and then pretend he had persuaded her to eat? Johnny, he nearly killed her!'

Silence. Jonathan stood very still, trying to take in what she had said. She looked so flushed, furious with herself because of the tears that were coming to her eyes because of the trauma of this moment. All the way here he had told himself that her letter meant she must have found out about his whoring. Though he could not understand how. But this was worse than that, much worse.

'Debbie, I don't understand you. Truly.'

'Then if you don't understand *her*, ask *me*.'

He had not noticed the door into the bedroom which had

been left ajar. Now he turned and saw . . .

A ghost.

'Sarah!' But it was not Sarah. This woman was too thin, too pale and anyway this is the wrong place entirely *she must be really dead as Debbie says . . .*

'Everything she says is true, Jonathan. Every word.'

'But . . .' He recovered, took a step towards her. 'My dear, is it really you?'

'Don't touch me, Jonathan!'

Well, that at least rang true.

'Why did you send that man to torture me? Debbie is right – I might have *died*. Do you hate me so much?'

'I don't . . . Sarah, why are you here? Have you been released, is that it?'

On the proud, beautiful face a wintry smile. No love though. 'I escaped. Don't ask me how.'

'I don't care how! My dear, you look ill. Won't you sit down? I can't bear to see you like this.'

Sarah paused, then sat. It was true, her legs were shaking. But maybe that was with anger. Very quietly, her throat hurting slightly with the words, she said: 'Jonathan, I went out to slash that picture as a political protest against the government's treatment of Mrs Pankhurst, but also because I had discovered what you were doing when you were visiting Martin Armstrong. You didn't really get treatment for a stomach complaint, did you? You were visiting prostitutes. Don't pretend – I know quite well it's true. You must imagine how much that hurt me. It would hurt any woman but especially me. Jonathan, you *know* how my father died. When I married you I believed that I had found an honourable man who would never, ever do such a thing, and yet—'

'Sarah, I did not—'

'You ran the risk of infecting me, Jonathan! Just as any man does who goes to such dreadful places. And worse than that, I discovered in prison that that man Armstrong whom you claim as a friend is actually a whoremaster who purveys young girls as merchandise for the sexual attentions of men such as my husband . . .'

For a moment her voice failed her. The tears got in the way.

'Sarah, I promise you this is not true—'

'Don't lie, Jonathan! You know it is. And not only that – you sent this man, this monster, to my cell to . . . to torture me. That's all it can be called. Stuff a yard of tube down my throat and pour cold soup down it until I vomit all over him. That's what he did and *you* sent him!'

'The devil he did!'

Jonathan swung round, glared for a moment at Deborah, stunned . . . She saw eyes wide with shock, fists clenched in rage. Then he knelt down in front of Sarah, took her hands in his . . .

'Let go of me!'

'Johnny, don't!' Debbie hovered over him, pushing him back. He turned, got up.

'I don't want to hurt you – my God! Sarah, are you telling me that man forcibly fed you?'

'Yes, Jonathan. That's exactly what I'm saying.'

'Then he lied to me! The utter, filthy slug – he told me he had persuaded you to eat. I told you that, didn't I, Debbie – it was the truth!'

'And you believed it? Knowing what sort of a man he really is?'

Jonathan stood quite still, staring first at his sister-in-law, then at his wife. He felt numb. As though a spear had struck him deep inside, where there are no nerves. Just heart and lungs and liver. And a man's soul.

Slowly, his mind searched through what they had said. He was a lawyer, even in shock. He took things piece by piece.

'You say that he force fed you – believe me, I did not know that. You say I visited prostitutes at his consulting rooms – that is true. But they were all medically clean, Sarah, I could not infect you. I took good care of that.'

'And some of them were children?'

'Some were . . . quite young, yes.'

He met her eyes briefly. Husband to wife, with the memory of all the years they had known each other. Thought they had known each other . . . Then he looked away, his face haggard.

'Sarah, none of this would have happened if we . . . if you . . . The women I went to, it was . . . for a medical problem, as

Martin told me. Perhaps I was foolish to believe it, but that was how it began.'

For a while there seemed no more to say. Once, Jonathan met Deborah's eyes and she looked down. Without thinking about it Jonathan said: 'I will kill him.'

'What?' Deborah gasped. 'Jonathan, what are you saying?'

'You heard.' He turned to Sarah. 'Clearly I have been a fool and betrayed you, my dear. If I were in your position I would not want to see a man like myself ever again. Perhaps you won't, I don't know. But, whatever you think of me, I value you and I have a score to settle with that man. When I have done that I shall come back and beg forgiveness perhaps, if I can. Till then, take care of each other and Sarah . . . I am sorry.'

The door closed and he was gone. The two women looked at each other.

'Does he mean it?' Deborah asked.

Sarah sighed. 'I don't know, Debbie. Somehow I doubt it, he's not that sort of man. But, to tell you the truth, at this moment I don't really care!'

On the way across town Martin Armstrong thought: if I can do the same here, I'll be safe. This is the only other place Sarah Becket knows about. If I can get all the girls out of here, the Commissioner of Metropolitan Police himself will be able to walk around this house and won't be able to prove anything!

It was rush hour, though, the end of the working day. Martin's motor taxi was blocked in a series of jams caused by motor omnibuses, horse-drawn drays, other taxis, trams, hansom cabs, cars, motor lorries, and even coster boys pushing barrows. The pavements were thronged with clerks, businessmen, and shoppers returning home. At one point a shire horse, pulling an omnibus in front of Martin's taxi, got its loose shoe jammed in the tram rails. The animal panicked, wrenched itself free of its traces, snapped the four-inch thick shaft of the omnibus, and kicked in the spokes of the wheel of a brewer's dray, which collapsed sideways, spilling barrels of beer all over the road. When the ensuing chaos and argument had lasted over half an hour, Martin paid off his taxi driver and got out to walk. But that proved a further mistake because he was not a fit man, and after a few hundred yards he was out of breath and his chest hurt. He did not find a free cab capable of moving through the streets until half past six, and it was nearly eight when it set him down outside the house in Red Lion Street.

The argument here was calmer, but not dissimilar to that which he'd had with Mrs Burgoyne. The madam, Mrs Stone, saw no reason why she should move immediately, and she had nowhere obvious to go. If Martin would pay to put herself and the girls up in a hotel or a boarding house for a week, she might consider it, she said. Otherwise, no. Anyway, there were customers in the house at the moment and others who had made appointments. She couldn't close down just like that! She was a businesswoman, she had a reputation to keep up. Surely a man like Martin, with connections in high places, could head off any unpleasant investigation that might take place?

Anyway, everyone knew that suffragettes were mad. No one in authority would take what they said seriously for a moment.

The conversation was interrupted by a scream from upstairs.

'Mrs Stone! Mrs Stone! Look out the window, quick! There's a terrible huge crowd outside, all pointing here!'

Martin felt the same shock to his heart that he had felt earlier that day when he had discovered Sarah Becket was missing. He swayed, clutched the back of a chair, and breathed deeply until the pain in his chest lessened and his pulse slowed. He walked to the window beside the front door, sweat prickling his forehead.

Outside in the street was an awesome sight. Thirty or forty women, all dressed in white, stood close together under the streetlights, holding placards and chanting. Martin read some of the placards.

End Child Prostitution
Close this Whorehouse.
Chastity for Men!
Stop Veneral Disease – End the Great Scourge!
Votes for Women!

Round the outside of the group of suffragettes was a crowd of onlookers. Some – a group of young shop assistants and delivery boys in flat caps and scruffy suits – were enjoying themselves throwing fruit and tomatoes, several of which had splashed on the suffragettes' white dresses. For a moment Martin cheered them silently, hoping they would drive the women away.

Then a delegation of women approached the front door. They were led by an elderly, determined looking woman with grey hair swept back severely into a bun under a small blue hat, and round spectacles on her nose. Behind her came four others. Three were in white dresses carrying banners; the fourth was a tall young woman in a plain brown dress whom Martin had seen before somewhere . . .

The wardress! Ruth Harkness . . .

Hurriedly, Mrs Stone locked the door and Martin stepped back from the window and turned down the light so that he could see and not be seen. The women outside hammered on the knocker. To his disgust, Martin saw that there were a number of shabbily-dressed young men behind them, earnestly scribbling into their notebooks.

The doorknob rattled. When the women outside found that the door was locked, one of them called out.

'Open this door, please! We represent the Women's Social and Political Union. We are campaigning for the purity of relations between the sexes, and we believe this to be a brothel which is responsible for the spread of venereal disease and the deliberate corruption of young children! We want to speak to the landlord, Dr Martin Armstrong.'

Martin groaned. He saw the young reporters scribbling frantically in their notebooks. Girls were milling around on the stairs behind him and two flustered middle-aged men came downstairs, hurriedly buttoning their waistcoats.

'What the devil is it, Mrs Stone?' one of the men asked. 'What's going on?'

Mrs Stone gestured helplessly towards the door. 'Bloody suffragettes! Blasted health and purity campaign, looks like! Caught *you* with your trousers down, haven't they?' Despite her annoyance, she couldn't resist a smile.

The man looked furious, pompous, and terrified all at once. 'I can't be found here, woman! I've got a family, a home, a reputation to keep up! Is there a back way out?'

Mrs Stone laughed. 'Yes, if you have to. Out through the yard by the dustbins. Show him, Jane, will you?'

As the two men hurried out, Martin looked about him irresolutely. Should he stay? After all, the suffragettes couldn't get in, unless . . .

There was a crash of breaking glass. The window next to the front door smashed and a stone rolled on the floor.

'Bloody hell!'

'Look out!'

'Stand back, there!'

'Open this door!'

'No!'

More windows smashed. Martin ducked out of the hall into one of the downstairs front rooms, but stones were coming in there as well. Two, three, six – there was shattered glass everywhere, all over the chairs and carpet. Shouts and cheers from outside, screams and yells from upstairs. He could see the stones going up to the first floor too.

Then the keen, piercing sound of a policeman's whistle.

I can't stay here, Martin thought. The police will come in and interview anyone who's here – I've got to get away. Whatever happens, this is ruin. Where shall I go?

He ran out through the kitchen and the scullery, into the back yard, past the dustbins and the outside loo. On down the filthy alleyway, panting, his heavy body unused to exercise. At least there were no women here – they had not thought to guard the back entrance. The shouts and screams were fading now. It was a long alley – at the end he could see a pool of light cast by a gas lamp where the alley emerged into the main street. Martin's chest hurt and his forehead was sweating. As he came near the end of the alley he slowed to a walk, breathing deeply, painfully.

Where now? he thought. Away from here. Home, to hide and plan and think. What good will that do? The scandal will be all over the press in the morning. What shall I say? The police are bound to go into that house now, even if they do arrest the suffragettes for breaking the windows. At least I wasn't there. If Mrs Stone lies convincingly they may not be able to prove any connection at first.

Oh my God!

He had forgotten his briefcase. It was there on the floor in

Mrs Stone's front room with all the accounts and photographs he had saved from the house in Kensington. And it was engraved with his name and address.

He dithered halfway along the alleyway. I shall have to go back and get it. No I can't – the police may be in there now and the suffragettes, too, for all I know. I hope they get arrested and their skulls split open by truncheons – *but what am I going to do*?

It's no good, I'll have to run.

He lumbered out into the street and almost bumped into two policemen. He turned to get away from them but one of them seized his shoulder.

'Just a minute, matey!'

'What are you doing? I—'

He turned, trying to be indignant, but, as he did so, the policeman shoved his right arm up his back, painfully, and the other bent to peer into his eyes.

'Yeah, this is one of 'em all right, Bill. Dashing out the back way to save 'is skin. You can see the guilt in his face!'

'But I—'

'Come on, sunshine. Save it for the Inspector at the station. You can make all your excuses there.'

Martin would have protested vehemently, but the pain of the arm twisted up his back was too intense. And then, as he thought of the briefcase he had left in the house another pain came sharp and fierce into his chest. He was gripped by a fierce cramp so that he couldn't breathe, and the harder he tried, the worse it became, so that he could feel his face turning blue and his tongue hanging out and then he flopped in the man's arms and fell face down in a puddle in the gutter, hunched over into a ball and twitching in agony as though with some huge effort his body might get his heart going again.

The two policemen bent over him, shocked, uncertain what to do.

'Blimey, George,' one of them muttered, awestruck. 'I think we frightened the bugger to death!'

Deborah had booked tickets on the night train to Holyhead which left at ten o'clock. She knew it would be a strain for Sarah but she thought it offered the greatest chance of concealment.

Once they were on board and in their sleeping compartment they could go to bed, and no one would disturb them until morning. If they had travelled by day they would have had to sit in a compartment with others, or go into the restaurant car, and in either place there might have been someone who would recognise Sarah, or simply comment on her unusually strained, starved appearance.

The difficulty was getting her to the station in the first place.

It was only a few hundred yards from the hotel, so they could easily have walked. But Sarah was in such a state of emotional and physical collapse after Jonathan had left that Deborah decided to ask Mrs Stewart to order a cab. At half past nine they sat in the front of the hotel downstairs, waiting for it.

Sarah wore a long black fur-lined coat which covered her body completely from head to foot, so no one would see how thin she was. It kept her warm, too – even indoors with coal fires Deborah had seen her shiver, and it was a cold night outside, windy with the threat of rain. She wore a small, veiled black hat, fastened under her chin with a ribbon as though she were a widow in mourning.

Deborah looked the cheerful one, with a pale blue coat and a feather in her hat with her hair up, but she was not. The scene with Jonathan had depressed her more than she had expected, and the cold dark night outside the window frightened her with its loneliness. She kept thinking of Rankin, walking away from her with his hands in his pockets under the streetlight on the embankment. Perhaps, if I go out now, he will be waiting at the station to see me off, she thought, and knew it was nonsense.

I am leaving London, I shall not see him ever again.

Only in my baby's eyes . . .

But at least now she had something to do, someone to care for. Sarah sat silent, reaching her hands out to the fire. She seemed to luxuriate in the warmth of the flames, as though she had never seen such a thing before. If she collapses on this journey it will be my fault, Deborah thought. We could have stayed another day . . .

'There it is!'

She saw the cab draw up outside and went out to the hall to show the cabbie which bags to take. Then she took Sarah's arm as they went outside, but Sarah climbed in without trouble.

'I'm not an invalid, you know,' she said. 'I could have walked.'

'I'm sure you could. But it's not necessary. Anyway, look!'

Outside the station were two large policemen, patrolling quietly up and down. Are they looking for us, or are they always there, Deborah wondered. She had never sheltered an escaped prisoner before, she had never thought to look. But coincidence or not, she was glad to drive past them in safety. It's going to be like this all the way to Ireland, she realised.

Mrs Stewart had collected their tickets earlier that afternoon so they only had to find a porter to carry their bags, and get on the train. When they were safely settled in their sleeping compartment, Sarah sat down quietly in the single armchair while Deborah unpacked their bags and brought out the nightdress and dressing gown she had brought for Sarah from Belgrave Square. Sarah watched her, smiling sadly.

'You're an angel, you know,' she said. 'To take all this trouble for me. I don't deserve it.'

'You never deserved to fall off your pony or slip on the ice when we were young, either,' Deborah answered. 'But I was there to help you home and bandage you all the same. I think I enjoyed it, at the time. Probably I just wanted to be loved.'

Sarah seized her sister's arm, and stared intently into her face. 'Don't mock yourself, Debbie,' she said intensely. 'You were here when I really needed you. That's not something to despise. I'm truly grateful. I hope I'll be able to repay it some day.'

Deborah looked away.

'None of us know what's going to happen in life, do we? Come on, let me help you out of that dress.'

Sarah stood up and turned her back so that Deborah could help with the fastenings. There was a whistle from outside and a chunter of steam from the engine. With a lurch, the train began to move out of the station.

'No, we don't,' Sarah said. 'And this year, too many dreadful things have happened that I never wanted. It's like a dream to me, to be going back to the peaceful countryside at Glenfee.'

Deborah helped her sister into bed, and then stood for a moment leaning on the wooden bar across the window, watching the lights flashing past behind clouds of steam. After a while, the glow of the city faded and the stars came out.

'Yes,' she said. 'It's always very peaceful, at Glenfee.'

PART FIVE

Glenfee

24

'That's it, sir. Tuck the stock tight into your shoulder. Elbows firm, like a tripod. Heels flat on the ground. Rock . . . steady.'

Simon Fletcher was aware of the mountains of Mourne in front of him, a faint blue blur in the distance. Nearer, fields, a line of elms in a hedgerow above a sunken lane, newly bursting into leaf. In the hedgerow, primroses, new ferns uncurling, some bluebells, a foxglove. And a small paper target.

Tiny, at this distance. Concentric circles, a black spot in the middle. Bring the foresight onto the black spot, hold it there, just in the middle of the vee of the backsight . . . damn!

The weight of the rifle, the tension, made his arms tremble slightly. The foresight wavered from the target. Simon took a long, shallow breath, and let it out slowly. Get it right, he thought. They're all watching. The sergeant, the other men waiting their turn. Charles, somewhere behind with his swagger stick.

Bring it back, that's it, just under the spot. Steady.

Now!

The kick in his shoulder, the enormous ringing bang in his ear, surprised him. The barrel pointed up, high, over the elm towards the mountains. Damn.

The instructor, Sergeant Cullen, knelt beside him.

'That's right, sir. Not bad, but you jerked the trigger. Squeeze it gently like I told you. And lean into the butt against the kick, to hold it firm.'

Simon's shoulder felt like a horse had kicked it. Grimly, he worked the bolt to bring another round into the breech, and pressed the butt against the bruise. Beside him, all along the line, other rifles went off, each flat crack seeming half as loud as his own. The scent of cordite, the sense of vast, lethal power, exhilarated him. I could learn to like this, he thought.

He brought the foresight down again onto the target, squeezed the trigger.

Five paces behind, Charles Cavendish stood, tapping his stick softly against the polished brown leather of his riding boots. He wore his khaki officer's uniform, revolver holster at his belt, a gleaming Sam Browne belt across his chest. Under the peak of his cap the grey eyes crinkled as they often did out of doors with the look of a soldier or countryman; and there was the hint of a smile on his lips.

The exercise was going well. When these men had finished, every man under his command would have fired ten rounds. The guns, brand new Mannlichers still in their travelling grease, were in perfect condition. The results of the shooting ranged from average to highly creditable. Some of the men – perhaps a third – were ex-Army, with a sprinkling of marksmen; but the rest, like Simon, had seldom or never fired such a high-powered weapon before. It was for them the exercise had been arranged. Most, under the skilled instruction of Sergeant Cullen, had landed at least half of their rounds somewhere on the target; and all, he felt sure, were immensely cheered and heartened by the exercise.

We must be the most powerful military force in Ireland now, he thought. If the government in London tries to impose Home Rule on us by force, they won't be able to.

Of course the Nationalist Volunteers, the Catholics who wanted Home Rule, had plenty of spirit; but they had little discipline and no arms worth speaking of. And the British Army, though well-equipped and highly disciplined, must have lost a great deal of morale after the Curragh Mutiny, when their officers had expressly refused to obey orders to march against the Ulster Unionists. That had led to the resignation of the Secretary of State for War, and an utter shambles in the British high command. And that was six weeks ago, when we were virtually unarmed, Charles thought. Whereas now, after the gun-running, we have the most modern rifles you can get. And the British Army in Ireland have only a fraction of the men we have.

And not a tenth of our spirit, Charles thought with a smile. I would hate to have a commission in the regular Army now. Half of their men would probably support us, if they dared.

'Sir! Sir – Colonel Cavendish, sir!'

He turned to see a young boy, a sentry, running towards him across the field.

'Yes. What is it?'

The boy reached him and saluted, panting for breath. Charles recognised him as one of a section which had been posted as scouts, to keep a lookout during the shooting. This boy had been with a corporal, at the edge of the field to the west.

'Sir, British Army patrol, sir. Heading this way. They're marching along the road, sir, from the west!'

'Good Lord! How many, boy? Where?'

'About twenty or twenty-five. Maybe a platoon, Corporal Duncan says. You can see them better from that hill over there. They're about a mile away, marching quite quick!'

'Come on then, let me see.' Charles strode across the field, not running, keeping calm. He had three times that many men in this field alone. But an imp of excitement and delight filled him. What if the British Army had really come out in search of trouble? To punish the UVF, perhaps, for getting the guns?

The boy was right. From the hillock at the edge of the field, Charles's binoculars showed a platoon of men, infantry, in full gear with haversack and ammunition pouches, marching with their rifles at the trail. In loose order, moving quite fast. An officer a few paces in front. As Charles watched, the man turned and waved an arm as if to urge his men on.

A pulse started to throb urgently in Charles's throat. They'll have heard the shooting – they can't fail to know we're here, he thought. It could be. It really just could be that the war for the freedom of Ulster will begin here, in this field, today! And I will give the first command.

Wouldn't that be a story to make young Tom proud!

Swiftly, he scanned the road in the other direction, and the fields north and south. No one else in sight, so far. Just the one British Army platoon. He turned to the two men beside him, gave out a string of orders.

'Right, you boy! I want you to take two men from that group over there who've finished shooting. Each of you go to one of the other three lookout posts and ask them to send one man to me with a full report on everything they've seen so far. *Everything*, you understand. You and the other two replace the men you send and make sure you keep your eyes peeled – I don't want to be surprised from any other direction. Got it?'

'Yessir!'

'Good! Now, Corporal, run to Sergeant Cullen and tell him that, as soon as those men have finished shooting, I want everyone except the scouts formed up in three ranks by platoons. And I want Robinson, Conroy, and McNeill sent to me up here, with rifles, right away. Off you go!'

'Sir!'

As the man ran, Charles took another look at the approaching platoon through his binoculars. He noticed his hand was shaking ever so slightly. I could start the war now if I wanted, he thought, very secretly to himself. Maybe these men will start it anyway, but, whatever they do, I could destroy that platoon completely and claim they fired first, if I wanted.

But that's not what my standing orders are. Charles knew them off by heart. *Do not fire unless fired upon and avoid all provocation. To avoid any possibility that the Army or police should attempt to seize your weapons, UVF officers should ensure that their contingents are of sufficient size to render any such attempt hopeless.*

Well, I've done the second, anyway, Charles thought. Now it's up to the British Army officer down there. He glanced behind him as he heard the first of Sergeant Cullen's barked orders and saw nearly fifty men hurrying into three ordered ranks. The three marksmen he had sent for came across the grass towards him.

'Right, gentlemen. I don't want you to draw attention to yourselves – and on no account are you to fire unless I give the order. But the rest of us are going to parade openly in front of that advancing platoon of the British Army. Do you see them, there? If by any chance I should give the order, and *only then*, you understand, I want you to be in a position where their officer and sergeant should be the first to fall. But you do not shoot unless I give the express order or fall myself. Is that clear? Now, let me show you where to hide . . .'

One of them spoke English, of a sort. Enough to negotiate with Mrs O'Donnell, at least. When Werner brought them to her, fresh from the ferry, they stood in the doorway of the little hillside terraced house and smiled. Blocking out the sunlight with their bulk, their heavy kitbags slung over their shoulders. All the little woman could see was three hulking shadows, the flash of teeth, and a glint of sunlight in their fair hair.

To Werner's relief she was undaunted. 'So, away in with you then. It's the three of them like you promised, Mr White, is it? Wipe your boots on the mat now and put your things in the two rooms upstairs – it's the ones on the right, you'll see them plain enough when you're there. And then if it's a meal you're wanting, it's on the table at half past six prompt, mind you, I don't keep it waiting and it'll go cold and be fed to the dog if you're not there, good hot food too, you'll see no better this side of the water.'

She kept on talking as she led the way into the narrow hall at the foot of the stairs, and had to back out of the way into the kitchen as the three big men followed her. Their shoulders scraped the walls and one kitbag brushed the single framed painting, of a little girl with beautiful curly yellow hair dancing on a beach in sunlight. At the foot of the stairs the first one, Franz, the only one who knew any English fit to repeat, stopped, clicked his heels, and bowed to Mrs O'Donnell as though she were a countess.

'It is a fine house, Mrs. I think we shall be comfort here. I hope your food is plenty hot and good too, so your dog get hungry, eh?'

Then he smiled and held out his hand, and the little Catholic landlady shook it, scowling a little to maintain her dignity, but pleased nonetheless.

'Don't you worry about that, now. I know what you boys

like. I've two sons of my own in the merchant service and another in the King's, and it's their rooms you're having while they're away. My boys write to me from Rio and Boston and Hong Kong, they do, they see all sorts of wonderful things, but never any cooking to match their old mum's, that's what they say in every letter I get, I'll show you sometime if you like, if you can read good English.'

'You show. I like that,' Franz said, and moved quietly away from her up the stairs, leaving the other two, monoglot Germans, to shake the old lady's hand and mutter '*Herrlich, gnadige Frau*,' and smile in their turn.

The house was a three storey one on a corner of the terrace, and the two rooms upstairs were surprisingly large. Two iron beds in the front room, one ancient armchair, and a window giving a view down a line of steep cobbled streets to Belfast docks. Werner wondered if he had been wise, choosing a landlady as talkative as Mrs O'Donnell. But she lived in a Catholic area where there would be no support for the UVF. And there should be nothing to arouse suspicion about three foreign sailors seeking lodgings so near the docks.

The three were called Franz, Karl-Otto and Adolf. They were all in their mid-twenties, six feet tall, and very broad across the chest. Franz had a charming smile and pimples on his chin; Karl-Otto had a nose that someone had pressed in, so that it zig-zagged puffily down his face. Adolf, the only dark one, had a thin face with receding hair and bony hands as strong as nutcrackers, with an anchor tattooed on the back of one and a ship in full sail on the other.

They sat down on the beds and the chair and looked at Werner, and he felt simultaneously reassured and annoyed.

Reassured, because each of them was clearly capable of picking up two Ulstermen and putting them in his pockets if necessary; annoyed, because the job might take a little more subtlety and training than that, and he doubted if these boys had either.

Despite his rank as Major, Werner had almost no experience of commanding men. The very nature of intelligence work meant that he worked on his own. He was not even sure how much these men knew, or what he should tell them. He had still less idea how he should establish a good rapport with his team, or make them trust him. The thought that he might have to give them instructions every day about where to go, what to do, came as a great burden to him.

He launched into a lecture he had prepared about Belfast, the people in the city, the political divide.

'The Catholic people around this house, like Mrs O'Donnell, may be counted largely as our friends, because although they have little active interest or sympathy for Germany, they are a minority oppressed by the ruling caste which is divided against itself – the Protestants of the Ulster Volunteer Force on the one hand and the British Army on the other. It is our job to provoke a civil war between the UVF and the British Army, so that they destroy each other and provide no threat to the legitimate ambitions of His Imperial Majesty Kaiser Wilhelm in Europe. Exactly how we are to do this I shall explain to you later. The first thing . . .'

'Major von Weichsaker?' Karl-Otto, the one with the zig-zag nose, raised his hand. Like a boy in school.

'Yes, what is it?'

'Where can we hide the guns?'

'Guns? What do you mean, man?'

'Well, I'm sorry to interrupt you, sir, but that woman downstairs, I know her type. She'll be in here searching through our clothes and cleaning up the minute we're out of the house. If she finds the guns it won't look good. Are we to carry them all the time or . . .'

'No!' Werner thought of the police, the way sailors could get into a drunken brawl, lose their temper. On the other hand . . .

'It's all right, Karl-Otto.' Franz spoke, his smile calm, radiating competence and control. 'I'll go down later and charm her. While I'm doing that you and Adolf can prise up one of these floorboards and put them under there. I've already noticed a loose one in that corner.'

Werner felt irritated. The men were supposed to be listening to *him*, he thought. But on the other hand he should be glad they had come all the way from Germany with their weapons safe, undiscovered by the customs. Perhaps they did know their job, after all.

'Yes,' he said. 'Do that. And I'll save the rest of the lecture until later, if you like. The main thing is to keep your mouths shut and your eyes and ears open. For the rest, behave like normal sailors. Franz can buy newspapers and translate them for you. I'll be in touch most days, so if you want anything I can help you to get a feel of the place. But for the moment your job is to establish yourselves here – and wait. My job is to plan exactly what is best for us to do, where, and when. Until I am sure of that, we can do nothing. So you just settle in, enjoy the hot meals, and live in comfort. But be ready to move any time I want you. All right?'

'Yes, sir.' The three heads nodded in unison. They did not salute – it would have seemed incongruous to all of them. But there was no sense in which they smiled or mocked him either. A small part of Werner expected that, always had done, because of his hand, which made him inferior to other men, unable to be accepted into the Imperial Army. To say nothing of what Charles Cavendish had done to him at school, all those years ago.

To his relief, these three, so far at least, seemed to accept him for what they had been told he was. A Major, a professional soldier in the service of the Kaiser. The leader of their operation.

He was beginning to sense, too, that they were not quite the boors they seemed. There was an air of quiet confidence about them, as though they had done these things before and were unworried by them. As though they knew their job, and trusted him to know his.

Let's hope they do, though Werner. After all, to ask just three sailors and a man with a ruined hand to persuade the UVF and the British to destroy themselves, that's not an easy task. If I can do it, it will be the triumph of my career.

He left them, walking out into the smoky, cobbled street, feeling curiously alone, and excited.

'What's happening, Sergeant?' Simon asked.

'Show of force, sir. And the Colonel's taking precautionary measures.'

'Do you think they mean to fight?'

Sergeant Ian Cullen was a short solid man with a face like a seamed cannonball. He had fought the Boers, the Pathans, the Zulus, and the Catholic Irish, but his most formative military experience had been five years on the North West Frontier. There, as a young man, he had discovered that almost every rock could hide a bearded tribesman with a long flintlock rifle, any waterhole could be poisoned, any tempting glance from a veiled, sloe-eyed village girl might mean her brother was hidden behind a curtain with a slim curved knife, hoping to slit your throat and present your balls on a plate to his sister. The message was: trust no one but your comrades, and believe most of them are fools, too.

He glanced briefly at the sparkling eyes of Simon Fletcher. In Sergeant Cullen's view, anyone with eyes alight like that meant trouble. The young ADC had just fired a high-powered rifle for the first time, and now he thought there was going to be a battle. Not only that, but he looked as though he might enjoy it.

'They might mean it, but they'd be mad to try,' he said shortly. 'I should go to the Colonel if I were you, sir. He might need you.'

As he watched the young man cross the field, Sergeant Cullen saw the platoon of British soldiers come into sight, along the country lane about a hundred yards away. Always, throughout his military career, it had been axiomatic that you trust your comrades; and now those comrades, British Army soldiers, were the enemy. Not only that, but Colonel Cavendish, like a Pathan chieftain, had snipers concealed in the hedge, to fire on them at any false move.

For a second the Sergeant felt a twinge of conscience. If this went wrong, he would be in open rebellion, liable, perhaps, to be hanged as a traitor. But that was all nonsense, he told himself. The government would never have the nerve, and anyway, it was they who were in the wrong, with their Home Rule that would hand the country over to a bunch of disaffected Fenian rebels. Some of the best men in the army were in the UVF. Colonel Cavendish, for one. The way he had organised the landing of the guns at Bangor was staffwork of a higher order, and this training session showed a commendable attention to the needs of young recruits. Now, in Sergeant Cullen's eyes, his instant decision to ensure their safety by covering the approaching men with an ambush showed a most commendable mistrust of appearances.

If a man was ready for things to go wrong, the Sergeant thought, he was more likely to survive when they did . . .

Charles met Simon halfway as he strolled back across the field towards the main body of his men. He was in clear sight of his hidden snipers all the way; he had a white handkerchief in his hand which he would drop if he wanted them to fire. But it was unlikely, he thought. There had been no reports of any other groups approaching to surround them, and it would be suicide for this single platoon to try to attack from the road. The most they might do was attempt some police action – demand the surrender of the guns, perhaps, which would make them look foolish. This is about propaganda and morale, Charles thought. I must manage this situation to gain the maximum psychological boost for my men.

He saw the young officer – a Captain – marching busily towards him at the head of his line. He's in a fix, too, Charles thought. If he ignores us, he'll look a fool; if he tries anything, he'll fail.

He wandered casually on towards his men, listening to the steady tramp, tramp of the British Army's boots approaching. Sergeant Cullen had drawn up the UVF soldiers in three platoons of three lines each. All stood rigidly to attention. A few – about a quarter, maybe – wore military khaki; the rest were dressed in rough workmanlike jackets and coats that approximated as closely as possible to the same thing. Many were in flat caps, a few in trilbies or bowlers. Several had wrapped puttees around their trousers and most had some kind of military-looking belt, with ammunition pouches, and haversack.

And all, now – every single one of them – had his own brand-new Mannlicher rifle.

Charles thought: if I was that young British Army captain, I wouldn't want to see that. I'd pretend I hadn't noticed.

He smiled, and glanced sideways over his shoulder. The hedge at the edge of the field was less than three feet high, so the two sides could see each other very clearly. The British platoon was nearly opposite them now, about ten yards away from the rigid lines of the UVF. They had shouldered arms, and kept up a steady, well-drilled pace. But none of them were looking to the front, as the drill-book said they should be. Every single eye in the British ranks was straying sideways, taking in the details of the UVF men they were about to pass.

Every eye, that is, except those of the young Captain, who was affecting to ignore them.

In his best, clipped, Sandhurst-style tones, Charles said: 'Sergeant Cullen! Order the men to present arms, if you please.'

'Sir!' Just as the tradition of the Army ensured that his commanding officer's voice was quiet, casual, polite, assuming that discipline was so absolute that an officer's request in the gentlest tones would be instantly obeyed, so Sergeant Cullen's parade-ground voice, assiduously cultivated over the years, was a high-pitched bullroar, so ear-shatteringly loud that no private soldier, even if deaf, blind, and afflicted from birth with congenital idiocy, could fail to be affected by it, and jump to obey.

'***Companeeeee! Prepare to salute! Preeezent . . . arms!***'

A cloud of rooks rose, flustered, from a treetop four fields away. Nearer at hand, as it had to, the head of the young British Army captain turned right to see what was happening.

He was being paid a compliment. The entire company, fifty men of the Ulster Volunteer Force, were saluting him in the traditional style of the British Army. Charles, Sergeant Cullen, and his half-dozen officers all had their right hands raised to their caps. The men in the ranks stood, ramrod-straight, one foot behind the other, with their rifles held vertically, directly in front of them.

Brand-new, totally illegal, German rifles. Better than the ones the British soldiers had. Held out, straight in front of them, in a position no one could possibly pretend to ignore.

As a salute. A loyal gesture of respect.

Charles could not quite keep the smile from his face. He guessed that there were probably several other smiles in the ranks behind him, as well.

He watched the young British Army captain. What do you do now, boy? he asked him silently.

For a moment the young man looked away, and Charles thought: by God, the puppy, he's going to ignore us! If he does that, the brat, I'll march behind him, all the way down the road to Ballygowan, and arrest him at the crossroads!

But the habit of military courtesy prevailed. The young man was, after all, being saluted not only by a force vastly superior to his own, but by a commander wearing the cap of a Colonel. The order came ringing back over the hedge.

'Platoon! Eye-es . . . *right*!'

The order was slightly superfluous. All the British Army soldiers were already gazing to their right, but now they had permission to do it. In the traditional response to the salute, they marched past the saluting UVF men, their eyes looking rigidly at them over their right shoulder, the young Captain with his hand raised stiffly to the peak of his cap in salute.

In Charles's left hand, he felt the white handkerchief crushed firmly in his fist. Fifty yards away, hidden in the ditch, his three best marksmen watched the scene, grinning to themselves over the sights of their guns. One of them could just see the young captain's eyes, tiny black dots at this distance, over the foresight at the tip of his barrel.

25

The lounge of the Imperial Hotel was comfortable, warm, extensive. An ample coal fire blazed in an impressive grate, surrounded by a fireplace of pink and grey marble. On the walls, solemn portraits of city dignitaries alternated with pictures of railways, docks, and shipyards. The room was full of armchairs and chesterfields, screened from each other by luxuriant potted palms and aspidistras. Waiters flitted discreetly between them, ministering to small groups of earnest businessmen and gossiping wives.

Werner sat in an armchair in a corner by the window, where he could look out into the street and keep an eye on anyone who came in through the main entrance. A newspaper lay unread on the low table in front of him, a cigarette smouldered in his left hand. A thin smile crossed his lips as he watched the solid citizens of Belfast moving and chattering between the potted plants, like beasts in a jungle. I am like a hunter here, he thought, hidden in the foliage, waiting for the perfect shot.

He flicked his ash into the ashtray, blew a smoke ring, and watched.

A young man entered the lounge.

He was very slim, in blue blazer and flannels, with a straw hat in his hand. His brown hair was cut fashionably short, and his profile, as he glanced around the room, was classically beautiful. Broad forehead, regular aquiline features, smooth rosy skin. He moved through the room with casual grace, like an athlete, a gazelle amongst hippopotami. At last he saw Werner, strolled towards him, and sat down on the sofa opposite.

'I couldn't see you. Were you hiding?'

'No.' Werner took a long drag at his cigarette, exhaled, smiled. 'Just watching.'

His manner, the long slow look from the unsettlingly cold blue eyes, irritated Simon Fletcher. He looked away, out of the window, to reassure himself that no one had followed him here. 'Well, I hope it amuses you.'

'Oh, it does.' It was the first time Werner had seen Simon in civilian clothes. Close to, he noticed that the blazer was slightly threadbare around the cuffs and elbows, the straw boater faded. This relieved him. He didn't want Simon becoming too wealthy, too independent. 'Would you like coffee?'

'Why not?'

Werner raised his hand to beckon the waiter and ordered. While they waited, he said: 'Our last interview was very useful. I was much praised for my articles in the *Neue Zuricher Zeitung*. My editor is coming to regard me as something of an expert on Ulster affairs.'

'How nice.' Simon lounged back comfortably in the sofa and raised an eyebrow ironically. 'That's what you wanted, isn't it? But then, I expect these things seem a little different from the perspective of Zurich.'

'Of course. Most of my readers are satisfied with a very superficial understanding. But for my own self-respect, I like to maintain higher standards. I need to know more.'

The waiter arrived and put a tray with silver pot and two cups on the table between them. Werner paid, bent to pour the coffee carefully with his left hand, then put the pot down and passed the cup to Simon with the same hand. Simon made no move to help him. As the young man took the cup Werner noticed him gazing contemptuously at his damaged right hand, the one he could never use for such delicate operations.

Simon sipped his coffee and smiled, looking perfectly relaxed, perfectly at ease, casually unaware of his own good looks. He said: 'I could tell you more, of course, if you like. If the pay was right.'

Werner finished pouring his own coffee, balanced it carefully beside him on the left-hand arm of his chair. 'The pay would be the same as before. The newspaper is quite happy with that.'

'I might need more.'

Simon let the words hang in the air between them, and watched a flicker of surprise cross the other man's face.

Werner felt a surge of anger, fuelling the contempt which he had felt ever since he had met this young man. But he controlled it, quickly. Simon Fletcher was the most useful informant he had found so far in Ulster. For the past two months they had been meeting regularly in different places, always with a straightforward, mutually profitable exchange of information for money. As ADC to one of the leading UVF commanders, Simon had access to and understanding of some of the most important plans of the organisation. As a talented young man of poor background with no moral principles, he was prepared to sell some of this information for money. On condition that it was published in Switzerland, attributed to no one, and shorn of certain precise details which might give the informant away.

Those were terms which Werner could happily comply with, since the most crucial details of Simon's information were not intended for publication at all. Instead, they went straight into the reports which Werner wrote for von Falkenhayn in Berlin. Any extra money Simon received would come straight out of the coffers of the German Chancellery.

I suppose they can afford it, Werner thought. The only question is, how much this smooth-faced little whore deserves.

The vital thing that Simon Fletcher did not know was how Werner had worked out that he would be a useful informant in the first place. Simon had no idea that Werner had known Chalres Cavendish at school. And even less idea what that schoolboy relationship had been like.

Werner smiled and said: 'Why more, Simon?'

'It's becoming difficult. We're better organised now, better armed and equipped. There are more people around all the time, more checks on everything, more security. It's quite possible the government will move against us any day, so we have to be careful. And if anyone was to think I was a police spy . . .'

He left the sentence in the air, but he did not shudder or look frightened at the prospect. Werner had the impression it was just something the boy said, for bargaining purposes only. There's real steel at the heart of this boy's selfishness, he thought. He'll take care of himself if he has to.

'All right, then. How much more?'

'Fifty pounds.'

Twice as much as before. Werner thought. More than half a year's wages for a dock labourer, as this boy's father had been. He frowned. 'That would depend on whether you could tell me what I want to know.'

'Which is?'

A middle-aged lady and three young girls settled themselves noisily into the chairs and sofas immediately behind Simon, and for a moment Werner did not answer. But there was a screen of thick-leaved foliage between the back of Simon's head and the young women, and when they were busy with the waiter Werner leaned forward and said quietly: 'I need to know about Sir Edward Carson.'

Simon looked surprised. 'What about him, exactly?'

'Well . . .' Werner hesitated. I'll try and do this as a journalist first, he thought, but if it doesn't work, there's always the other. This is the time to use what I know, if I have to. It's safer if he still thinks I'm a journalist, though. 'Carson was over here in Ulster shortly before the gun-running, wasn't he? I saw him making speeches. And your unit was guarding him.'

'Some of the time, yes. So?'

'Well, as you say, it's quite possible the government could attack you at any time. Or even arrest Carson. You must have thought of that.'

'Of course. That's why we guard him.'

'Quite. Well, my editor would like an article on that. The security aspect and so on. How exactly you organise it, how many men are involved at each stage, where he sleeps, what you think the major risks are, that sort of thing. It would be an interesting article to read; it would make clear to everyone what an important man Sir Edward Carson is, and how seriously you people take things.'

Simon frowned, thinking. 'Well, I suppose I could tell you in general terms . . .'

Werner shook his head. 'No, you don't understand. In general terms I could write it myself, already. Any journalist could. To make it authentic I need to know the exact details of his next trip to Ulster – dates, times, the units involved, everything. Don't worry, I wouldn't publish it until the day after his trip was over, to safeguard you. But I need to have accurate details in the first place. That's what would really give colour to the article, make all the difference. It would help my career. After all, it's only going to be published in Switzerland. None of your colleagues are ever going to read it.'

Simon hesitated. The girls behind him looked at the plate of cakes the waiter had brought, and one exclaimed: 'Ooh, Mummy, you shouldn't!'

Simon said: 'I don't know. I think the best thing would be if I told you everything about how we guarded Carson last time he was here, before the gun-running. That would give you colour all right but there would be no risk to us . . .'

'No.' Werner stubbed his cigarette out decisively in the ashtray. 'That's no good at all. You don't understand the newspaper business. If I tell my editor what happened last month it's no use to him at all – it goes straight in the bin. It's only today's news, or better still, what's going to happen *tomorrow* that he wants to know. It's got to be Carson's next trip or nothing.' He took out a notebook. 'I imagine there will be a round of speeches soon to celebrate the safe landing of the guns. When is he coming over from London?'

'This Saturday, I think.' Simon hesitated, watching Werner write it down.

'Good. Where, what time?'

'I don't know. I'd have to check. You know these things have to be secret. I'm not even sure . . .'

'If it wasn't secret, I wouldn't have to ask you.'

'I know.' Simon sat very still for a moment, his soft hazel eyes fixed on Werner's. There was a slight flush on his cheeks. Don't try to pretend you've got principles now, boy, Werner thought. It's too late.

Simon said: 'I don't think I can tell you that. It's too risky.'

'Think of the money, Simon. I might even pay more than you ask.'

It was the wrong thing to say. A tight, hard look came across the young man's face, and Werner glimpsed for the first time the cruel little guttersnipe hiding behind the perfect features. And mixed with the cruelty, suspicion and cunning. It was a look he had seen on the faces of boys at Eton, long ago.

'I don't believe you want this for a newspaper article at all, do you? You're in the police, aren't you? Either that or a German spy.'

So the journalist idea has failed, Werner thought. He said, coolly: 'And if I am?'

'It would have to be a lot more money.'

'I can pay.'

The two men stared at each other in silence, recognising the change in relationship. One of the girls behind Simon said: 'You meet such interesting people here, don't you, Muriel? That's why I come.'

Keep him here, whatever you do, Werner thought. If he gets up to go now you've lost him. He said, carefully: 'I always wondered how a young man like you could fit in with the Orange movement.'

'What the hell are you talking about?' Simon stared at him, his voice low and urgent with tension. '*Are* you a spy or not?'

'Sssssh.' Werner put his finger to his lips, nodding significantly in the direction of the young ladies a few feet away behind the potted plants. 'Never mind who I am for the moment. I'll tell you that in a minute when you've answered my question. Don't worry, I'm not insulted.'

Werner's coolness, the odd menacing light of amusement which flickered in his eyes, disconcerted Simon. 'Answered what question, exactly?'

'How an intelligent young man like you can work and survive in a military organisation dominated by a religious movement, the Ulster Presbyterian Church.'

'I don't see what that's got to do with anything. I go to church like other people. Anyway, the Orangemen are just cannon fodder, rank and file. They provide the bodies and the organisation, and industrialists provide the money. But the UVF is actually run by professional soldiers, aristocracy. Men of the upper crust. Mostly Anglicans, actually.'

'Like Charles Cavendish?'

'Yes, if you like. I don't see what the hell this has got to do with . . .'

'One minute, and you will.' Werner held up his crippled right hand, one finger extended like a warning. The finger seemed to fascinate Simon. Werner said: 'So when you and the aristocratic Colonel Cavendish hear some of the fundamental Orange preachers holding forth about Old Testament values, how do you feel, Simon? When they talk about Sodom and Gomorrah, for instance? After all, Sir Edward Carson is a fine speaker, as I heard for myself the other day, but he is very morally correct, too, is he not? I believe it was he who prosecuted the poet, Oscar Wilde, for . . . what some people call unnatural vices, some twenty years ago. He does not seem to me a man who would look kindly on any . . . immorality . . . amongst his followers. I wonder if that is a strain, sometimes, for a young man such as you.'

For a moment Simon sat quite still without speaking. He seemed very cool but a flush flared on his cheeks and then drained away. There was a vicious look in his eyes, like that of a weasel who has been cornered by a terrier and will bite if it comes any closer. One of the girls behind said: 'Oh, Belinda, you really can't have another! It's sinful, that's what it is.'

Simon murmured: 'I don't understand you.'

'Let me make myself clearer then. If I wrote in my newspaper, or better still in a letter addressed to Sir Edward Carson, House of Commons, a paragraph to say that Simon Fletcher was a sodomite, committing sin and buggery with Colonel Charles Cavendish of the UVF, what would be his reaction, do you think? What would happen to you? It is a crime that carries a two-year prison sentence, I believe.'

For the first time Simon appeared flustered by the proximity of the young ladies behind him. Werner had deliberately raised his voice a little louder than it needed to be and Simon glanced nervously over his shoulder to ensure the women had not heard. Then he turned his head this way and that, as though looking for a way to escape.

'If you leave now I shall do exactly what I said. Sit still.'

Simon shuddered, then took a deep breath and gripped the

edge of the sofa firmly. He met Werner's eyes with a look of hatred.

'How did you know?'

'That is none of your business at the moment. Let us just say I am older than you, and . . . you are not quite so invisible as you seem to believe.'

Let him sweat, Werner thought. He had no intention of revealing his schoolboy connections with Charles Cavendish. That would only give Simon a weapon to turn against *him*. After all, knowledge was power. If he had not known from his own body what Charles was like, he would not have watched him for weeks with the intense gaze of hatred. Would not have seen that he had a young, handsome aide-de-camp who was constantly with him. Would not have approached that aide-de-camp to test his loyalty – and found it wanting. Would not have tested it further with the inspired guess that he had made just now.

There was no doubt it was true. The fascinated horror in Simon Fletcher's eyes, the fear and honesty that went into his response, put it beyond doubt.

'What do you want me to do?'

Werner took his time. He extracted a fresh cigarette from the silver case in his pocket, lit it left-handed without offering one to his victim, and said: 'No more than I have already told you. I want you to get me a full itinerary of Sir Edward Carson's next visit to Ulster. Date of arrival, people he'll meet, speeches he'll make, houses he'll stay in. I need a precise time and place for all those. Also, exact details of how he'll be guarded – which unit, how well armed, how many men, how often the guards change, that sort of thing. It shouldn't be too hard for you. A matter of detailed staffwork, that's all – and that's what your unit's good at, isn't it? Part of your job.'

'I can't find out all those things! They don't write it all down on one sheet of paper, you know. They keep it secret and change their minds at the last minute, sometimes, for security.'

'You're part of that security, aren't you? You and your lover boy?'

'Yes, but—'

'Then make it your job to find it out! If it's difficult, that's too bad. You know what the alternative is.'

As the shock of discovery sank in, Simon struggled to get control of himself. He felt as though he had stepped through a looking-glass, into the sort of situation which he recognised, but in which he had always previously been in control. He had to find out what the rules were, what were the limits to Werner's blackmail.

'Why do you need to know? You *are* a German spy, aren't you?'

This time it was his voice that was raised slightly higher. He noticed Werner's eyes flicker momentarily past him, to check if they had been overheard. Two can play this game, he thought.

But then we both lose . . .

Werner said: 'You can think that if you like, it doesn't matter to me. I've always regarded myself as a humble journalist.'

'Liar!'

Werner stared at him coldly, noticing a hint of courage return to the young man's face. But it was the courage of desperation, the weasel trapped with nowhere to run. He exhaled smoke across the table.

'You can insult me if you like, little pederast, I am impervious to that. But I give you two days, that's all. You must come up with the bones of the information by then. I shall look it through and possibly ask for more details. If there is any backsliding or failure, then you and your Colonel will provide the biggest scandal the national press has seen this year. And for all I know Sir Edward Carson himself will lead the case in court for the prosecution. It will do the cause of Ulster Unionism no good at all. Rest assured, young man, I *am* a genuine journalist, and your story would further my career just as well as the other.'

'Why don't you just publish it then?'

Werner smiled. He was aware that it was not a nice smile but he was enjoying the situation. His dislike for Simon and everything he stood for was intense – and he was also aware just how viciously the young man would fight back if he got the chance. It was not a chance Werner had any intention of giving him.

'Let's just say that I understand and sympathise with your perversion, shall I? And that it would pain me to think of a sensitive young man like you being beaten and buggered all day by strangers in prison. Or does that appeal to you, perhaps?'

Simon's face had gone quite white, and his hands shook as he stood up, quite involuntarily, quivering in front of his accuser. Werner thought he might have gone too far. But then they both saw a waiter, hovering uncertainly, and the moment when Simon might have attacked him was gone. He turned abruptly to leave.

'Simon!'

It was a pleasure to Werner to see how his voice brought the boy up short, like a dog on a leash.

'Yes. What now!'

'You forgot this.'

He held out the faded straw boater. Simon reached for it but Werner held it back. As the boy bent towards him, Werner hissed: 'At the Royal Ulster, on Monday at six, as before. And remember, I shall write the article beforehand and leave it in an envelope ready to be posted if I do not return. Don't pretend to have principles, will you?'

'Can I have my hat?'

'Here.'

As Simon snatched it and strode away through the jungle of potted plants, Werner leaned back in his armchair and took two deep, satisfied breaths. That young man will dream of killing me tonight, he thought. Slowly, he held his cigarette at arm's length in front of him, watched the smoke curl lazily up towards the ceiling, and smiled.

His fingers were not shaking at all . . .

26

Summer has come early, Charles Cavendish thought.

It was an unusually perfect day. The sun sparkled out of a cloudless blue sky, a cool crisp breeze blew in from the sea over the waving green corn, and all along the hedgerows the trees were in their first flush of new leaf. Charles lounged in the back seat of his open-topped chauffeur-driven Lancia as it bowled along the country roads towards Lough Neagh. They drove past fields full of sheep and young lambs, bouncing after each other like long-legged white rubber balls; woods with a sudden hazy, limitless carpet of bluebells under the trees; a deep swirling river where a single fisherman stood, up to his thighs in water, like a silent, watchful heron; a meadow where a hare stood up on its hind legs in alarm and then ran, zig-zagging left, right, and away, out of sight behind a herd of stolid munching cows.

This is my country, Charles thought. In its way it is the most beautiful place on earth . . .

The wind on his cheeks was cooler, softer than the breeze on the high veldt, or the harsh dusty blast of oven-heated air that came down the Khyber Pass in summer; but this was the place that mattered most to him. Those other places were for travel and adventure; this was home.

They drove through a small village of a few dozen thatched and slate-roofed cottages with a large Catholic church with a spire like a small cathedral at the end of the street and he thought: it is their land too in a way. But they are not fit to govern it, no more than peasants in the Sudan or Zulus or Muslims in Lahore can be expected to rule themselves. It is not their place in life, nor will it be for a hundred years. If the government gives way to them all the energy and prosperity of Ulster will be lost, we will sink in confusion and savagery.

But it isn't going to happen.

The Lancia bounced and swayed down the long rutted track towards St Andrew's Preparatory School, and Charles glimpsed an orderly pattern of young boys in white between the trees, with a little crowd of spectators clustered by the pavilion and the scoreboard. In the sudden silence as the chauffeur stopped the car and switched off the engine outside the front door of the school, Charles heard the sound of his own boots scrunching across the gravel, sparrows chirping in the ivy, the crack of bat on ball and young boys cheering in the distance.

There was no one about. He made his way quietly through the garden to the cricket field. As he appeared near the pavilion the headmaster, Dr Duncan, rose from a deckchair to greet him enthusiastically.

'Colonel Cavendish! What a marvellous surprise, sir, marvellous! Your timing couldn't be bettered – your son is next in to bat, I believe. Yes, that's right! Fifty-three to get off eight overs with four wickets in hand! They have a wickedly good off-spinner but we're still in with a chance, I think!'

'Splendid!' Charles glanced up the steps of the pavilion to where his son, in cricket whites and pads, sat with his bat clutched tensely across his knees, staring out across the field. At first he thought Tom had not seen him but then the boy turned his way, and his eyes widened with surprise and delight. Charles walked up the steps towards him and Tom got awkwardly to his feet.

'Hello, Father.'

'Hello, Tom. Thought I'd drop in, see how the old team was getting on.'

'It's a bit stiff. They were a hundred and thirty two all out and we're eighty for five, and one of their bowlers is . . . oh crikey, look at that. He's going to catch him!'

Charles turned to see a young fielder running slowly backwards with his hands raised high, intent on the flight of a ball which came down to him, safe into the hands which clutched it to his chest. There were cries, groans, and applause from the crowd.

'Help! I'm in! Where are my gloves?'

'Here, I think.' Charles picked them up from the floor and handed them to him. 'Good luck. Play a straight bat, Tom.'

'I will if I can.'

And then his son was gone, out onto the field, still fumbling with the gloves, his bat held clumsily under one arm. The pads, Charles thought, were a little big for him – the straps flapped and clinked as he walked. There was polite applause as he passed the batsman on the way out, and then Tom was there at the crease, taking his guard at the umpire's directions while the bowler waited impatiently.

Charles was astonished at the sudden tug of emotion the sight wrought in him. The boy seemed so small suddenly, so vulnerable – only a foot or two taller than the stumps he was standing to guard. I hope he does well, he thought, in front of all these people – and me. I could have put him off by arriving just at that moment. That would be awful.

He was suddenly aware that more than half the spectators and boys were watching *him*, rather than the game. He was in full military uniform, right on the front steps of the pavilion. Quickly, he stepped down and went to an empty chair right at the back of the crowd, to make himself less conspicuous.

Tom survived the first ball and the next, and Charles began to breathe more easily. The third spun off the outside edge of his bat and Charles groaned, but the boy in the slips dropped the catch. Off the last ball Tom drove the ball for two runs and Charles heaved a sigh of relief.

Over the Easter holidays, father and son had become, for the first time, friends of a sort. It was a new emotion for Charles. He had been away abroad so often while Tom was young, and when he was at home on leave the boy had seemed either afraid of his father or indifferent to him, more interested in collecting worms or beetles or stealing cakes from the kitchen. Then, Tom had been Deborah's concern. Now, at the same time as he was finding his relationship with his wife harder and more repugnant than ever, Charles had come to feel new pride in his growing son.

That boy in white out there with the flapping oversize pads

will grow into a youth and then a man and will one day inherit Glenfee, he thought. I shall never have another son. The sort of man he grows into will depend a great deal upon me.

When two more overs had gone and Tom had scored ten runs, Charles began to relax. The headmaster came over to talk to him and Charles responded civilly. His son, he learned, had settled in well this term and, in every department except Latin, was up to scratch. Dr Duncan was chiefly interested to learn what shape the UVF was in and Charles told him, curtly, that they could now take military control of the entire province overnight if they wished. Then Tom, to his father's vast delight, hit a four, and both men applauded.

When the match was over Charles obtained permission to take his son out for a drive in the car for a couple of hours. The chauffeur drove them along the shores of Lough Neagh until they came to a small village where a stream joined the lake. Charles remembered from a previous visit with Deborah that there was a pub here which also sold gloceries and could be induced to provide a cream tea. Father and son sat out in the garden together, watching a small brown-sailed fishing boat drift slowly in the distance.

'You did well,' Charles said. 'Though it was a little ambitious to try to knock that spinner for six. You deserved to be caught making a cackhanded swipe like that.'

Tom grinned. 'It *was* a bit wild. But Hale and I had a bet on it. He mucked it up too.'

'Hale?'

'The team captain. Didn't you see him? Big fellow, fair hair, went in number four. His brother's in the first team at Haileybury.'

'Oh. Decent sort, is he?'

'I'll say!' For a while Charles listened as his son rattled enthusiastically on about the exploits of Hale and his other school friends, and he thought, this is a whole world the boy has which I know nothing of. Or rather, I know nothing of *these* particular boys. The general atmosphere of Tom's school life sounded much as his own had been.

'How about you, Father?' Tom asked. 'Was it very dangerous landing the guns?'

Charles smiled. The sudden intense, shy eagerness in his son's face touched and amused him. 'Not really, no. More a matter of careful staffwork and forward planning, you know.'

Tom looked disappointed. 'But didn't the others – the government army – try to stop you?'

'They didn't know anything about it.' Charles relented, and told the story of the phantom army of British soldiers which had marched out of Holywood Barracks and vanished into the night when they had landed the guns at Bangor. Then, seeing the spark in his son's eyes, he told the story as carefully as he could of how the guns had been landed and where they had gone, and of how he had outfaced a British Army patrol a few days later. After that, somehow, they got on to his exploits in Egypt and the Sudan, and the day, many years ago, when he had ridden forty miles through the desert alone, in danger of being captured by hostile tribesmen at every yard. Tom demolished his scones and cake and listened, his eyes alight with romance and pride.

I am a hero to this boy, Charles thought suddenly.

It was not a thought that he had consciously been aware of before. It brought with it immense pleasure, and a slight, hidden fear. He did not want to think about the fear. There is no reason, he thought, why Tom should not be proud of me. Especially now that I am here at home in Ulster, fighting for something I believe to be right. If Tom believes in it, too, that makes it all so much more worthwhile.

On the way back to St Andrews he told Tom of his own time at school when he had been in the Eton team which had beaten Harrow by three runs and of another, stranger match on the North West Frontier, which had been brought to a sudden, untimely end when the pitch was invaded by a wild band of Waziri horsemen, who rode across it at a mad gallop firing flintlock muskets at the players.

In his dormitory Tom introduced his father to Hale, his cricket team captain. The boy shook Charles's hand politely and accompanied them downstairs as Charles took his leave. Charles shook hands with them both on the front steps of the school and got into the back seat of the Lancia. He felt proud and happy, pleased that he had come. The open-topped car scrunched away across the gravel drive, and he turned in the seat for a final wave.

But the boys had already turned their backs and were going into the house. Hale, the bigger boy, had slung his arm casually across Tom's shoulders.

An eel started to gnaw at Charles' spine. He shivered suddenly in full sunlight, and was tempted to order his chauffeur to turn the car round, so that he could sprint back across the gravel and wrench the two boys apart. But he gripped the back of the seat and did nothing. The car carried him smoothly through the lovely countryside, away from his son.

Surely not, he told himself. They're both far too young, that boy Hale's only a year older than Tom.

But in a few short years . . . I remember a boy who looked a bit like Hale once. In my study at Eton. The one with the beautiful hips and the broken hand. If *I* could love other boys, then sooner or later Tom . . .

He had not thought of Tom in this context before. But once the idea had occurred to him, it had to be faced. Charles prided himself on being a logical man, clear-thinking, direct. It was that which had led to his success as an army officer. That, combined with a less logical love of the thrill of personal danger, a delight in the daring risk.

What would I feel if my son preferred men to women? As I do.

The answer stunned him with its violence and finality. *I will not have it! It cannot be allowed. I would ache with grief.*

Why?

He sat back in his seat, watching a herd of cows wending their way homeward through the long evening tree shadows, and thought, it is mostly jealousy. I could not bear my son to be used like that by a man or another boy.

What if he enjoyed it?

He wouldn't, at first. Be honest, Charles, he told himself, none of the boys I knew at school enjoyed it initially. They had to be trained, coerced, persuaded.

Corrupted, the world would say . . .

Charles knew, from some of the Greek and Latin poets he had read at school, that there had once been a time when sexual love between two men, soldiers even, had been acceptable. Achilles and Patroclus, perhaps. Hermes and Lysander. The point was interesting, but academic. In the real world of the British Empire homosexuality was a crime punishable with instant dismissal from military service, imprisonment, social ostracism. Not so long ago the penalty had been life imprisonment.

Do I want that for my son?

Of course not. No father could. If the boy grows up like me in this he will be condemned to secretive, snatched, hidden affairs, often with different men, usually brief and guilty, enlivened only by the thrill of lust and the horrible, appalling danger of discovery and instant utter ruin. Little tenderness, love, security – where is the room for that, in all the fear, suspicion, danger?

And an impotent marriage, too. I am lucky to have a son at all. Deborah was right, I suppose. I have been cold to her since I came back from Egypt and it must be hurtful to her and impossible to understand. Even if it is repugnant to me it is my duty to give her the chance to have a family. To give myself another son.

Only . . . I wanted to be faithful to Simon.

For once in his adult life, after so many years of rigid celibacy and occasional secret snatched encounters with strangers, Charles had believed that in Simon Fletcher he had found someone to love. A boy who was not only beautiful and discreet, but who could return tenderness and trust and love, whom he could have by his side constantly, and not be afraid of losing.

There is no fool like an old fool, Charles told himself.

I am nearly forty years old, there is grey hair in my moustache and my forehead is higher than it was because my hair is receding. I am still fit enough but my body is leathery and hard and scarred in places by sabres. In cold weather I limp because of the knee that was crushed when the polo pony fell on me. There is no beauty in me for the boy to admire, only my power for him to cling on to.

As the Lancia swept into the drive at Glenfee Charles thought, what would I do if Tom found out about me and Simon?

Would I sit down and explain it to him like a father, as I talked about cricket this afternoon?

Or take out my revolver and shoot myself in the head?

Simon Fletcher was furious.

All his life people had been taking advantage of him. Usually they succeeded at first; always they failed in the end. He knew all about blackmail; he had used it half a dozen times against men who had deserted him. The power of blackmail gave him a thrill which warmed him all along his spine. It was an addiction he loved. But he had never dreamed that it would be used against himself.

What was infuriating about it was the sense of helplessness. The sense that he was about to lose control of his own life; to become a doll, a puppet in another man's game. To do something that meant nothing to him, and a great deal to that German, Werner von Weichsaker.

As Simon cycled back to Glenfee along the quiet country lanes, the expression on the German's face, and the curious ugliness of his crippled hand, obsessed him. He remembered the malicious confidence of the man; the way Werner had enjoyed teasing him by raising his voice, summoning him back when he wanted to leave. That was only the beginning. If I do what he wants now, it will only get worse. There will be more demands, more hoops to jump through.

I won't do it.

He's threatening Charles as well as me. No one else has a right to do that. He's my lover. I should protect him.

I will . . .

Loyalty was a new emotion for Simon. It made him feel virtuous, almost saintlike. He cycled in through the gates of Glenfee in a glow of good feeling. He was less sure how practical it was . . .

He saw the chauffeur polishing the Lancia in the carriage shed where it was housed, and deduced that Charles must have recently arrived home.

What shall I do? Tell Charles? No – no point; it would just make him miserable. I'll deal with the Kraut myself, somehow or other. For now I'll just go in to Charles and be pleasant to him.

*

The letter had arrived late in the day. Charles sat in the library, reading it. It was brief and disappointing.

Belgrave Square
29 April 1914

My dear Charles,

I was pleased and touched to receive your letter this morning. With all the difficulty and danger of landing so many guns it must have been hard for you to find time to write, but I am relieved to learn that you are safe and that it went well. Let us hope that the increased strength of your soldiers will not lead to war, but to a decent, negotiated peace.

I had an uneventful journey over and Jonathan is well. Neither he nor I have been able to see Sarah yet and may not for a month, but I live in hope. I will write more later.

In haste,
Your wife,
Deborah

It was unusually short for her letters, and said nothing, really. Charles read it twice, frowned, and flung it dejectedly into the fire. She had taken three days even to write this much. Perhaps he had no right to expect more from her, but he had tried, in his own last letter, to apologise for his coldness. He remembered the words and the thought they had cost him. *You will forgive me if I seemed a trifle abrupt at our last meeting. You and I are going through choppy waters at the moment but so long as we keep our chins up we shall not go under!* Surely that was clear and decent enough – what more could any man have said? Women were supposed to be the experts in matters of the heart and keeping a marriage going, but she hadn't even bothered to reply to that part of his letter. Can't blame a chap for trying.

'Good evening. Mind if I join you?'

Charles looked up. Simon had come into the room. It was his day off, so he wore civilian clothes – white shirt, blazer, grey flannels. As always, he looked slim, lithe, graceful. Not in any way effete – Charles would not have been attracted to that – but a fit young man who had been gifted with unusual physical perfection.

He walked to the mantelpiece and stood there, lighting a cigarette. Charles sat back in his chair, surveying him. The last scrap of Deborah's letter turned to ash in the fire by Simon's leg.

When the cigarette was alight and Charles had still not spoken, Simon said: 'Well? Did you have a good day?'

'Extremely pleasant, thank you. I drove over to see my son.'

'Ah.' A little twinge of jealousy crawled like a gnat on Simon's skin. He smiled and brushed it away. 'And is he well? It's the cricket season, isn't it?'

'Yes, indeed. He's in the team. I saw them play.' Charles would have liked to go on, to describe the scene, but not . . . not to Simon. It would have besmirched the memory, somehow, and anyway he had the sense that Simon's interest in the game would be feigned. 'What about you?'

'Oh, I just . . . went into town. Mooched about.'

'See any unusual activity by the army or police?'

'No.' Simon smiled. 'We've got them on the run, haven't we?'

'I hope so. We'll see next week, I expect. When Carson comes over.'

Don't remind me of that, Simon thought. But the subject had a certain fascination, after all. 'Why then?'

'Well, if they were going to make any kind of stand, that'd be the time, wouldn't it? Try to prevent the man from parading in front of his own armed troops, don't you see? If I were Asquith I'd have Carson arrested before he left London. But I doubt if the man's got the guts.'

'Probably not.' Simon exhaled slowly, thoughtfully. 'What's Carson's itinerary, exactly?'

'He arrives at Larne first, then on to the Old Town Hall, Belfast, and after that Craigavon. He'll spend one night there, and after that he's due to spend Sunday with a friend of his – Ferris – just outside Dundonald. He gives another speech at Bangor on Monday night and leaves next morning from Belfast.'

'Oh. So he'll come near us then?'

'Too true he will. I've been given the job of picking him up on Sunday morning at Craigavon and guaranteeing his security for the rest of the day. I've been on to Ferris already and warned Sergeant Cullen to detail half a dozen of his best lads. We'll need two cars, besides our own – I was going to put you on to that in the morning.'

'I see,' Simon said softly. 'A big responsibility.'

'Indeed. A great honour for our boys, as well. He must have liked what he saw of them when he was over a fortnight ago.'

'Yes.' Simon thought: I'll tell him now. But if I do, Werner will write that article, and we'll both be ruined. Wait, until I've worked out how to deal with Werner.

He smiled at Charles and said: 'You look tired.'

'No.' Charles said after a pause. 'A little sad, only.'

'Sad? Why is that?' Simon strolled over from the mantelpiece and perched on the arm of a chair a few feet from Charles. He dared not come closer. It was a rule they almost always observed, never to touch where there was the slightest risk of discovery by servants or others. Simon had a room at his disposal in the East Wing of Glenfee, where he was sleeping tonight, but only two or three times had they dared to come together there. Mostly they met in Simon's old lodgings, which he had kept on in Belfast; once in a hotel in Donaghadee. It was a furtive, secret, terrifying business.

Charles said: 'Because I have made a decision which pains me.'

Simon laughed. 'You sound very solemn for so late at night. Was it so hard, then, with your son at the school?'

'No. Not at all, it was very pleasant.' Charles looked away from Simon, into the fire; then made up his mind and faced the boy calmly. 'Simon, you are much younger than me; you don't know what it is to have a son. Perhaps I haven't known all these years, as well as I should have, but something brought it home to me today. It's a responsibility. I can't do just as I wish because every action of mine has an effect on Tom as well as on myself. I suppose all this sounds obvious to you, but I have not felt it so strongly before . . .'

'Not obvious,' Simon said coolly. 'But very solemn. What are you trying to say?'

Charles took a deep breath. 'I am trying to say, Simon, what I have perhaps hinted once or twice before. That . . . it is not sensible for me to carry on a relationship with you as I have done. And I mean it this time, Simon! *Please hear me out*!'

His voice rose sharply as Simon stood up and strode to the mantelpiece. He flung his cigarette into the fire and stood with his back to Charles, but Charles went on nonetheless.

'It is not good for me because I cannot be a decent father if I have such a relationship – and I risk losing everything my son has any right to expect, for just a few minutes' stolen pleasure. And it is not good for you Simon, either, if the truth be told.'

'Not good for me? Oh, wonderful – how do you work that out?'

'Because . . . you build hopes on me that can never be fulfilled. We cannot have any sort of life together, Simon, you must realise that. And also, I am pleased to say, you are turning into quite a decent soldier. I have seen that in the past few weeks. You are efficient, you have the gift of good organisation, you are always smart, well turned out and are learning to shoot like a veteran. You are enthusiastic, too – no one can say any of your duties have been neglected or skimped. You have a great future . . .'

'And this is a reason to cast me out?' Simon turned suddenly and stared at Charles incredulously. So pompously he sits in that chair, like a judge or my old headmaster. *What right does he think he has?*

'Yes, of course. Listen for a moment, and *think*. This is painful for me too, Simon, truly. You are young enough to make a success of your life, and you can do it as a soldier in the UVF. Later, when all this is over and the government has backed down as I believe it will, you could go on into the regular army or whatever other field you chose. With my recommendation you would get a good start, go far.'

'You would do that to get rid of me?'

'No. Simon, listen – and for God's sake don't raise your voice. What I am saying is that discovery would be ruin for you just as much as for me. And sooner or later, my boy, believe you me – we *will* be found out. Then all your young life will be ruined, and mine too, and Tom's. It is not worth it – the world is not made for people like us. Until I met you I had not . . . been with another young man for years. I thought I never would again. Celibacy is the best way, Simon, for both of us. If the Catholic priests can do it, my boy, surely we can.'

Charles sat quite still in his chair, not getting up, not daring to come close to Simon and embrace him as part of him longed to.

'And all this came to you as the result of a visit to your son?'

It was not said kindly; Simon had a bitter, sarcastic edge to his tongue. It was a sign, Charles thought, of immaturity; not the part of the boy's character he was trying to appeal to.

'That was what brought it on, yes. But it is the fruition of something I have been thinking for some time, now. You know we have discussed this before.'

'Yes. Do you remember what I told you?'

'That you could go to another man? Yes, I remember. Of course I would hope you would not do that. Simon. But it is your life, you are free to choose.'

'And you wouldn't care?' I came here to show him my loyalty, Simon thought, and then he does this to me. His fists clenched at his sides, as though he wanted to leap on Charles and hit him. But that was not Simon's way, he had not the skill of it. There were better ways by far to gain revenge.

'Of course I would care, Simon. Think for a moment what I've said, what I've offered you. I've been a soldier a long time now, seen a lot of young men. People in high places would respect my judgement if I put it on paper – they'd give you a chance. *That's* how I care. Not for what we do together, which is an obsession, a danger to both of us. But for everything else about you – for your future.'

'So long as I stay clear of your son?'

Charles sighed. 'You don't have to stay clear of him, Simon. I don't think you're a monster – I care for you. I just want you to . . . stay clear of me, if you want to put it like that. As I shall of you.' His voice hardened slightly. He had been a commanding officer for many years: he realised it was time to bring the interview to a close, to give Simon time to reflect on it before he said anything unfortunate, as he so easily might.

'You are still a valuable member of the UVF, and I shall expect to see you around me carrying out orders in the coming weeks as efficiently as before. You are my ADC, so it will be convenient for you to keep your room in this house for the time being. But that is all there must be between us from now on. I know it is hard, but I want you to reflect on what I have said. In a week or two, when you have done so, I shall ask you about it again, and we shall see if we can devise a plan for your future where my connections can be of most use to you. Until then, that is all, so goodnight.'

Simon's face was aflame with anger. But below that was the knowledge that he had been in this position many times before, and that revenge was never obtained at once. Only later, with planning and detail and much deeper, fuller satisfaction.

But he had come here full of good intentions, caring for this man. Revenge would be easy but he had meant to try to avoid it. He made one final effort.

'So that's all, is it? You think you can end it just like that, before we run the risk of any scandal? Charles, there is something very important I have to tell you—'

'I don't want to hear it! Not tonight, not tomorrow, not for at least a week until you have had time to reflect and cool down. It's for your own good—'

'But Charles—'

'You don't call me that here. That is all, Simon. Goodnight. *You are dismissed*!'

Simon stared, his mouth half open, about to speak. If he hears about Werner that will change his mind surely, he thought desperately. It will bring us together to fight the very danger he fears.

He doesn't deserve to hear.

Abruptly, Simon turned on his heel and strode for the door.

All love ends like this, he thought. Ever since my father I have known it. Attraction, lust, pleasure, rejection, betrayal. And then, always, the bitter-sweetness of revenge.

He strode away down the corridor, his mind full of images of Charles, and Tom, and the key he had turned in the front door of the house where he had found his father in bed with a woman. His father, whom he had loved more than any man before or since.

The flames of that burning house flickered in his eyes . . .

The train reached Liverpool at five in the morning, but the passengers were allowed to stay in the sleeping compartments until eight if they chose. Deborah had time to send a telegram to Charles at Glenfee, and then she and Sarah embarked on the ferry in time for breakfast. They found a quiet table in the corner of the first-class dining room, and sat eating boiled eggs and muffins as tugs whistled and hooted on the Mersey and the great grey Liver building slipped by outside the porthole.

'I don't think he suspects us,' Deborah said nervously, as she watched the waiter crossing the floor towards them with a fresh pot of tea.

'Of course he doesn't. Relax,' Sarah smiled at the man as he gave them the tea, and ordered two more muffins. 'Anyway, the man's Italian. What would he know? Look here.'

She passed across a copy of the *Daily Mail*, which she had bought from the purser's office as they came on board. Deborah read:

FEMALE HOUDINI VANISHES

SET THEM ALL FREE, SAY PANKHURSTS

No clues have so far emerged as to the whereabouts of Mrs Sarah Becket, the militant suffragette who escaped from Holloway prison two days ago. Theories as to how she escaped vary. 'It is possible she was provided with a skeleton key and a disguise,' a police source said. 'But she may also have climbed a ladder over the wall, or even escaped in a laundry basket. We are keeping an open mind.'

Meanwhile the WSPU have been proclaiming the escape as a triumph. Miss Christabel Pankhurst, speaking in Paris, said: 'This brilliant escape shows that it is impossible to cage either the body or the spirit of a free, independent woman. I call upon the government yet again, in the name of decency and justice, to release all female political prisoners today, and give women the vote.'

The Liberal MP, Mr Jonathan Becket, said that he knew nothing of his wife's whereabouts, but claimed he would be seeking assurances from his friend the Home Secretary that his wife had been humanely treated while she was in prison.

'Humanely treated!' Deborah said. 'He *knows* you were force fed!'

'Yes, of course,' Sarah said sadly. 'But it would damage his reputation to say so, wouldn't it? He would have to disagree with the government, and that would lose him any chance of becoming a minister.'

'Is that all he cares about?'

'It seems like that to me. He's talked about it enough over the past year, at any rate.'

Deborah sighed. 'That would explain why he won't support female suffrage in Parliament, any more.' She told Sarah about the speech Jonathan had made, that day when she had watched him from the Ladies' Gallery in the Commons.

Sarah said nothing. She buttered her muffin carefully and then cut it into squares with quick, vicious strokes of her knife. Deborah wished she had said nothing.

'At least he hasn't told them where you're going,' she offered.

'No. It seems he hasn't done that, anyway.' Sarah pushed the muffin away irritably, then leaned forward with both elbows on the table, cradling a cup of tea in her hands. 'You know, Debbie, it may sound awful to say this, but I truly think I could bring myself to kill him, if he did.'

'Don't, Sarah.' Deborah saw the tears well up in her sister's eyes. 'You're still not strong. You'll wear yourself out with emotion if you start thinking like that. You ought to relax, and eat.'

'Always the motherly type, weren't you, Debbie? And now you've got a real live invalid to look after.'

Deborah winced. She had suffered frequently from her sister's sarcasm in her youth and had never developed a strong defence against it.

'I don't think of you as an invalid, Sarah. Just someone who needs help and protection for a while, that's all.'

'Yes.' Sarah reached out impulsively across the table and touched her sister's hand. 'I'm sorry, I didn't need to say that. Your help's appreciated, too, don't think it's not. It's just that it's a bit of a surprise to come out of prison and find my sweet little sister included in the rabid ranks of the militant suffragettes.'

'Sssssh!' Deborah looked over her shoulder, alarmed. But the table nearest to them was empty and no one seemed to have heard. Sarah laughed out loud.

'Look, Debbie! The purser's coming! He's going to have you thrown into the Mersey for making seditious remarks!'

Despite herself, Deborah looked behind her. There was no one there. She blushed. 'Laugh if you like. You *could* be arrested at any time, you know.'

'I do know – and I've no intention of letting it happen. Rather than that I'd jump into the river.'

'You can't swim!'

Sarah stared. 'That's true. I'd forgotten. You know me too well.'

'Yes.' It was Deborah's turn to smile. 'Listen, Sarah, promise me one thing, will you?'

'Anything. What?'

'When we get to Glenfee, don't attack Charles.'

'Attack him? What do you think I am? A raving Amazon with a cutlass? Look at me, I can hardly stand.'

To Deborah's eyes, Sarah was already looking a lot better. Still thin and hollow-cheeked, but there was a brightness in her eyes and a flush in her cheeks that had not been there last night. She had walked quite firmly from the train to the ship and taken a turn among the deckchairs on the promenade deck before coming in to breakfast.

She remembered how strong and energetic Sarah had been as a child. She had regularly won races at village fêtes, each year. But it was not Sarah's physical strength that concerned her now.

'I don't mean that, silly. Just don't go for him with all your suffragette propaganda. You know how he hates that sort of thing. And it won't help, you won't convert him.'

Sarah raised an eyebrow. 'Isn't that just the reason why all men keep their outdated attitudes? Because no one ever challenges them?'

'Perhaps . . . Oh, I don't know! Perhaps it's being challenged all the time that makes them worse.'

'Oh, come on now, Debbie, really! That's *exactly* the government's line. If we all believed that—'

'Please, Sarah.' Deborah held up her hand. To her surprise, her sister stopped. 'You may be right, I don't know. But in Charles's case, I . . . I've got a reason why I don't want to antagonise him right now. It's going to be hard enough to persuade him to shelter you, an escaped convict, but I'll make him do that, don't worry. But . . . things haven't been too good between us and, if you could keep him sweet in every other way, it would be a favour to me, that's all.'

Sarah looked at her quietly for a moment. Deborah's features had always seemed to her like a reflection of her own but slightly softer, somehow, less sharply defined. It was not just the fair hair and the slightly broader face, it was also a gentleness, a placidity which she did not see in her own mirror. Perhaps some of it comes from being a mother, she thought bitterly, but not all. Some of it was there as a child, too – that's why I could always dominate her.

And yet there were certain things, she knew, that Deborah felt very passionately about. Her quiet country home, her son Tom. Exactly the things I have never had.

She said: 'Always the same old Debbie, eh? Anxious to preserve the appearance of things. Well, don't worry. My marriage may be a heaving cesspit but I haven't come to break up yours. If Charles protects me under his roof I will smile and curtsey and make demure polite remarks about his brave rebel soldiers. Nothing else.'

Deborah breathed a sigh of relief. 'Really? You promise?'

Sarah laughed. 'I promise. Honestly, Debbie, it will be a relief to me, too. I don't want to destroy your home. Don't you know that I've always seen Glenfee as a haven of peace and security?'

'Have you? Oh, good.'

Tears started suddenly into Deborah's eyes, and, to hide them, she gazed out intently through the salt-smeared porthole, to where the docks of the Mersey were fading slowly behind them.

A haven of peace and security, she thought.

Just the place for a child to be born . . .

27

The Royal Ulster Hotel. Monday evening. Five minutes to six.

Werner sat comfortably in the foyer, reading the evening paper. In the Balkans, there were fears that the Serbs were about to attack the Albanian Moslems. A suffragette had been arrested for slashing the portrait of the Duke of Wellington in the Royal Academy. There was no trace yet of the other escaped suffragette, Sarah Becket. In his Budget speech the Chancellor of the Exchequer, Lloyd George, had announced a supertax of 1s 4d for those earning over £7,000 a year. The Kaiser had been present at German Army exercises in Westphalia. Bernard Shaw's play *Pygmalion* was playing to packed houses in London.

There was nothing about Sir Edward Carson visiting Ulster.

Werner looked up from time to time, to check on those coming in and out of the hotel. It was a busy time. Two groups of travellers had just arrived from the station and were checking in at the desk while the porters carried in their bags. Several others were coming in and out, waiting either for an appointment or for the restaurant to open for the evening meal. Werner wore a dark well-cut woollen suit, with shiny elastic-sided boots and a clean shirt and tie. His bowler hat and thick tweed coat hung on a hook near the door and his injured hand was concealed in a soft light brown glove. He felt comfortable, prosperous, successful, perfectly in tune with the atmosphere around him.

Only that morning he had bought a new car, courtesy of the Imperial German government. It was parked in the street behind the hotel. Some time in the next few days, if all went well, he would use it as part of his plan to kidnap and murder Sir Edward Carson.

I wonder what will be on the front page of the evening paper that day, he thought with a smile.

The long case clock in the hall started to chime. Six o'clock. A waiter drew aside the red rope at the entrance to the hotel dining room. Simon Fletcher walked into the foyer and stood in front of him.

'Ah. So you made it.' Werner folded up his newspaper and threw it down on the arm of his chair. 'Have a seat.'

'Thank you.' Simon sat down on the edge of the armchair, leaning forward, his arms resting on his knees. He was wearing the same blazer and flannels as before and he swung a small leather briefcase between his knees. He did not look afraid, but quiet, resolute, determined.

Werner glanced at the briefcase. 'Have you brought what I asked?'

'I think so, yes.'

'Good.' Werner did not ask to see what Simon had brought; that would come. Probably the young man has some further condition he wants to make, Werner thought. He has been thinking about it all night and worked out a plan. They usually do. All in good time.

'Have you eaten?'

Surprise registered on Simon's face. 'No, I haven't actually. But—'

Werner got to his feet and gestured hospitably in the direction of the hotel restaurant. 'Well then, why don't we go in? I took the liberty of reserving a table in a discreet corner, just in case. I have had nothing since breakfast myself.'

He led the way across the vast half-empty dining room to a table by a wicker screen and some long red damask curtains. When they were settled and had ordered, Werner raised a slim glass of sherry in his good hand and said: 'So. I hope for both our sakes you have succeeded. Was it difficult?'

'No, not very.'

'Good. May I see what you brought me?'

'Yes, of course. But there are conditions, first.'

As I expected, Werner thought. He sighed, and tucked a napkin under his chin as the waiter brought the soup. When the waiter had gone he said: 'Do you really think you are in a position to make conditions, young man? Remember, I have already written an article about you and your handsome lover. It makes a highly entertaining and scandalous read, and it will be posted to my editor if I do not return. Or if you do not co-operate.'

'That's what I mean,' Simon said. 'You think you have to coerce me. That may not be necessary. I might want to co-operate.'

Werner put down his spoon and dabbed thoughtfully at his mouth with his napkin. This *was* a surprise. 'How do you mean, exactly?'

'Well, I've been thinking about what you said when we last met, and wondering why you might want this information. It isn't for your newspaper in Switzerland – you can stop pretending that, I don't believe it. I think you're a German spy and, if you are . . .' Simon held up his hand to forestall a protest. '. . . then it may be that I want to help you.'

'Want to help me.' Werner stared at Simon calmly for a few moments. It is a beautiful face, he thought, I can understand Charles Cavendish being attracted to it. But there is something strange there, under the skin. This is a boy strong and hard and utterly sure of himself. A few days ago he was furious with me and now he wants to co-operate. I don't think I want to know.

'You *are* helping me by bringing those papers,' he said mildly enough. 'That is, if they *are* the details of Carson's visit as I asked. That's all I want, just now. If they are satisfactory, they may be all I need, and no one need know of your . . . affair with Colonel Cavendish. There is no need for any other involvement from you.'

Simon picked up the slim leather briefcase from below the table and flicked open the catches. His cool grey eyes never left Werner's. 'All right, then. Maybe not. Nonetheless, when you've read them I'd like to know if they're what you wanted or not. If you need to know more, I may be able to help. But first,

I'd like you to listen to what I have to say.'

Werner shrugged. It seemed a strange way of bargaining. 'I agree, of course.' He held out his hand.

The two sheets of paper which Simon passed across the table exceeded his expectations. In small, neat, meticulous handwriting, Simon had listed not only the dates and times of Carson's planned arrival and departure at various places on his four-day visit to Ulster, but also all the secret orders for Carson's security, including the number of companions he was expected to take with him, which unit of the UVF would be responsible for guarding him at each stage, and, where possible, the number of troops who would be involved and the officer responsible. He had also hazarded an educated guess at which roads Carson would be likely to take at each stage of his journey, and the estimated time of departure and arrival at each point. Werner read each page with interest and delight.

He put them down on the table and smiled.

'Where did you get all this?'

'Various places. It took some time. The main details were circulated in an order to Colonel Cavendish, though, because he's involved.'

'Yes, I see that.' To Werner it was the most interesting detail of all. Next Sunday morning Charles Cavendish was due to pick up Sir Edward Carson from Craigavon at nine-thirty. He would be in his six seater Lancia, and would command a security detail of three armed soldiers. They would transport Sir Edward to Mount Stewart on the Ards peninsula, where Sir Edward would be spending the remainder of the weekend. From Craigavon, Simon estimated that Sir Edward might either take the main road through Belfast or go south via Ballynahinch, but given Colonel Cavendish's preference for country roads he might also go through Hillsborough, Drumbo, Moneyreagh, Comber, and Newtownards. But whichever way he came, he was certain to travel the last part of his journey along the eastern side of Strangford Lough between Newtownards and Mount Stewart.

So that, Werner thought, is where I should go for a drive tomorrow morning with my three young German sailors. Unless . . .

He looked at Simon curiously, while the waiter cleared away

their soup plates and brought the main course.

'You've earned your meal, at least, young man. What is it you want to say?'

Simon met his eyes calmly. He had thought this out thoroughly over the past couple of days. He had no qualms. If his guess was correct, this man with the sharp bitter face and intense blue eyes could be an instrument in his own revenge. In which case Simon would no longer be dancing to another man's tune, but would have turned the situation to his own advantage. Which was the way he liked it.

He said: 'You're planning to kidnap Carson, aren't you?'

Werner started. Am I so transparent? He put down his knife and fork carefully before answering, with a laugh that sounded forced, even to him.

'What makes you think that?'

'All these questions you ask. When is he coming to Ulster, where is he going? And then the fact that you're German.'

'I write for a Swiss newspaper. The *Neue Zuricher Zeitung*.'

'So you tell me. But it's not what you want to know all this for, is it? People in Zurich don't want to know which roads Carson travels on.'

Werner waved a hand, dismissively, as though the point no longer mattered to him. 'All right, perhaps not. But what possible reason could I have for wanting to kidnap Sir Edward Carson?'

'Because it would help Germany in some way. Embarrass the British government, cause trouble to them. I expect it would lead to riots and some fighting, at least. Does Germany want that? I don't know. It doesn't really matter to me.'

Werner poured himself a glass of wine and sipped it curiously. 'You surprise me, young Simon. I thought you were a loyal member of the UVF.'

'Perhaps I was, a few days ago,' Simon said. 'Things change.'

'So suddenly?' Simon did not answer. 'I see. How strange. You will tell me you are getting married next.'

'If you mock me you'll learn nothing, will you?'

'I suppose not.' Werner's curiosity increased, outstripping his contempt. 'Well, come on then. Tell me, young man. What is it that matters to you, if it is no longer loyalty to the cause of Ulster Unionism?'

'What matters to me,' Simon said slowly. 'Is that whatever you do is going to hurt Charles Cavendish. Is that right?'

Werner sat back. 'It might do, yes. I have my own reasons for that. You wouldn't understand. But if you co-operate I'll see that—'

'I want to hurt him, too.'

'Sorry?' Werner was startled. 'What do you mean?'

'What I say. I don't care one way or the other about Carson, I told you. But if your plan to get at Carson will damage Charles Cavendish, I want to help you with it. In any way I can. Perhaps I can make it better.'

'But why? I thought—'

'You thought we were lovers. So we were. But all that has changed now. And when things like that change, they change absolutely. With me at least. So I want to offer you my help. But if I'm to be of any use, I have to know your plan.'

Werner sat quite silent, thinking. It was an appalling risk. Simon could easily be inventing all this, playing a part. If Werner confided in him and was betrayed he could easily be caught, locked away in an English gaol. On the other hand, Simon had guessed a lot already. And if Simon did betray Werner he'd be damned himself, by that story he had left in a sealed envelope in his hotel room, to be posted if he did not return.

Cautiously, Werner asked: 'Is that all you want?'

'No, not quite. If your plan is as important as I think it is, and it succeeds, I couldn't stay here. I'd want to be paid. In marks which I could spend in Germany.'

Greedy, too. And vindictive as well. What a treasure Charles Cavendish has found himself, Werner thought. A devil in godlike form.

'The German Empire is not poor. If you served it well it could afford to repay you.'

'Good. And I could come back to Germany with you?'

'Perhaps. We have not discovered yet how you could serve the German Empire.'

'To find out about that you have to trust me with your plan.'

Quite, Werner thought. And this could be where I lose everything, to a mind sharper and more devious than my own.

For a while he said nothing. He finished the food on his plate, dabbed at his lips with his napkin, sipped his wine, and thought. When I knew him at school, Charles Cavendish was insensitive and perverted, he thought, but he was not particularly devious or underhand. Of course he tried to conceal what he did to me, but that was the end of it, really. Otherwise he was upright and honest, a perfect public schoolboy in the grip of an illicit passion. I can't imagine him trying to deceive me with a story like this. If Simon had told Charles about me, he'd have come straight here to arrest me.

So that means it all comes from this boy's own nasty, vindictive mind. Is he telling me the truth, or not?

Thoughtfully, he asked: 'Why did you fall out with Cavendish?'

'That's my business.'

'No, it isn't. Not if you want me to trust you by telling you my plan. I have to understand your motivation.'

Simon frowned. There's a definite petulance in that face, Werner thought. But it's so strong it's frightening rather than contemptible. That poor fool Charles! Still, serves him right.

'It's simple, as it always is. He cares more for his family than me. He went to visit his son and started to feel guilty, so he decided to cast me off. They never learn.'

They, Werner thought. So there have been other victims before Charles, have there? 'What happened to the ones before him?'

'Accidents. One died in a fire, another fell off a ship at night. One went back to his wife but her hand had been caught in a mangle, like yours; and then he had an accident with a shotgun. They have accidents, you see. It must be unlucky to leave me.'

For the first time that evening, a smile crossed Simon's face. Only briefly, but it fascinated and terrified Werner, more than anything that had gone before. There's something missing in this boy's mind, he thought. I'd be a fool to trust him. And yet . . .

'Are you planning to kill Carson or just kidnap him?'

The waiter padded across the room smoothly on soft shoes, to clear their plates. Werner waited while he did it, then ordered biscuits and cheese and coffee. On the other hand, he thought, someone clearly as focused and maniacal as this might just be useful. And it would be poetic revenge on Charles, after all.

He made up his mind.

'My purpose is to remove Carson, so that the UVF will believe he has been arrested by the British police or army. Then they will be bound to attack the army and police to get him back, particularly if a rumour spreads, as it will, that Carson is held in, say, Holywood Barracks.'

Simon frowned. 'Why would a rumour spread about that?'

Werner shrugged. 'I am a journalist, after all.'

'So then there will be fighting, and that will benefit Germany in some way, is that it?'

'Yes. You don't need to know how.'

'I don't care.' Simon thought for a moment. 'So then you'll have to kill Carson, won't you, because if he was ever released he'd say it was all a German plot, and nothing to do with the British government at all?'

Werner nodded slightly. 'You are very astute. Does that frighten you?'

'Not at all.' Again Simon smiled his unnerving, perfect smile. He poured himself some coffee. 'So how will you do it?'

Werner patted the two sheets of paper on the tablecloth beside him. 'That's why I asked you for these. Until you walked into this hotel I didn't even know that Carson was coming to Ulster this weekend. But it seems to me that the most likely time is either over the weekend, at Mount Stewart, or on Sunday when he's on the way there.'

'In Charles Cavendish's Lancia,' said Simon softly. 'Yes, why not? Do you have enough men to attack it?'

'I do. Three, to be precise. I shall be waiting for him, somewhere along the road beside Strangford Lough. I suggest you make sure you are not in the car with them. Unless you really want to help, in which case you could be driving the car, to make sure it slows down . . .'

'Perhaps,' Simon said. 'I often drive it. I could do that if you wanted, of course. But it's dangerous, a difficult thing to attack a moving car successfully, when it's full of armed men. There might be another way.'

He thought for a while. Werner lit a cigar and the smoke

curled lazily up between them. An idea began to hatch in Simon's mind and he smiled as it crawled from its shell.

'Surely it would be better if Charles could be persuaded to help us.'

'Help us? How?' This is a waste of time, Werner thought. The boy's afraid to be in the car and he's trying to find a way out of it.

Simon's teeth gleamed through the smoke and candlelight. 'Oh, I think Charles could be persuaded to. He wouldn't want to, of course – in fact it would hurt him like hell, but there's no way he could possibly refuse. What you may not know about Charles, you see, is this . . .'

Deborah had sent a telegram to Charles from Liverpool, and to her relief, the Lancia was waiting on the docks in Belfast for their arrival. Charles's chauffeur, Robinson, helped them into it with their bags.

'Good to see you back, Mrs Cavendish,' he said. Robinson was a lean, dour young man in his mid-twenties, with a passion for anything mechanical and an intense commitment to the Ulster Volunteers. He spoke hardly at all, so Deborah was touched by the unsolicited warmth of his greeting.

'It's good to be back,' she said. 'This lady is my sister, she is coming to stay.'

'Ma'am.' Robinson touched his cap, shut the back doors carefully behind them, climbed into the driving seat, and began to ease the long car smoothly through the tangle of carts and trolleys and passengers and suitcases at the dockside. Deborah had deliberately not mentioned Sarah's surname, and if the chauffeur knew that she was the famous escaped suffragette – the female Houdini, as the *Daily Mail* had it – he gave no sign. Anyway she had no doubts about his loyalty, or that of any of her servants. So long as Charles agreed that Sarah was welcome in his house, not a word would be spoken.

As they drove through the soft green countryside, she could feel Sarah begin to relax, even as her own tension grew tighter. By the time they turned off the lough side road and cruised up the long gravel drive towards the house, with the large trees in the parkland to their left, and the woods and pheasant runs on their right, Sarah lay back in her seat, smiling, one hand held out beside the car to feel the breeze. Deborah sat upright beside her in her blue coat and feathered hat, staring intently ahead.

Charles was not there to meet them, but he arrived at midday. By that time the butler, Smythe, had installed Sarah in a large bedroom facing south-east across the lough, the housemaid had aired her bed and lit a blazing fire, and the cook, Mrs Hubert, had prepared a pheasant stew. Charles came into the dining room as they were about to sit down to it.

'Ah, there you are, my dear,' he said. Deborah stood up and smiled, although inside her stomach was fluttering terribly. He was wearing khaki, as usual, with polished Sam Browne belt and riding boots, but it was the lean, cold look on his face that concerned her. He did not smile or advance to kiss her.

'Yes. I got your telegram. You said you were bringing a guest but you did not say who.'

He glanced at Sarah. As she had promised Deborah, she smiled winningly back. 'There was a reason for that, Charles, you see. I am . . . in need of some privacy at the moment, and Debbie was kind enough to offer it to me. I hope you don't object.'

Despite himself, Charles smiled faintly. The old, lopsided smile. It's going to be all right, Deborah thought. At least about Sarah.

'I see I am to be asked to harbour an escaped prisoner.'

'Yes.'

Deborah said, quickly: 'Charles, Sarah is my sister, we *have* to help her. She was forcibly fed in that prison and drugged with bromide. If she had not escaped she might be dead by now. I have promised her she will be safe here – and I cannot break my word.'

He raised an eyebrow. 'Without asking me?'

'There was no time, Charles. We had to move quickly. It was an emergency.'

'But we *are* asking you now, Charles,' Sarah said, still determinedly on her best behaviour. 'I would very much appreciate it if you could extend your hospitality to me at Glenfee for a few days at least. If you feel you cannot, then of course I will go.'

'Where to?' Charles asked, sardonically.

'Oh, there are suffragette groups in Ulster. I am sure I could find one willing to put me up, if I had to. But—'

'Charles, please!' Deborah stood directly in front of him, forcing him to look at her. 'I don't often ask things of you, but this is extremely important. If you had seen Sarah when she came out—'

'I can see her now. Thin as a rake.' He looked at his wife, and the odd, lopsided smile did not fade. To her surprise he actually seemed to be amused. 'All right. Even if she is the black sheep of your family and behaves liked a crazed hottentot, I suppose she is still part of it. You may stay on two conditions, madam.'

'Yes?'

He looked at Sarah and his smile broadened in a way that Deborah had not seen for some time. 'Firstly, Mrs Becket, there are a large number of old pictures in this house, some of them of my ancestors. I would appreciate it if they were left unscratched.'

Sarah flushed. 'Why yes, of course. You don't think—'

'And secondly . . .' He glanced towards the table, where wisps of steam were curling towards the ceiling from a shining silver tureen. '. . . that you make every effort while in this house to eat the food that is put in front of you, beginning with what Mrs Hubert has provided today.'

'Well yes, of course, I agree.'

'In that case, you are welcome.'

Sarah sat down in her chair, demurely, as she had promised, and Deborah picked up a plate and lifted the lid of the silver tureen.

28

The sun appeared briefly from behind grey, hurrying clouds as Simon turned off the road and began to nurse the car down the long, rutted track towards St Andrew's Preparatory School. As he passed a wood the sunlight caught the building briefly, making the bricks of the old red house glow warmly amid the surrounding green fields. The windows flashed like mirrors, and the ivy on the walls shone brightly. It's like a church, Simon thought, a holy place that I'm about to raid.

Then the sunlight passed and it was just an old dull house amid drab fields, waiting for the rain that was about to sweep in over Lough Neagh. Simon had driven most of the way with the canvas cover raised, ready for the downpour that was bound to start before long.

He turned the car in a circle on the gravel drive outside the school's front door, so that it would be facing away, up the drive, when he left. Every little detail was important, he knew, on occasions like this. It was a pity about the car itself – Werner's new Daimler, rather than Charles's Lancia, which would have been more convincing, but that couldn't be helped. Anyway, he had an explanation ready.

He got out of the car, tugged his already smooth uniform jacket straight, strode briskly up the main steps, and rang the bell. The immaculate uniform, the gleaming Sam Browne belt, the cap with the badge of the UVF, would impress the headmaster more than anything else, he hoped. He remembered how keen the man had been to talk to him last time, when he had come dressed like this with Mrs Cavendish to deliver the boy at the beginning of term.

The bell echoed away inside the school and there was no response. For an awful moment Simon thought there was no one there, that they had all gone away. Then the door opened slowly and a woman peered out.

'Yes? Can I help you?'

'My name is Simon Fletcher. I've come with an important message from Colonel Cavendish, about his son. Is Dr Duncan here?'

'He's taking prep at the moment. Can you wait half an hour?'

'I'm afraid not. It is *very* urgent. I have to be back in a couple of hours.'

The woman sniffed. She was large and formidable, dressed in a long woollen skirt and cardigan. Dr Duncan's wife, Simon supposed. She looked him up and down; then, seemingly impressed by the uniform and look of dutiful urgency on his face, nodded.

'All right. Come in and sit down there. I'll see if I can fetch him.'

Simon sat on a chair in the hall, staring silently for a moment at a moth-eaten tiger's head above a row of photographs of past cricket and rugby teams. He heard the murmur of voices from far away. A distant door slammed and footsteps approached. Dr Duncan stood before him, in an old brown suit with a row of pens in the top pocket, and a shabby chalk-stained gown. The grey hair and side whiskers stood out more wildly than Simon remembered.

He stood up and held out his hand. The headmaster shook it brusquely.

'Well, young man? You have an urgent message from young Cavendish's father, I hear.'

'Yes, sir. It's . . . rather serious, I'm sorry to say.'

'Step in here.'

Dr Duncan opened a wood panelled door to the right of the tiger's head and ushered simon in. There was a large desk, rows of books, several ancient chairs and sofas with cricket bats and pads piled on them, and a rack on the wall with a number of thin, pliable canes. Simon shivered, remembering a similar room in his own school days. Dr Duncan sat behind his desk, indicating a hard, upright chair in front of it.

'Well, what is it? Serious, you say?'

'Yes. It's the boy's mother, I'm afraid. She's very ill.'

'Mrs Cavendish? I'm sorry to hear it. She looked well enough when she came here.'

'Yes. It was an accident. She, er, fell from her horse and hurt her head. The doctors are very concerned. Only a matter of time, they say.'

Dr Duncan sighed, pursed his lips, and pressed his fingertips together in front of his face. 'Dear me, how very tragic! Such a pleasant young woman, too. Well, well. You want me to break the news to the boy, I suppose.'

'Well, no sir, it's not exactly that. Apparently she's been asking to see him, and Colonel Cavendish has sent me to bring him home.'

Dr Duncan thought for a moment, then shook his head. 'I'm not sure that's wise, young man. Serious injury and death can have a very traumatic effect on the minds of boys of young Cavendish's age, you know. They don't have the maturity to cope with it. In my opinion it might be best to keep him on at school, where he is surrounded by friends and has plenty of work to keep him busy. Take his mind off it, stop him brooding.'

Simon opened his mouth, closed it again, swallowed. He had thought he had anticipated everything but not this. He had forgotten the stubborn, bloody-minded, stiff-upper-lip attitude schoolmasters of the old style could adopt. He forced his face into a conciliatory smile.

'You're probably right, sir, of course. But it's not for me to decide, I'm just here to obey orders. Colonel Cavendish's express instructions were that I should bring the boy home to see his mother, tonight.'

Dr Duncan bristled. 'It's termtime, and I am in *loco parentis*. In the absence of the Colonel himself, it's for me to decide.'

Simon stared at the man, saying nothing. Outside, there was the sudden thunder of a group of boys rushing upstairs, and a teacher shouting at them to be quiet. Simon felt a surge of all the hatreds and resentments of authority he had felt in his own school days, and thought, irrationally, I could take out my revolver and shoot this old fool in the face if I wanted.

But that would be no help at all.

Softly, he tried to insist. 'She is very ill, sir.'

'So you say.' Dr Duncan hesitated. 'I don't want to be unkind, but in my experience misplaced softness at this point can make matters much worse in the future.' He glanced at the telephone, hanging in its stand on the right of his desk. 'Perhaps I should speak to the Colonel myself.'

Simon was prepared for this. 'He is extremely distraught, sir. Also, he is very busy with UVF business; he won't be home until eight this evening. And he gave me express instructions to have the boy home before then. I can't disobey an order, sir.'

Dr Duncan frowned at him, then sighed. 'Well, I understand that. As I say, I think it's unwise, but we all have to submit to discipline. I'll write the boy out an *exeat* for a week, and send for him now. But tell the Colonel what I said now, will you?'

'Yes, sir. Of course.'

Dr Duncan grunted and leaned back to pull a bellrope behind his desk. The woman came in.

'Fetch Cavendish here, will you, my dear. And tell him to bring his coat.'

When Tom came in, in grey flannel shorts and pullover, with his tie slightly awry and fair untidy hair, Dr Duncan stood up portentously and came from behind his desk to put his hand on the boy's shoulder. That lean, freckled face with the smudge of ink on the cheek, Simon thought bitterly, this is what Charles valued above me. A miniature of himself, an officer and gentlemen in the making. Let's see how he takes this news.

'I'm afraid I have something unfortunate to tell you, my boy,' Dr Duncan said. 'You recognise this young officer?'

Tom glanced at Simon, eyes wide with wonder. 'Yes, sir.'

'Well, he has brought me some unfortunate news. It seems your mother has had a fall from a horse and is seriously ill. Your father feels it is best that you should go home to see her at once.'

'Oh no! But – Mummy?' Tom glanced about him wildly. 'She hardly ever rides.'

'That's just it, Tom,' Simon said smoothly. 'She put the side saddle on old Punch, and he shied at something in the hedge. She couldn't hold him. He reared and came down on top of her, I think.'

'But what happened? Is she badly hurt?'

'Quite badly, yes. She's hurt her head. That's why your father sent me to fetch you, now.'

'Oh, I see. Yes, of course. We'd better go.'

No tears, Simon noticed. Just wide, dark eyes in a slightly paler face. The freckles stood out more clearly than when he'd come in. Perhaps there was a slight quiver of the lip.

'Here's your coat, Cavendish.' Mrs Duncan helped Tom put it on as they went out onto the front steps. Her husband said: 'I've given you an *exeat* for a week, boy, but tell your father you can come back earlier if he thinks fit. It may be better to be here with your friends and your work to take your mind off things. Also there's a match next Saturday, we'd like to see you play in that.'

Tom wasn't listening. As Simon had anticipated, he was staring at the Daimler.

'That's not Father's car. Mr Fletcher, why have you brought that?'

Simon had his answer ready. 'The Lancia broke down yesterday, Tom. It needs a new cylinder or something. Couldn't be fixed overnight, anyway, so your father hired this from a garage in Bangor. The owner's in the UVF. We have to keep the show on the road, you know. You'll enjoy riding in it – it's a dream to drive.'

Perhaps it was a little too complicated an excuse, but at least it was enough to overcome the time while Simon opened the front door and installed Tom in the passenger seat. Then Simon sprang round quickly to the front, cranked the handle, and leapt in beside him. They were away.

As they reached the end of the lane the rain came down. A few large pregnant drops on the windscreen at first, then floods of it, thundering off the canvas roof, swooshing across the windscreen, bouncing off the bonnet in hundreds of tiny fountains. Simon turned up his coat collar to shield himself against a stream trickling through the roof. If it doesn't stop the engine this could be a bonus, he thought. At least no one will hear us arrive in a downpour like this.

Beside him on the seat, Tom shivered in the sudden chill caused by the rain. Simon grinned to himself. You'll be a lot colder than this before the night is over, my boy, he thought. That stiff upper lip of yours might get frozen solid!

He smiled to himself at his joke, and felt no pity at all . . .

On the way back to Glenfee Tom said little. Once, when the rain had slackened and they could hear themselves speak, he tried to ask about his mother, but Simon did not encourage conversation.

'I wasn't there. I didn't see it myself,' he said. 'You'll find out soon enough when we get you home.'

As planned, Werner was waiting for them in Dundonald. He had a black bag in his hand and was standing outside the hospital. When he got into the back seat of the car, Simon said: 'This is Dr Marcus, a specialist in head injuries. Dr Robinson has called him in for a second opinion, and your father asked me to pick him up here on the way back.'

Tom said little then, either. He seemed cold and stunned more than anything else. Shivering, with his arms folded across his chest for warmth and his wide dark eyes staring earnestly forward through the rain as though to will them onwards. Not until they came to the walls around the park at Glenfee and turned right instead of continuing straight on along the side of the Lough, did he turn to Simon in alarm.

'Where are you going? This is the wrong way!'

Simon had an answer for that too. 'There's a tree down in the drive. We have to get in round the back.'

It was an unlikely answer, because there had been no wind, only rain, and anyway, the road to the back of the estate would still leave them with a ten minute's walk across sodden grass to get to the house, but it kept Tom quiet for another couple of minutes until they turned left along a muddy track that led into the woods at the top of the hill.

Then he said: 'But this is stupid!'

Simon drove round a bend out of sight of the road, stopped the car, leaned over, and seized Tom's arms, pressing them against his sides so that he couldn't move. At the same time Werner reached from behind with a damp sponge which he pressed over the boy's nose and mouth. For a few moments Tom struggled, wriggling and kicking frantically, but it was no use.

The squeaking under the sponge faded, and the little body in Simon's hands relaxed. The reek of chloroform filled the car. For a few moments longer Werner held the sponge in place, then slowly, cautiously, he took it off. Tom's body flopped feebly to one side on the front seat, head lolling. He lay there, eyes closed, breathing quietly and slowly.

Simon put the car in gear, and drove on slowly up the muddy track into the woods.

For a long time Werner had been unable to work out what it was that annoyed him about English country houses.

After all, there were plenty of fine castles in Germany, providing a similar lifestyle. Werner himself had spent part of his youth in one. They were the birthplaces of the aristocracy – the von Moltkes, the Falkenhayns, the leaders of the Empire. Despite their occasional stupidity they had a place in the world – there were very few of them, and they were born to lead. He accepted their way of life as odd, but natural. He was impressed by his visits to the homes of his father's friends, and enjoyed them.

So why did their English and Irish counterparts annoy him so much? He had visited several as a boy, when his father was planning to send him to Eton; and many more since he had returned to the country, to work as a newspaper man.

It had taken him several years to realise that they annoyed him precisely because they were *not* counterparts of the German schlosses. There were far more of them, for a start – nearly everyone he had met at Eton seemed to have a country house. And then, when he went to them in anticipation, they were so much scruffier than he expected. Many of them stank of cats and dogs; they would have a few decent rooms and the rest would be cold and draughty, with thunderous plumbing and stuffed lion's heads presiding over faded wallpaper and peeling paint. Shamefully neglected, in fact.

But it was the inhabitants that really annoyed him. Even the poorest of them acted as though his rural slum really was a castle, and he himself entitled to rule the world from it. As, indeed, the wretched people did. While Germany was penned into the centre of Europe, the confounded English went out from these country houses of theirs, full of icy draughts and dogs and sjambok heads and photos of cricket teams at Allahabad, and ruled an empire on which the sun never set.

If it ever rose, that is, Werner thought. His thick Ulster coat had become thoroughly sodden waiting for Simon outside the hospital in Dundonald, and the car itself, the new Daimler that he had bought earlier this week, had leaked in half a dozen places so that he wondered how long it would be before mould and mushrooms started to grow in it. As he drove up the long drive between the dripping trees he tried to imagine what mental aberration could possibly have persuaded Charles Cavendish to return from India and the Sudan to fight to keep control of such a miserable place as this.

He wondered if Charles Cavendish would remember him.

If he did not he would find out soon enough.

Through the rain and evening gloom he could make out that Glenfee was a moderately large three-storey building with an imposing pillared porch, and what looked like a stable block and several coach houses around the back. There were lights shining dimly through the rain from several of the downstairs rooms, none of which appeared to have curtains drawn. He parked his car on the drive at the front of the house, and hurried up the steps to the front door.

After a pause, a butler opened it. 'Yes, sir?'

'I have come to see Colonel Cavendish.'

'Indeed, sir. Then you had better come in.'

'Thank you.' Werner stepped gratefully into the hall, his coat dripping on the floor. He noticed that the hall was, as he had expected, large, dimly lit from some hissing oil lamps in the corners, and featured several vast oil paintings of ancestors on the walls.

'Is the Colonel expecting you, sir?'

Werner grinned, the pale blue eyes in the thin wolfish face

laughing at the man. 'No, but what I have to say is very important to him. It's a message about the UVF. He will see me, I'm sure.'

'No doubt, sir. Do you have a card?'

'Of course.' Werner fumbled in the pockets of his coat. Damn the English and their wretched formality, he thought. At least in Prussia we have something worth being formal *about*! He produced the card and was left to stand dripping in the hall. He heard a piano somewhere to his left, and a woman singing softly. After a moment the butler returned.

'If you would follow me, sir. And perhaps I could take your coat?'

A trace more warmth, perhaps? If so, why? Had Charles recognised the name on the card he had sent in? If so, what did he feel? Guilt, after all these years? Or amusement, that a man he had abused as a child should care enough to seek him out? Werner followed the butler along a narrow, dark corridor to a door at the end. The man stood back, showed him in.

'Mr von Weichsaker, sir.'

It was a small room, about twenty feet long by about ten square. There were ledgers and box files on shelves all along one wall, and two filing cabinets in a corner next to a typewriter on a table. A few pictures here and there – of Carson, addressing a rally under a huge Union Flag, and another of some young men in regimental uniform in a hot country – India perhaps. To Werner's relief there was a warm coal fire blazing in the grate, but there were no curtains in the window, and rain rattled against the glass out of the blackness of the night. Most of the floorboards were bare, but there was a thin, worn rug in front of the fire. At the far end of the room, near the window, Charles Cavendish sat at a desk facing the wall under a lamp, reading.

It's as drab as his study at Eton, Werner thought suddenly. In all these years he hasn't changed at all.

As Werner came in Charles looked up. The face was the same – thin, sharp, with that proud hooked nose and thin firm mouth. Older, that was all. With receding temples and hair that was greying rather than black. And an air of natural authority that had increased, if anything, since he was head of house at school. Not a man to be trifled with.

And what about me? Werner wondered. Do I look the same to him?

Apparently he did not. No recognition flashed in the cool grey eyes. Just a frown, a polite puzzled glance. Charles stood up, held out his hand.

'Good evening, Mr – von Weichsaker, is it not?'

'Yes, that's my name.' Deliberately, Werner peeled back the glove from his crippled right hand before holding it out. All the time he watched Charles's face. The look of cool, polite disinterest persisted for longer than he had expected, almost, in fact, to the point where Charles was about to take the hand and shake it. But then, he froze. Looked down at the hand, then up, searchingly, into Werner's face.

'Good Lord! So it *is* you?'

'Yes, Charles. It is me.'

Werner had been prepared, to an extent, to feel anger, but not this sudden wave of red fury. Perhaps it was the callous, calm voice in which Charles announced his surprise, as though it was a matter of minor interest which need not detain him long. Perhaps it was the arrogance, the untouchable sense of superiority which cocooned the man even in this old, damp house at the end of the world. Or perhaps it was the way Charles avoided his hand as though it was diseased . . . He stepped back, as though now he had decided Werner was not a gentleman, not even a person to be welcomed into the house at all.

If I could knock him down and shove a red-hot poker up his arse, Werner thought, I would.

But there's no need. Whatever he says or does I can take my time. I've got something to say which will hurt him far far worse than that.

'Well.' To do him credit Charles had at least paled slightly. 'After all these years. Whatever brings you to Glenfee out of this dark, rainy night?'

'I wanted to see you, Charles. I have something important to say.'

'Indeed? Well, you've chosen a damned inconvenient time for it. But now you're here you'd better sit down.' He indicated a shabby leather sofa. 'Can I offer you a drink?'

'Yes, please. Whisky, if you have it.'

Charles opened a cupboard and poured a small amount into two cut-glass tumblers. 'I'm afraid I don't have ice, water, that sort of thing. Neat do you?'

'Certainly.' Werner took the glass and drained half of it in one go. The warmth spread gloriously through his veins.

Charles sat in the chair by his desk and smiled awkwardly. 'I hope I don't seem too rude. It's a bit of a shock to get used to, seeing you as a fully grown man after all this time. What do you do for a living?'

'As it says on my card. I'm a journalist.'

'Oh, I see. Well, what do you want from me? Inside knowledge about the UVF, I suppose. If so, I warn you it's no go. The reason we're such a tight effective organisation is that we know how to keep a few secrets.'

Werner smiled. 'Yes, I know that. As a matter of fact I happen to know one or two of your secrets as well.'

'I beg your pardon?'

Werner took a deep breath. That was silly, he thought. This was where it would all begin. The important thing was to handle it calmly, so that Charles did not lose his temper completely and do something foolish.

'Forgive me. Perhaps I exaggerate. But I regret to say that . . . I have a rather difficult request to make of you. It is of the utmost importance that you listen to me carefully, and think before you react. If you do not, something terrible may happen which you will regret for the rest of your life.'

Charles put his whisky glass down carefully on the desk. 'I'm not sure I understand you.'

'Of course not. Not yet. Let us take it step by step. It is very simple, really. I think you should read this letter.'

As he took the letter out of his pocket, Werner could not stop his hand shaking slightly. He stood up before he gave it to Charles, and then stepped back slightly to be a little out of Charles's reach, near the door. It was rather like passing over a piece of dynamite, in its way. He put his left hand back in his pocket, where the automatic pistol was.

The letter was in a crumpled white envelope. There was nothing written on the outside. Charles picked up a paperknife and slit it open.

Inside was a single sheet of lined paper, apparently torn from a child's exercise book. On it was some writing in grubby pencil. The letters were shaky, not always the same size, smudged in places.

Father,
These men have caught me and shut me in where you can never find. Please do what they say or they will kill me. I am sorry.
Tom.

Charles did not take it in at first. When he did, needles of rage pierced his brain. He sprang to his feet, pushed back his chair, turned upon Werner . . .

'*Stand still*!'

Through a red mist of rage Charles saw the round, black muzzle of a pistol pointing unwaveringly at his face. Werner stood with his back to the door, two yards away, out of reach, with the gun at the end of his fully extended left arm. Behind the gun were two ice-blue intense eyes freezing him into stillness.

'Sit down. Please.'

Charles stood, his hands clenched into fists, shaking with the sudden rush of fury. Surely this German was no marksman, would not dare . . .

'Do what I say. Now, please. If anything happens to me your son will die as well. *Sit*!'

Slowly, never taking his eyes off Werner for a second, Charles backed towards his chair, reached behind him with his hands, sat.

'You unutterable bastard!'

'Say what you like.' Werner lowered the pistol slightly, but did not move away from the door. 'But when you have finished, listen to me. If you love your son at all it is important to do that.'

'Love him *at all*? What do you know of it, you slug? *Where is he*?'

'You read the note. Safely guarded, where you cannot find him. But, unlike you, I do not make a habit of abusing small boys. If you listen to me and do exactly as I say, then by tomorrow night I will return him here. Safe. Completely unharmed.'

'And if I don't?'

'You will, if you love him. Be warned, Charles Cavendish. I am not a monster as you seem to think, but the man who is guarding Tom is. His orders are to kill the boy if I do not return – and I am perfectly sure he will do it. So do not even try to disobey.'

There was a silence. The rain rattled on the window and the coal spluttered in the fire. Far away, faintly, Charles could hear the sound of Deborah playing the piano and singing. As though this place had become a home again, he thought, uselessly.

'What do you want me to do?'

That's better, Werner thought. The first sign of a return to reason. Still standing out of reach by the door, he began to explain. He spoke very slowly and clearly, aware that he was dealing with a man whose judgement might be clouded by emotion, who might be overcome by rage at any moment and forget what he said.

'It is very simple, really. At nine-thirty tomorrow morning you are due to pick up Sir Edward Carson at Craigavon and transport him in your car to Mount Stewart. Is that correct?'

'How the devil do you know—?'

'I asked if it was correct. Is it, or isn't it?'

Slowly, painfully, Charles nodded. 'It may be.'

'Good. I also believe that you intend to leave this house, Glenfee, at seven o'clock tomorrow morning in your car with your chauffeur. You will then pick up an armed escort of three UVF soldiers in the village three miles down the road and proceed to Craigavon. Is this correct also?'

'Someone has told you—'

'Of course. Now, it is a good plan but I wish you to change it slightly. You may still leave this house at seven o'clock tomorrow morning, but your chauffeur and the men from the village will not be in it. Instead, I will accompany you with an armed escort of three men of my own. At the same time as we leave, you will send your chauffeur to the village with a written order cancelling the duties of your escort. Do you understand?'

Charles stared at him, with loathing. 'But why?'

I've seen a rabbit stare like that at a snake, Werner thought, with satisfaction. He smiled at Charles, enjoying the sense of power. 'Ah. Well now, that is the interesting part. You see, we will all go in the car to Craigavon to pick up Sir Edward Carson as arranged. You will play the role of the officer in charge, as though I and my men are your soldiers. You will be very careful not to betray us in any way, because if you do, your son will die. Is that clear too?'

'Everything is clear, you monster, except what you hope to gain by doing this.'

'What I hope to gain is a little acceleration in the course of history, no more. You and Sir Edward will not, of course, arrive at Mount Stewart after you leave Craigavon. Instead I have arranged a little holiday for you in the country. A rumour will spread that Sir Edward has been arrested by the British Army and is being held in Holywood Barracks. If you want to know why we are doing this, think about your colleagues in the UVF for a moment. What are they likely to do, when they hear such a rumour – and find Sir Edward is missing?'

Charles did not answer. He remembered some of the fiery conferences he had attended only last week at Craigavon. Again and again, a number of junior officers had urged an immediate pre-emptive strike on all the military barracks and stores in Ulster, so as to make the UVF's threat of controlling the province a *fait accompli*.

The orders for such an operation – a three-page document entitled *The No.1 Scheme* – were already drawn up. They detailed the occupation of Belfast by a flying column of 5,000 men, a 'sudden, complete, and paralysing blow'. There were plans to cut railway, telegraph, and telephone communications throughout the province, to block all roads that could be used by British reinforcements, and to capture all British Army and police depots. Every UVF unit in Ulster had already practised its role in this plan for months but until recently they had not had the guns to put the plan into action. Now they had.

Last week in Craigavon several officers had argued strongly that it should be put into immediate effect *now*, while the time was ripe. The Liberal government was surprised and demoralised by the success of the gun-running and the mutiny of its own officers at the Curragh last month, they said. It was very tempting. Only the more mature officers counselled caution.

If Carson were arrested, everyone in the UVF would believe the British government were trying to attack them. They would want to strike back. The pressure to rescue Carson and take over the province before it was too late would be irresistible.

Charles himself had argued for putting this plan into effect. It had never occurred to him that it might be useful to the Germans. He had realised it might lead to a brief civil war but he believed the UVF would win it and that the Liberal government would back down and reverse their nonsensical policy of putting Ulster under an Irish Home Rule Parliament in Dublin. He remembered discussing this in the car with Simon on the way back from Craigavon.

Simon! Could he be behind this? The thought hurt him almost as much as the piercing pain about his son. He remembered how bitter Simon had seemed whenever he had tried to end their relationship. How an unpleasant, vicious side to the young man had surfaced . . .

A side which Charles had tried to ignore.

He glared at Werner intensely. 'Who told you all this?'

'All what exactly, Charles, old boy?'

The calculated familiarity of Werner's manner enraged him. It was deliberate – an attempt to remind Charles of their school days together, when . . . he had been as fond of Werner as he had recently been of Simon. And now they had both done this to him! Charles gripped the sides of his chair, trying to retain control.

'Who gave you all this information about my orders to collect Carson tomorrow? And made you think that the UVF might stage a coup if Carson were abducted?'

Werner laughed. 'As for the second, it is obvious enough, isn't it? I worked it out for myself even before I saw the secret orders. But I got hold of those and the details about tomorrow, because – you're afflicted with a certain weakness, aren't you, old chap?'

So it *was* true. Simon – that smooth-talking little devil. And only a few days ago I offered to write letters of recommendation for him, too. '*Why*?'

He hadn't realised he had shouted aloud. But Werner seemed happy to answer.

'Why did I come to you, do you mean? Why choose you as the weak link in the highly moral force of loyal Ulstermen? Well, Charles, why do you think? I knew what you were like from all those years ago when we were at school together. Do you remember? When I was put into your study for protection and you forced me to do those things that . . . no decent man would think of. I haven't forgotten – I don't think I ever will.

'Then I was sent back here and the first thing I saw was you, parading all proud and disdainful with a young smooth-skinned ADC by your side. Perhaps it seemed normal to most people but I thought, nothing has changed, has it? So I thought I would ask that young man a few questions, just to see where his loyalties lay. Oh, you chose a jewel this time, Charles, didn't you? Young Simon couldn't give a damn for you or the Union, not in a thousand years! That boy cares only for himself. And now, I'm afraid, he seems to think you've insulted him – apparently you have a gift for it. So, just like me, he wants to hurt you.'

Charles stared at him, hurt, bewildered. 'I thought . . . we were friends, at school.'

Werner laughed. It was a cruel, mocking sound. 'For a leader of men you know very little about people, don't you, Charles? You thought we were friends because you wanted to think it. It was never true, not after you started to touch me. You had the power and you used it to degrade me. You never even cared what I thought.'

'So you're doing all this just to hurt me, just for something that happened at school?'

So casually he says it, Werner thought. *Just something that happened at school.* As if a boy could be buggered once a day for two terms and then cast off, forgotten, unharmed. He never wrote, never cared when I left. Passion can't touch this man. Just sarcasm, cruelty, blackmail.

Coldly, he said: 'Oh no, Charles, you're not that important. I'm not doing it to hurt you at all. The fact that it does just adds to the pleasure.'

Silence. Werner was pleased to see that Charles's initial rage seemed to be cooling. The man was less likely to try to spring up and try to throttle him now than he had been a few minutes ago.

No doubt he was thinking hard, instead, of more devious ways to evade the trap he was in.

As quietly and calmly as he could, Werner said: 'Let me explain what is going to happen between now and tomorrow morning. Listen carefully, it is important for your son. He will be kept where he is, well-fed and guarded, until tomorrow night. If all goes well and I return safely to speak to his guard before eight o'clock tomorrow night, he will be released and brought back here. Otherwise he will be killed. So it is in your interests to see that nothing happens to me.'

He paused, waiting for a response, but none came. Charles sat silent, unmoving, staring at him with concentrated disgust.

'Tonight I will stay here in this house. No doubt it will cross your mind to try to send a message to someone for help, but I would advise against it. It would cause the death of your boy – and it would also lead to the death of the messenger. My men have surrounded this building and have orders to shoot anyone they see leaving it. I suggest you advise your servants of that at once. I see that you also have a telephone, but you will find you are no longer connected to the operator. Do I make myself clear?'

'Perfectly.' Despite himself, Charles reached out casually for the telephone at the end of his desk and put the receiver to his ear. After a few moments' silence, he put it down in disdain. 'It seems you have planned well.'

'I believe so. Now, if you will show me around the house and find me a room for the night, I need trouble you no more until the morning. If no harm comes to me, no one needs to be hurt.'

'No one except Carson,' Charles said. 'And me too, I suppose.'

'I beg your pardon?'

'*A little holiday*, I think you said, didn't you, Weichsaker? Carson and I would be taken away for a little holiday? Have you thought what Sir Edward will say when he is released and finds the whole country plunged into civil war because of a plot organised by a foreign power? He'll turn the whole force of the UVF against you, and the British government will do the same with their forces! Then you'll see a war far worse than anything that could happen in this small corner of the world. What good will that do you or anyone else?'

Werner smiled thinly. Franz, Karl-Otto and Adolf had already dug the two graves which were the solution to that problem. One for Charles, one for Carson. But it would encourage Charles to mention them now.

'That is a matter for politicians, not me,' he said. 'After all, holidays can be long or short, according to need and circumstances. In any case, I suppose that your wife and servants will be here tomorrow night to welcome your son home, even if you and Sir Edward Carson have to be detained a little longer.'

29

Playing the piano had given Deborah unusual pleasure. She was no great pianist, but she had always played, ever since she was a child. She liked romantic ballads and lullabies mostly, which she could sing in a clear, low contralto as she accompanied herself. The songs and soft chords gave her comfort. She had played the same tunes to Tom when he was at home, and tonight she shared them with Sarah, who sat quietly on a sofa in the drawing room, leafing through a newspaper and listening. Sometimes, when Deborah looked up, she saw a relaxed smile stray like a ghost across the thin, strained face in the firelight, and she thought, this will do us both good.

Not just the two of us either. Always, she was conscious of the child growing inside her. This music is for my baby, too, she thought. It will help him sleep and grow quietly inside me, safe, secure, knowing nothing of the dangers and troubles of the world into which he will be born. I must shield him from that as long as I can.

As long as I can . . . Once, towards the end of the evening, Charles had looked in. With him was a tall thin man with startlingly pale blue eyes and a crippled hand. Charles had introduced him as Werner von Weichsaker and said he would be staying the night. But neither had stayed to talk. Charles's introduction had been curt, brief almost to the point of rudeness, and Deborah had guessed the man's arrival had been an unwelcome extra burden to her husband's many military duties. Charles looked unusually tense, she thought, his face pale, strained.

So tonight would not be the time to tell him of the baby.

For three days now she had put it off. Each day seemed to her like a reprieve, a last blessed hour of sunlight before the storm that had to come. She told herself that Charles was too busy, he was in the wrong mood. That Sarah was too weak to face the inevitable row. That she was being kind to her baby to let it grow in peace another day longer. She even told herself that she was being kind to Charles.

Soon the excuses would run out.

As she went to bed the rain had stopped. She opened her bedroom window and stood there in her nightdress for a moment, looking out into the darkness across the grounds. The clouds were passing and there was a patch of clear sky over the hills to the west where the moon shone down, surrounded by a sprinkling of stars. She could make out some of the trees of the park and the woods on the hills; the field where the cattle came down to the pond that they sometimes called a lake, where she had played at boats with Tom and where the poor children from Dublin had tried to catch ducks; the summerhouse near the oak in which Tom had built a tree-house; the woods with the little gothic pavilion and the ice-house and the badger setts and the tunnel under the road where she and Tom had played hide and seek long ago.

This is my home, she thought. Despite all its frustrations it is where I belong. When I tell Charles what I have done, I shall lose it all . . .

An owl hooted near the stables. Deborah shivered, closed the window, and climbed into bed. She blew out the candle and lay quietly, watching the small rosy shadows of the firelight flicker on the ceiling. She remembered how she had lain here longing for Rankin only two short months ago. Her lover whom she would never touch again.

Her doorknob clicked. The door opened slowly in the dark. A man came into her bedroom. Deborah gasped, and sat up, startled.

'What – who's that?'

'Sssssh. It's only me.' The dark figure closed the door softly behind him.

'Who?'

'Charles.'

Charles? She could hear the creak of the riding boots, so he was still fully dressed, in uniform. *But Charles never comes into my room!*

'What do you want?'

Even as she said it she thought how unwelcoming, how harsh the words sounded. He must want something from me or he wouldn't have come, and I should be glad of it. It is the source of all our problems that he never seems to need me so I shouldn't drive him away. Perhaps he even wants to make love – even now it might not be too late to persuade him that the child is really his. *Oh God I don't want to I'm not in the mood it would be harsh and dry and tearing but if he wants to of course I must it's my last chance . . .*

'Charles?'

'I have to talk to you. Do you have a light?'

'Yes. Here by the bed somewhere.' She reached out, fumbled for matches, lit the candle. He came and sat on the chair between her and the window. She could see the profile of his face in the candlelight – the proud hooked nose, thin high brow, smooth grey receding hair, hollow cheeks, more lined than usual. She could not see into the darkness of his eyes.

'I have something dreadful to say.'

He knows, she thought. How can he possibly have found out?

'It's about Tom.'

'Oh!' Not about me and Rankin then. But his voice sounded so grim, weary, bitter. 'What has happened?'

'He has . . . Deborah, I am very sorry to tell you this, but Tom is in serious trouble.'

'What – at school, you mean? Has he done something wrong?'

'No, not at school, Deborah. He's not there . . .'

The voice was not just bitter, but frightened, she realised. 'Charles, what's happened?'

'Don't scream, woman. It's very important that you don't scream. Please control yourself.'

'*Will you please tell me what has happened to my son?*'

She was sitting bolt upright in bed now, glaring at him.

'He has been . . . kidnapped.'

'What?' It was beyond her comprehension. She was not sure where she was or what she was doing; she felt faint. He was holding her hand, a thing he never did.

'Please, Deborah, don't scream. It's very important that you don't scream. That man might hear you.'

'What are you talking about?' Desperately, she focussed all her energies on trying to understand what he was saying, to believe it was really happening. His voice was low, insistent, urgent.

'Listen to me now. That man who is staying here, Werner von Weichsaker, he is one of them. He came to me tonight to tell me. His men have taken Tom from school and hidden him somewhere. They are German agents, you see. They want to capture Carson, perhaps kill him. And they want to force me to help them, so they have kidnapped Tom.'

It was too much to take in all at once. Floundering, she said: 'How do you know they have Tom? They may be lying. Dr Duncan wouldn't let him go, surely?'

'He gave me this.'

Charles gave her a crumpled scrap of paper. She read it.

> *Father,*
> *These men have caught me and shut me in where you can never find. Please do what they say or they will kill me. I am sorry.*
> *Tom.*

The tears came. She couldn't help it, they were just there. Welling up inside her, misting her eyes, shaking her chest so that she sobbed. They were no use, she didn't want them, they didn't help. Fiercely, she said: 'What are we going to *do*?'

He explained again, patiently, what Werner had said, what he wanted. This time she took some of it in. She said: 'But why – how do they know all this?'

Charles did not answer at first. He had hoped to avoid this but – it was impossible. It was bound to come out now. Anyway, Tom was her son as well as his; she had a right to know how his weakness had brought the boy into danger.

'I'm afraid – I think Simon told them.'

'Simon?' Deborah had never liked the young man, but . . . 'Why? He's one of your soldiers, isn't he?'

'Of course, but . . . it seems he has taken a dislike to me and been selling information to these Germans. It may even have been him who persuaded the headmaster to let the boy leave school. Dr Duncan would recognise Simon, wouldn't he?'

'Yes, I suppose so. He drove me there at the beginning of term. But why would Simon dislike you, Charles? You've always been kind to him, haven't you?'

'Yes, but . . . Deborah, I am very sorry about this, but . . .' He hesitated. The words were there, in his throat, to tell her, explain why he had been so cold to her all these years. *I am afraid I have not behaved entirely properly with him* . . . Perhaps, if he said that, she would understand, accept him for the man he really was.

But he could not do it.

'. . . It seems the boy has been paid. I am afraid I am not always the best judge of men. And these Germans have used him.'

'So – Simon has helped in this kidnap?'

'I don't know. I am not sure who is guarding him, but it may be that Simon has a hand in it. Anyway, we have a choice.'

'What do you mean – a choice?'

The shock was too deep for tears. Deborah suddenly felt a surge of furious energy, a desire to hit someone or run far away and leave all this behind her. But she could do neither. Instead, she got abruptly out of bed, stepping carefully past Charles so as not to touch him. She took a dressing gown from her wardrobe, wrapped herself in it, and walked up and down by the dying fire.

'We have to find Tom!'

'I don't think we can, my dear.' In a grey, weary voice, Charles explained what Werner had told him. 'So you see, there *is* a choice, though no one would wish to face it. If I do what they say, Tom will be released – probably – but Carson will be captured, possibly killed, and a wretched civil war will break out which will benefit Germany and kill hundreds, perhaps thousands, of soldiers; or we prevent all that and our son dies.'

She stared at him incredulously. 'You can't mean it, Charles! You don't have any choice at all. You couldn't risk Tom's life!'

Bleakly, he said: 'It is not only Tom's life at risk, you see. I have a duty to all the other lives that may be lost as a result of this wicked scheme.'

'A duty?'

'Yes. Tom may have a similar responsibility one day, if he becomes an officer.'

'But it's his *life*, Charles! Anyway, I thought you were happy for a civil war to start.'

Charles sighed. 'I have advised in favour of a considered military action, yes. But only if it has been agreed on by our leadership; not as a result of Carson being kidnapped, perhaps killed by the Germans. To support that would be treason, woman – don't you realise that?'

Silence. It was so like Charles, she thought. No one else could be so cold, so logical and correct, in a horrendous situation like this. Perhaps that is how you learn to behave, as an army officer. But this is our son we're talking about – how *can* he be so calm? I am married to a man I don't understand at all.

'So what do you intend to do?'

Charles leaned forward intently, his elbows on his knees. As though it was important to convince her of some academic point.

'I think there may be a solution. A way of fighting back while minimising the risk, at least.'

She strode to the window frantically, staring out into the night. Hurrying low clouds had hidden the moon again and there was a spatter of rain, the rustle of wind among dark, shadowy trees. She pressed her hands against the glass.

'Tom's out there somewhere, Charles. We've got to get him back!'

'Yes, of course – I'm trying to do that. But not at the price of betraying my conscience! Listen, Deborah, von Weichsaker says he has the house surrounded, but I don't entirely believe him. He can't have that many men, and they won't know the grounds. So it might be possible for me to get away from the house and go down to the village and summon help. And if I could do that, I *would* have enough men to surround the house. Men who know this area very well indeed.'

She gazed at him helplessly. It all sounded futile to her. A boy's game of soldiers. That was the world Charles lived in.

'But how would that help Tom? If you do that, they will kill him. Tom says that in his note, doesn't he?'

'Yes, but nothing will happen to Tom until tomorrow night, he said. Only if he, von Weichsaker, doesn't come back safe from the operation against Carson, *then* something will happen to Tom. Not before. That may prove to be their mistake. You see, if I can get to the village tonight, I can get Sergeant Cullen to organise a detail to arrest von Weichsaker and his men when they come here and try to get in the car with me at seven tomorrow morning. It might be dangerous for me, but it won't hurt Tom. And then, if von Weichsaker sticks to what he says, nothing will happen to Tom until eight tomorrow evening, when Werner fails to turn up where they're holding him. Which means we'll have over twelve hours to look for that hiding place – and try to persuade von Weichsaker to tell us where it is. My guess is that when he realises he's been beaten, he'll understand there's no point in killing an innocent boy.'

She looked at him coldly. 'And so you intend to leave me alone in the house with this monster, and go down to the village to collect your soldiers. What do you think this Werner von Weichsaker will say when he finds out you're not here? He'll probably take me hostage, as well.'

'That's why you'll have to keep quiet tonight. When it gets light I want you to warn all the servants, tell them to stay inside the house. I'll be back by morning – I'll have to be. It'll only take me a couple of hours at most to get to the village and back.'

'And if you're wrong? If you're shot by the men surrounding this place?'

'That's a chance I must take. At least it'll mean von Weichsaker's scheme will fail; it can't work without me in the car. So again, there's a chance they'll release Tom or that he'll be found in time.'

There was a long silence. They stared at each other, conscious suddenly of the sounds of the house at night; the fire burning in the grate, the occasional creak or groan of old rafters, the wind siffling around the eaves, a slight patter of returning rain on the windows.

'Charles, I don't like this! It's too risky. I think you're making a mistake.'

Charles got to his feet, a thin smile on his face. 'Don't worry. I am a soldier, after all. I've moved past the Matabele at night before now. I'll be gone in a few minutes, and I should be back well before daylight. I didn't come for your advice, but to tell you what's happening because you have a right to know and in case anything goes wrong. And also to say, whatever happens – I am sorry.'

'About what? You couldn't have known.'

'No . . . Of course not. Wish me luck then, my dear. Goodbye.'

He walked past her to the door. He did not touch her and she did not speak. Then he was gone, and she sank slowly into a chair by the fire.

'And if he doesn't come back?'

'He will. He's a soldier, of course he will.'

'Soldiers get killed. All the time. In a way, I think he wants to.'

'Debbie! What do you mean? That's not like Charles.'

'No, I know. It's just . . . something he said. Oh God, Sarah, I hope I'm wrong! He seemed so grim – resigned, almost.'

'Don't talk nonsense. You're imagining things.'

The two women sat huddled together in Sarah's bedroom, whispering earnestly together by the light of a candle. The window was open, and they could hear the soft hissing of the rain on the grass outside, and the sighing of the wind. So far, no sound of what they were listening for – the sounds of a fight, whatever that might be. A shot? Shouts? A scream? Deborah didn't know.

Deborah was not sure how long Charles had been gone. It was difficult to measure time when your mind was in such turmoil. For a while she had stayed in her own room, but the sense of utter helpless panic had been intolerable. She knew it was wrong to burden Sarah with things like this, but what else could she do? Call the cook? Run out into the garden herself? Go and plead with that man Werner in his room?

At least Sarah had not fainted. Indeed she seemed excited more than anything else. More alive than she had been since she came here. And she saw the problem with slightly more detachment than Deborah could manage.

Now she asked: 'What made you think Charles wanted to die?'

'He apologised to me, Sarah. He never does that.'

'About what?'

'This man kidnapping Tom, I suppose. I don't see why it's his fault except he brought that awful young man Fletcher into the house.'

'But why did *he* do it?'

'Oh, I don't know. Sarah, I don't know!' Deborah shook her head hopelessly. 'I just want my son back!'

'Of course. Of course you do.' Sarah's mind was racing, trying to think of a way out of this appalling deadly puzzle she had woken into. 'There are guns in this house, aren't there? We could go downstairs, find some, kill this German . . .'

'And condemn Tom to death? As Charles may be doing right now?'

'Yes, I see. Well, where could they have taken him, do you think?'

'How should I know? A house, an empty cottage somewhere – there must be hundreds all over Ulster. Perhaps a barn up in the hills.'

Sarah sighed. 'And all you've got is this note?'

'Yes.' Deborah sat with her head in her hands. Her chest ached and the tears trickled pointlessly through her fingers. She had never felt so useless.

Sarah looked at the note, hoping it might tell her something. What would you do, if you were a young boy scared out of your wits, forced to write a letter like this, she wondered. Write a note on the back, perhaps. Or the envelope. She turned the paper over. Nothing. Just the blue printed lines and the red of the margin – normal exercise book paper. 'Have you got the envelope?'

'No. Charles must have it. I never saw it.'

So much for that. Sarah studied the writing. Nothing useful there. Just an uneven, pencilled scrawl. 'Poor boy. He must have been terrified.'

'Yes, of course he was.' Deborah got up and took the note out of Sarah's hand – almost possessively, Sarah thought. She stared at it closely, then crumpled it in her hand. 'Wouldn't you have been?'

'I was,' Sarah said, very softly to herself, glad that Deborah couldn't hear. The Black Maria, she thought, the cell, the day I was shut in that basket. The poor little boy – how old is he? Eight? He must be scared out of his wits. At least I knew what I was doing it for, but even I nearly went mad. He's just a victim, doesn't know anything at all. Probably they haven't even told him what it's all about. 'The worst thing is not knowing when it will end.'

Sarah hadn't realised she had spoken the last thought aloud, but Deborah turned as though she had heard.

'What do you mean?'

'Being imprisoned, as I was and Tom is now. You can bear anything if you know it's going to end, but when you're at someone else's mercy you can't know that. Anything longer than a day seems like forever.'

'Don't!'

'I'm sorry.' Sarah got up and walked quietly across the room, put her hand on Deborah's shoulder. She was still in her nightdress and even walking was still not so easy for her. But if I could find a way to do something about this, she thought, I would find the energy from somewhere, whatever it cost later. It's like those little girls in London, only this is a boy, even younger.

'When he was about four or five,' Deborah said softly, compulsively. 'We used to play hide-and-seek round the grounds. It's a good place for it, there are lots of hiding places. And then one day I couldn't find him, the little beggar. I looked for *hours*. I called and called – I thought he was just being naughty – but in fact when I found him he'd lost the key and was nearly frozen to death.'

'Why?' Sarah stroked her shoulder softly. 'Was it winter?'

'No. It was nearly May. He was in the ice-house.'

Tom had been given two blankets but he was still cold. He sat on the steps most of the time, with the blankets wrapped around him like the pictures of squaws he had seen in books about the Wild West. They helped, but not much. The steps were cold and damp and there was a draught that came whistling under the door and made his back and legs ache. But at least it was better than the ice in front of him.

He couldn't see the ice because it was dark, but he knew it covered all of the floor. It was at least a foot deep, maybe more – he had thrust his hand down into it as far as it would go, and had not found bricks. Goodness, it was cold! His hand went numb afterwards, so that the bones ached right through to the wrist; and even when that had warmed up he felt he had lost some warmth which he couldn't afford. His teeth were chattering most of the time and he could feel goose pimples all round his knees. He was wearing grey flannel shorts, long grey socks, a bright orange jumper and a school blazer – and it was not warm enough, not by a long way!

He wondered if he was meant to die in here, and told himself not to be stupid. People go to the Antarctic, and that must be much colder than this. Some of them die there of course, like poor Captain Scott. But at least he reached the South Pole first, and he didn't whinge about the cold – no Englishman would. His men probably trained in places like this. I'm lucky, really. I'll be able to lead an Antarctic expedition when I get out!

If I get out.

To stop himself getting into a funk and thinking panicky thoughts like that he got up every ten minutes or so and walked around the floor of the ice-house. He tried to pretend he was on an Antarctic expedition and sometimes it worked. The floor of the ice-house was perfectly circular, and it was about six yards in circumference. It was quite dark in here, and the ice scrunched and slithered beneath his feet, but that was all right; it just helped him to pretend he was in the cold and dark of an Antarctic winter. Anyway, he knew what the ice-house was like; he had been in here before in daylight. The walls were made of brick and quite thick, and the whole thing was sunk several yards below the ground for insulation. That was why there were steps, winding down from the door, which was locked. Even to approach that door from outside you had to open another door first and go down a little cold tunnel. The roof was well insulated, too, and since the house was in a wood under trees which never let through any sunlight it was very, very cold.

Cold enough to keep ice in throughout the summer. Ice that was used to cool bottles of wine and champagne in buckets, or to pack around meat and fish which cook wanted to keep fresh for a few days before cooking.

It was a luxury that only a few country houses had, and Tom knew his parents were quite proud of it. Sometimes they bought ice to fill it, from fishing trawlers which had been up to Iceland in midwinter; in other winters, when it was cold enough in Ulster anyway, they had it chopped out of the local ponds and water-butts and brought it up here in a cart.

The ice-house was always supposed to be kept locked, but everyone knew the key to the outside door was kept under a slate near a yew tree, and the key to the inner door hung on a hook in the tunnel. Once, when Tom was younger, he had taken the first key, gone inside, locked the door from within, and then taken the second and opened that door too. It would have been all right if it had gone to plan – he had only meant to fool his mother. The trouble was that he had lost the key to the outside door under the ice somewhere, and nobody could hear his shouts. He had only escaped when he had found the key after nearly two hours, and then by a superhuman effort unlocked the door and staggered down across the lawn to the house, his legs almost rigid with cold.

The memory of that day encouraged Tom and frightened him too. You *can* escape from this place, he thought. I did it before. Only then when I came in here to hide from mother, I had the key, and now I haven't. That man Simon Fletcher has got it and he didn't say when he was coming back. And if he doesn't come back I *will* die of cold. People do. Scott did . . .

No, Father will rescue me because I hid a secret message in my letter. That was very clever of me – just like Sherlock Holmes. When Father comes to let me out he'll say I'm a plucky little chap, especially when he learns I didn't cry. I'll tell him I walked halfway to the South Pole while I was waiting.

The only thing that troubled Tom about the message he had sent to his father, was that really it was the sort of message his mother was more likely to understand. And, knowing his father, he might not want to upset his mother by showing her what he had written.

The best thing to do with thoughts like that is to ignore them, he told himself. Think about what Father would say. Chin up, old man. That's the spirit. Never say die. Play up and play the game. Show the world what an Englishman is made of.

Shivering, he dragged himself to his feet, and for the fiftieth time began to stumble around the floor of the ice-house, a tiny figure shrouded in blankets.

South, towards the Pole.

It was true that Charles had once crept through the lines of the Matabele but that was twelve years ago now. And even then he had had the services of a skilled African tracker who had led the way. This time he was on his own.

When he left Deborah he went back to his own room and took off his riding boots. The leather would creak and they might shine in the moonlight, he thought. Instead he put on an old pair of marching boots and puttees, and then pulled a thick pair of grey socks over the boots to muffle the sound of the nails.

The rest of his clothes would do, he thought. Khaki jacket and trousers would not show up in the dark, but he left off his officer's cap with the gleaming brass badge and put on a long, dark, riding coat against the rain. He spun the chamber of his Webley service revolver to check that it was fully loaded, and slipped it into the holster on his Sam Browne belt, leaving the flap loose so that it would not get in his way if he had to draw it quickly.

But a shot would make too much noise. If he really did come across any of Werner's men then the last thing he would want to do was call down all the rest by firing a gun. A knife would be better. He glanced quickly around the room and took a knife from the wall. It was a kukri – one of a pair that he had bought from a Ghurka in India. The blade was nearly a foot long, curved, heavy especially towards the point, and razor sharp – he had once seen a diminutive Ghurka soldier slice the head off a bull with one in a single blow. Smiling grimly, Charles buckled it on to his belt. A kukri is not supposed to be taken out of its sheath unless it draws blood, he thought. And if one of these bastards tries to stop me tonight there'll be enough blood to float a ship.

He stepped quietly down the back stairs to the kitchen door. This was some way from Werner's room, so it should be all right, but still he moved slowly, cautiously, listening to every creak and groan of the floorboards. He had forgotten how deafening silence could seem when you were listening for every sound – he could even hear the singing of blood in his ears.

Outside, darkness enveloped him. He moved quickly through the yard towards the stables, and then past the walled kitchen garden behind. So far, so good. None of the horses had whinnied, his boots had not sparked on the cobbles. This far he knew the way without thinking, so he had moved quickly; from here on he would have to go more slowly, with care.

He waited under a tree, letting his eyes grow accustomed to the darkness. There were two obvious ways to the village: either down the drive at the front of the house, or along a cart track that ran from the stables at the back, west and north around the outskirts of the estate, eventually going past a small wooded rise and down onto the loughside road a mile further on than the drive. It would be foolish to take either of these; if there was any truth in Werner's claim, then both would be guarded.

There were three other routes. He could go straight across the park and down to the road that way: it would be quick, and quite easy if the darkness held, because there would be nothing in the way but a few hedges, grass and cows; but if the moon came out he would stand out clearly, an obvious target. He could go west, away from the house in the opposite direction to the village. There were quite a lot of hedges and small hills here, good cover; but he would have to make a long loop round to his right after he had crossed the track, four or five miles across country in order to return to the village from the north, and that would take time.

And time was what he did not have. To be sure of taking Werner by surprise he wanted to give his orders to Sergeant Cullen and be back in the shortest time possible, so that Werner would have the least chance of realising he had gone. The less Werner suspected, the safer it would be for Tom. So he had to go quickly.

He decided on the third route: north through the mile and a half of woods and coppices that led directly to the junction of track and road, half a mile outside the village. The woods were thick in places, but he knew them well. And, when he approached the road, the trees would give him good cover to look out and see if anyone was watching.

When his eyes had adapted well enough to distinguish the trunks of trees ten or fifteen yards away, he set out.

Inside the woods the darkness increased. He was surrounded by the dank dripping sound of water falling from leaves. The rain had almost ceased, but water was still making its way from the trees to the ground. The sound, Charles thought, would deaden any noise his feet might make on the damp turf and leafmould underfoot. His greatest care must be to avoid stepping too sharply on a rotten stick or crashing into a bush.

There were paths through the woods. He thought he knew them well. He had come in here once or twice with Tom only a few weeks ago, in the Easter holidays. He remembered how shocked the boy had been when they had come upon a line of vermin strung up on a fence by Charles' gamekeeper – half a dozen rotting crows, a sparrowhawk, a weasel, and two magpies, all hanging in various stages of decomposition from a branch not far from the pheasant runs. It *was* disgusting, Charles had agreed, but they were there to deter others. Vermin had to be killed, to make the woods safe for pheasants and songbirds.

And children, Charles thought. He wasn't sure what the legal penalty was for blackmailing parents by kidnapping little boys, but it ought to be death. If I saw that Werner strung up on a line rotting like a crow I wouldn't care, so long as Tom was safe.

And would Simon hang, too? Now, as he pushed his way slowly through the dark dripping trees, the enormity of what had happened came over Charles and he began to weep. He could not remember weeping ever in his life before, but that must be what it was. There was a pain in his chest and his breath came harshly and he thought: *I did this to my own son*. It is because I trusted that boy Simon and gave way to my passion with him and with Werner, when I knew it was wrong, that all this has happened. If I had restrained myself, as I ought to have done, then no one would have dared to blackmail me with the life of my only son.

Sweet Christ forgive me! Just a day ago Tom thought I was a hero. If I get this wrong now, they will kill him. And even if they don't, one of those devils will probably tell him his father has done something he could never, ever understand.

He stopped for a moment in a glade, and for the first time noticed a sound like a man in pain. Abruptly he held his breath. The noise stopped at once, and he realised with shame it was the sound of his own sobbing. If I make a noise like that because I can't control my own emotions I deserve to be caught. For God's sake, man, get a grip!

Softly, he moved out of the glade along a dark grassy path which led to the pheasant runs. The moon had come out, and a pale silver light began to filter down between the trees. Ahead of him he could make out a row of low wooden hutches where the keeper kept his pheasant poults. Two hundred yards beyond that, down a slight slope, would be the road. In ten minutes at most I should have made it, he thought. And then, if there's no one on the road itself, in five minutes more . . .

'Halt! Stand there, please – still!'

The voice spun him round as though he had touched an electric battery. Who was it? Where? It came from the left, just ahead and to the side of the hutches – yes! Six or seven yards away under the trees, the figure of a man.

His first instinct was to run, but even as he took the first step he saw the figure had a rifle. And the voice said: 'Halt there! Still, or I shoot!'

Charles stopped, five yards from the man, thinking: It's no good to run. Even if I get away they'll know I've gone now and that may mean death for Tom. The only thing is to stop this man now, quietly, so that no one knows what's happened.

Silently, as he stood in the semi-darkness, he slipped his hand under the long riding coat and slid the kukri from its sheath . . .

'It sounds silly, but I was terribly frightened then, ' Deborah said. 'He was so little, and he could easily have died, simply frozen to death in there. I mightn't have gone there for days. I made a rule he shouldn't ever go in a place like that again. I called it never find.'

'Never find?' Sarah stood beside Deborah, gently stroking her shoulders and back. She was only half listening to the words, more to the tone of them – the compulsive, terrified hysteria that made Deborah go on and on, talking about a problem neither of them could solve or forget.

'Yes. Like some medieval dungeon, you know. The ice-house and places like that were out of bounds for hide-and-seek because you might never be found there, you know. Anyway, we hardly ever played hide-and-seek after that. Sarah, why am I telling you all this?'

'Why? Because it was the last time you lost him, I suppose. And now this, which is much worse. Listen, Debbie,' Sarah stopped rubbing Deborah's neck, and sat down on a stool in front of her. She held Deborah's hands and stared quietly into her eyes. 'Charles knows the countryside round here quite well, doesn't he? So if he thinks he can get into the village he probably can. And once he's got his UVF soldiers to round these kidnappers up, there won't be any point in their holding on to Tom, will there? No one makes war on small boys.'

'Don't they? What if only one of them knows where he is, and that one gets shot or runs away? We'd never find him!'

Deborah's eyes looked haunted in the candlelight. I have never seen her upset like this, Sarah thought. She's obsessed by the horror of it all, as I was when I found out about Jonathan . . .

Forget that! Don't think of that now, it's all past.

As comfortingly as she could, she said: 'Charles is a soldier. He knows what he's doing, Debbie.'

Deborah said: 'Never find . . .'

'What?' She'll lose control completely if I can't reach her, Sarah thought. 'Of course we'll find him, we've got nearly twenty-four hours yet . . .'

But Deborah wasn't listening. Frantically, she took her hands away from Sarah's and scrabbled on the chair, on the fireside table, in the pocket of her nightgown. Looking for something.

'Here!' She took out Tom's crumpled note. 'Don't you see? Look, there!' She pointed to some words at the end of a line. 'Never find!'

Sarah read the note again.

Father,
These men have caught me and shut me in where you can never find. Please do what they say or they will kill me. I am sorry.
Tom.

'What do you mean, Debbie?'

'It's not proper English, is it? If you or I were writing that sentence we'd say, "where you can never find *me*", wouldn't we? And Tom's bright, he doesn't make mistakes like that. He's done it on purpose.'

'Debbie, you're imagining things. He was probably just frightened and confused and left a word out, that's all. Anyway what could it possibly tell you?'

'That . . .' Deborah got up abruptly and paced across the room. 'I know it sounds crazy, Sarah, and you'll think I'm making it up, but I don't think Tom's far away at all. I think they've brought him here and shut him up in the ice-house!'

'But why would they do that?'

'Because . . . it's near and it's easy and it's very secure and no one would think to look there, perhaps. I don't know. I'm just telling you that's what those words mean, to Tom and me. It's not a mistake, it can't be. He and I used those words hundreds of times – they're a sort of family joke.'

'Wouldn't Charles recognise them?'

'I don't know – no, probably not. He was away in India at the time, so it wouldn't mean so much. Sarah, he's *there*. I know it.'

Sarah stared at her, bemused. 'It's a possibility, I suppose, but – what are we going to do about it?'

'We could wait for Charles, tell him when he comes back.'

'Will he believe you?'

'Probably not.' Deborah shook her head frantically. 'Oh Sarah, I know it sounds crazy but I *know* he's in there! And we can't just leave him. Even if they don't kill him, he'll freeze to death!'

'All right. Let's go there and let him out.'

'What? Just you and me?'

'Yes.' Sarah smiled. 'You and a few other ladies got me out of Holloway, didn't you? This should be a lot easier than that!'

Charles stood quite still, waiting. He could see the silhouette of the man in front of him, five yards away under the trees, shadowy in the moonlight. He could distinguish the shape of the rifle, but not the face; just a pale grey blue under a cap. If the moon goes in, he thought, I won't see even that.

And he won't see me.

Charles felt the weight of the kukri in his right hand, under his coat. Heavy, perhaps one and a half pounds in weight, solid, razor sharp. A single blow from it would sever the man's arm or neck, leave him stretched, twitching on the ground, pulsing his life's blood into the leafmould. It would be a terrible thing to do – but for my son, he thought, I will if I have to.

The man was still five yards away, just out of reach. Deliberately, Charles took a step forward.

'Halt!' the man said. 'Stand still there.'

Charles realized he still did not know definitely who the man was. Certainly the accent was not local, probably foreign, but before killing a man one ought to be sure. If he was just a poacher and I sliced his head off . . .

'Who are you?'

'To talk not. Back to house. *Verstehen*?'

Oh yes, I vestehen all right, Charles thought. Just come a little closer and you'll see. 'Which house d'you mean, old chap? I went out for a midnight stroll and got lost, don't you know?'

He took another step forward.

'Halt! Stand there!'

The man took half a pace backwards to keep his distance, into the low overhanging brush of the surrounding trees. Charles thought, I can move forward faster than him, but one false move and I've had it. The gun barrel was pointing straight at his chest, and the man's voice sounded distinctly nervous, uncertain what to do next.

Any moment now.

'Hilfe! Hier! Adolf! Schnell!' The man turned his head and yelled loud over his shoulder, into the night. At the same moment the moon went in, and he almost disappeared in the sudden blackness all around him. Charles ducked and stepped forward, swinging at the rifle barrel with his left arm to lift it up and away, harmlessly over his head. At the same time he drew out the kukri in his right hand and, as he felt the rifle barrel slide away, raised himself to his full height and swung the kukri down and forwards with all his strength into the darkness where the man had been.

He felt a jar all along his arm and a crack as though the kukri had sheered right through something.

But it was too high! It was not in the right place for an arm and there was not the soft, sticky blood smell or a scream. Instead there was a curse, not where the knife had struck but a little further away, and a shadow moving under the trees. God damn it to hell, Charles thought, I hit the branch of a tree not the man. He lifted the kukri again and stepped forward but another branch whipped him in the face and before he could focus on the shifting indistinct shape in front of him there was a sudden red flash and a blinding roar and . . .

'There's a man there!'

'Where?'

'Sssssh! Look!' Deborah reached out and touched Sarah's arm, pointing down between the trees. They were on a little hill about half a mile west of the house, with large well-grown cedars and beeches stretching high above their heads. Immediately in front of them and below them was a thick bank of rhododendron bushes, which Deborah hoped would screen them from view. The ice-house was just below them to the right, screened by the rhododendron bushes and a number of other shrubs. As the moon peeped from behind a cloud, she had seen the shape of the man.

Sarah peered along the line of Deborah's arm, but it was hard to see what she was pointing at. It was very dark, and a thin, drizzling rain was still falling. The brief flash of moonlight filtered through a confusion of trees and branches which were unfamiliar to her; she was not even sure she could distinguish the ice-house.

She was beginning to regret her impulsive suggestion that the two of them should come out here. They had no clear plan, other than to look for the key, unlock the door, and see if Tom was inside. Despite Deborah's certainty about the words in the letter, Sarah thought the chances of finding Tom were highly unlikely. She had only suggested they come in order to humour her sister and help her break out of the self-destructive weeping and panic which had begun to engulf her. At least it was action, and Sarah was in favour of that. It might lead to something, and if not, at least they would know they had tried.

The moonlight faded, then returned. Sarah peered harder in

the direction Deborah had pointed. There *was* a low building there – she could see part of its roof between the rhododendrons, wet slates glistening silver. And something else, about ten yards to the right of the building. Was that a man, standing very still and dark beside a leaf-covered path, or had Deborah imagined it? It might be only a tree stump, or a small fir tree, perhaps?

Fir trees don't move.

The figure turned, took several paces idly along the path, as though going nowhere in particular, then came back. She thought she could make out the coat now, and a peaked cap like that of an officer.

'It *is* a man!' she hissed fervently. 'You're right, Debbie – standing guard outside the ice-house!' Sarah was impressed. Perhaps Deborah's intuition had been right after all.

'What did I tell you? Tom's got to be in there!'

'Well, what're we going to do now?'

'Sssssh! He's looking this way!'

'Oh my God, so he is.'

The two women froze. At least we had the sense to put on dark coats and hats, Sarah thought. Surely he can't see us? If he has, we can't possibly fight him. I only just managed to make it up this hill. Maybe it's my gasping for breath that's given us away.

Deborah was almost certain who the man was. He was slim and he had that officer's cap on – certainly he wasn't a poacher, and she couldn't believe any German spies would dress like that. Anyway, surely their caps were different? So it *must* be Simon Fletcher, and that proves everything. He has a stick in his hand too, or is it a rifle?

As the young man looked up, and then began to climb the slope cautiously towards them, Deborah thought, if it is him I can't run, that would be deserting Tom. Maybe I can find a fallen branch somewhere to hit him with, or I'll walk straight up to him and jab my fingernails in his eyes . . .

She had never fought anyone since she was a child, and she had little idea what to do. But no one had threatened her son before, and that made everything different. She thought: everything's possible if you have the courage. The main thing is to attack . . .

The dank silence under the trees was shattered suddenly by a scream far away in the woods to their left, and a shot immediately afterwards. The two women froze and the woods around them echoed with the sound. Then there was another scream, high-pitched, distant like the first. This time Deborah thought she could make out some of the words.

'*Hilfe! Hier! Adolf!*'

It was about a mile away, in the woods by the road where the pheasant runs were. My God, she thought, it's Charles!

On the slope in front of them the dark figure of the young man stood quite still, staring to his right where the sound had come from. He seemed to hesitate for a while, and Deborah thought, if I were a man I would attack him now. While he's still not sure we're here, while he's not thinking about us. But I'm not: he's too far away and I still haven't found a stick.

Then the young man made up his mind. He turned abruptly and walked away from them, back past the ice-house and out of sight. For a couple of minutes Deborah listened, in the oppressive silence that seemed to have descended around them even closer than before, like a damp dark blanket. She thought she heard occasional footsteps going away, down the slope and through the trees towards the house. If he was going into the house then surely there would be the scrunch of gravel . . .

There! Wasn't that it?

She had to take the risk. 'Come on!' she whispered to Sarah. 'I'm sure he's gone. We've got to try the door!'

Simon was good at waiting, but only when he saw the point of it. If there was a man to be killed – tipped from the passenger deck of a ship into the grey midnight sea or incinerated in his own mistress's house – then Simon could wait for hours, immobile, waiting for precisely the right moment and thinking only of the task in hand. Then he would strike, swift and silent as a snake, and be gone. The waiting was part of the joy of successful revenge.

But tonight was different. He had not chosen to wait outside the ice-house, and he saw no point in it. The boy was shut in behind two locked doors. He could not escape, and no one would come to rescue him because no one knew where he was. Simon wanted to be in the house. He wanted to see the expression on Charles's face when he learned what had happened. He wanted to see the knowledge seep in, like poison, that this was Charles's punishment for having rejected Simon's love. It was what happened to all men whom Simon met, in the end. And he wanted to see Charles's face when he realised that his son, whom he said he loved above anything, was a hostage in Simon's hands; and that, because of this, he was going to have to betray every principle he had ever held dear.

It was a more subtle, crueller revenge than any he had devised before. That was why he had proposed it – that, and the large pension from the German treasury that Werner had promised him, if the plan succeeded. But all his pleasure would be wasted, if he was not allowed to witness the effect on Charles . . .

Werner had insisted Simon stayed by the ice-house, partly to guard Tom, partly to ensure that no one left the house to give a warning, and partly, so he said, because he felt that the sight of Simon might so enrage Charles that he would be unamenable to reason.

None of these reasons impressed Simon, but in the end he had given way. Now, alone in the dank night, he wished he had not. He had considered going in to young Tom and favouring him with a detailed account of exactly what his heroic father did for sexual gratification; but the pleasure in that, also, would be small if he were not able to witness the meeting later between father and son. It had also occurred to Simon, later in the night, that Werner's plans excluded him from the trip to Craigavon the next day. One of Werner's men was to drive the car; he, Simon, was to stay here. The more Simon thought about that, the more foolish he thought it was. He knew the roads and the car better than any German sailor; and any suspicious sentries they met would recognise him as Charles's ADC. And, most important from Simon's point of view, he would be there to watch Charles squirm as he carried out Werner's orders.

All these thoughts were going through Simon's head when he heard a sound in the woods above him. At first he thought it might be a fox or a badger rustling through the leaves – he had heard several already that night. Then a stick cracked and there was a sound that might have been whispering; though it was hard to tell, with the rain and the wind through the leaves. But if it was someone, trying to move through the trees into the back lane and on into town, then he had been placed here to stop that.

He climbed hesitantly up the slope. He was not an experienced soldier or used to fighting in the normal sense. He had his rifle, the Mannlicher which had been smuggled in from Germany, with the long bayonet hanging from his belt, but he was not fool enough to think he was expert in using it yet. Still, it would at least do to make a noise and summon help.

He was still hesitating when the scream and the shot came.

The sounds terrified Simon. He was alone here and one of the voices sounded like a German calling for help. Perhaps Werner had got it wrong – perhaps Charles had somehow got out a message asking for help and there were UVF soldiers all around him now in the woods! Or perhaps Charles had been shot and was dying.

Either way, Simon could not bear to stay alone here any more under the dark dripping trees. If Charles was dying or had to be killed then he, Simon, wanted to be in on it. And if he was not and the whole operation had gone wrong then he wanted to know, so that he could make his escape.

Quickly, not caring how much noise he made, Simon ran down the slope and across the wide lawns towards the gravel drive and the dark, looming shape of the house.

'It's not here!'

Deborah felt frantically with her hands under the slate by the old yew tree near the ice-house. There was no key! Not under the slate, not on the grass or the roots nearby. She searched quickly, carefully, kneeling on the damp muddy ground as she patted with her hands everywhere, but it was not there.

'Are you sure this is the right place?'

'Of course I'm sure! It's always here. That's where it's kept!'

'Then that man's got it!'

'Yes. Simon, the devil!'

Deborah got to her feet and ran back to the outer door of the ice-house, banging with her fists against the old, mossy wood. She called in a low, anxious voice, 'Tommy! Tom! Are you in there?'

They both listened carefully but there was no answer. She banged and called again but the result was the same.

'I could scream louder,' she muttered. 'But it wouldn't help and someone might hear. We've got to get this door open!'

'Yes, all right, but how? We need some sort of tools, at least.'

Sarah felt the edges of the door in the darkness. In places bits of old rotten wood could be peeled off but there seemed to be plenty more solid stuff underneath. She could get her fingers into the gap between the lock and door jam but that was no use; nothing moved when she pulled.

'Perhaps if we could get a bar or a spade in there and lean against it – that might lever it open. But where could we find something like that?'

'I don't know!' Deborah was nearly weeping with frustration. Her son was in here, she was quite sure of it. But if she couldn't get this door open soon that monster Simon Fletcher would come back and apart from that, the shot might mean Charles had been killed, for all she knew. Charles, the stupid arrogant fool, prattling on about being true to his conscience and his duty – *why isn't he here*!

'In the Middle Ages they used to smash doors in with battering rams.'

'What? Don't be silly, Sarah – where would we find a thing like that?'

'A big log, perhaps, or a stone. There must be something, somewhere.'

'All right, let's look.'

At first it was impossible. There were trees all around but no logs; for the first time in her life Deborah cursed her garden staff for being too efficient. Only little stumps and twigs and masses of useless bushes and leafmould. They searched around on all sides of the ice-house but they could hardly see. Time was passing, Deborah realised; soon someone would come up from the house and then all her efforts would have been wasted. Her son might be killed because now she knew where he was and who had kidnapped him . . .

The moon came out, bathing the woods in clear silvery light. At least it was clear now and they could *see* they were wasting their time.

'Here!'

'What is it? Where are you?' Deborah rushed towards the

sound of Sarah's voice. She was near the path under one of the rhododendron bushes.

'Look, there's a big stone. If we can just get it out of the ground . . .'

'Let me help.' The stone was one of a number that the gardeners had dug into the ground at the side of the path, presumably with the idea of marking the route and possibly having a little wall on either side in the end. It was big, a foot or more in height and six inches thick. But Sarah was right, it ought to be possible to get it out. Maybe the rhododendron roots had loosened it, or the rain. They seized it with their slippery, muddy hands, tugged with all their force, grunted . . .

'It's coming!'

'Yes!'

The stone lay on the path, loose, like an extracted tooth, and Sarah collapsed gasping beside it. For nearly half a minute she lay there, wheezing. Deborah tried to lift the stone herself, failed, tried again. This time she moved it two feet and then dropped it, weeping with frustration.

'It's no good – it's too heavy!'

'No it's not!' Sarah was back on her feet, and the two of them got their hands under the stone, lifted it, carried it together up the path to the door of the ice-house. Then, backs, breaking, they put it down.

'We can do it. We've *got* to,' Sarah said. 'Look, when we pick it up, we'll take two steps back and then swing it as hard as we can against the door, just by the lock there. If we do that enough times it's bound to smash. Only don't drop it on your toes!'

'No,' Deborah laughed, a brief, harsh laugh. Then they bent to pick up the stone. The first time they swung it there was a disappointing slithering smash, and they did indeed drop it with a soft plop into the leafmould by Sarah's foot. Deborah felt the door but nothing seemed to have happened to it at all. Sarah leaned against the wall, clutching a finger which had got crushed.

'It's no good,' Deborah said. 'It's too heavy and we're not strong enough. You shouldn't be doing this anyway.'

Sarah gasped for a moment, her breath coming too harshly for speech. Then she said: 'Nonsense! Good exercise . . . make me strong. Anyway, when you've been in prison you know . . . how important it is to get out.'

'All right. Thanks.' They bent to lift the stone again and this time they managed much better. The stone hit the old iron of the door with a thunderous crash and they didn't drop it but swung it back again for another blow. And a third. Then they put it down, gasping, to examine the damage.

It was not as much as Deborah had hoped. The iron of the lock was bent and the wood around it splintered in places, but although the door rattled it held nearly as firmly as before. This is going to take time, she thought. And time is like strength – something we don't have much of.

Even as they paused, breathing heavily, she heard voices down by the house, and lights came on in the windows. Then there was the sound of footsteps, walking outside on the gravel.

'Come on,' she said, bending to pick up the stone. 'Four more good swings this time. Just there, on the edge of the lock.'

'I'll do my best,' Sarah whispered grimly. But even as she stepped back for the first swing she staggered, and nearly fell . . .

30

Werner had not gone to bed that night. It seemed too risky and he felt vulnerable in his enemy's house, even though he was convinced he had paralysed Charles with his threats. Instead he sat quietly in an armchair by a low fire with the automatic pistol on his left knee, gazing into the flames, thinking.

If all went well tomorrow he would have fulfilled every jot of the plan he had submitted to von Falkenhayn. Carson would have vanished – spirited from the very gates of the Unionist headquarters, Craigavon, into nowhere. The Unionists would be shocked, furious; they would be certain that the British government were behind his disappearance and no amount of official denials would convince them otherwise.

Tomorrow morning, to reinforce this belief, an article, already written by Werner, would appear in the *Neue Zuricher Zeitung* at the same time as Carson's abduction. The article would say that the paper's correspondent had exclusive information that the British Special Branch were planning to arrest Carson and keep him incommunicado in a police station near Belfast for several days. Werner had arranged for copies of this article to be sent to the London *Times*, the *Daily Telegraph*, the *Irish Times*, and the *Daily Mail*. When the news of Carson's disappearance broke, one of these would be bound to report on Werner's article even if they did not believe in it completely.

No amount of government denials would destroy the avalanche of suspicion which, Werner felt sure, would lead to a flood of attacks by Ulster Unionists upon police stations and British Army barracks throughout Ulster. The remaining Unionist leadership would be powerless to resist it. The civil war would have begun.

Carson, meanwhile, would be in one of two graves already dug in a bog on a side road not far from Craigavon. Charles Cavendish would be in the other. It was an isolated, lonely spot; the bodies might rot there undiscovered for years. By late afternoon Werner, Adolf, Karl-Otto, and Franz would be on the ferry to Stranraer, and Simon on a train to Dublin, from where he would take a ship direct to Germany. Their tickets were already bought.

No one would return to Glenfee to free the boy Tom, as Werner had promised. It was too risky. Instead the keys would be posted to the house with a note, in block capitals, telling Mrs Cavendish where to look.

Of course, it could still all go wrong. But Werner did not at the moment see how. The most dangerous moment might be at Craigavon, when Charles might be tempted to do or say something to arouse Carson's suspicions. But Werner had looked into Charles's eyes tonight when he had told him of the danger to his son, and he felt sure that Charles Cavendish would put his love for his son first, his duty to Carson second.

After a while he dozed and fell asleep. He dreamt that he had returned to Germany, and that the Kaiser himself was awarding him a medal. He raised his right hand to salute, and as he did so he realised that it was whole again, undamaged. He was seated on a gleaming black cavalry horse being honoured by Kaiser Wilhelm II in front of a review of the entire German Army, and his dead father was beaming at him proudly from behind the Kaiser's right arm . . .

The shot awoke him instantly.

He sat up, staring around the room, the automatic in his left hand, pulling back the safety catch with his thumb. But there was no one here; the room was silent, empty. Probably the shot had not come from inside the house at all. He tried to remember exactly what the sound had been like, but it was hazy, confused by his dreams. Had he really heard a shot, or only dreamt it?

Then there was a cry, thin, high, distinct, from somewhere out in the grounds.

'Hilfe! Hier! Adolf!'

He ran to the window and looked out. But it was dark – a thin rain falling, wind. He would see nothing. He forced himself to think. Clearly someone had disturbed Franz or Karl-Otto. Either someone coming towards the house from the village, or someone going away from here, trying to take a message. Which he had believed Charles would not dare to do.

If there was someone coming towards the house then it was important to get hold of Charles. He could order whoever it was to stop, go away, tell them that it was all a mistake and everything was all right.

If it was someone going from here to the village then he still had to get hold of Charles. To find out if he had sent anyone – to check if the man was still here at all!

Werner hurried out of his room into the corridor. He had forced Charles to show him where he slept earlier that night. Perhaps he should have kept Charles with him all night but he had thought that would be too provocative, make Charles so angry that he would attack Werner out of simple rage, forgetting the consequences. Werner had decided to leave him alone in the hope that he would cool down.

That could prove to have been my worst mistake, he thought as he hurried along the corridor, past the main staircase.

As he had feared, Charles's room was empty. The spears and assegais hung on the wall, the fire was cold in the grate, the bed unslept in. Werner's feet echoed on the bare floorboards. He thought: damn!

Now what do I do? He hurried down to the library and the study but they were empty too. Someone had lit the oil lamps in the corridors and main stairs. In the front hall, he met the butler, Smythe, in a dressing gown.

'Ah, good evening, sir. I thought I heard a shot, and someone shouting, in the grounds.'

'Yes. I heard the same.' What do I do about this, Werner wondered. He noticed that the butler was staring at the automatic in his hand. 'It's all right, don't worry, Colonel Cavendish has already gone out to deal with it.'

'Perhaps I should wake Johnson, the chauffeur, and go out to help him,' Smythe suggested.

'No, that won't be necessary,' Werner said quickly. 'Colonel Cavendish gave express instructions to me, in fact, that everyone was to go back to bed and not trouble themselves. I am here to guard the house if there is any . . . ah, good evening.'

They both turned as a young man came in the front door with a rifle in his hand. Simon Fletcher. He looked cold, damp, frightened. 'What the hell's going on?'

'It's nothing.' Werner stepped quickly towards Simon, so that the butler was behind him and could not see his face. He stared at Simon meaningfully and flashed a glance over his left shoulder. 'I was just explaining to the butler here that there is a UVF night exercise taking place in the grounds, and so there is no cause for concern.'

'What? Oh, I see – yes.' Simon took a deep breath and got a grip on himself. 'Yes, it's all right, Smythe. It's just night training, that's all. No need for concern. Didn't Colonel Cavendish tell you?'

'No sir, I'm afraid he did not. I fear that the cook and the chambermaids . . . '

'Yes, that's right. You go and explain to them now, would you? And tell them all to stay in bed – that's the safest place to be, by far.'

'As you say, Fletcher.'

Smythe went out, with, Werner thought, just the faintest show of suspicious reluctance in his manner. When he had gone, Werner dragged Simon through one of the side doors into the library.

'What the devil are you doing here?' he asked furiously. 'You're supposed to be guarding the boy!'

'I came because of that shot, of course. Someone's out there – one of your men's in trouble. What's going on?'

'It's Charles Cavendish, I think. He's not in the house.'

'Oh Christ!' Simon gazed at Werner incredulously. 'You mean you let him go?'

'I didn't tie him down, if that's what you mean. I told him the boy would die if he tried to get help. I thought he would have enough sense—'

'Well, if he's gone out and got past your men, your scheme is wrecked anyway,' Simon said bitterly. 'You can kill the boy or not, it won't make any difference. I told you, you should have let me come into the house and talk to him . . . '

'Quiet!' Werner said. 'What's that outside?'

There was the sound of feet, dragging on gravel, and a sort of sick moaning. They both rushed to the window and looked out.

In the light from the oil lamps in the main hall, a group of men appeared moving slowly across the gravel drive. There were three of them – two apparently strong and healthy, supporting a third with a bloodstained, bleeding face, who stumbled feebly between the others, with an arm around each of their necks.

The shot seemed to go on and on for a long time. Whenever Charles tried to think, the only picture in his mind was the shot exploding out of the night in front of his face. There was yellow and red and white fire and a noise that went on and on and on, straight through both eardrums and round and round inside his head and down his spine and through every part of his body. He tried to think of something else but there was only that, the rifle shot exploding out of the night in front of his face, yellow and red and white fire . . .

Then once there was the sense of falling. Down over a cliff through midnight air, turning and turning with the noise still in his head and the sense that there was nothing below him or above or in any direction at all, just an endless vacuum through which he fell and . . .

A blade of grass up his nose.

It tickled. He shifted his head and sneezed, and he realised his head was wet everywhere. Cold wet underneath because he was lying on grass or mud or leafmould, and hot sticky wet on top and all across his face. He didn't know what that was and he didn't like it. He had a sense that he should keep the cold wet and the hot wet apart, but to do that he would have to split his head in two and *Ah God the noise again!* And the shot in front of his face, yellow and red and white fire . . .

A shout, somewhere above him: '*Hilfe! Hier! Adolf!*'

Where did it come from? He realised he had hands and tried to move one. It crawled in the leafmould near his face like a crab. In order to see if it was really one of his own he pushed against it with what might have been his arm, and it lifted his face up so that he could see for the first time. The moon had come out and there was a boot a few inches away from his nose. He opened his mouth to speak, but the hot, wet, sticky stuff trickled in, and before he could swallow it the boot lifted up out of his sight and came down between his shoulder-blades, crushing his face into the leafmould again.

'Lie still. *Hilfe kommt.*'

The weight of the boot was many thousands of times stronger than any strength he might have, so he lay and felt the hot wet trickle down from somewhere on his right forehead to join the cold wet under his left cheek. After a while he opened his right eye again and saw shadows and silvery bits of leaf and grass, so he decided he was not blind. He decided he was not dead either, because neither heaven nor hell could be like this. He tried to remember what there had been in the world before the shot, but the noise came back and his head throbbed and he closed his eye and prayed *please God stop it now!*

And God answered with a small voice that said: Tom.

Tom is my son. He will be killed now. I have to rescue him.

He was not sure yet why Tom would be killed or who would do it or where he was, but he knew immediately that it was very urgent and he tried to get up, but that only resulted in his head turning over and more pressure from the boot and the hot sticky liquid trickling straight down over his right eye and his left eye being free to see things for a change.

What it saw was a knife blade.

The knife blade was about a foot long and two inches wide, bent in two at an angle halfway along. It was one or two feet away from his head, and the point was stuck in the ground. The moonlight shone on it and was reflected straight off the gleaming blade into his eye and it went on into his brain, where it dispelled the noise and the fog and illuminated his memory.

Charles thought: Kukri. That knife is a kukri and I used it to try to kill this man, this German spy who has his foot in my back and was trying to prevent me from going to the village to raise the alarm. I have to raise the alarm because they are going to kidnap Sir Edward Carson and start a war, and to persuade me to help them do that they have kidnapped my son Tom. Oh

God, what will they do to him now?

There was a crashing noise through the leaves and then two more boots came and stood by his face. There was a conversation above him in German and then someone bent down and struck a match and held it close to his head. Then there was more conversation and then they picked him up.

'Can you stand?'

'No, I—'

Charles staggered and flopped against one of the men. Each of them put an arm round his waist and laid his weak floppy arms across their necks, and they began to move through the wood. They were more or less carrying him, but occasionally, one of his legs moved, and after a while they both did, and one of the Germans said: 'Is better now, uh?' and let him down a little so that he bore a bit more of his own weight himself.

As they came out of the woods and onto the drive, Charles thought: maybe my strength is returning a bit. If I really had to now I might be able to stand. I've got an arm round the neck of each of these two bastards – if only I was strong enough I could throttle them both.

But that was utter nonsense, as he found when he tried to move his right arm even a few inches. Someone seemed to have unstrung all the muscles inside it, as though it belonged to a rag doll. And the Germans were built like a pair of buffalo, they weren't even breathing heavily after carrying him almost a mile.

They carried him up the front steps of Glenfee, and as they came into the hall the library door opened and there were Werner and Simon. Oh sweet Jesus in heaven, Charles thought, perhaps they didn't need to send me to hell when I died, they just sent me back here . . .

'Put him down over there,' Werner said. 'Under that lamp.'

Franz and Adolf carried Charles into the library and sat him in a chair. His uniform was filthy; there were streaks of blood like matted hair all over his face and neck, and his skin was as white as paper. When they let go of him he slumped against the back of the chair as though he would have fallen out of it had there not been a headrest there. But his eyes were still alive.

They moved from Werner to Simon, dark with hatred.

'What happened?' Werner asked Franz in German.

'I saw him coming through the wood and told him to halt. He jumped at me with a knife so I had to shoot him. I don't think it's very bad – the bullet must have just grazed his skull.'

'Let's have a look.' Werner switched to English. 'Someone had better get some water from the kitchen – Simon, it had better be you, the servants know you.'

'Why treat him at all?' Simon asked coldly. 'Your scheme's ruined anyway, he might as well die.'

There was a slight movement in the chair, as though Charles had tried to sit up. His hot dark eyes focused on Simon, his mouth slightly open in shock.

'Nonsense,' Werner said sharply. 'If it's only a graze we can dress him up and take him with us. Soldiers are always getting wounded, Carson will be impressed by his dedication to duty.'

'In *that* uniform?' Simon asked.

Werner looked at Charles's jacket. It was streaked with mud and blood. 'If necessary. But he must have a clean one somewhere. Get the water when I tell you to, damn it!'

Simon went, and returned. While Franz held the bowl, Werner bathed Charles's face and forehead carefully. It was as Franz had said – a narrow wound about an inch long on his right temple, which bled profusely. 'Do you have any first-aid equipment in this house?' he asked Simon. 'Bandages, iodine?'

Sullenly, Simon brought it. Charles winced when the iodine was put on, then Franz applied a cotton dressing and wound a quick, competent bandage round Charles's head.

'There.' Werner took a deep breath. 'And you say he was going *towards* the village when you shot him, not coming back from it?' he asked Franz.

'Yes.'

'Then so far no one knows anything about us.' He looked at his watch. It was twenty to four. 'We will dress this man up in clean clothes and continue with our scheme as planned. Your wound, Colonel Cavendish, will provide an interesting topic of conversation for you with Sir Edward Carson when you meet. You had better work out an innocent story to tell him.'

Very faintly, Charles said: 'Don't be stupid. I can't go with you now, man. I'm too weak.'

Werner stared at him. 'Stand up!'

Charles made what seemed to be a feeble move to get out of his chair. He slumped back after his head had moved a few inches.

'I can't. Sorry, old man. It's no go.'

Werner felt the sweat trickling under his arms and on his upper lip. So near, and yet so far. And now this arrogant sod had the gall to mock him with his own weakness. In that upper-class English drawl.

'In that case, I shall kill your son.'

Werner felt the electricity of the room focus on him. Franz and Adolf were watching him, shocked. Simon had an odd smile on his smooth handsome face. Charles sat up, much more sharply than he had done before. His voice was stronger too.

'You can't do that! You daren't! He hasn't done anything to you – he's only a boy!'

'I made a promise and I shall keep it,' Werner said. 'Except that it will not be me who does the killing. Simon shall have that pleasure.'

Charles sat back, breathing in quick short gasps. 'But I can't move. Really, I—'

'Then you had better get your strength up. Simon, go and fetch the boy. Call Karl-Otto in too – he is in the fields to the west of the house. In the meantime, Colonel Cavendish, we will fetch you brandy and clean clothes, and let you rest. When we leave this house to pick up Sir Edward Carson, your son will come with us in the car. So will Simon Fletcher. I am afraid young Simon does not like your son, but you have my word no harm will come to him so long as you summon up enough strength to do exactly as I say. When we get within a mile of Craigavon, Simon and the boy will get out. We will pick them up on the way back. If Sir Edward is with us the boy will be unharmed. Otherwise, Simon will cut his throat.'

Charles stared, horrified, as Simon Fletcher walked out of the room with a satisfied smirk on his face. Hell is all around me, he thought.

The stone was huge and heavy and slippery and hard and it tore at the muscles in their arms and shoulders and backs and legs as they swung it, but they would not give up. Their hands were slippery and muddy and sweat trickled down their faces and under their arms and between their breasts, but each time the stone smashed into the door there was a crunch and rattle that seemed to loosen something further, and they thought, surely *this* time it must break.

The moon came out from behind a cloud, shining through the soft drizzling rain, and they put down the stone to examine the door more closely.

The handle was broken, and the wood all round the lock was smashed and torn into splinters. The metal lock was twisted and bent so that two of the screws had dropped out, but still, when they pushed against it, the door refused to open. It was loose, it rattled back and forth, but something held it.

'One more try,' Deborah said. 'Can you manage?'

Sarah nodded, without speaking. Her breath came harsh and raw into her throat, and she was so exhausted by the effort of lifting the heavy stone that her hands were trembling violently – but she had no intention of giving up. She had never seen Deborah like this, so desperate, so determined. But it was also a joy to be *doing* something at last, not being a victim. I may be weak but I *will* overcome it, she thought. Not just for Tom, but for all children.

The moon went in. A gust of wind brought stronger rain from the west. They picked up the sodden slippery stone, stepped back, swung forward together – smash! It nearly fell from their hands, but nothing moved. They stepped back, swung forward again – the same. A third time, the last before they would have to drop it and rest – and this time as they hit the door it gave! Something wrenched out of the wood inside, the door fell open in front of them, and they staggered forward into the tunnel, carried forward by their own impetus, nearly dropping the stone on their own feet before they collapsed on the floor beside it.

They lay there for a moment, breathing heavily in short gasps of triumph.

'Are you all right?' Deborah asked.

'Yes. We did it!'

'First part, anyway.' Deborah stumbled to her feet. The passage was quite dark, blacker even than the night outside. I should have thought to bring a torch, she thought. But she had been here in daylight, she knew the shape of what should be behind the door. She walked forward, one hand on the black slippery wall. Three paces, slight turn to the right, down two steps – a door. Locked, of course. She banged on it with her fists.

'Tom! Are you in there?'

Silence. Just their own laboured breath in the dank narrow passage. And, oddly, the confused echo of voices from outside, far away. Oh no, Sarah thought. It was all for nothing.

Deborah shouted again. A higher pitch to her voice this time, a note of panic.

'Tom! Are you in there? Answer me! It's Mother!'

Again silence. Sarah felt her breath sobbing from a new pain in her chest. It's too desperate, she thought, too futile. Surely someone was shouting outside, too? It sounded like a man's voice.

'*Karl-Otto!*'

Then there was another sound. A tapping from the far side of the door. Not loud – like a mouse far away. Then a voice, small – 'Mummy!'

'It *is* him!' Deborah said. 'Tom! I'm here, with aunt Sarah! We'll get you out. Are you all right?'

'Yes,' the voice said. 'But I'm cold. Be quick, Mummy, please!'

'Don't worry, we will!' Deborah shouted. Then she turned. 'Though God knows how, if they haven't left the key.' She scrabbled back with her hands along the right-hand side wall, fumbling for the place in the darkness. 'It's usually here, on a hook somewhere. This is it – oh God, it's missing! Heaven help us! We'll have to smash this door in with the stone as well!'

'Just a minute.' Sarah reached out and gripped Deborah's shoulder in the darkness. 'Ssssh! I think there's someone outside!'

Simon strode out of the house across the drive and the lawn that led to the wooded hill where the ice-house was. He had the Mannlicher rifle slung over his shoulder and the bayonet at the belt by his side. As he came near the hill he shouted out to the dark, silvery fields on his left.

'Karl-Otto! Hey, Karl-Otto! Come to me here! Karl-Otto!'

He saw no need for silence or secrecy any more. Whatever Werner said it seemed to Simon a desperate plan to try to force the wounded Charles to go in the car to Craigavon. But nonetheless he was prepared to bring Tom to confront Charles in the house. There could be some pleasure in that. If Charles resists or tries to rescue the boy then I'll kill him there and then, and perhaps his loathsome little son as well, Simon thought. And then I'll flee to Germany.

It was revenge which interested him, not Werner's plot against Carson. That was just a means to an end.

He shouted again: 'Karl-Otto!'

As he approached the wooded hill he saw a dark figure approaching him in the distance. It was still some two hundred yards away across the grey moonlit fields. A voice came back to him faintly, but clear.

'Ja. What is?'

'Go into the house. Von Weichsaker's orders. I have to fetch the boy.'

The man's English was not good but Simon hoped he understood. He changed direction slightly and began to head across the fields towards the house. Simon carried on up the hill under the trees, towards the ice-house. As he came nearer he remembered the sounds he had heard here before, and glanced ahead nervously. For a moment he thought he saw a shadow move, but surely that was just imagination. He fumbled in his pocket, brought out a small electric torch, and shone it around under the trees. Nothing.

Then he shone it on the door and stopped, thunderstruck.

'What . . . '

He stood for a moment, irresolute, outside the broken door. It was quite silent. He unshouldered the rifle, cocked it, and pointed it forwards in front of him. Then, holding the torch clumsily alongside the barrel, he bent his head and stepped forward cautiously into the tunnel.

Almost immediately he stumbled and nearly fell. Swearing, he looked down by the light of the torch and saw a large stone on the ground just inside the door. From inside he could see how the lock of the door itself was smashed and shattered as though by a massive iron bar. Simon's stomach squirmed.

Who can possibly have done this? he thought.

The torchlight wavered, glimmering on dank, moss-covered walls. He took it away from the rifle barrel, shone it ahead of him down the passage.

'Simon Fletcher?'

He jumped. There, in front of the door, was a figure. A woman, perhaps, though she was so dirty and bedraggled it was hard to tell. In the dim light of the torch he saw a face streaked with mud and bedraggled brown hair, a filthy brown muddy dress, dark eyes staring at him with a wild intensity like a trapped ferret.

He stood nervously, a yard or so away from her. The rifle wavered in his right hand, pointing at her breast. 'Who the hell are you?'

'Don't you know me? I'm Tom's mother. Have you come to let him out?'

'Yes.' He shone the torch more carefully and smiled to himself with relief. It was true, it *was* her. Deborah Cavendish. Surely he could handle her, she had never been any threat to him before. But tonight she looked different – more like a savage gypsy woman in the mud and the rain. And there was a cunning look in her dark fierce eyes as well – like a trapped weasel.

She straightened up, stepped towards him.

'About time too,' she said. 'But now I'm here you can give me the key. I need it to unlock the door and set him free.'

She held out her hand.

'Oh no.' Simon stepped back cautiously, still aiming the rifle clumsily in one hand and holding the torch in the other. 'I have to take the boy down to the house. He's a prisoner, like his father.'

Deborah stood still, peering at him over the glare of the torchlight. She knew it was Simon by his voice, but she could only see the outline of his face indistinctly, and the dark gleam of the rifle barrel pointing towards her. She felt a hand clutch her heart.

'What do you mean, a prisoner like his father?'

'What I say. Your husband was caught trying to run away through the woods. We've brought him back, and now I've come to fetch his son.'

Deborah's mind had been racing ever since Simon had come in. When they had gone outside because of the noise they had heard, and seen him coming up the hill, she and Sarah had hatched a plan. Sarah would stay outside, hidden behind a tree. Deborah would stay inside the passage and try to persuade Simon to give her the key. If that failed, at least she could distract him until Sarah came in. Then they would both attack him and grab the rifle from him if they could. Two of them might manage it, if they both went for him at once. But they hadn't counted on the way the torchlight would dazzle her, so that she could see virtually nothing beyond it. She had no way of knowing whether Sarah had followed him into the passage yet or not.

They had also had the hope that Charles had succeeded in getting to the village, so that if only they could rescue Tom and keep him hidden for a while, help would come.

Now they had failed to rescue Tom in time, and no help was coming. They were on their own.

Deborah said, in a wheedling voice, despising herself: 'He's only a little boy, for heaven's sake! You can't make war on children.'

Simon laughed. 'Can't I? I can do what I like!' The laugh was outwardly pleasant, suave and confident, as most of Simon's phrases and actions always were. Here, in this dark passage with a rifle in his hands, that frightened her more than anything else. There was a coldness, a certain empty quality in it that terrified her even more than she had been afraid before. There is something missing in this young man's mind, she thought.

She tried one more time. He is a man, he has a gun. Sarah is crazy to think we can fight him. But if he can't be persuaded we must. '*Please*, Simon. Give me the key.'

His left hand, holding the torch, moved back to the side of the rifle barrel, which he advanced slowly until it was pointing directly into her mouth. 'If you don't get out of the way, woman, your son won't have a mother at all.'

She stood very still for a moment, trembling. She was not afraid, but furious because she could do nothing. If she stood still he would kill her and then she would have no way of protecting her son; but if she moved aside she would not be protecting him either. A flood of hysterical tears threatened to rise within her but she suppressed them instantly. Tears were no good now – nor was reasoned argument or cajoling. She felt like a savage – a wild woman of the Stone Age faced by a snake or a bear. Then she heard footsteps shuffle on the leaves behind him and thought: Sarah was right. There is only one way after all.

To distract his attention she smiled at him in a way that she hoped looked more frightened than cunning, and stepped away from the door, towards his left side.

'All right,' she said. 'But don't hurt him, please, will you?'

'Oh no,' he said mockingly. 'Now, just move back out of the way, and I'll open the door.'

As she came past the beam of the torch she saw, for the first time, the long bayonet hanging on his left hip like a short sword, and thought, I can threaten him with that.

He reached out his hand for her left shoulder. As he did so she screamed: '*Now!*' and lunged for his side, knocking him off balance. She grabbed the hilt of the bayonet with both hands, trying to pull it out of the sheath. At the same time Sarah swung at the back of his head with the stick she had found, knocking him off balance against the wall by the steps. Simon groaned and fell forward, dragging Deborah forwards with him. Then he lurched clumsily to his feet again. The torch clattered to the floor, sending a bright intense beam against a brick on the side wall, and plunging the rest of the passage into darkness. Sarah screamed and hit Simon again, and Deborah felt the rotten branch shatter against his shoulder just in front of her face, spraying her with damp splinters. Simon stumbled but didn't fall. Deborah felt him staggering under her grip. She held on to him but he was trying to turn round and stay upright and keep hold of the rifle all at once.

'Get the gun!' she yelled to Sarah. Sarah grabbed hold of something but there was a clatter as though he or she had dropped the gun, and none of them knew where it was in the panic and the darkness and the lurching, stumbling bodies.

Deborah felt herself slammed back against the wall but she held on to the hilt of the bayonet grimly. In a moment he will break free, she thought, and then he'll kill us both and Tom too. If I get this bayonet out and threaten him with it he'll see sense and calm down.

But the bayonet wouldn't come out. She couldn't understand what on earth was wrong with it. Instead of pulling it out of the sheath she was dragging the whole belt upwards, tilting him further off balance. He punched the side of her head with his left hand but she felt nothing because all her attention was focussed on her fingers around the hilt of the bayonet, pulling and tugging to get it free, and then he grabbed her hair and she screamed but she still didn't let go.

Her fingers had worked out the problem. The hilt was fastened to the sheath by a little button clip that went over the guard. Her fingers found the button and wrenched it free, tearing a nail as she did it. Then Simon swung round in a complete circle, his fist swinging out in the darkness with a wild punch that caught Sarah hard in the stomach and doubled her over on the floor.

Deborah was flung free, back against the wall, but the bayonet came out of the sheath as she fell, free in her hand. I've got it now, she thought. But what do I do with it? Sarah was groaning on the floor somewhere near her feet and Simon was somewhere in the gloom a few feet further ahead of her. She saw his body moving in the dim light of the torch; she could hear his short, harsh, desperate breathing, mixed with her own gasps and Sarah's groans. She stood, half crouched, with her back to the wall like a trapped animal, the bayonet held out in front of her in her right hand like a shield to ward off evil.

Then she realised the torch was near her left foot. An idea came to her. She dived forwards, snatched it up in her left hand, and shone it towards him.

He stood with his back to the right-hand wall, fumbling with the rifle in his hands, pointing it towards the dazzling glare of the torch. As she watched, he shouted, high, frightened, breathless. 'Get back out of the door! Quick, or I'll shoot you both!'

But even before he had finished shouting a shadow lunged out of the darkness towards him, knocking him off balance again. Sarah screamed: '*Now!* I've got his legs, Debbie! Grab him!'

But Deborah stared, paralysed, not knowing what to do with the bayonet . . .

And then the gun went off, a foot in front of her face.

The noise was enormous, shattering, like a thunderstorm inside her own head, and there was white and yellow fire in front of her face. She stood quite still, rigid, thinking: I'm not hurt at all. He missed me. In a minute he'll shoot again.

In the feeble yellow light of the torch she could see he was still standing, struggling to stay upright with one hand against the wall to keep his balance and the rifle raised in the other to club the woman who was on her knees with both arms round his legs, pushing, clinging, straining against him with all her strength to wrench his legs out from under him and knock him over before he could fire again.

Deborah snapped out of her trance and thought, if he hits Sarah with that he'll break her skull.

She ran forward with a sudden scream and, as she did so, Simon finally lost his balance and fell forwards towards her so that her stab with the bayonet went right through his coat and into his stomach and on up under his rib-cage through a lung and his heart until it grated against his backbone and jarred and twisted in her hand.

He collapsed on top of her, his already dead weight slamming her hard against the ground. She lay there for a moment, stunned, her legs twisted painfully under him. Then Sarah grunted, and with a huge effort heaved him to one side. The torch, from where it had fallen, shone up into Sarah's face. It was pale, sweaty, savage.

Sarah leaned forward, grabbed Simon's head by the hair, and thumped it hard against the floor. Then she knelt beside him gasping, her hands still entwined in his hair, to see if he would move.

The body gurgled once, twitching, and lay still.

Deborah dragged herself to her knees, shaking, and picked up the torch. She shone it on Simon's once-beautiful, perfect head. Thick red blood was pouring out of his mouth and nostrils.

'Oh my God!' she exclaimed. She felt sick. She grabbed his

arm and heaved him up on to one side, and there was the bayonet. The hilt of it was buried in the front of his jacket, low down below his rib-cage. The point came out of his back, just below the shoulder-blades.

The two women stared, breathing heavily. There was nothing to say. The body twitched once or twice, and more blood came out of its mouth. Otherwise there was silence. Then a small voice came from behind the door at the end of the passage.

'Mummy? Mummy, are you all right?'

'Dear God,' Deborah said. 'The keys!' Mechanically, her hands fumbled in the pockets of Simon's jacket. Not this side, they had to roll him over again. The front of his jacket was slippery and warm with blood. 'Here.' She took out two keys, shone the torch on them, chose one. Then she got up and stumbled to the door at the end of the passage.

Her hands were shaking so much that she couldn't get the key into the hole. She dropped the torch, picked it up, and tried again. At the third attempt she made it. The key turned and the door opened. A wave of icy air flooded into the passage.

A small boy stood in the torchlight at the foot of the steps, shrouded in blankets, shivering. His fair hair was ruffled and untidy, his thin anxious face stared at her with wide dark eyes. 'Mummy?'

'Yes, Tommy, it's me.'

She went down the steps and wrapped her arms round him. There was frost on the outside of the blankets and the torchlight sparkled on the round icy floor.

'I heard a shot. Mummy, you're shivering.'

'It's all right, Tommy. You're all right now.'

'But wasn't there shooting? Was there a fight?'

'Don't talk about it, Tom. Everything's all right. I'll take care of you now. Come outside.'

She pushed him ahead of her up the narrow steps, and shone the torch deliberately at the wall on the left, so that he wouldn't see the body on the floor.

'Sarah,' she said. 'I've got him.'

But to her surprise Sarah wasn't in the passage. She flashed the torch quickly around it to make quite sure. No one; only Simon, sprawled on the floor. Tom walked ahead of her, a tiny figure huddled in his blankets, towards the moonlight outside the door at the end of the passage. She had one arm reassuringly on his shoulder.

At the doorway he looked out and paused, frightened.

'Mother, I don't like it.'

'It's all right, Tommy,' she said. 'We're safe now.' Her body was shaking all over but underneath that was the warmth of gratitude, tears of triumph that would burst out in a flood at any moment. *I have saved my son!*

'Sarah?' she said softly. 'Where are you?'

She stepped out of the door and saw two men, standing silently under the trees. They were both very large and the moonlight glinted on the barrels of their rifles. They stared at her quietly for a moment.

Then one said;: 'Ja. Is the boy and his mother. You go with us now please. Down to the house.'

31

Sarah stood beside a beech tree halfway up the slope, appalled. She could not understand how it had happened, or why they could not see her, or what she should do.

She saw Deborah start to protest, but immediately one of the two men seized her by the shoulder and propelled her in front of him down the hill. The other man slung Tom over his shoulder and followed after. They were both big, broad-shouldered men, at least a foot taller than her and even taller than Deborah. Both were armed with rifles and Sarah didn't have even a stone or a branch. If I rush at them, she thought, perhaps that man'll drop Tom and he'll run away. But he can't, not in all those blankets, and anyway where would he go? It's more likely they'll shoot him and then what? At least I'm still free, I should be able to help in some way, but what? I'm too weak, my stomach hurts and there's something wrong with my eye and I can hardly stand . . .

She was still dithering by the time the men came out of the wood and on to the grass thirty yards away, and then they were going across the grass towards the house and it was far, far too late.

A minute ago we thought we had saved Tom. How did this happen?

When they had killed Simon and Deborah had got up to unlock the door, Sarah had staggered outside because her stomach hurt where Simon had punched her and she couldn't stand the sight of all that blood and she wanted to be sick. She had stumbled a few yards up the hill and vomited on the ground, and then, when she had stopped retching, she had heard some voices further down the hill. So she had climbed up further to a point where she could look down upon the house, and when she had turned, she had seen the men already outside the ice-house. How they had got there without seeing her she didn't know, but they had, and she had been so paralysed with shock and indecision that she hadn't moved out of the shadows where she was until they had taken Tom and Deborah and marched them away.

She remembered there was a rifle in the ice-house, Simon's rifle. I could take it and try to shoot them, she thought. But she might hit Deborah or Tom instead. Anyway, she didn't know how to use a rifle, she had never learnt.

That's one thing I really do need a man for, she thought grimly. But who? Charles, he's a soldier. *Oh God they've captured him too*! She remembered what Simon had said to Deborah as she stood just outside the passage only a few minutes ago. '*Your husband was caught trying to run away through the woods*' – something like that. So no one knew these people were here. Even though Simon was dead, no one could stop them.

An idea came to her.

Charles was trying to get to the village to fetch his men from the UVF, she thought. Deborah said his sergeant lives there and so do a lot of the men. Probably they have their rifles with them . . . *I could go and warn them instead*!

How?

I can't go past the house, they might see me. But there's a lane, isn't there, at the back of these woods. I remember I went for walks there with Jonathan on our honeymoon long ago. Where is it?

She began to climb up the hill, but almost immediately she stumbled and fell on her hands and knees. She felt exhausted. her breath came in short harsh gasps and her chest and stomach hurt and there was bile in her throat and tears flowed down her cheeks. She clenched her hands in the leafmould and thought: why am I like this?

I have just helped to kill a man – is that it?

That's not it – even when I was being force-fed I wasn't as weak as this. It's because we failed. All that effort wasted. Tom and Deborah and Charles are in the hands of these devils and I've turned my back on them. I'm running away.

That's not true. You have to believe in what you're doing, then you find strength. You're not running away, you're running to fetch help. Convince yourself, believe it. Make your legs move. They *have* to move. It doesn't matter how weak they are. They're the only hope now.

She dragged herself to the top of the slope on her hands and knees, and then stood up. Her legs were shaking uncontrollably and her chest and stomach hurt as though they were being rasped with a file every time she breathed. It had begun to rain again and she was wet and shivering with cold. But the track she was looking for was only ten yards ahead. She could see the moonlight glistening on a wet gatepost.

Grimly, she stumbled towards it. When she had got onto the track the ground began to slope downhill. Digging deep into her resources, she began to run along the dark muddy road, her legs in the long damp skirts wobbling like rubber beneath her . . .

To Werner, it seemed that the war had already begun. Each time there was a shot outside in the darkness matters got worse. First Charles was dragged in wounded and bleeding; now Karl-Otto and Adolf came in with the boy and the news that his bedraggled, bloodstained, hysterical mother had murdered young Simon. The ferocious look in her wild dark eyes suggested that she would do the same to the rest of them if she got the chance.

Karl-Otto strode into the library and flung the boy down on a sofa. His mother immediately broke free from Adolf and stood protectively over him. Charles forced himself out of his chair and took three paces towards them before he was restrained by Franz.

Werner listened to their story, appalled. It had to be true; the woman's dress was covered in blood. This place is looking like a battlefield casualty station, he thought.

Charles was staring at Deborah, his face white with disbelief, horror and – could it be admiration? 'You killed him?' he whispered.

'Yes,' she said. 'I had to. He wouldn't give me the keys.'

'The keys?' It made no sense to Charles. But it didn't matter. Tom was here, safe. That must be Simon's blood on Deborah's dress, not her own. She seemed to him like some avenging angel out of the Old Testament. A witch. A saviour. My *wife*.

With an effort he turned to Werner. The man was standing quite still, watching the two of them. He looks as shocked as I am, Charles thought. He decided to press his advantage.

'You must realise your wretched scheme is finished now,' he said as coolly as he could. 'There's your guide and chief torturer dead already, before you even leave the house. That second shot must have woken half the county. I suggest you surrender your weapons to me, now, before anyone else is hurt.'

He stepped away from Franz, and held out his hand for Werner's gun.

Werner hesitated for a second. He's right, he thought. How can I carry on like this? It's like trying to pick up quicksilver with a fork – the harder I try the more things run away. He became aware that his men were looking to him for orders, anxiously.

But if I surrender now we're all lost. We'll hang, probably, or spend years cramped in some filthy prison. And this arrogant sod will have beaten me again.

He wrenched his lips into a grim smile, and said: 'On the contrary, I see my plan has worked, Colonel Cavendish. The arrival of your son has cured your weakness and given you new energy. I have no need of a guide, I know the way to Craigavon quite well. Now, we will spend the next hour sprucing up your uniform and providing some food for your son, while Franz brings the car round to the front door. As for your wife . . .'

He stared at the haggard, bloodstained figure on the sofa, her face streaked by tears, her arms wrapped protectively around the fair-haired boy in the grey blankets, whose big eyes stared at him in horror. Werner's heart almost failed him.

'. . . she had better clean herself up as well. She is an affront to humanity.'

Deborah wrapped her arms tighter round the boy, almost squeezing the breath out of him. 'I am not leaving my son,' she said. 'You can do what you like to me, but you shan't touch him.'

The cold blue eyes facing her blazed with an icy determination that made her stomach freeze within her. 'I shall do what I like, Mrs Cavendish,' Werner said. 'To you or anyone else who gets in my way. I suggest you remember that, for whatever short time you may have left upon this earth.'

If only I had kept the bayonet, Deborah thought. But I couldn't do that again, it was too foul. And anyway, there are four of them. I wish I knew where Sarah was. But she's all alone, she can't help now. If only I wasn't so tired. I never knew fear made you tired but it's true. But I have to fight back. Not for myself or Charles but for Tom.

Her gaze did not shift from Werner's eyes. In a grey, bleak voice she said: 'That's what young Simon said, only a few minutes ago. There is still a God in heaven, Mr von Weichsaker. If you lay a finger on my son, what happened to Simon Fletcher will happen to you, as well.'

The lane was longer than Sarah had ever believed possible. It seemed to her that she had been running for hours and her body wasn't working any more. She had stopped several times for breath, and twice she had sat down in the mud in the middle of the lane. Once she was down, there was a strong temptation to sleep. But each time she dragged herself to her feet and stumbled wearily on.

It seemed to her that the lane twisted and turned more than she had remembered. Perhaps that was only the dark, or perhaps she herself was weaving hazily from one side of the lane to the other. She knew she was doing it a little, but she had no idea exactly how much. It didn't matter anyway, the main thing was that she was going on. It doesn't matter how slowly I'm going, she thought defiantly, even a snail would get there in the end so long as it kept going in the right direction.

In the right direction.

The horrible thought struck her as she tottered around another bend and saw nothing in front of her but a further stretch of dark road between trees, with the puddles on the surface reflecting the lightening grey of the sky above. She sat down abruptly on the line of tussocky grass which ran down the centre of the lane, and dropped her head between her knees, while her legs trembled and the breath rasped painfully into her lungs.

What if I'm going the wrong way?

If I turned the wrong way when I first came into the lane all this effort will be taking me further away from the village, not nearer. I couldn't have done that, could I?

She knew she could. She had been born and brought up in a city and she had never had a good sense of direction. She had often got lost in the country, even around Glenfee. She remembered playful arguments about it with Jonathan on their honeymoon. It had been a joke, all those years ago, but not now.

If I can't be trusted to find my way in the daytime, how can I be sure I've got it right in the dark, in a rainstorm, when my body's broken because of prison and my mind's all hazy because we killed that man?

She dragged herself to her feet and took a few steps further down the lane. But it was so hard, and what was the point if she might be going the wrong way? She stood still, irresolute, wondering what to do. Rain still dripped down the back of her neck, and she shivered with cold. She noticed the grey hurrying clouds above were getting lighter, and realised she could see the track ahead more clearly than before. There were still dark trees on either side, but she could see a strip of grass running down the centre of the lane, puddles in the ruts on either side, a farm gate some fifty yards ahead. Dawn must be on its way.

Perhaps if she got to the gate she would be able to look out across the fields and catch sight of the village or the house. Then she would be able to work out where she was from that. But she would have to hurry. Dawn was around six o'clock, she thought and Deborah had told her that Charles's car was expected to leave for Craigavon soon after seven. Even when she got to the village it would still take time to round up the men to stop them.

But when daylight came, she might meet someone – a farm labourer, perhaps – who could help her.

With the dawn the wind had got up. Vast gusts of it blustered through the trees, setting them swaying and creaking beside her like the sea. As she lurched towards the farm gate an unusually large gust howled through a gap in the trees, caught her sodden skirts, and sent her staggering sideways into the ditch. I can't stand much more of this, she thought, my body just won't take it.

As she stumbled to her feet again a car came round the corner behind her, its headlights glistening through the driving rain. This is it, she thought. Someone who can help me at last!

She tottered out into the middle of the lane, waving her arms frantically. The car would have to stop; she was on the grassy patch in the middle of the lane and there was no way round. The driver saw her and applied the brakes, the back wheels sliding sideways through the mud. It stopped about ten yards away from her.

Sarah sobbed with relief. There were two men in the car, wearing leather driving helmets and goggles that covered their faces. One of them lifted a gauntleted hand, opened the door, and got out. His companion got out the other side.

She started to walk towards the car, then paused. There was something odd, something familiar about the car, she thought. What was it?

Fear crawled like worms in her stomach. That car – it was Charles's Lancia – the one the Germans were going to take to Craigavon! And one of the men – the one climbing out of the passenger seat – was holding a shotgun in his hand.

Shortly after dawn the rain stopped. But the grey clouds still scudded eastwards over the grounds, chased by a loud, boisterous wind that bent and tossed the tall trees near the road, and churned the waters of the lough into miles of white horses and short, choppy grey waves.

The wind rattled the windows of Glenfee Lodge, and piercing draughts hissed and scurried through the rooms. Werner stood with arms folded at the end of the library, scowling as he stared out into the cheerless light of day.

It was nearly seven o'clock. He would have to decide in the next few minutes whether to go ahead with his mission or abort it. They would have to leave on time – with a gale from the west like this the journey east to Craigavon could easily take longer than expected, to say nothing of the risk of the engine stopping if it began to rain again, or of the car sliding off the road in the wet. He had sent Karl-Otto and Franz in search of the chauffeur and the car. They would bring it round to the front door any minute now.

Certainly enough had gone wrong already for him to justify aborting the mission. Charles wounded, Simon dead, several of the servants and that other woman, his wife's sister, apparently vanished – he had been able to trace neither the butler nor the housekeeper so far this morning – and the boy's mother was completely intractable. No one could blame him if he estimated the risks were too great at this point to continue, and withdrew with his three subordinates still unharmed.

But failure will not further my career, Werner thought. There will be no medal. No presentation from the Kaiser. Charles Cavendish will live to laugh, and mock me again.

But if we go ahead, what can I do with the boy's mother? She had not let go of Tom once since she had come into the house, and Werner's men had been reluctant to prise them apart. Werner had been about to order them to do it once, when they had brought her a clean dress, but she had marched upstairs with the boy's hand gripped tightly in her own, and he had seen a look in his men's eyes which had made him change his mind and order them to follow her and stand guard outside the door instead.

They were brave men, but sentimental. They would kill Carson or Cavendish without a thought, but a mother and a child was a different matter. I ought to shoot her myself, he thought. After all she's a murderess, she killed Fletcher. But if I do I may have a rebellion on my hands, just when I need maximum obedience and devotion to duty.

In the next few minutes I shall have to decide. If we go ahead we can't take her with us, and I daren't leave her behind.

He glanced over his shoulder at the far end of the library, where Charles, Deborah and Tom sat together round a small fire which Franz had lit. Like the ideal happy family, Werner thought bitterly. Guarded by Franz, watching them quietly with a cigarette in his mouth and a cocked rifle resting on a chair in front of him.

Charles had not thought it was possible to feel such pain. Not the pain from the bullet that had grazed his skull. That was an ache, merely. Ferocious, but bearable. He had born many worse wounds in his time. In battle, in skirmishes on the North West Frontier, even in falls from polo ponies. They had all been wounds he had born with honour.

The pain that hurt him was in his whole body – behind his eyes and in every muscle of his face and especially, deep in his chest. It was unbearable. It felt as though his face were melting into tears that ran down inside his skin so that every tube and sinus and pore was suffused and bloated with ugliness. It felt as though a red-hot wire brush was scraping the lining of his lungs. It felt as though he was standing alone in the middle of a regimental square of sand, watched by all the soldiers he had ever commanded and by his parents and grandparents and family to the twelfth generation, while his badges of rank were stripped from him and his ceremonial sword was broken and flung in the mud at the feet of his son.

The name of the pain was shame.

His son sat opposite him, his dark eyes haunted by fear, clutched in the arms of Deborah whose eyes were hot and dark with anger. Charles was ashamed to look at either of them.

I wanted my son to see me as a hero, he thought, but I do not deserve to have a son at all. None of this would have happened to him if it had not been for me. I was so blinded by lust for Simon's beauty that I saw nothing of the monster within. Even now I am *grieved* for his death!

I am not even a competent soldier. Only Deborah – *Deborah*! – has managed to fight back. Even now, Charles could scarcely believe it.

Awkwardly, only briefly glancing up from the fire, he asked: 'Did you mean to kill him?'

'Does it matter?'

She was not looking at him; all her attention seemed divided between Tom, at her side, and Werner, brooding by the window near the door.

'No, not really. Only . . .' he drew a deep breath, through the pain of shame in his lungs and his face. '. . . I suppose I should say that you were perfectly right to do it.'

She glanced at him briefly, and tears started in her eyes. 'There was no time to think of what would happen. Of course we would have avoided it if we could. There was . . . so much blood, Charles.' She shuddered and glanced at Tom, then lifted her head determinedly to stare warily at Werner. 'And there will be more, if these devils have their way.'

He nodded, and forced himself to look at Tom. 'Don't worry, old son. Chin up. We'll beat 'em yet.'

Tom forced a brief, pale smile which wrenched his heart. Do the old lies still work for him, then? Surely even Tom is old enough to recognise disgrace when he sees it.

But apparently not. It seemed that Tom trusted him, even now. Of course Tom had no idea what hold Simon had had over his father, or why Werner had chosen him of all the officers in the UVF to blackmail. Not yet. He still thought his father could do something to save him. With honour.

Abruptly, Charles stood up. Franz cocked his rifle warningly but Charles ignored him. He strode unsteadily across the room towards the door until Franz barred his way physically, holding the rifle across his chest.

'Mr von Weichsaker.'

Werner turned to look at him. He had unfolded his arms and slipped his left hand inside his pocket for the pistol.

'Yes? What now?'

'I want to talk to you.' He jerked his head back over his shoulder at Deborah and Tom. 'Just you and me together.'

Werner considered. His lips curled in a sarcastic smile. 'I would be loathe to part you from your beloved family, when they have just brought about such a remarkable improvement in your health. A little while ago you couldn't even stand.'

'That's what I want to talk about.' For a long moment Charles watched his enemy, taking in the startling pale blue eyes, the raised mocking eyebrow, the sarcastic insolent smile. Does he want me to *plead* with him? he wondered.

At last Werner shrugged. 'All right.' He nodded to Franz, who moved his rifle aside. 'Step outside into the hall, then. For a couple of minutes only. But remember – if Franz hears a shot or a shout, he will kill these two immediately. The woman first.' He stared meaningfully at Franz, intent on beating down any suggestion of resistance or scruples. Once let those show and we're lost.

Outside in the hall, Charles shivered suddenly. The cold

draughty wind whistled over the wooden floor. Or perhaps it was fear.

He said: 'Look, Werner, I have a bargain for you.'

'A bargain? Do you honestly think you're in a position for that?'

'I don't think any of us are in a good position. You *must* realise by now that you can't go through with this.'

'Must I?' It was exactly what Werner feared, but he wasn't going to show it. Or allow Charles to defeat him.

'Yes. You're a sensible man. Too many things have gone wrong. But look – if you call the whole thing off, and drive away from here, I undertake not to raise the alarm or come in pursuit for . . . two hours. That should give you enough time.'

Werner laughed. 'And would this promise bind your wife as well? She seems the force to be feared, at the moment.'

'She is my wife, of course she would agree.' Charles flushed. 'All she cares about is the boy.'

'She would be even better behaved if we took the boy with us.' Those cold blue eyes watched him levelly.

'Oh no.' Despite his efforts at self-control Charles felt his face flush, his hands clench by his sides. 'You're not taking the boy.'

Werner watched, impassive, assessing the rush of emotion coolly. 'So, the boy still matters most of all to you.'

'You unfeeling beast—'

'Please!' Werner raised his right hand, the crooked fingers waving irritatingly in Charles's face. 'No insults or shouting. Remember, Franz is in there with your son and heir.'

'All right. But you are not taking Tom with you. I forbid it!'

Werner did not trouble to answer. He let the words hang in the empty hall between them, like the memories of pride and power that gazed down at them from the large oil portraits on the walls. Past, gone, irrelevant. Whatever happens, I have had part of my revenge already, Werner thought. This moment, in this cold, draughty hall. All the power has come to me.

And power is addictive. The more you have, the more you want. At that moment he made his decision. I will not go home with half a victory, he thought. Half is only the beginning. Forget Fletcher, he was an irrelevance. I can still do it all, on my own.

His voice, when he spoke, was calm, clear, determined. Like the head prefect of a school talking to a junior fag.

'Listen to me, Cavendish. I am not going to run away or take your son to Germany with me. So you can put your mind at rest about that. Instead, I am going ahead with the plan exactly as I described it to you, with a few minor alterations to take account of the, er, changed circumstances of this morning. I will tell you these alterations now.'

Charles said nothing. Werner even detected a faint, almost imperceptible nod. The sense of power tingled in his veins like champagne.

'First, you are obviously fit enough to walk and talk and lead Sir Edward Carson to the car. That is all you will have to do, and you will do it well. I congratulate you on your swift recovery.

'Second, not only your son but your wife will accompany us in the car to Craigavon. I see no alternative to that, because I am too much of a gentleman to shoot her – and after tonight I do not trust her to remain confined in any place I might leave her. Since you are so particularly attached to conventional family life, you may perhaps take some comfort from this.'

Still no reply. Charles stood quite still, almost like a soldier at attention before his commanding officer. Werner noticed a slight swaying in the legs, and thought: he will have to learn to control that, for his son's sake.

'Third, when we come within a mile or so of Craigavon, I myself will get out of the car with your wife and precious son. That is because I regret to say I do not entirely trust my brave German sailors not to take pity on them, at the last moment. But I trust myself, absolutely. If you do not return with Sir Edward to the place where you leave us in a given time, I shall shoot them both dead, and make my escape alone. Do you understand?'

Charles shook his head. 'No. I do not understand how any man could even think of behaving like this.'

The faintest trace of a flush crossed Werner's face, and was gone. 'You are a soldier, you are not required to understand why. Only what you have to do, and what will happen if you disobey. Now, time is pressing. I suggest you go in and explain things to your wife, and be prepared to leave within a few minutes.'

As Charles went back into the library, Werner heard the car draw up on the gravel outside, and went through the front door to meet it.

It was the wrong car.

To his astonishment, Karl-Otto and Adolf appeared not in Charles's Lancia, as they had been specifically instructed, but in the black Daimler which Werner and Simon had driven here yesterday. And the two German sailors were alone – there was no chauffeur.

The car jerked unsteadily to a halt. Karl-Otto got out of the driver's seat, an anxious frown on his stolid boxer's face. Werner dashed down the steps towards him.

'No, no, not this one! The Lancia, I said – where is the Lancia?'

'Not there, sir. It has gone. And the chauffeur, too.'

'What? God in heaven!' No sooner was one problem solved than another arose, like the heads of a hydra. If the chauffeur had gone, Werner thought, then he might be trying to summon help. He gazed wildly down the drive, as though a regiment of soldiers might appear there at any moment. Then he took a deep breath, tried to recover himself. 'Are you sure? Did you look everywhere?'

'Yes, sir, of course.'

'But it *can't* be gone. We would have heard it go.'

'Well, not necessarily, sir. You see there's some sort of bridle-path behind the stables that leads out between the fields. It probably joins that track where I was keeping guard last night. We went to look. There are tyre-marks in the mud.'

Werner swore again. He had asked Simon to call Karl-Otto in – when? It couldn't be much more than an hour ago. But an hour would be enough for whoever was in the car to get clear and pass a message to Craigavon. Had it all gone wrong?

He stood quite still for a moment on the drive, turning the possibilities over in his mind. Could they still go to Craigavon in this car instead of the Lancia? Yes, probably. People who saw Charles would expect him to be in the Lancia but he could cook up some plausible explanation for that, if forced to. Could they still get away from Glenfee? Yes, if they hurried. What would happen when they turned up at Craigavon? Ah, that was the problem. If the chauffeur had gone only to fetch help to Glenfee, then there would be no danger. But if he had known enough to pass a message on to UVF HQ at Craigavon, then whoever went there would be walking straight into a trap.

Whoever went there. That was the key to his decision, Werner realised. As the plan stood, it would be Franz, Karl-Otto, and Adolf who would turn up at Craigavon with Charles. Not Werner. He himself would be safely hidden beside the road some miles away with the woman and the boy as hostages.

So it's still a risk worth taking, Werner decided.

'Right.' He smiled at Karl-Otto and Adolf coolly, trying to dispel the anxiety on their heavy, honest faces. They looked to him for leadership and it was his duty to supply it.

'Don't worry, boys, it's not your fault. The operation goes ahead as planned. We'll just have to take this car instead, won't we? Come in now and fetch the prisoners, then we'll be on our way.'

As he turned, a shot rang out from the library.

Charles stepped back into the library and stared at his wife and son.

It was a haunting sight. Deborah was in a long brown dress with her fair hair pinned up roughly into two wide swathes at the top of her head, and her hot dark eyes watching him anxiously. She had one arm round Tom, who was still clutching the blankets over the grey school shirt and orange pullover and tie and shorts which he had worn all night in the ice-house. He still shivered occasionally and his face was unusually pale, but his eyes were alight and his chin was raised defiantly as though there was still hope.

When there is none, Charles thought. There should be a portrait of those two sitting like that, mother and son, because they will soon be dead, like all the other sitters in all the other portraits round the wall. And if they are not portrayed like that, no one will see them as they should be remembered.

They will be dead either way. Werner will shoot them if I refuse, and if I agree he will still shoot them in the end because I will fail. I am bound to fail, I am no actor. However hard I try I shall never be able to go up to Carson in Craigavon with a bandage round my head and persuade him to walk beside me to a car full of men who will kill him. It is just not possible.

So Deborah and Tom are bound to die.

He walked towards them slowly across the room. As he did so, another thought came to him.

There is only one armed man in this room.

Franz was watching him calmly, backing away a little towards the windows so that he could cover the three of them easily with his rifle. He didn't look unduly worried, but most of the time the rifle was trained towards Charles, not Deborah or Tom.

What had Werner said? *I cannot entirely trust my men to kill women and children*. Something like that.

There were a number of small tables in the library, with vases and books and oil lamps on them. To reach the armchairs and sofas round the fireplace, Charles had to pass close by one of these tables with a small expensive black china flower vase standing on it. The vase was about eighteen inches tall, with a long narrow neck and a wide bulbous base to hold the water. There were a number of tulips and ferns in it.

Franz was on Charles's right, the vase was on his left. As he passed the table, Charles moved his right hand across his body, seized the vase by its neck, and flung it back-handed straight into Franz's face.

It was a perfect shot. The base of the vase hit Franz full on the nose, and shattered into a dozen pieces. Water and flowers sprayed everywhere. Franz's head snapped backwards, almost breaking his spine, and his feet took two tottering steps back as well before the momentum of the blow flung him over on his back so that he fell, cracking his head hard against a windowsill behind him. As he collapsed, he pulled the trigger of his rifle.

The bullet ripped into a portrait of an elegant eighteenth century lady and her child on a Shetland pony over the mantelpiece. Deborah screamed. Charles gasped, staggering from the force of the throw which had sent him off balance. His head was reeling, dizzy. But he recovered enough to see Franz lying propped against the wall with his head slumped on his chest and the rifle rolling forwards out of his nerveless hands onto his knees. Charles bent down and picked it up.

Instinctively his military training came into operation. He went down into the firing position, one knee on the floor behind him, the other raised with his elbow resting on it and the rifle pointing towards the door of the library. He flicked the bolt back to eject the used round, and forwards to load a new one. Then the library door opened and Werner ran in with an automatic pistol in his left hand shouting: 'Franz? *Was ist los?*' and Charles shot him through the chest.

Werner lurched, the force of the bullet carrying his chest backwards while his legs still carried him forward, and then he skidded, fell flat on his back and crashed into a table. Charles flicked the bolt back to eject the used cartridge and forwards to load a new one, saw the massive bulk of Karl-Otto coming through the door with his rifle raised, and fired again.

Karl-Otto stumbled forwards and fired his own rifle into the floor. Charles's shot had taken him high in the left shoulder, but he was not dead. He crashed face down onto the floor on top of Werner, his rifle still clutched in his massive right hand. Charles flicked his bolt back and forwards again, searching for the third target, Adolf. But Adolf took one look through the door and then backed away, flat against the wall in the hall outside. Charles waited. One to go.

He stayed exactly where he was, kneeling in the firing position, rifle cocked, finger on the trigger, butt pressed into his shoulder, staring at the door. One second . . . two . . . five seconds . . . ten . . .

Tom let out a tiny, strangled whimper as though he might be hurt. Charles glanced swiftly over his shoulder and saw Deborah with both her arms wrapped round him and Tom peering out over his blankets with eyes black with utter terror. Charles frowned at them both, meaning: Keep down! Keep quiet! and turned his eyes back instantly to the door. Nothing. No sign of Adolf. He waited.

Karl-Otto groaned. Charles risked another swift glance away from the door. Karl-Otto was hard to see. He was lying face down on top of the inert Werner, half-hidden behind a small desk, and an ornamental table had collapsed on top of his head. He groaned again, and moved a little bit, and Charles saw the big brawny right arm that still held the rifle shift slightly. He couldn't quite see the rifle though, it was hidden beneath a pile of papers and the remains of a potted fern that had fallen on top of him with the tables. But he thought the rifle was moving.

Cautiously, making no sound, Charles rose to his feet and took a single step forward, swinging his rifle round to his right and downwards as he did so. He was right – there was Karl-Otto's big determined face looking up at him as the German rolled onto his left side. Karl-Otto's rifle came up in his massive right hand until the little dark muzzle of it was wavering upwards like a single deadly eye pointing at Charles's face . . .

Charles fired.

The bullet smashed straight into Karl-Otto's chest. His huge body leapt like a clubbed seal, and his hand twitched and fired his rifle upwards into the ceiling. His legs came up and folded briefly into the foetal position, and then he slid off Werner's body and lay face upwards on the floor beside him.

As Karl-Otto's rifle clattered to the floorboards, Charles flicked his own bolt back and forwards and looked up towards the door, but it was already too late as he had feared it would be, because Adolf leaned round the doorpost with his rifle cocked and ready and all the time Charles was raising his own rifle – so slowly it seemed, as though moving underwater – he could see Adolf's finger tightening on the trigger and then he felt the explosion in his chest and saw the flash of light together and then nothing more ever on this earth.

Only when Charles lay face upwards on the floor at her feet did Deborah move. Slowly, she stood up. She did not let go of Tom for a moment but forced him roughly behind her so that she was shielding him with her own body.

She stared at the man, Adolf, standing in the door.

He was tall, bonier than the others. He had a thin face with dark receding hair and the hands that clutched the smoking rifle had tattoos on them, an anchor on one and a sailing ship on the other. He had dark brown eyes that looked as frightened as her own.

For a long moment he stared at her, while the blue smoke from his rifle barrel drifted up towards the shattered ceiling, and she waited for him to lift the gun again and point it at her. Then something unfroze in his mind.

'*Ach nein*,' he said. He shook his head once, and then again more definitely, stepped back into the hall, and closed the door. She heard his boots on the steps outside, and, a moment later, the ignition firing in the Daimler. Then came the sound of the wheels on the gravel and the car's engine receding down the drive.

Tom crept out from behind her but she did not let go of him; she did not think she would let go of him ever again so long as she lived. The room reeked of blood and cordite. The two of them knelt beside Charles, pale, frozen, while the portraits of his ancestors smiled down at him from the walls . . .

32

The Lancia crawled cautiously up the drive towards Glenfee. It was overburdened – there were eight people jammed into its six seats, and four more hung outside on the running board. All of these except two – the driver and the woman – held new Mannlicher rifles, cocked and pointed in the air, ready for action, so that the car crept forwards across the gravel like a porcupine, its spines raised to defend itself.

As if this were not enough, two motor-cycles growled behind it, the pillion passengers similarly armed. Behind them came a third motor-cycle with a small machine gun mounted on a side-car, which the gunner swivelled warily from side to side as they went through the gates and drove past the wide lawns towards the house.

Sarah Becket sat in the front seat of the Lancia, between the chauffeur and Sergeant Cullen. Very soon, she knew, she would collapse with exhaustion; but for the moment she was simply terrified. If the Germans were still here, there was likely to be a gunfight with Deborah and Tom in the middle of it; if they had already left, they would probably have taken Tom with them, and he would be in worse danger than before.

Nonetheless, she had done her best. She glanced gratefully at Robinson, the chauffeur, beside her. When the Lancia had stopped for her in the lane, an hour or so ago, she had felt certain the two men in it were Germans. But they were not. The man with the shotgun had been Charles's butler, Smythe, who had realised that something was terribly wrong in the house when he had looked out of a window and seen two men he had never seen before carry a wounded Charles into the library. Then there had been shouts, and another shot. He had distrusted Werner from the first, and had not believed these men were soldiers in the UVF. So he had gone on his own initiative to rouse Robinson, and the two of them had pushed the Lancia quietly down the back lane, past the stables, until it was too far away from the house for the sound of its engine to be heard. Then they had driven towards the village with the idea, like Sarah, of seeking help from Sergeant Cullen.

Sergeant Cullen had been roused many hundreds of times before dawn in the African veldt and the North West Frontier. He had learnt, long ago, that speed of thought and action meant the difference between life and the broad blade of a tribesman's spear through your neck. Within ten minutes he had sent a despatch rider speeding towards Craigavon; within twenty he had a convoy driving back towards Glenfee. But he was not accustomed to dealing with hostages.

As the Lancia scrunched to a halt in front of the wide front steps and the verandah, Sarah thought the house had a dreadful, deserted feel. Birds were singing energetically from the trees, but there were no fires lit, no smoke from the chimneys, no faces at the windows. We're too late, she thought. They've gone.

Four men leapt from the running boards and dropped to one knee in the firing position, their rifles aimed at the house. Four others jumped out quickly to join them. Sergeant Cullen barked orders to the motorcycles to drive on round the back.

The front door of the house opened. A woman came out, with a small boy clutched to her long skirts.

Deborah and Tom.

With a little cry of relief Sarah leapt from the car and ran towards the steps to join them, but Sergeant Cullen caught her arm and held her back.

'Wait! Just a minute, Mrs Becket,' he said. 'It may be a trap.'

Deborah walked very quietly forward to the top of the steps and gazed down at them. There was no emotion on her face, none at all. Just a pale haunted weariness, as though she found what was in front of her eyes too hard to comprehend. She saw the lines of armed men and ignored them.

'Sarah?' she said. 'Sarah – come up.'

'Wait.' Sergeant Cullen said again. He called out: 'Mrs Cavendish? Where is your husband, ma'am?'

Deborah looked down. 'Oh, it's you, Sergeant,' she said. 'You've come too late. My husband's inside, but he's dead.' She waved her hand briefly towards the door, and moved it back quickly to clutch Tom as though she feared he might escape unless she held him. 'They're all dead, except one, and he . . . there's too much blood.'

Sarah saw her sway again, and this time the Sergeant let her go, so she ran up the steps and put her arms round Deborah gently. Soldiers ran past them in their heavy boots, pushing the door open warily and stepping inside. Sarah guided Deborah to a garden seat on the verandah, between an urn of geraniums and a sculpture of a small lion. The seat was wet with rain but it didn't matter.

Sarah said: 'What happened?'

Deborah sighed, staring out across the park to where the great trees waved by the road in front of the grey squally waters of the lough.

'Charles shot two of them, and then . . . ' Slowly, piece by piece, the story came out.

'He would have got them all if . . . ' Tom's thin, shocked, high-pitched voice piped up for the first time, and the two women stopped, waiting for him to finish. But he didn't finish, his voice tailed away.

There are no ifs, Deborah thought. Only what happened. Those endless seconds when he raised the rifle too slowly. And all the waste of our lives before that.

Ifs don't matter . . .

The sunlight hurt her. It was bright clean sunlight, gleaming out of a clear blue sky on to fields and woods that were still sodden with yesterday's rain. There was still mist along the streams and rivers and in all the dips and valleys of the fields, and the newly-washed leaves on the hedges and trees beside the road glittered and sparkled as they drove past. Despite the sunlight the road was still damp, and sometimes spray whooshed up from the tyres as they drove through puddles where branches overhung the road, and occasional rivulets of water splashed down on their heads and trickled icily under their collars and down the backs of their necks. Yet all the time the sunlight warmed their faces.

If only the sun had shone like this yesterday, Deborah thought bitterly. But on the day of Charles's funeral the rain had come down in torrents. She had stood beside the sodden grave, throwing mud on the coffin instead of dust, and had squelched, shivering, past the honour guard of drenched UVF soldiers with her soaking son's hand clenched tight in her own. There had been so much rain she had not known if there were tears on her face or not, but she must have been crying because of the pain in her chest and throat.

Sir Edward Carson had been there. He had spoken to her kindly and given Tom a little Union flag with the Red Hand of Ulster in the middle. He still held it proudly in his hand now as he sat between Deborah and Sarah in the back of the Lancia on his way to school.

He was proud of his father, Deborah knew. That was the greatest gift Charles had been able to give the boy. He had died like a hero; Tom had seen that. Yesterday Sir Edward Carson had come to Glenfee and said to Deborah, in front of Tom: 'If it had not been for the heroic actions of yourself and your husband, Mrs Cavendish, not only would I probably be dead, but, far more important than that, this province would have been plunged into the unnecessary chaos of civil war, which I still pray God we can avoid. Not only Ulster but the entire nation is in your debt.'

It appeared that the government in London agreed with him on that if nothing else, because the police had confirmed to Deborah that, because of her sister's part in the events at Glenfee, no attempt was to be made to secure her rearrest. Quite apart from certain embarassing disclosures in London, newspaper interest in the deaths at Glenfee had been intense, and the government would have been extremely foolish to imprison anyone who had played a part in foiling the German plot.

Of the two surviving Germans, one, Adolf, had escaped, and

the other, the injured Franz, confirmed what Charles had told Deborah, that Simon Fletcher had been promised a fortune in German marks to betray UVF secrets and kidnap his commanding officer's son. Sometimes, in her prayers, Deborah had asked God why this thing had had to happen to Charles, instead of any one of dozens of other senior officers of similar background in the UVF. But the only one who knew the answer to that was Werner, and he was dead.

As they approached St Andrew's Preparatory School Deborah clutched her son's hand more tightly. *I can't do it*, she thought, *I can't let him go again*. But the headmaster, Dr Duncan, was there with his wife on the main steps to meet her, and Tom was clearly so embarrassed by his mother's concern that she had to let go. Dr Duncan himself was crippled with guilt and determined to make amends in any way he could.

'Under no circumstances, madam,' he repeated endlessly as they toured the building and settled Tom down again in his dormitory, round the door of which peered the wide, curious eyes of half a dozen of his friends. 'Under no circumstances whatsoever will young Cavendish or any other boy from now on be allowed to leave the grounds of this school without being accompanied by a member of staff – and Tom will not be allowed home unless you personally come to fetch him. It was a most dreadful thing, dreadful, and I am determined it will never happen again.'

Of course it won't, you silly man, she thought wearily. My husband's dead, no one would want to kidnap Tom now. And, in a strange way his pompous, pointless assurances helped her to deal with her own anxiety. Life had to go on, Tom had to grow up, he couldn't stay tied to her skirts forever.

Nevertheless Tom allowed her to kiss him, and she saw tears well in his eyes, briefly, as she left. In the car, Deborah waved and waved until the car turned a bend in the rutted track and the old ivy-clad school was out of sight. Sarah touched her arm.

'He'll be all right, Debbie,' she said. 'Truly.'

Deborah dabbed at her eyes with a handkerchief. 'Yes,' she said. 'I know he will. Oh, that stupid man!'

'Who? Dr Duncan?' Sarah smiled. 'I expect if any German comes he'll bite their legs like a bulldog.'

'And make them write a thousand lines.'

'Yes.'

The sisters smiled at each other. The chauffeur, Robinson, drove stolidly along the country track and out on to the road beside Lough Neagh. After a while they came to a small village where a stream joined the lake and Deborah leaned forward and touched Robinson on the shoulder.

'Pull in at the grocer's shop, will you please? If I remember rightly, we can get a cup of tea there and stretch our legs in the garden.'

The grass was almost dry now, and the woman agreed to serve them tea outside at a small wooden table. While they were waiting, Deborah and Sarah wandered down to the shore. The sunlight sparkled on the waters of the lough, and little puffy white clouds floated high in the warm blue sky. A few hundred yards away, a heron stood motionless in a bank of reeds.

'You are lucky, living here,' Sarah said. 'In London, one forgets.'

'Yes.' Deborah took a deep breath. 'Sarah, there is something I have to tell you.'

'So serious?' Sarah turned to her, surprised. 'Debbie? What is it?'

'I . . . ' She hesitated. It is a secret that does not have to be told at all, Deborah realised. Not now. Charles is dead, and I am an honoured widow. Everyone will assume that the baby is his.

Unless . . .

Maybe I'll come over and see you some time. And we can meet . . .

Rankin's words had sounded so callous when he said them. Standing with his hands in his pockets under the street lamp, watching her walk away. She had hated him then. But now Deborah knew that some day, some time, she would have to see him again. Not for passion. That was all gone, a fever that had passed. But to let him know . . .

What?

That she was glad they had been lovers. That she did not hate him any more. That he was right; his child would be brought up in a good home, with all the advantages which wealth and education could give. And that she would love it, with a love as fierce and protective as she had for Tom.

I would like to tell him that, Deborah thought. And that if I had not taken his advice, I would have lost Tom also. But if he does come, and Sarah is here? I shall have to pretend, and deceive her.

Still Deborah hesitated. She thought of Sarah, who had wanted children so much and would probably never have any now. She would probably stay married to Jonathan for form's sake, but they wouldn't live together, not any more. She was likely to be hurt, jealous even, when she learnt that Deborah was pregnant; if she learnt about Rankin too she might never speak to her sister again.

But Deborah was tired of lies. She realised how much she needed someone in her life to whom she could speak honestly. Who would love her for what she really was. Charles was dead, and anyway, she had never been able to talk to him. Even if Rankin came, he would go away again after an hour or a day or a week – she would never be able to rely on him.

So if not Sarah, who?

I could go and whisper my secret to a shell on the seashore, she thought. And what good would that do?

I don't want her to go back to London, and leave me alone with my guilt and my memories. I want her to stay here with me at Glenfee, at least for a while. When my baby is born I want someone to share the moment with me. I want there to be at least one person, apart from myself, who knows everything about where it came from and how it was conceived, and who still loves it, for all that.

I want that person to be Sarah, my sister.

I want her to know the truth.

So she began.

'A while ago I met a man . . . '

The two rich ladies, Mrs Devlin thought, did not seem to know their own minds. They had ordered tea at eleven o'clock in the morning, but when she had laid a cloth over the wooden table in the garden and set out two willow pattern cups with the sugar bowl and the milk jug and the tea pot which was only a little chipped at the spout, and a selection of cakes with some hot soda bread fresh from the oven, they had not come to sit down.

They just continued pacing up and down by the shore of the lough, the fair-haired one in the blue coat doing all the talking, while the slim dark one in the grey skirt and jacket and straw hat listened quietly, until all the heat had gone out of the soda bread and the tea in the pot would be tepid and stewed for sure. At times they frowned and looked very solemn, and once the fair one cried, so that Mrs Devlin felt certain all the good food would go to waste, but the dark one put her arm around the fair one and started talking earnestly, and they walked right the way up to the reeds so that the heron flew away in disgust.

Mrs Devlin was just wondering whether to clear the table and brew fresh tea, or give it all to the chauffeur, when the two ladies suddenly came and sat down laughing and ate and drank as though it was the most delightful meal they had had in their lives.

Mrs Devlin didn't like to interfere. She just stood at the stone sink in her kitchen and watched from the window until they had finished, and marvelled. All that money, so that they could have a chauffeur in a big shiny six-seater car just sitting outside the shop by the roadside reading the newspaper until their ladyships were ready, and yet they understood nothing about good food and drink. Perhaps it came from living in a big house, Mrs Devlin thought, where everything would be stone cold anyway by the time it reached the table from the kitchens. Maybe rich folk grew to like their food and drink like that.

Anyway, the two ladies had certainly found plenty to talk about, Mrs Devlin couldn't deny that. They spent nearly two hours in her garden, and never let up for a moment. And when at last they came to pay and left her a two shilling tip, they were both smiling and laughing all the time, as though the good Lord had just granted an extra birthday to the pair of them.

Mrs Devlin came out into the garden to clear the table, and stood watching wistfully as they drove away out of sight, in the back of the shiny black car.